THE SONG OF THE RED RUBY

AGNAR MYKLE

THE SONG
OF THE RED RUBY

TRANSLATED BY
MAURICE MICHAEL

NEW YORK
E. P. DUTTON & CO., INC.
1961

My day demanded to see my passport and take my finger prints.
But I had a hidden identity.
My day searched me.
It did not discover my tenderness.

*

Will the young people of the future cultivate the Earth?
We are not united in a longing for dead planets.
We are united in a longing for the palms of the hands.

*

This book ought to be read twice.
It also contains a message.

THE SONG OF THE RED RUBY

The Park with the White Swans

When you turn out of the street in the quiet, empty spring night and direct your steps towards the public park, when you stand in front of the high wrought-iron gates and raise your hand to take hold of the big, worn bronze latch, you will feel a catch in your throat.

This may be because it is night, for night is an unlawful time. An old thief, you turn imperceptibly and glance hurriedly at the houses on the far side of the street. The houses are asleep. In their hundred windows, with drawn blinds, there is not an eye to be seen. The town is asleep.

It may also be because it is a secluded place which you are about to enter. A deserted park fills you with a vague feeling of mystery and of guilt. In our childhood and early youth we have all done things in a public park. We did them when it was spring, when it was dark, when it was night, when the air was filled with the smell of earth and trees.

Or it may be because there is something implacable and unalterable about a park: once inside, it takes an exorcism, or a resolve, or a fine to get you out again. Of course a public park has the peaceful green shimmer of an oasis about it, but only when viewed from outside. When you go inside you discover the oasis has a tall iron fence round it; you are imprisoned; the wave of a wand has turned the oasis into a cell. Did you go in because you wanted to force a meeting or a decision? The great eye of the night will be gazing upon you searchingly and will reveal what your heart is worth. Everyone trembles before that possibility, and you will always feel that catch in your throat when you face the gates of a deserted park on a spring night.

But most of all it is because you are a student and twenty-three, because the Spring Term Ball has just ended; because you still have the melody of 'Sing the Student's Happy Life' in you; because the basses sang 'No Storm yet in our Minds doth dwell', and this made you feel wicked and evil, because you loved the truth, because it is two o'clock in the morning, because it is a mild and silken-soft spring night, because you are standing there with the young woman you have searched for all your life and who has just been your partner at the ball, because you have asked her if she would go for a stroll in the park and she has said yes, because you are a timid young man, because you admire and worship this young woman more than anyone on earth, because you have never dared to give her the least hint of your inmost feelings and your wild, wild hopes, because she is an angel and you a centaur, because you hope that a miracle will happen in the park and you will find the courage to tell her; and you realize that if the miracle happens and she shares your feelings, you will not know how to deal with so much happiness.

Any of us can stand up to grief. Only the strong can stand up to good fortune.

May night, May night!

When it is spring in Norway people's hearts weep tears of melting cold; it is a grim, fitful, poignant happiness, like when a frozen limb thaws. For spring is so violent and so cruel in our country. We can not only see it and smell it, we can hear it. It whispers and chatters and murmurs in our ears; there is the dripping of melting ice from the gutters of the houses and the branches of the trees; the streams chuckle and the bursting rivers bluster; the wind whistles in the air and the skipping ropes of little girls smack on the pavement; spring sings to us from the throats of birds and trills in the brittle ring of bicycle bells; spring whispers in the sprouting grass and beneath last year's withered leaves; spring seethes quietly in the dark soil and rises like fermenting wine in the stems of the plants, in the trunks of the trees and in people's limbs: sap and milk and blood and semen. Spring purrs its low menacing song as if it were a giant cat asleep in the bowels of the earth. And then the cat wakes up and stretches.

Spring is a promise, but first and foremost it is a demand. A wild, impossible, heart-rending demand. For who can make the close of the year as magnificent and majestic as its beginning? Spring is a demand that is made upon us, and in our hearts we all know that we shall fail. That is why spring is so cruel, that is why there are tears in people's hearts in the spring.

The ends of the tall iron bars of the fence stood out against the faintly shimmering night sky like flattened spearheads. On their way there they had wondered whether it would be open at that hour. They had a vague idea that public parks were usually shut at night.

He laid his hand on the heavy bronze handle, turned it and pulled. The gate opened. For a moment he was aware of its heavy, tremulous weight in his hand.

They both shuddered as the gate creaked on its hinges. They waited a moment in the silence, holding their breath. They looked at each other. He held the gate open for her. She gave him a smile and a gay look, but he could see that she was tired. It was now two in the morning and it had been a long day for her. Perhaps this is what I wanted, he thought in surprise, to tire her out. Tire her to the extent that in the end she will collapse on the seat (there must be a seat we can sit on?) and ask if she can put her head in my lap. If she does that, then it is as good as done, then I shall be at liberty to stroke her cheek, then she will have answered without my asking. Or tire her to the extent that she falls down in a faint? Then I shall have an excuse for putting my arms round her and lifting her up, an excuse for holding her in my arms, for holding her hand in mine, for stroking her hair, for expressing all the tenderness that I now carry unsaid inside me.

She went in and he closed the gate behind her and he knew that he was not going to have the courage to tell her what was in his heart.

Slowly they walked up the gravelled path. On either side stood tall, dark trees: beech, poplar, birch, silver fir and some exotic kind of conifer with branches like swaying tigers' tails; it was like walking beneath a vaulted roof.

He made a startled movement as she stopped and broke the silence. She said,

'Shall we go and see if the swans are awake?'

He nodded and forced a smile.

'Swans swimming are one of the loveliest sights I know,' she said as though to herself.

So they walked to the pond. But the swans were not to be seen.

Slowly, exchanging occasional remarks, they walked back to the path. He pointed to a seat.

'Shall we sit down?'

'M'm,' she said.

'Wait,' said he, 'you might dirty your coat.' He took out his handkerchief and wiped the dew off the planks. It made his handkerchief so wet he could almost have wrung it out.

'Thanks,' she said, 'that was nice of you.'

'Uhuh,' he said.

They sat down.

He crossed his legs and sat there waggling one foot; but that drew attention to his foot, and as he did not have patent-leather shoes to go with his dinner jacket, but just ordinary black calf, he uncrossed his legs again. Then he leaned back and stretched out his arms and let them lie on top of the backrest. That meant that his right arm was just behind her neck: if he lowered it just an inch it would be round her shoulders. He said:

'Would you like a cigarette?'

'Yes, please,' she said.

He held out the packet, and lit a match. He had to close his eyes as she moved her face to it, she was so near. And they were alone in the night, alone in the park, she and he, and he could not speak.

His heart was leaden with impotence. He was a born speaker; she had heard him lecture and debate; that evening she had sat beside him while he proposed the toast of the ladies. Afterwards some students had even come up and congratulated him; but now, in the night, he had lost his tongue; now, alone with this young woman, he could not speak. He could only chat, could only make conversation about things of no importance: the weather, the outlook for the summer, brands of cigarette, swans, swing records, the old professor who was reputed to have written ballads in his youth, the strange atmosphere of a spring night. It was as though he were split into two people: one made conversation, smiling and polite and laughing, like an automaton; the other was full of despair over the pointless farce. He smoked cigarette after cigarette, and became sore and bitter and dry in the throat; he was filled with a paralysing fear and did not know what had caused it.

He wanted desperately to open his heart to her, his need for tenderness was so strong that he had a queer feeling in his midriff; but he could not, dared not. All was at stake where he was concerned; it was the hardest gamble he had let himself in for. He began a sentence to himself, began it over and over again; inwardly he was furious with himself. Now, he said, now I'll shut my eyes and say it, now, now, one two three, now. But he did not say it. He thought: If I say it and for some reason or other she turns me down, if for some reason or other she does not feel the same for me as I for her, if she has to refuse me, politely and unhappily, if she says that she does not love me, but that we can be friends (is there anything more wretched and pitiable than 'being friends'?), if I propose and she cannot accept me, then all is lost. I can bear a life lived with an unexpressed hope; but I can never bear to live with defeat pronounced. Best say nothing. Then at least I have the hope. Just say that I am going to France tomorrow. And that it is such a long time till the autumn, till I can meet her again.

'Not feeling cold?' he said once.

'Oh, no,' she smiled.

Then he gulped. He would so gladly have taken off his coat and put it round her shoulders. There was nothing he would have liked better than to take her in his arms. But she was not feeling cold. Pity!

'A cigarette?'

'No thanks, I have smoked so many this evening, it has given me a bit of a headache.'

So he lit a cigarette for himself and looked at her, worried. He could put his hand on her forehead and massage it; there was nothing he would have liked better than to massage her temples,

but of course that was out of the question. If only he could just
stroke her hair. He was on the verge of screaming.

Dimly he sensed that if he tried to explain his feelings and
his powerlessness, she would not understand. Dimly he sensed
that an older woman might understand a young man being
paralysed by love and adoration, but not a young woman.
Understand it with her mind, perhaps, as a scientific fact; but
not admit it emotionally, and not surrender. Dimly he sensed
that a young woman wants to be conquered, that she only sub-
mits to a man who is full-blooded, strong, his throat full of
laughter, a man who does not ask, but triumphantly demands.
He could be like that to other women, to women who did not
mean so much to him and whom, perhaps, he slightly despised.
He could put an arm round their shoulders and let them know
what he wanted.

But not here. Not with the girl he loved. He couldn't touch
her. He couldn't speak to her. And he was too proud to beg.

He sat with his hands in his lap. He had a queer feeling in his
jaw muscles. He had to fight to keep his teeth from chattering
out of longing, fear, cold.

A faint hint of morning light was beginning to appear, but
it was still night. The park was on an eminence; on one side of
it lay the town, still and asleep; on the other the harbour with all
the sleeping boats. They were sitting on a seat under the tall
dark trees. He could smell the bitter, voluptuous smell of spring
night, of moist spring night; it came billowing from the soil,
from the grass, from the flowers and the trees, and from the
swans' muddy little ponds; from the distant hills surrounding
the town came the belated smell of winter, of the patches of
snow still lying on the summits; from the harbour and the fjord
came a salt gust of cold, cruel, deep water. But from the sky and
the air and the tops of the trees came a quivering warm breath
of nascent summer. And from the young woman at his side he
caught the faint warm smell of her body and her scent.

He thought: I'm not going to get it said. Not unless a miracle
happens. Not without her fainting so that I have an excuse to
take hold of her. I'm not up to saying it. Some time later. In a
year, perhaps. Perhaps not for five years. But, he thought despairingly, it is now that it should be done, it is now—at this

moment—that the wonder exists. What will it be like in five years' time? Who is going to guarantee that she will become mine in five years, when I have become strong enough and mature enough to propose? She may be married to someone else by then. She may be married and have children!

He thought: Why don't I stretch out my hand?

He ventured to glance down at her hand. It lay in her lap, so small, so strong, so brown, so warm. It was only a hair's breadth from his own. He sat there as though under a spell, looking at her hand. He began to tremble. Just to lay his hand on hers, that would break the spell.

Only a hairs-breadth separated him from wonderful life.

He gulped and began, stuttering, to talk about France. He had just read an uncanny book by a French author, Louis Guilloux, called *Le Sang Noir*. It had also come out in Norwegian. It was about an old schoolmaster in a French provincial town who was so abject and full of doubts about himself that his pupils ended by tyrannizing him completely. They forced him to stand guard by the door to warn them if the Head came along, while they played poker in class! The old master went by the name of Cripure. His subject was philosophy and his speciality Kant's *Critique de la Raison Pure*. His pupils had twisted this in *Cripture de la Raison Ticque*. Hence his nickname. Had she read the book?

'No,' she said, 'but it sounds awfully grim.'

'Yes,' he said, 'it's a horrifying book. A book about a man who has mastered philosophy but has not acquired the ability to live.'

He added, for this was 1939 and dark war-clouds were already drifting in over Europe: 'When I read it, I had the feeling that in his heart of hearts Guilloux was not writing about an old schoolmaster called Cripure, but about a country called France.'

They sat for a while. Then she turned to him and said with a smile, but he could see that there was a veiled challenge in it:

'Do you know which philosopher I loathe most?'

'No?'

'Schopenhauer. He said: "Life is a sad affair and I will spend mine thinking about it." Have you ever heard such a thing? Let me have a cigarette, please. I get so worked up when I think about that loathsome Schopenhauer.'

He gave her one with a rush of thankfulness. Then he said :

'I don't think I agree with you. Yes, perhaps, where your view of life is concerned. But of the philosophers it is only the great, dyed-in-the-wool pessimists who grip me. The ones that preach the transience and vanity of life. The others, the semi-optimists, the nice, kind ones, seem false to me, like artificial vanilla sauce or an Oxford Group preacher. Christianity without tears, so to speak. The worst I know is that optimistic American, William James, the father of pragmatism, the practical philosopher, who says that truth is the term for everything that it is good and useful to believe in. He defined truth as the "cash-value" of a concept.'

He spat on the gravel.

'No,' he said, taking a deep breath, 'give me rather a confirmed pessimist. I feel sick when I read James. Give me Schopenhauer, he who gives me no hope. By not giving me hope, he forces me to fight : his own hopelessness rouses the opposite in me. You dismiss James with a shrug of the shoulder. You get angry with Schopenhauer. So it is Schopenhauer, the pessimist, who has a stimulating effect. You see,' he said and smiled to her, 'the very fact that you are angry with Schopenhauer proves that he is a philosopher.'

'You are odd,' she said and smiled.

'Am I?' he said and looked despairingly at her hand.

'What about that French book you mentioned,' she said, 'about the old schoolmaster. That's pessimistic too, I take it?'

'Very much so. You feel like weeping at the end of it.'

'And you mean that it is a valuable book because of its pessimism?'

'Immensely valuable. Unfortunately it is so well written that it can never reach the masses. But if it could be read by everyone in France it would do more to strengthen the morale of the French than the entire Maginot Line. One can endure the thought of the Maginot Line, one can be cosy and snug behind its fortifications. But one cannot bear to think of the dissolute, degraded old Cripure. He is the writing on the wall. France . . .'

He got no further.

He had again glanced at her small, brown, soft, strong hand; it lay just a hairs-breadth from his own; he only had to reach out and the whole rich and wonderful world would be his. And as he sat numbed and unable to stretch out his hand, a thought came to him: Oh well, there are girls in France too. And in the moment of thinking that loose, submissive thought, he knew that he had brought himself to the verge of defeat. For the man who at a decisive moment thinks of what he may have to fall back on, is not exerting all his strength to win a decisive victory. That man has lost already. He gulped with despair and turned his head away so that she should not see the tears in his eyes; for of one thing he felt perfectly sure: a young woman has no respect for a young man who weeps. A socialist does not weep.

He sat with averted face, staring down at the grass. His gaze came to rest on the section of his trousers visible below his overcoat. He looked at the shiny black silk stripe down the outer seam. He had paid fifteen crowns for the hire of his dinner jacket. Suddenly he knew with bitter, firm conviction, that this was the last time, the first and last time he would wear a dinner jacket. By God, there was no more ridiculous garment than a dinner jacket. His wrath gave him a certain relief.

I shall ask her after all, Ash thought. I'll ask her now. One two three. Now.

A Vesuvius on Two Legs

There is much that man can grasp, much that he can comprehend, but time is the great enigma.

Time and destiny and eternity, and again time.

While the author was writing these lines, and while the reader was reading them, the earth was spinning on through space, and where were we thirty seconds ago?

Man is homeless in time. Salvation from the madness of this enigma of time does not lie in our believing in God, but in now and again looking at a clock. The clock, of course, is a miserable deception, and we all know that time shown by the watch a man looks at in Norway is hopelessly different from that shown by the watch a man looks at in Japan; yet without watches and clocks we are lost. Without the seeming security of a clock face and its two hands we should die, we should be delivered up to the intangible emptiness and terror of time. And as a clock seizes a second and shows it to us, so art takes an instant out of eternity and holds it fast. He who enjoins a moment to tarry is certain of death. But some must die, so that others may live.

Every moment is the fruit of two hundred million years. The days roll along, minute by minute, like flies buzzing home to die, and every second is a window on to all time.

Here is one moment:

One autumn morning in 1938 a tall, heron-like Norwegian, just turned twenty-three, boarded a ship in his native town on the coast of Norway. In the last day or two he had signed various letters and documents, including a bond for a bank that had been kind enough to lend him two thousand crowns (against security). Under his signature he had written with a secret little thrill: 'Stud. Merc.' which showed that he had been accepted as student at his country's College of Political and Economic Sciences. This had been in existence for only a year, but was already known as The College. It was in another, larger town on the west coast. The journey there by mail-steamer would take two days and nights.

His baggage consisted of a cabin trunk, a rucksack and a violin case. In the trunk were a suit and a winter overcoat, underclothes, shirts, ties and books; in the rucksack shoes and slippers and socks and a 'hussif' and two jars of raspberry jam (a parting gift from his mother, accepted with reluctance); and in the violin case a violin and bow.

The combination of these two facts, that the young student (whose name was Ash Burlefoot) was going to a college that trained stalwart breadwinners—accountants and business managers—and that he was taking with him a violin on which he really played, were sufficient to indicate that here was a young man with a difficult time ahead of him. For the world and Norway are such that you can become a good accountant with a fine salary, but only on condition that you do not stray into

the unreal world of Paganini; or you can become a clever
musician and composer, but only on condition that you do not
get stuck in the realistic world of business with its columns of
figures, balance-sheets, profit and loss accounts and electric
calculating machines.

Thus, it could safely be predicted that this young man was
in for a conflict and a painful choice—between office stool and
music stand. That, however, was only one of the many struggles
in which he was about to become involved. The college to which
he was now going was a state university and as such non-
political, neutral and strictly academic in character. But it was
an open secret that the initiative for its creation, as well as a
considerable part of its funds, had come from conservative
private business interests. Thus it was safe to assume that the
economics promulgated from its chairs would be liberal, bourgeois economics. Student Burlefoot, however, was a socialist
and he shuddered at the thought of the next two and a half
years. Should he, in this nest of capitalists, at once declare himself a socialist and adopt an aggressive attitude from the outset,
or should he say nothing of his political convictions and study
there as a guerrilla in disguise? In which way would he best
serve socialism? He did not know and there was no one to
advise him.

He did not belong to any socialist organization, but he had
decided to join one in the town he was going to—and felt
thrilled at the thought. In his home town he had been content
to join the others in applauding the socialist speakers who took
part in the school debates. The socialists were the best speakers
and he admired them immensely. He was never to forget the
retort one of them made in a debate: it became a nail in the
ship of his life.

At one meeting, the chairman of the Students' Society had
congratulated one of the younger socialists, a solicitor called
Jespersen, on his appointment as town councillor, an important
position. Dr. Munkestad, a conservative, then rose to his feet:
'I cannot echo those sentiments, for it seems to me that Mr.
Jespersen is far too young and inexperienced for such an exacting position. I can only express the hope that where God has
given a post, he will also give understanding.'

The young socialist, Jespersen, stood up and in a quiet friendly tone of voice, said :

'Mr. Chairman, can no one get Dr. Munkestad a post?'

For two seconds there was silence in the great hall; then a roar of laughter burst forth from the eight hundred students.

Young Ash Burlefoot had had a demonstration of the power of *words* that he never forgot.

What did being a socialist mean? Ash Burlefoot could not have told you off-hand. He was not well versed in the theory of socialism; he had not read much of Marx and he neither understood nor could say he agreed with the materialist interpretation of history. For him socialism was something very simple —liberty and bread. For himself and for everyone else on earth. He had made up his mind to become rich, at any rate richer than his father; he was the son of a municipal streetcar driver and a not inconsiderable part of his childhood and youth had been spent listening to cold, bitter, interminable discussions between his father and mother about cutting down the housekeeping budget about the price of potatoes, margarine, coke and fish, about patching and altering clothes, about the advantages of slicing cheese thinly and of putting money in the bank and of not smoking cigarettes. Yes, he intended to be rich; he had learned this much—that kindliness, culture and goodwill go by the board when the family budget is so restricted that panic breaks out when the elder son goes off and buys something so luxurious and unnecessary as four new strings for his violin. But the wealth he was to acquire was not to be taken from others, it would be gained in common with others. Hence he was a socialist.

When his thoughts ran on these lines he became serious and moral, and that did not suit him, for in his heart of hearts, in the core of his being, he was a laughter-loving fellow with a vast appetite for life, an adventurer, a poet, a robber baron, a gay pagan. As a child he had for many years been kept at home and indoors by a prosaic, but painful bronchial illness; for many now forgotten years he had regarded life from indoors, through a window-pane, he had sat philosophically and scratched in the earth of his mother's flower-pots in the window with a miniature brass rake, had sat reeking of turpentine, with a perpetual cold, with heaving, laboured breath, while his fellows were playing outside on the pavement in the sunshine and the wind. This prison existence of his childhood had stored up in him such a hunger for liberty and a longing for action, that now—unwittingly—he went about like a Vesuvius on two legs.

He was a worshipper of life, he drank in life with all his senses, he could sob with pleasure over life's wonderful smells and essences; he never knew which he liked best: to be sitting bent over a juicy red steak or lying with his nose snuggled into a girl's armpit. He hungered for music, literature, the whole world's culture, for friendship, companionship; and he wanted to perform great deeds himself, to win fame. (This last, however, he never dared admit.) He could go far at a party, a dance or a drinking bout or some similar orgy, but he shrank from the vulgar and brutal. (He had a secret horror, a horror of the beast in people.)

All this titanic, subterranean volcano was hidden, however, beneath an obliging, friendly, smiling, shy nature. He was a thin, tall young man, far above average height; and on that pole of a body his head seemed almost small and fine. His face was pale, intense; his forehead very high, and as smooth as a peeled almond; his nose was straight with nervously quivering nostrils. Some of his sensuality was apparent in his powerful chin and thick red lips; but the first quick impression of strength and resoluteness was destroyed when you looked up from his mouth and saw his eyes: they were blue-grey, as timid as a doe's, and his lashes were as long and thick as a young girl's.

It was a smiling, dreamy, innocent face crowned with a shock of corn-yellow, wavy hair. His laugh was delighted and spontaneous, so uncontrolled that to his despair he always made himself conspicuous in cinemas and other places of entertainment.

From fifteen to twenty his face was covered with pimples. For three years he had been convinced that he was the ugliest person in the world. Now the pimples had gone, but he still had a lingering horror of looking young girls in the face, he was afraid of seeing commiseration or repulsion in their eyes. Gradually he had also acquired a certain fear of middle-aged women; what he read in their eyes was quite different; a certain moistness could come into the eyes of middle-aged women when they looked at him : why?

He stood on the deck of the big ship that was taking him to a new town and a new life, a young first-year undergraduate, with a sea of difficulties and unresolved conflicts of conscience ahead of him, but the future was his, the salt sea-wind whistled in the ship's rigging and his heart pounded; at that moment he had all the qualities necessary to triumph. Why was it, then, that he did not stride forward, proud and strong, into the bows and hurl his youthful challenge across the water? Why did he stand under the superstructure, squeezed against the wall, with wavering gaze and hat pulled down over his eyes, as if he were a fugitive and a criminal?

He was a young man with a past, a young man who had stumbled decisively in life's first heat and now, with set jaw, was preparing for its second heat. He no longer sparkled with happiness, for he had been reduced to that racking of the brains that gives rise to a sense of guilt. He was a very lost sheep who had mustered the remains of his strength and risen to his feet, refusing to be lost.

When this young eagle had been offered an independent job running a commercial school in the provinces, he had given up his studies at Oslo University and delightedly winged his way to what he thought was life's great adventure: a well-paid job with his own office and private accommodation in a strange town where he was free from the tyranny of parental supervision. He had quickly got himself a passionate, fiery mistress with long, glistening raven black hair (if it was not she who had got him). She was called Gunnhild and was the local vamp and six years older than he. After some months of violent love-making he had put her in the family way (if it was not she who had arranged to become so). After that, his doe's eyes did not have the same light in them as before and his laughter was no longer so innocent and pure. He couldn't persuade a doctor to give her an abortion; in his despair he fled to a small town near the first, where he was offered a job running a new school; there he met a little divorcée of thirty-seven called Siv. She had flaxen hair and a melancholy mouth and warm hands; she was so short that she reached only to his solar plexus. She took him under her

motherly wing and he rewarded her gentleness and thought-
fulness by promptly putting her in the family way too (if it was
not she who succeeded in becoming pregnant). Then he almost
went out of his mind and one night—it was the eve of his
twenty-first birthday—he had stood sharpening his razor with
every intention of castrating himself. Since then he had limped
about the earth, afraid of the light, ashamed, with bowed head.

A man who has been in hell never forgets it. He bears for all
time a crown of melancholy and bitterness round his brow,
however fair and curly his young hair may be. The experiences
mentioned here had driven a breach in his self-confidence. He
was afraid lest people find out about his past and condemn
him. All the last year that he had spent teaching in his native
town, he had scarcely dared look at a young girl, he felt broken
as a person and a man; in his loneliness he had recourse to the
poor form of love-making on which he had lived in puberty:
the joyless solitary rite, and that in its turn merely increased his
self-contempt and did nothing to make him pull himself together. Solitary love-making was poison, he had learned that,
but he had also learned what the other could lead to. He had
laid in an arsenal of contraceptives, but he did not know what
use he could make of them. He had grown frightened and
shunned the light, any complaint made with assurance convinced him that he was at fault.

Now, at the age of twenty-three, he had already begun to be
apologetic. His face paled every time he saw a man in uniform
or a policeman, he always thought that they were coming to
take him to prison for being behind with his maintenance payments, that the black-haired Gunnhild, who was an animal,
unscrupulous, as hard as nails, and without a particle of mercy,
had made good her threats and broadcast an appeal for him,
because he had not fulfilled his obligations punctually. Yet he
had a sort of built-in stoicism and that saved him; he kept his
secrets to himself, never told anyone of his fears.

In his heart of hearts he refused to admit that his defeat was
in any way a moral failure; he was convinced that the earth was
green and fertile and good, and that it was more than rich
enough to take two new-born babies. He was utterly convinced
that in other and more spacious circumstances the birth of two

children would not have been a sin and a disgrace, but, on the contrary, a source of joy. He was convinced that he was not at fault, but that the fault lay with society, with its lies and fear of sex. Thus he came increasingly to hate his parents, the institution of the family, hypocrisy, the little golden ring, the clergy and especially the concept called God.

In this state of mind he had turned to socialism. It is true that in his country socialism had begun to assume a character of practical striving for material benefits, that it had passed into the hands of the trade unions for whom progress never means anything but higher wages and security of employment, but that he did not realize. In his over-excited state socialism was to him the wonderful renaissance of the twentieth century, the re-discovery of man's sovereignty, the epitome of culture, greatness, freedom, beauty and wit, for he had listened only to the intellectuals. ('Mr. Chairman, can no one get Dr. Munkestad a post?') And at this period of his life there were two people in Norway, they shall be given their true names, who by their fearlessness and uprightness made an indelible impression upon him; they became the heroes of his youth, and as he now stood on the deck of the mailboat that was taking him to start his life's second heat, his idealized picture of them was the most precious thing he had with him, more precious than his beloved violin.

The first was the Norwegian writer Arnulf Øverland. Ash had read his polemic *Christianity, the Tenth Plague* and it had left him gasping for air and sobbing with excitement. Then there came a time when he read one of Øverland's poems. Reading it, he had felt as if a dagger had come whizzing past his ear from behind and buried itself in the wall before his face, a gleaming dagger with a red ruby glowing at the end of the haft. That was at the verse:

> Tear the cross of Christ off your flag
> And hoist it red and unadorn'd
> Let no one fool you with their brag
> That to us a saviour has been born.

He was never to forget those lines; they were to burn for ever in his blood, sweet and proud; if he should ever manage to get on his feet again and become a man, he would be a man like Arnulf Øverland.

And the other hero? This was a heroine. Her name was Tove Mohr and she was a doctor, and one evening she had stood, tall and straight, in a dark dress, and lectured in favour of legalized abortion and the establishment of Birth Control Clinics all over the country. He had heard about her before and read of her untiring work; but that evening, sitting among eight hundred other students listening to her, he couldn't believe his own ears. He had become filled with a quiet sense of reverence; he had been so moved that he had to bury his face in his hands. Her voice was educated, calm, soft, academic; for some reason or other he was tremendously impressed by her standing there speaking in the cause of the unfortunate and tormented, not because she herself was involved, not because she was a woman of the proletariat with some personal wrong to avenge, but because she was possessed by compassion and charity. There was no *need* for her to speak on behalf of legalized abortion, but she did so all the same.

The woman's personal courage also made an overwhelming impression on him. He himself knew women who, in private, behind locked doors, and in hushed tones, could maintain a woman's right to interrupt pregnancy. But if he had asked them to say it publicly, to write to the newspapers about it, lecture about it—they would have shrunk in terror from society's condemnation and from what is perhaps the severest punishment that can be meted out to a woman: to be thrown to women. Yet here stood a woman openly discussing the disgraceful thing, speaking without a tremor in her voice of the most unmentionable thing of all: the unwanted child. . . .

There was a discussion after the lecture. He didn't dare take part in it; he was afraid his voice would break, afraid the emotional volcano he had in his breast would erupt. He sat there, mute and unhappy, until twelve o'clock; then he could endure it no longer, but got to his feet, trembling with nervousness, and asked the Chairman if it were not possible for the Students' Society to send a resolution to the authorities in order to speed things up.

Chairman: Am I to understand your question as a proposal that a resolution should be sent?

Ash: Yes.

Chairman: Then we must vote on the resolution.

Voice from the hall: We must first know the terms of the resolution.

(Ash goes pale at the thought that perhaps he will have to frame the resolution.)

Another voice from the hall: The vote would not be legal. Before a resolution can be adopted, two-thirds of the members must be present, and most people have gone home.

Ash looks round the half-empty hall: it is true. For a moment, through the curtain of tobacco smoke, his eyes meet those of the woman doctor; he looks down and resumes his seat. He has lost. But he prays a silent prayer that *she* may not give up the fight.)

A very young man.

Time, and the ship, and the ship again. (Always there is a ship and where is it taking us now?) Cruel time has the answer, but time has no mouth and in his powerlessness and humility the young man glanced at his watch: three minutes left.

A young man with a naked, sensitive heart (like the quivering skin on the flank of a thoroughbred) his longings extended to all points of the compass, his soul swung like a compass needle but had not the latter's ability to find a direction, a very young man in search of education, strength, service (for he did not want to command, he wanted to serve, to become part of something greater than himself), in search of love (oh, love), in search of honour, honour and again honour, and an honourable life. His soul was that of a butterfly, his body an elk's, he stood on deck (two minutes left) with his bundle of ignominy and his dream of fame; in one half of his heart a violin, in the other a cash register. (Never before had he bothered about money, but he had obligations as a father; necessity had made him secure with a safety-pin the inside pocket where his poor little pocketbook lay; he was embarrassed by the safety-pin and no one must see it.) He would so gladly have stormed the heavens, but he was held back by a safety-pin. A very young man, musician and accountant (vine leaves and rates of interest), poet and socialist (the Nine Muses and Karl Marx), wanting beauty and justice, filled with a vision of the future (young men will always see visions), a young prophet with his face turned back in sorrow, a young man seeking joy, pure joy, the joy that is unfailing (if it exists, but it must exist! And he must find it! Let no one fool you that the saviour has been born!), a young man, embarking on life's second heat. He had descended to the realm of the dead and dug himself up again; now he wanted to find the joy that is unfailing; in his dreams he searched for a red ruby. That young man with gentle roe-deer eyes and set jaw was going to find the red ruby if he had to dig in all the mountains of the world and move each one, find it even if it did not exist, even if he had to make it himself—did he shrink from becoming an explorer or alchemist?—such was the young man, Ash Burlefoot, on that day in the early autumn of 1938 as he stood on the deck of the mail-steamer in a moment lifted out of eternity.

When the ship's bell rang for the third time, he shuddered and tightened the belt of his macintosh.

Slowly the ship slipped down the fjord, the world rolled sickeningly on its way through endless space, and endless space journeyed on through time.

He gripped the brown-varnished ship's rail and held tight.

I Wonder how the Middle Classes Live?

The salt sea breeze blew him awake, his gloom left him as he heard the thump of pistons from the engines in the bowels of the ship, it was like kettle-drums in a great symphony of destiny, and he felt like dancing on deck.

What is the secret of the dull, honey-sweet sense of well-being that fills a person on the first day of a voyage? The quivering, bland awareness of adventure in the body? Is it not perhaps the feeling of being cut off for two whole days and nights, cut off from land?

No sooner had the ship rounded the first headland, so that he could no longer see his home town, than he was overwhelmed by a huge, senseless, mad desire for food. He had caught a smell that was streaming out from the corridor. He inhaled with wide, quivering nostrils, a cry rose in his throat, he thought he knew that there was going to be fried halibut, *fried halibut with lemon*!

King or beggar, conqueror or fugitive—as long as a young man can stand on a ship's deck and reel with hunger, there is hope.

A little later in the day, in front of the ticket window, someone beside him said, 'Hullo!' Turning, Ash was surprised to find himself looking into the face of a former classmate. Ash gulped; far from being pleased, he was secretly horrified. This horror was caused by the past, no matter what part of it; the past was a thing from which he was fleeing and of which he did not wish to be reminded; a familiar face and a voice that said hullo were as terrible as the sight of a policeman. (He had a tactical plan for his life, which was this: for five years I shall remain in seclusion, in the shadows, with my hat pulled down over my eyes; *then* I shall come forward with the knowledge and strength that I have been acquiring secretly; I shall emerge like a thunderbolt as a musician, scientist, politician, the surprise will knock them over and paralyse their memories, the very thunder will keep them from remembering my past.)

A second's hurried calculation told him that his old schoolmate must be quite ignorant of his recent degradation. It is true that he came from the part of the country where Ash's defeat had taken place, but Norway is larger than anyone realizes and so far Gunnhild had not carried out her threat to broadcast an SOS for him.

So Ash smiled. 'Hullo,' he said and: 'Where are you off to?'

The other, a thin, swarthy, quiet youth called Daniel, pursed his lips almost apologetically and said that he had passed into The College. That was where he was going.

Ash Burlefoot gaped open-mouthed.

Ash had been the best in the class. He had the best reports, the best recommendations, the best qualifications for studying at The College, yet he had lived the last few months in fearful doubt whether his qualifications were good enough. While waiting for the results, The College had become for him a sort of Olympian school which only young, golden gods were allowed to attend. He had nearly died of pride and joy the day he got the letter telling him that he was accepted.

But Daniel, rather slow and lethargic, had been the born also-ran. He had done a year at Oslo University, just got through the preliminary in phonetics, but failed resoundingly in Latin. What qualifications were those for The College? What remained of its Olympian glory now? And what about young gods?

The next instant his disappointment turned to relief. If a man like Daniel, with such mediocre abilities, could be accepted, it meant that The College must be an easy place, its exams child's play; to work his way through the future would be as easy as cutting butter with a hot knife. If the moment before he had been hurt in his vanity, now he was brimming over with relief; perhaps the work would be so easy that he could take spare-time jobs and earn a little! Perhaps he could even combine work at The College with a course in harmony and counterpoint at the Conservatory!

He rubbed his hands and slapped Daniel's back; he was so delighted that he discovered he could afford to stand Daniel a beer in the saloon. In the saloon he became so above himself that he looked round blithely to see if there were any pretty women there, but there was no one but a fat peasant woman with a bearded wart on her chin and a kerchief round her head, and a thin old townswoman with grey skin and a lace collar and a cherry-strewn hat pierced with a menacing hatpin; but that damped neither their pleasure nor their hopes nor their visions of the future. The apathetic Daniel thawed and over the beer they agreed to try and get a room together when they arrived (it is cheaper when two share and also it provides company) and they felt they were well-off indeed when later that evening Daniel, who knew the captain, came and said that they might move from the third class and have a two-berth cabin in the first class without paying extra. It was outside the tourist season and there were many empty cabins in the first class.

That evening they stretched out in good mahogany bunks, feeling if not like gods, at any rate like lords.

Ash knocked the ash off his cigarette into the cardboard container fixed by the edge of the bunk, and with a feeling of profound well-being asked into space:

'I wonder how the middle classes live?'

When a Man Goes A-Journeying

He woke to a new day with a calm sea and was tremendously hungry. He could smell bacon and eggs and steaming coffee as soon as he reached the door of the dining saloon and he swallowed hungrily and walked in. As his knife cut through the yolk so that the yellow ran out, as he was raising the first aromatic forkful to his mouth, a thing happened to him that had happened many times before: he thought of a little girl without a legal father whose mother was so poor that she had to threaten the father that she would broadcast an appeal for him. Breakfast in the dining saloon cost two crowns; that was two crowns taken from a fatherless little girl. He gulped and let the piece of egg sink back on to the plate. For five such breakfasts he could have bought a child's dress and posted it to her. Of course, he would have got it back by return of post: Gunnhild would have said that she was not going to be fobbed off with trifles. She would have nothing to do with *bribes*.

Irritated, he again raised the aromatic piece of egg and bacon, and this time he swallowed it.

If I don't manage to get the better of this sense of guilt, he thought, it will end in catastrophe: either I'll kill myself or I'll work it off on other people: I'll start a revolution or a war, I'll sweep round me with a scythe. Perhaps, he thought, not only my salvation but that of all mankind lies in our being able to keep our sense of guilt *moderate*. Neither more nor less than to achieve a moderate sense of guilt.

He ate the rest of his breakfast tranquilly, in a sort of gay, excited serenity, because he had glimpsed the beginnings of a very interesting and important philosophy.

All the same: philosophy does not provide a child with clothes. He did not tip the steward.

Later, Daniel and Ash spent most of their time in the big first class saloon. It was raining slightly. The saloon was almost empty. The two of them read. Ash had lent Daniel a textbook on the analysis of balance-sheets.

'Do you understand any of this?' Daniel asked, looking up from the book and across at Ash.

'Heavens, yes,' said Ash, lowering the local newspaper he had got himself at the last stopping place. 'I even taught it for a year.'

Daniel sighed:

'It looks horribly difficult.'

'Child's play,' said Ash.

The next moment he shuddered: again he had been reminded of personal matters.

Was it early or late in the evening when their attention was attracted by the two girls? Afterwards, when he thought about it, he couldn't remember.

The two girls in overcoats and kerchiefs rushed about so restlessly; at one moment they were perched on the edge of a table in the saloon, the next they had run out on deck leaving the door open behind them; then they could be heard talking with one of the crew out in the corridor and giggling loudly; then they were back in the saloon, looked round, whispered cryptically to each other, exploded with squeals of laughter into each other's kerchief and rushed out again. Draughts and tumultuous gaiety accompanied them. Ash felt profoundly irritated by them, all the more as they obviously sought company. One was plain, but the other was quite pretty; but because they always ran hand in hand they made a pair of indeterminate character and appearance. There was something noisy and calf-like about them and then that perpetual giggling; Ash loathed people who could not behave in a public place; he felt that he wanted to

could not bear his gaze and pulled his head down again; and in the midst of his own ecstasy he had to investigate this phenomenon, asked if it were happening now too. Yes, she whispered. And now too? And again she whispered, 'Yes.' He had never seen anything like it; he now felt that he couldn't keep it going much longer; the realization that she was having those countless orgasms had aroused a little devil in him: he would show her! but now he felt that the end was near; he felt it from his toes to the roots of his hair, he was like an element with a thousand expectant volts. Then there was a knock at the door.

First he was terror-stricken: a ship's cabin is like a hotel room, you can never know what is allowed and what forbidden; perhaps it was the captain or the mate standing there! But the next moment he realized that it couldn't be as bad as that; it was either Daniel or the other girl or both of them; so then he became hilarious, hysterically excited, went to the door, right up to it and called:

'Wait! I'm asleep. Come back in half an hour! Come back in the early morning! Ha, ha!'

He heard nothing outside; reassured, he went back to the bunk. On the way he lifted his jacket from the chair, searched in a pocket, found what he wanted, had to open the little envelope with his teeth as his hands were trembling so, and at the third attempt managed to put the thing on. She had turned her head to see what he was doing and turned it away again as quickly. As he came into her again she whispered that he need not have worried. He paused and asked what she meant; she said that as far as she was concerned he could just as well have taken a chance.

At first the wantonness of her invitation made his blood race; it was as if molten lead had been poured into his veins. Then he came to himself and drew free. He got off the bed, stood on the floor, felt his cheeks go pale and taut.

He began to speak in a husky voice, stuttering with fright and fury. He lectured the girl and she curled up under the eiderdown and looked at him fearfully. Did she not know anything of the laws of Nature? Did she not know how a pregnancy was started? Had she no inkling about sperm and fertilization? Well, did she? Would she be so very kind as to tell him what

she had meant by asking him not to bother? Was she bent on
having a child, was that it? Had she private means that would
allow her to give a child a decent home and bring it up
properly? No? Well, neither had he; he was a student and had
only enough for dry bread for himself and he did not intend
to have children right and left! He lashed her with his words,
he walked round the floor in just his shirt, holding forth.
Heavens above, how he lectured her! Did she not realize what
tragedy a woman can cause when she doesn't take precautions?
Irresponsible, that's what he called it, criminal behaviour, yes
that was it, criminal! He shook his fist at her, he frightened the
wits out of her; she lay there terrified, looking at him round-
eyed and in the end she began to cry. That pleased him, some
of his anger ran from him then; he had aired much that he had
been bottling up inside, the lecture had done him good and it
would certainly be a useful lesson for her too. Excellent. He
stood there and realized that he was stone sober; all at once
he began to feel badly about the girl in the bed; perhaps she had
not meant it the way he had taken it, heaven knows what she
had meant, to hell with everything; now of course he had
spoiled the whole' thing and only succeeded in making her
unhappy.

He handed her a handkerchief which she took; then he
glimpsed a little smile on her face and he swallowed; and tiny
ants began crawling up his veins. To strengthen himself he
reached out his arm and took a gulp of the tepid brew in the
tumbler; it even tasted refreshing; he held the tumbler out to
her, she took it and drank a little. And for a little while they
said nothing. He sat down beside her. After all the agitation he
had to take a deep breath every now and again. He laid his
hand on her neck, she put hers on his. Her skin was so warm
and throbbing, he let his hand slide slowly down over her breast
and the eiderdown slipped off her and she did not hinder him,
and he was sick with restrained lust and she was a mountain of
pink willing flesh and he quivered with a thousand volts and
clasped her full breasts and cried aloud as the explosion came
and it was so good that it sent sparks up his spine, and he could
not remember it ever having been so good.

They dressed a short while later, for they had heard steps in the corridor outside. They looked at each other and smiled. Then there was a knock on the door.

'One moment,' said Ash.

He drew the girl up from the bunk and hastily smoothed the bed-clothes. Then he stood looking at her. He took her hand.

'Thanks,' he said quietly. 'Thanks most awfully.'

'Thank *you*,' she said, bashfully.

There was another knock. He glanced hurriedly round the cabin to see that it was all presentable. Then slowly his jaw dropped: it was not his and Daniel's cabin they were in! Nor the girls' either! It was another cabin, quite unused, except for the bed, there was not so much as a clothes-hanger on the wall or a toothbrush on the shelf! Before he had time to tell the girl of this astounding discovery, she had opened the door a little way and stuck her head out.

It was the other girl. Inquisitive and giggling, she burst in. Ash shut the door behind her. The two girls sat down on the bed for a moment. Ash felt that he must join in the conversation. He sat down on the chair by the bed; as he did so he saw what the other girl also saw at that very same moment and she looked from the little paper envelope lying on the carpet up at him; her nostrils distended momentarily and she looked at him with a half scandalized, half merry smile; she wasn't a pretty girl, her body was quite shapely but her face was common and sharp, and when she smiled he could see that she had bluey-white dental cement between her front teeth: she had been attending to her teeth herself instead of going to a dentist. Ash could not meet her knowing smile, so he used the old method of raising his eyebrows; and after a short while he got up and wished the girls goodnight.

Back in their own cabin Daniel was lying on his back snoring.

Ash undressed and washed. He had scarcely got in between the sheets before burning, redhot desire for the pink girl mounted in him again. Trembling, he got up and went quickly to the door, carefully he drew the curtain aside and opened the door, peeped out into the corridor. He heard the thumping of the great engines deep in the ship, he held his breath with excitement and intolerable desire, his heart pounded in time with the engines, which cabin was it that the girls had?—Had they gone to bed?—Dare he venture down the corridor in pyjamas? —What door should he try?—Suppose one of the stewardesses came along, or one of the crew? So he stood in the doorway and had to hold on to the jamb to keep his quivering body under control.

All at once they came walking along, the two of them, perhaps from the lavatory. He sagged at the knees, feeling rather faint, yet he managed to stretch out an arm and wave. 'Hssst!' he said and in the stillness of night it sounded as if he had blown a bassoon. She detached herself from her friend and came hesitantly towards him. He took her by the arm and drew her beseechingly into the doorway. He said nothing, he couldn't speak, he groped for her face and in the gloom he could feel that she felt as he did, but she made excuses: her girl-friend did not like being left like that; whispering and weakly resisting she stood there beside him, no, she couldn't go in with him, no, it wasn't Daniel she was thinking of, she could hear that he was sound asleep all right, it was her friend, she couldn't be away long. And all the time he had been pulling up her skirt and then his hands were there and she whispered into his ear that if he was quick, if he could do it standing up . . . and he went gasping in search of his toilet-bag, stubbed his bare toe on a leg of the chair and danced a silent dervish's dance on one foot while clasping the other; tears came into his eyes and he couldn't see, yes, now he had one; he was afraid she might have gone, but she was standing waiting for him, a little strip of light from the corridor shining on her dark hair, and his trembling hand groped over her and then her breathing was coming in the same gasps as his.

Afterwards she righted her clothes and slipped out through the door, turning as she did so to whisper a hasty goodnight; he stroked her cheek.

He sank to his knees on the floor of the cabin throbbing with happiness and thankfulness; finally he could endure it no longer, he had to groan or burst. Daniel stopped snoring and turned on his side.

When Ash again lay in bed, it struck him with singular force: he had no idea what the girl's name was!

Life is queer, he thought. He covered his face with his hands and groaned with pleasure and thankfulness as he inhaled again the bitter-sweet smell of her body, life was infinitely better than its reputation.

Then he lay on his back and clasped his hands on his chest, like a child saying its nightly prayer to God. Languid, heavy, happy, innocent, for the first time for an eternity innocent and without the least hint of bad conscience. This innocent child of God, for whom the bunk was so short that his feet stuck out over the end, smoked a blissful cigarette, and noticed how his hand still trembled, as though in after-pains. Then he stubbed out the cigarette in the cardboard spew-cup (the next morning he would write to the shipping company to thank them and say how practical it was having such a thing at the head of the bed); then he turned on his side, murmuring: 'When a man goes a-journeying ...' The sentence was never finished, he fell asleep like a stone sinking in a bottomless well.

He woke next morning feeling that something was wrong. For a few seconds he lay confused, sore, with gummed-up eyes, listening to the outside world. Why did he have that quivering feeling of something being wrong?

Then all at once he knew: he had overslept! He looked at Daniel's bunk: empty. He looked at his wrist-watch: a quarter to eight. According to the time-table the boat was due in at eight: he had told himself that he was going to get up at seven to see the fjord as they sailed in: the city itself was said to be a sight from the fjord. Damn it! Only a quarter of an hour before the boat would be in and he really ought to shave. Why hadn't Daniel woken him, the stupid idiot? Now, of course, Daniel was up on deck, freshly shaven, enjoying—yes, *enjoying* the sail up the lovely fjord. Daniel's suitcases stood neatly together on the floor, all packed, everything tidy, heavens how he loathed tidy people! Especially when they left their friend dead to the world, so that he would have to shave and pack in a ghastly hurry and arrive on deck, breathless and confused and angry and sweating and with a blood pressure of over two hundred, just in time to see that the boat was tied up, all the passengers gone ashore and not a porter to be seen on the deserted quay. And now he heard the telegraph ring down half speed; they were there!

He got up on deck just as the gangway was being lowered. Suddenly he caught sight of the pink girl standing with her friend in the queue on deck. He was immensely surprised that she did not seem to recognize him, did not reply to his discreet little nod; there might have been the shadow of a smile on her face, but he wasn't sure; she was seeing to her luggage and tickets in such a businesslike way. She and her friend were by the rail, dignified and aloof. It was as though they had never been little wantons running giggling through the corridors and saloons; there they now stood, ladylike, unapproachable, refined, like statues, and Ash clasped his head and wondered confusedly: Was it a dream? He rubbed his lips with his hand and caught the faint smell that lingered on it: he hadn't been dreaming.

He felt suddenly happy. But the next moment he was unhappy, for of course he did not know where the girl was going. Under the circumstances he couldn't go up to her and ask her name and address. Were she and her girl-friend going to look for jobs in the city? As waitresses, children's nurses, maids, or shop assistants? Now she was walking down the gangway, now she was on the quay, now she was going out of his life. A man had met them on the quay, he shook hands with them both, but smiled more warmly at the lush, pink one, and Ash swallowed and said to himself: Well I'll be damned!

As he walked down the gangway his heart was quivering and wondering. As he stepped out on to the round cobbles, it was the future he had beneath his feet. He stopped and stood there in the crowd. There were gulls' cries in the air and a clean sky. He had begun life's second heat. He had reached the city. His heart began to quake and a man said close to his ear:

'Elsa came home from the hospital yesterday.'

The Wild Boar

The first day in a strange town!

Quivering joy, snuffing nostrils, open eyes, light springy step, ears turning like animal's ears to listen to all the new words, the new melody of the city people's speech. . . .

Yes, all that. But first and foremost a feeling of smallness and fear of the great chaos, the houses, streets, addresses, telephone numbers. This town was so modern that the telephone was automatic, you only had to dial five numbers and you were through, but then you fumbled with the coin that had to be put in and pressed the button far too early and you broke out into a sweat, for you had not so many coins that you could afford to lose any in the telephone's greedy slot. A big city, twice the size of his native town, beautiful, clean, well-regulated, with style about the high modern office buildings in the centre and style about the old, white-painted, well-preserved dwelling houses in the side streets, mountains round about and sky above, an open and a free city, an old capital with churches, castles of stone and medieval houses on the wharves, a modern, live, enterprising commercial twentieth-century port.

A thousand mysterious, exciting smells poured over him from warehouses and sheds and office doors and café windows and from the streets themselves; there was the smell of tar and hemp of herring and dried fish, of oranges and cabbage and onions, of pepper and curry and cloves and cardamoms and dill, the door to a bakery opened and shut and for an instant he was enveloped in the warm wonderful smell of new bread and hot rolls, he caught the smell of steaming malt from a brewery and the sour smell of new leather from a tannery; the stuffy smell of cloth and clothes from a tailor's workroom and that of burned rubber from a vulcanizing plant; the smell of oilskins when he barged into people on the street, for it was drizzling and the place was famed for its rain and in a momentary

economic panic he thought that he would probably have to buy
an umbrella and how much did an umbrella cost! the smell
of salt, of hot iron from the rails where a streetcar squealed on
a curve (and as the son of a streetcar driver he had already
noticed that the streetcars were made by Siemens-Schuckert,
the same as his father's at home); a smell of boat's smoke from
the harbour, of motorcar exhaust in the streets, and from a
flower shop came a heavy smell of roses and moss and warm
mould as a sudden reminder to the young man that it was
autumn and that life ends in death, even for kings.

The streets, the houses with their Nordic *grandezza* and styl-
ishness, the trim octagonal pond in the centre of the town with
its surrounding lawns and sculptures—it struck young Ash that
surely this must be the loveliest town in Norway (later in life
he was to know that it was); and before he could say knife he
and Daniel had reached The College which stood on an eminence, and they both took their hats off as they went into the
office, for they had not realized that it was such a magnificent
place. They had a bewildering impression of mahogany doors,
soft thick carpets (and their shoes were muddy!) brass stair-
rails shining like gold, marble steps, huge wall mirrors in rococo
frames. They would not have been surprised if a butler had
appeared and asked for their cards. They were both whitefaced
with timidity when the college secretary asked them to be seated
while he got the forms. Well, thought Ash as he sat with
his hat on his knees, looking round, if they think they are going
to soften me up with marble stairs and mahogany, they're making a big mistake. If they want my opinion, there's a faint odour
of the upstart about this building; it's overdone, it reminds me
of Hadrian's Villa in ancient Rome; the shipowners must have
had bad consciences to have built a place like this. So much
the better: he would tell them about the dictatorship of the
proletariat, indeed he would and (since the secretary had momentarily gone into an adjacent room) he let go a fart to confirm
it. The next moment he blushed, as a young, plump girl clerk
with ash blond hair stuck her head round the partition behind
which she had been sitting out of sight and looked at the two
of them.

Daniel was to spend the first night at a hotel, Ash with some distant relatives of his mother. Then the following morning, they were to meet and go hunting for a room together. Daniel hadn't said a word about how he had spent that last evening on the boat and Ash did not like to ask if he had got anywhere with the other girl. For Daniel's sake he rather hoped he hadn't, even though easy girls do not grow on trees in Norway.

During the morning Ash had rung up his relatives and been told that he was most welcome and must come to lunch. Ash had accepted, though with considerable misgivings: he had met the husband, a grocer, some years before and thought him an ass. Now he was to have to meet the whole family and give them greetings from his own.

It was a visit that he was to remember for a long time. He met the wife first, a middle-aged, colourless, quiet woman whose handshake was strangely limp and almost apologetic. Ash felt as if he had taken hold of something dead. Her husband, how-ever, was quite different: a short, stoutish, muscular man of about fifty with a tanned skin, shamelessly white, strong teeth in a broad mouth with underhung jaw. The little creature bristled with vitality and hair; his body was almost pear-shaped (stalk up), with steeply slanting shoulders, protruberant pot-belly and broad hips; despite this almost feminine contour—or perhaps just because of it—he seemed doubly muscular, almost brutal; there was tremendous strength in his short bull's neck and short, thick arms; he came in smelling of pickled herring and strong green cheese and freshly roasted coffee, and Ash had no difficulty in imagining the little man lifting a herring-barrel weighing a hundredweight with the utmost ease; later in the day he discovered that the man's favourite contribution to a social gathering was the performance of feats of strength: he took chairs by the back and raised them till they were hori-zontal in the air, cracked walnuts in his fingers, lifted the piano with one hand and challenged Ash to a trial of strength. Ash declined when he saw the man's forearm; he had rolled up his sleeve and his arm bulged with muscle and was as hairy as a baboon's; Ash made the excuse that his forearm was twice the length of his host's and it would not be a fair test because of the principle of leverage.

The man's name was Sivert Nielsen (and Co.) but because he had jagged white teeth and bushy hairs growing out of his nostrils, Ash at once christened him the Wild Boar.

He had taken an immediate dislike to the man's boastfulness. He had scarcely got inside the door and shaken Ash's hand, before he was dragging him round all the rooms pointing out his treasures: 'What do you think of that, eh?' And every time Ash had to say that it was fearfully nice; which he did to the drawing-room furniture and its two paintings and piano and the bedroom furniture and the children's room and the radio and the bookshelves with their books, and the Wild Boar told him the price of each single item and what a bargain it had been, and he rubbed his hairy butcher's hands and told Ash that he had got his house at an opportune moment and only paid thirty crowns a month in rent, then he gave Ash a punch in the ribs and, beaming at him out of grey-blue, rather protruberant eyes that looked as though they had been a long time in herring brine, told him that he too could have all that, once he had passed his exams at The College, provided he just *worked*, and Ash felt beside himself with horror at the mere thought that the aim of his studies should be to have a home like the Wild Boar's; he would rather die than set up house with such things around him; he was unable to express his burning young hopes and visions, but among them was beauty and quiet, big light windows and simple furniture (preferably things he had made himself), there were flowers and restfulness and smiles, a beautiful woman (oh, who was to be the woman in his life and what would she look like?—he didn't know, but she would have dry, small, warm, strong hands and her handclasp would not be limp), and when he asked people home, it would not, most certainly *not* be in order to boast of what he had paid for the various pieces, and as he stood there beside the little, puffed-up, self-satisfied cheesemonger he had a vision, possibly because the Wild Boar's deep dangerous power, his tireless energy, reminded him of another person who also had had strength and energy and a strong will, a person from a stock of men who picked up lengths of railway line with ease and set them in place single-handed.

He thought of black-haired Gunnhild by whom he had had a child; if he had married her, her ideal of a home would have coincided exactly with the Wild Boar's. And she would have had the strength of will to see that she got what she wanted. If he hadn't known before, he realized at that moment with a tremendous rush of conviction that he had been right to run away and become a fugitive. Feeling almost relieved, he looked down again at the busy cheesemonger who had pulled out his gold watch and kept opening the cover and snapping it shut again, till he could be quite sure that his young visitor really had noticed this wonderful treasure: a golden gold watch made of gold!

Later, Ash thought: why do I have such an intense loathing of people who boast of their possessions? Is it that I find it morally reprehensible? Or is it that I am sorry for them, because deep inside they are so poor that they have to bluff with external things? Or am I secretly afraid of them and envy them their animal appetite for life?

Then the son and daughter also returned home. The son was a pale, slightly drooping stalk; there was something white, wrinkled, cowed and sunless about him that made Ash think of the shoots that potatoes put out after a winter in the cellar; he was a couple of years older than Ash and worked in a bank, and Ash got the impression that secretly he envied Ash for getting into The College. This vague feeling was rather depressing, especially as Ash had been told that he would be sleeping in the son's room, where a bed had been made up for him on the sofa. The idea of spending an evening and a night with a secret envier was far from pleasant. The daughter was seventeen and going to the Commercial High School; fat, strong, healthy and stupid, she was exactly like her father. Ash's heart was in no danger there. Ash was told with boastful bluster how she was in her School handball team and how, the year before, she had been with her class on a trip to Oslo. Ash nodded politely. He took a stealthy look to see if she too had hairs in her nose: she had. They were small and fair, but in time they could become big and dark, like her father's bristles. She was going to be a sight, Ash thought.

They took their seats at the table and the Wild Boar clasped his hands for grace, and so did the others. There was a moment's embarrassment, because Ash could not bring himself to follow their example. It was so awful that he could have screamed. The Wild Boar and God, it was too incredible! But why, actually? Wasn't God for all time bound to the industrious, the thrifty, those who bargained and counted their money? Richard Baxter, the late eighteenth-century writer of Puritan tracts, said that of two ways of doing business the Christian would also be the more lucrative! Why should he be so surprised at the Wild Boar saying grace? For a long time now, ever since he had celebrated his twenty-first birthday by resigning from the Church, he had known that it was the world's millions of Wild Boars who kept God going, and God them! Control your aversion for such scenes; one day you may go to Arabia and there the master of the house will probably go down on his knees with his face towards Mecca before he tucks into his food. Just smile, a slight, polite, calm smile, and look down into the fish soup and keep your convictions to yourself. It's all very well to tear the cross of Christ off your flag and hoist it red and unadorned, but there's no need to do it just at this table. Besides Mrs. Wild Boar's soup smells divine and there's boiled fresh fish and liver to follow.

The Wild Boar did not use his knife and fork, but pulled the steaming pieces of fish apart with his fingers and arranged them on his plate. He then sucked his fingers clean with much noisy smacking of the lips. Ash was tremendously impressed, chiefly because it had never for a moment occurred to the man that this was bad manners. No thought of self-criticism could penetrate that flint-hard skull.

Towards the end of the meal, when the stewed plums came on ('Genuine Victoria plums from my warehouse, you can tell that can't you?' asked the Wild Boar, and Ash nodded politely, while he wondered whether there could be such a thing as spurious, fake plums) conversation turned on Ash's plans for the future. The Wild Boar wondered whether Ash was thinking of starting up on his own after he had taken his exams, perhaps in the grocery trade. Well, Ash had to admit that neither wholesale nor retail trade entered into his plans, the nearest thing would be if he happened to get a job in the Co-operative movement.

A dreadful silence followed that remark. The Wild Boar swallowed a plum stone and his eyes nearly popped out of his head. Had he said the *Co-operative* movement?

It took Ash only a couple of seconds to realize what a brick he had dropped: there is the same mortal enmity between a capitalist cheesemonger and a Co-operative shop, as between a clergyman of the State Church and a chapel preacher. He would gladly have covered it up, but it was too late. The Wild Boar took a drink of juice and water and bent over the table towards Ash. In a voice trembling with hatred and the gravity of the situation, he said prophetically:

'Do you know what is written in Revelations?'

'N-no!' Ash had to admit that he was not very well up in the Bible. But wait: suddenly he remembered something he had heard in a discussion some time before, which had stuck in his mind, and, smiling, he added:

'Doesn't it say, in Chapter eight I think, that when the Lamb opened the seventh seal there was silence in heaven for about half an hour.'

The Wild Boar opened and shut his mouth.

Ash went on:

'I have often wondered whether they had watches in heaven or just went by guesswork.'

Ash felt that he could venture that little joke. To his boundless surprise he noticed that the son, the potato shoot, quickly put a piece of flat bread into his mouth to hide a smile. That made up for a lot; it was the first breath of warmth and understanding that had come his way in that house.

'That was not what I meant,' said the Wild Boar, 'I was thinking of something else. It says in the Revelation of St John the Divine that when the last day is approaching, the earth and all people are to be bound.' He straightened up and drew a deep breath after the effort of talking like a book, then he bent forward again, tapped a hairy finger on the table, lowered his voice and said in a conspiratorial, menacing tone: 'Do you know what they are to be bound with?' He did not wait for an answer, whispered: 'Co-operation.' Then it became too much for him: he shouted the word 'Co-operation!' drummed on the table with his short, fat, baboon-like fingers and bellowed: 'Co-operation!'

Ash glanced across the table at the Wild Boar's son; again he thought he could see the ghost of a smile on the young man's face.

'Well,' said Ash, 'perhaps not everything the Co-operative movement does is as good as it might be.'

'Good!' exclaimed the Wild Boar, his belly dancing with agitation, 'it's the work of the devil, boy. Co-operation is the Beast itself.'

'Wasn't it being bound you mentioned a moment ago?' Ash asked cautiously.

'That and the Beast. Both of them.'

'So we must just hope that the Beast will get entangled in its own toils.'

'Yes,' groaned the Wild Boar, 'God grant it be like that.'

There was no doubt about it now, the young man on the other side of the table had smiled about his father, smiled in secret understanding with Ash. Ash left that table in considerably better spirits than when he sat down.

Not much happened that night; Ash found the young man a far more pleasant and interesting person than he had thought at first.

'Well I never,' said the young man and pointed.

'What?' said Ash, sitting in pyjamas on the edge of his bed; he looked down at his foot.

He gasped as he saw what the other had seen: his big toe was unrecognizable; he had never seen such a toe; it was all purple, almost black. Cautiously Ash prodded it with a finger and tears came into his eyes from the pain of it. Each hour of love you get on earth, he thought, must be paid for with grief. Frightened, he said:

'What if it's gangrene!'

'Oh,' said the other with a smile, 'that's not going to drop off. Tomorrow it'll be green, the morning after yellow and after that it will be white again.'

'Thank you,' said Ash, who had taken a liking to the other.

That potato-shoot appearance covered a modest, wise and questing mind; they lay and talked for a while before turning out the light. The young man was very well-read, largely in fields that one would never have expected of somebody who was

not only a clerk, but also the son of a cheesemonger and enemy
of the Co-operative movement. He had read Aldous Huxley
and T. E. Lawrence (not the Lawrence, Ash was told, who had
written *Lady Chatterley's Lover*, but the one who had nearly
succeeded in conquering Arabia for the Arabs during the First
World War); he had read the writings of a German called
Rudolf Steiner, of whom Ash had never heard, and also (this
rather shyly) a Danish translation of the Koran. The whole
Koran? The whole Koran.

Ash was to meet the young man later on various chance occasions, but he never went back to the house. He did not want to
meet the Wild Boar again, the sight of whose red, glistening,
self-satisfied face filled him with a profound, dull loathing, for
after that evening he had for the first time in his young life had
to ask himself quite seriously whether one is entitled to kill
another person? Not legally, of course, but morally? Are there
circumstances in which it is right to kill? Are there people who
must simply be classed as vermin?

That evening the Wild Boar and Ash had been alone together
for a while. Ash had remarked on how different the Wild Boar's
son and daughter were. The Wild Boar had cleared his throat,
looked round, and lowered his voice; they were alone. The Wild
Boar said: 'The boy's not my son.' Ash wanted to know whose
son he was. The Wild Boar dropped his voice still lower and said
that the boy—oh, well, you see—when he, the Wild Boar, met
the woman who was now his wife, she had a child born out of
wedlock. He, the Wild Boar, did not know the father; later, he
had adopted the boy. Ash opened his eyes wide at this highly
unexpected revelation of understanding and charitableness in
the cheesemonger. The Wild Boar clasped his hands over his
little pot-belly and sighed piously. Even he was impressed by
his own goodness. Then he leant forward, laid a hand on Ash's
knee (he never forgot the sight of that hand) and in a low, knowing, confidential tone of voice, said:

'I don't regret it. She's *dutiful*. She never grumbles.'

His yellow eyes were brimming with assurance, confidence,
brutality and iron-hard covetousness. Ash's heart began to bleed
at the thought of that grey, silent woman without character
whose handclasp was so apologetic and limp; and he got to his

feet, deathly pale, and stammered the excuse that he was fearfully tired. He never went to the Wild Boar's house again, and
many were the nights in that strange town that he lay awake
wondering if it were permissible to take a person's life.

The Fifty Blond Wolves

The next morning came and Ash set off for town and found
Daniel and together they went hunting for rooms. After four
hours (they had been given a list of addresses at The College)
and looking at thirty rooms, they were so exhausted that when
they came to the thirty-first, Ash said to the elderly woman who
opened the door, 'Have you a room vacant?' and when the
woman quavered 'Yyyes,' Ash fell into the hall crying 'We'll
take it.'

The students' office, and The College office.
The curriculum.
The curriculum.
Where was one to start?
How small and bitterly forlorn a young man can feel, when
he finds himself having to choose one of eight hundred books.

On the very second day, after he had been to the first few
lectures, he got into a panic. For a couple of years now he had
been teaching, had done the talking himself, and he had lost
the ability to sit and listen. Not only that, but what the professors and lecturers had served up in those first few lectures
seemed to him obvious, trivial and commonplace. He was horribly afraid that all his energy and keenness and his vast
enthusiasm would drain away, if he were to sit through a hundred such soporific lectures. Being violently impatient, he
wanted to get down to things straight away, that very moment,
to whet his brain and sharpen his wits; he had not gone to The
College to potter, he had come to fling himself into the hardest

and most important of struggles, that of the young man to become adult. There he sat together with fifty other young men at long modern desks of smooth polished oak, trembling with ghastly anxiety. It suddenly struck him that these lectures were only the cud of chewed-over books. These professors and lecturers were superfluous; in his socialist terminology they were unproductive middlemen! If only he could get at the books himself—and quickly—he would be face to face with the enemy and at grips with his real opponent.

The next few days only increased his bewilderment and appalling uncertainty. The curriculum was as long as a series of bad years and listed a sea of books, both required and optional reading. (Merciful heavens, what did they mean by optional reading? Who was to choose? And to what extent did the optional books count in the exams?) The bulk of the written material for the first year was in the form of stencilled sheets full of corrections and typing errors. (Aha! So that is why we have to attend lectures: to go through the sheets with the lecturer and correct the mistakes. We have to suffer, because some ass couldn't check the typing properly.)

That The College was new was obvious in everything, its organization and administration, even in the persons of the professors and lecturers. They knew their subjects all right, but they were not sure how to serve the matter up; they did not know how much the students knew already, nor what they were expecting to be taught. As a result, they often faltered and stuttered, especially the younger ones, broke the chalk when writing on the blackboard and made mistakes in calculation, and towards the end of the lecture, sweating and flushed, they would take panic-stricken refuge in reading out of a book. As this was always in either Swedish, German, English or French (there being no Norwegian literature on the subject), they were translating unseen, and often very faultily, stammering and scratching their heads and looking desperately up at the ceiling, as though expecting to find the Norwegian equivalent there. It was both embarrassing and frightening, and their whole audience quivered with suppressed desire to help.

To crown it all, the Professor of Business Administration, the most important subject, was a foreigner brought in from outside, there being no Norwegian capable of filling this important post. The country of this professor's birth was unknown, but he came from somewhere in Central Europe, perhaps Hungary, and had studied in Germany and been for a time in business in Sweden. After that he had spent some considerable time in the USA where he had been both professor in a university and economic consultant to various large concerns (tinned foods and electrical equipment). He was a man whose record made the students gasp with admiration. His record perhaps, but not his ability as a lecturer. He had learned a sort of Swedish and now struggled manfully to dilute it with Norwegian expressions, as a result quite a lot of the time was spent discussing the meanings of words. He had no idea how to teach and was the worst lecturer Ash had ever heard. Ash found it difficult to reconcile his record with his performance: the students simply did not understand any of his equations, calculations and graphs, especially as his writing on the blackboard was hurried and careless, almost that of a sick man. It was Ash who discovered the solution. One day when they were all sitting exhausted and bewildered after one of the man's lectures, Ash said to the others: 'The man's *too* clever, that's what it is.'

The professor was fair-haired, fat, mild and boyish; he might have been between forty and fifty. His smile was kindly and angelic, but at times it seemed somewhat warped and melancholy, as if he harboured some grudge or hid despair beneath his mask of love. He was like a monk trying to play the sporting priest. In order to get on with the students he sat on the table with dangling legs instead of standing behind it, sat there and smiled like a middle-aged scout-master. Ash shuddered with embarrassment; his idea of a professor was a man who knew his subject inside out and who kept behind his desk. If he wanted to be friends with the students, and they with him, the place for that was outside the lecture-hall. Ash had come to learn business administration, not to enjoy the sight of a professor's grey socks below dangling trouser legs. The professor who crawls to his students, he thought, ends by undermining their respect for his subject: the definition of a professor is a man who has the courage to be disliked by his students.

(Ash suddenly remembered a German master he had had at
school; he had filled them all with mute terror and unqualified
admiration; he never smiled, but he knew his subject perfectly;
Ash had him to thank for the fact that he could write and speak
German like a native. How they had hated the man! And how
lonely, bitterly lonely, the man had been. Any accomplishment
of value, Ash thought, comes from iron loneliness! And no
sooner had he thought that than he paled in horror: there was
nothing in the world he feared more than loneliness.)

This professor, the man with the gentle, feline face and forced
laughter and the boyish lock of hair that fell over his forehead
(Ash itched to cut it off, because it was always dropping down
and the man was always brushing it aside, and this was appallingly distracting for the students), this man belonged, it trans-
pired, to a religious sect which was then called the Oxford
Group and has since changed its name to Moral Rearmament.
Ash could have forgiven him this if he had kept his religious
convictions to himself, but he found it more difficult when the
professor brought them into his lectures and based economics
on the principle of human kindness.

It appeared that the guiding principle of both the professor
and economics was 'to serve mankind'. When he heard this,
Ash felt cheated. The purpose of economics was to produce the
maximum output at the minimum effort and cost. Any fool could
see that. Economics was a technique and it was this technique
Ash had come to learn. 'To serve mankind?' All right; he intended to do so one day, the socialist way; he shared the same
goal, but it was the economic *means* he had come to study. And
what was the good of these covert sermons about morality,
human kindness and consideration for others? Morals are not
something you can read up or listen to, but an attitude acquired
in real life, a practical method of associating with one's fellow
beings, something that comes of itself, not a thing to lecture
about. All talk about morality merely arouses antagonism to it.
Morals are the result of people coming to terms with each other
and rubbing their roughness off against each other. (Occasionally people just cannot team up together; then one either kills
the other or takes to flight, as Ash had fled from the black-haired
Gunnhild; that too is morality, he thought, morals in practice;

all the clergymen in the world could not have got me to live in wedlock with her.)

Mankind's greatest and most fateful delusion is that people will be better and nicer to each other if children at an early age are made to swot up the ten commandments that the old desert chieftain Moses tried to knock into the heads of his bedouin-vandals a couple of thousand years ago. These strict, unrealistic and above all incomprehensible commandments are the main cause of people going about like secret criminals, and the reason why most people with delighted vindictiveness take every chance offered them of having other gods than God, taking His name in vain, not keeping the sabbath holy, not honouring their father and mother, killing, committing adultery, stealing, bearing false witness, coveting their neighbour's house, ass, servants and wife. The salvation of the world lies, thought Ash, in stopping all this talk about morality; little did he know what a singular philosophical idea he had thus propounded.

And there was no one to hear it; Ash was then far too bashful and timid to open his mouth.

When fear and uncertainty are present, evil enters into people's hearts and they do not take it out of those who are the cause of their fear and uncertainty (the professors), but become bad-tempered with each other. They are like animals snapping at their own kind; they watch and listen; because they are suffering, everyone else must suffer too. There's a law about this, a law of snapping, which applies to all who feel insecure and see no way out of the mess they are in.

Ash became aware of this now and again during lectures. When one of the students seemed to have found a word, a light, help in something that the professor had said and, from sitting back listening, bent quickly over his notebook to scribble down his newfound wisdom, his activity was greeted with irritable smiles from the others. They raised their eyebrows: 'Thinks he's discovered something!' They stuck their thumbs into their ears and waggled the rest of their fingers most eloquently. 'What's he trying to get us to believe?' They even went so far as to snatch the fountain pen from the wretch's hand and pass it round: 'We can't allow him to write down that *nonsense*!'

It was even more evident during the breaks, when all the

students stood in little groups under the great leafy chestnut trees in the grounds.

Ash was most sensitive to groups of people, especially men. It was amazing and sometimes frightening, as though he had a special sense that enabled him to listen in to the moods of the different groups, to take X-ray photographs of their minds; it was as though this sense was a bird, a wheeling hawk that allowed him to see everything; no, it was more like being able to go about on invisible stilts. Sometimes this feeling set him above the others; he did not want that, but it came of itself; and then he became frightened, feeling not only superior but apart, and he so badly wanted to be one of the others, hungered so fiercely for comradeship.

Between lectures the students stood about conversing in small groups; some ate buns, some smoked pipes, others rolled cigarettes; now and again they cast an absent-minded glance across the wall at the girls' school lower down the hill, where, on its grey, sand-strewn playground, little girls walked round and round arm-in-arm, while others played at hopscotch and others again skipped. The students stood seemingly relaxed, with their buns, pipes and cigarettes, but Ash was intensely aware how wide awake their brains were, razor-sharp, how they were listening like wolves. And what was their everlasting, quivering, unspoken question? This: *Have any of the others got on to anything?* Has anyone made a secret start? Alert blue eyes watched beneath fair, bushy nordic eyebrows: Had any of the others got going? Really got going? Who had they got the tip from? From last year's lot? From the profs? Had they gone to the profs privately and got the secret out of them? What were the others doing, those who, like themselves, had not got on to anything?

No one trusted anyone. Least of all when one of them said what textbook he was then working on. It might just be bluff. A manœuvre made to lure a poor devil into a blind alley. Getting a poor devil to spend weeks reading a useless book, while the others triumphantly got well ahead of him.

The fifty young men in this new year, who came from all parts of the country, all seemed to be career-hunters. They were all going to rise in society, to run businesses; it was their hope

and resolve that one day they would belong to the upper hier-
archy of business, they were the men of the new age. Therefore
they all went about their studies seriously and with a determin-
ation; they saw, listened, registered. Even though there was a
slight upward trend in business—partly caused by the growing
threat of war in Europe—jobs still didn't grow on trees. The
College was so new that many heads of private business looked
askance at the queer Martians it turned out; private business
didn't need academic theorists who no doubt knew the difference between annuity and accumulated interest, but were
unable to tell sago from semolina.

Therefore the students had not only to storm the citadel of
the examination, but while studying they must also lay plans
for overcoming the distrust of private business. This meant that
early on they had to decide on a definite branch, preferably a
definite concern, work on it, soften it up (this was best done by
applying to the concern for permission to write a thesis based
on conditions within it). Thus, in the fullness of time, one could
present oneself as the one person in the world able to save this
concern from its old-fashioned, cosy muddle, waste and chaos
and bring it safely over into the new era of streamlined, profit-
yielding, scientific management.

So, it was essential from the very first to keep oneself informed
of what the other students were doing, what books they had
started reading, what plans they had for specializing, what professor they were in with, what firms they had contacted.
For—oh, horror!—suppose the day after the final exam *two*
newly hatched economists presented themselves in the office of
the director of the *same* ready-made clothes factory expecting
a managerial post to fall into their laps like a ripe orange! Two
or three years' intense study just to discover that you have
chosen the wrong target.

The game, then, was to get to know the plans of all the others,
without giving away any of your own; to be such a good diplomat that you outplayed all others in this game where the stakes
were so high and the play so complicated that you were per-
petually fraid of tripping yourself up. What if all the others
were as diplomatic as yourself? Much has been written and
said about oriental cunning; but it cannot possibly be more

cunning than the nordic cunning that was displayed by the students of The College in its first few years.

The bell rang, the groups drifted towards the entrance; the fifty young Norwegians (*were* there fifty? Had some devil perhaps taken advantage of the break to have a private talk with the rector?) went in for the next lecture, quivering with excitement, the effort of shamming, uneasiness, fear, uncertainty. They were a pack of wolves. But they had to wait several years, till after the exams, before they could howl.

In a strange way Ash was almost relieved to find this materialistic career-hunting attitude among his fellow students.

It is true that ever since he went to grammar school he had despised the attitude to life that only counted victories on the surface, that knew the price of everything and the value of nothing. Now and then it occurred to him that his contempt for social position, wealth, medals and honours was a veiled reaction against his mother, who suffered from petit bourgeois admiration for all that was 'good class'. In his childhood he had been very dependent on his mother and strongly attached to her. She was the only person in the whole world to whom he could turn when he was ill in bed; she was the angel of light.

Later, in his youth, the relationship changed; from having been a stay for the sick child, she became a burden on the healthy youth now wanting to be a man. She had possessed the child and she had wanted to own the young man as well. Her son was to make good all that she had lost or missed in life; he was to build her the house of her own she had never had; he was to make her presents of the jewellery and fox furs she had only seen on other women, he was to raise her out of insignificance: he was to cover her with glory by reason of the prominent position he was to occupy. Already she was saying: 'My son at the university,' and she was just waiting to be able to say: 'My son, the bank manager,' or, giddy thought: 'My son, the minister.' *He* was the one who was to compensate her for the ignominy she had suffered every time her trolley-driver husband had neglected to apply for promotion. She meddled in all her son's affairs, decided everything from the way he did his hair and the clothes he wore to his friends and girls (though

she was not always successful in the latter), and every time
he thundered against her misplaced interference—which was
tearfully sentimental and strongly resembled idolization—her
inevitable answer was: 'But I only did it for your own good,
Ash!' Oh, if only she had had the honesty to admit that it was
her own good she had been thinking of!

Because of that Ash loathed sentiment and always preferred
people who used dry, unemotional words to express themselves.
Possibly this was one of the reasons why, despite his many
poetic qualities, he had never written poetry even for his secret
diary. The only two lines of verse he ever committed to paper
were

> Much more than any other
> I hate my own dear mother.

It is possible that it was this relationship to his mother and
her uncritical idolization of him that made him, hungry as he
was for recognition, so suspicious of praise. In his mind praise
was suspect, a present he was given just in order to catch him
in a secret snare; praise became synonymous with having done
something nice and harmless. This had led to that twist in his
character that was to make him, both as a student and later in
life, spoil a certain success at the last moment in order to avoid
becoming the fat bemedalled pillar of society. That too was
why he was subconsciously attracted by the unconventional,
by those who lived on the fringe of society—gipsies, prostitutes,
drunkards, thieves, writers (the rebels, not those who wrote
pretty stuff for confirmations and silver weddings), and felt a
sympathy for the poor, for invalids, pacifists, divorced women,
negroes, Jews, communists, socialists.

But was he not himself out for a career, a position? Yes, indeed, but it was to enable him to achieve the *good* life, not
the *dashing lavish* life. He knew even then that, just as it is
impossible for a poor, overworked wage-earner to wrest from
the day the time needed to get and enjoy the good that is called
culture and which is a state of mind (paradoxically enough the
only occasions in those days when a wage-earner could come in
contact with culture were when he and his union were on strike,
for then he had time to go to the public library and read
a book!)—so too the busy head of a business is caught in the

same net. It is almost impossible for a man with a family and an income of four thousand crowns to enter the realm of culture and beauty; but is it not just as difficult for the company director earning four hundred thousand a year to do so, when for the sake of his position he must go on earning the same amount in the years to come? What becomes of freedom then, and freedom from care?

In view of the inner life I intend to lead, Ash told himself, my future income will be somewhere between four thousand and four hundred thousand a year, but considerably nearer four thousand than four hundred thousand. I shall earn enough to have what is necessary. Anything above that 'cometh of evil'. Let my mother and the Americans believe that happiness lies in external things. I know better. And I must disappoint my mother because she will never get a house of her own or a silver fox, at any rate not from me. There is no need to tell her that now, while I am a student and badly need the pocket money she may be able to send me; she has exploited me for so many years that I can exploit her now without my conscience pricking me; but one day she will be surprised to see how low her precious son remains on the social ladder, it will be her cross that her genius of a son never became director of the Bank of Norway.

In a strange way, then, young Ash was almost relieved to find the materialistic attitude so strong among his fellow students. Thus he knew what lay ahead of him; he knew that there was no question of sentiment, but that it was trample or be trampled. After the ethical and idealistic soul-searchings that had made him so unhappy during the last year, it was refreshing, even a relief, to have fallen among wolves. The only discordant element in that blond wolves' paradise was the professor of economics smiling his forced saintly smile over his fifty yapping students, while in a meek and somewhat uncertain tone he exhorted them in broken Norwegian to 'serve mankind'.

But with Ash this restlessness went deeper than with most of the others. He had so little to live on that he went white if a shoelace broke, requiring an immediate outlay; the shadow of his loan from the bank hung over him like the knife of the guillotine: those two thousand crowns were to last him two, nearly

three years, and after that they had to be *paid back*; the thought
of that debt, of the loss of freedom which every crown he spent
implied, sometimes depressed him so that he swore he was going
to live on bread and water (as he did periodically with the humiliating and demoralizing result that he exploded with hunger,
went gasping to a good and far too expensive restaurant where
he gorged on roast lamb and vegetables to the tune of eight
crowns). He had so much to build up; he must get up into the
light quicker than the others and achieve the independence
and glory that only money can give; quicker than the others
must he settle accounts with the past by making a future for
himself.

Sometimes when he looked at his fellow students and saw
their bright open faces and heard their clear, self-assured voices,
they seemed to him to be unwritten pages. Their foreheads
were smooth and their eyes clear and blue; they did not all come
from well-to-do homes, yet all seemed to have escaped the
branding iron of dishonour, no one was threatening to broadcast
an SOS for them. Sometimes in his heart he sadly envied them.
Why could he not be as untouched, as uninfected, as strong?
Why could this not have been life's first smiling heat for him
as well? Why did he alone have to start with a broken back and
the ball of dishonour fettered to his leg, why, why? Could they
not moderate their laughter a bit and their arrogance? Must
they so ostentatiously produce photographs of sweethearts who
were so particularly pretty and whom one day they were going
to marry and have sweet legitimate children by?

The Blue Book

There is a song about one Kalle Petterson who was jilted by his
sweetheart Josephine. This was one of the many songs the
students sang in their basement club and which Ash accompanied on the piano, with the result that he was invited to start
a students' choir and later a students' orchestra and to be leader

of them both. These musical activities became the one real bright spot in his life at The College. To quote Kalle Petterson:

> Today I sing from a joyous heart, tra-la-la,
> I've no wife and it's all the same to me, tra-la-la,
> None to nag when I come, nor to scold when I go,
> I'm a man without wife, a bachelor gay, tra-la-la!

Freedom is a good thing, but absolute freedom is as bottomless as the black night of space. Where the lectures were concerned, Ash felt like Kalle Petterson: he could attend if he liked and he could stay away if he liked; yet far from making him happy, he found that this freedom tortured him with doubt. Like all young people he was accustomed to school being compulsory and study meaning a fixed amount of work which you had to do, and on which the master heard you to make sure you had done it. Here there was nothing of that and such boundless liberty was slowly sending Ash off his head.

After ten days his feeling of panic was such that he forced himself to do something about it. He went up to the reading-room and began looking through the Business Management shelves. Here he got in among German reference books and in the end took down a book in a light blue binding, an enormous book as fat as a Bible and with as many pages. Among the book's many sections he found one of two hundred pages with the most seductive title *Industrial Accountancy, Technique and Method.* It was the word 'Technik' that particularly attracted him and set him trembling with anticipation. Cautiously he looked round at the other tables: had his discovery of this treasure been seen by any of the others? Evidently not. For a moment he clasped the treasure to his chest, offered up a prayer of thankfulness to God and began to turn the pages. Oh, this was far better than he had dared hope!

The text was set in a nice small type with two columns on every page and was stuffed with sample calculations, equations, diagrams, accounts, etc, etc. It seemed to deal with every conceivable economic aspect of a big industrial concern, it was the work of a German professor with a good name and a chair at a famous university in Germany, it seemed to be good, solid, concentrated academic work in which everything was neatly and elegantly set out, and there wasn't a single printer's error on any page and no chit-chat, not a word about serving humanity, nor—to Ash's great relief—was it even hinted that the task of the science of business management was to serve Hitler; in fact, the article was a piece of good German work in the best sense of the term, it was just Ash's cup of tea and his own secret. Eyes bright and shining he told himself: Here I've got Business Management in a nutshell!

His delight and relief were boundless: here at last was something he could get his teeth into. His heart was thumping as he sat down to read. Sadly and not without malicious pleasure he thought of the other unhappy forty-nine sitting there in the lecture-room, the sport of the lecturer's inadequacy.

It was not long before he began to have a sneaking suspicion that perhaps this two-hundred page article that he had so miraculously discovered did not contain *all* that he needed to know on the subject; that the other forty-nine in the lecture-hall were picking up occasional grains of wisdom that were not to be found in this German wonder-treatise. This doubt he thrust aside as quickly as it came: in his rootlessness and panic he *had* to have something to cling on to, *had* to wall himself in with this blessed synthesis.

That first day made him fearfully determined. He swore that having taken the decision, he would not rest till he knew the whole article inside out, through and through, and could quote it word for word, drunk or sober, awake or asleep. He was going to have the basis of business management crystal-clear in his head; then, he would always be able to hold his own because he would be able to compare any problem of detail with the conspectus the article had given him. He would be able to stand up in the lecture-hall and say: 'Sir, may I be allowed to point out that . . .'; with calm assurance he would be able to say: 'This question of course must be seen in conjunction with the *whole* economic structure of the firm. It is scarcely enough to regard it as a mere problem of accountancy, for it is most intimately bound up with costing.' Hm. He would have his feet on firm ground, and there's no better feeling than that in the whole world.

For the next month he did nothing but sit over his book in the reading-room. He guarded his blue book like a jealous lover his beloved; he got there at the crack of dawn, reeling from lack of sleep, and was the first one in when the reading-room opened; he had to restrain himself from rushing to the shelf to assure himself that the book was still there; with trembling hands he took his wonderful blue book from the shelf and went and barricaded himself with it behind a desk in the farthest corner; he was like a monkey in a zoo that has managed to grab a banana and huddles into a corner in order not to attract the attention of the others and almost chokes to death because it cannot stuff the banana down its throat quickly enough.

Every day he brought a German dictionary with him and translated the entire article into Norwegian, word by word, sentence by sentence; he wrote the translation in a special book with all the diagrams, equations, examples, everything. He wrote all day in beautiful copper-plate and at home in the evenings he read over what he had written and tried to learn it off by heart. 'What's that you're doing?' Daniel asked. 'Oh,' said Ash, clutching the precious notebook to his bosom, 'I'm just looking over my notes.' Sometimes, as he sat in the reading-room writing, he thought: I could have stayed at home and read this! At other times, he became a prey to despondency because of the things in the book that he did not understand, especially the specimen calculations, many of which he could not make head or tail of; the German author had a nasty habit of using higher mathematics and Ash was no mathematical genius; he chafed, but of course he could not consult any of the others without giving away the secret of the article and then anyone could have come and copied it. He was like a woman who daren't tell any of her friends where she bought her new hat, for he would have been blazingly angry if he had discovered someone else with the same treasure. Yet he was altogether too young, too ambitious, too preoccupied with himself, to see how ridiculous his secretiveness was. It was many years before he could see that taking oneself very seriously is tantamount to being profoundly unsure of oneself.

After a month of this ant-like industry, a change came. It came suddenly, swiftly, like an avalanche. It was like someone

knocking a hole in his skull, through which voices reached him:
all at once—it was like a vision from Hell—he knew that the
other forty-nine sitting down there in the lecture-room were
really *learning* something. While he sat up there buried in his
book, dead to the rest of the world, the other forty-nine had
sat down below stuffing themselves with endless knowledge
about economics, commercial law and foreign languages!

He dropped the blue book as suddenly as he had taken it up.
Once it had seemed to him to be a miraculous revelation, an
Aladdin's lamp, but now he regarded it as a work of the Devil,
a poison that had befuddled his mind and dulled his understanding; and in that crazy state he had let himself miss his only
chance of properly learning and preparing for the exams; there
he now was with his splendid wonderful matchless (and how
matchless!) article, of which he hadn't been able to complete
more than half, because it is a gigantic task to translate heavy
German mathematical matter and at the same time learn by
heart what you have translated—while the other forty-nine
were in the lecture-hall below and had made a month's progress, a month, heavens, thirty whole days—along the only right
road—they had a lead of thirty days—while he was left with
half a matchless article that he would never have any use for
and about which nobody would ever ask him. It was all in vain:
those beautiful diagrams he had drawn in red ink on graph
paper, all his beautiful sums and equations, all done for nothing
—he was the greatest idiot there was, a cousin of jackals and
brother of donkeys, a cosmic fool, he deserved to die and
heartily wished that he could. Good heavens, perhaps they kept a
record of attendances at the lectures. Perhaps they had seen
that he wasn't there, perhaps they had made a note about him,
perhaps there were rules that you were not allowed to take an
exam unless you had attended a certain number of lectures,
perhaps he had forfeited his chance to sit for the exam!

He dropped the blue book as though it were a skunk, a dead
rat, a piece of human excrement, and ran. With his white doctor's
coat—the student's uniform—flapping round him and his eyes
black with fear, he tore down the stairs like an outcast angel,
burst open the door of the first lecture-hall he came to and flung
himself in. From that moment he went to *every* lecture, popular

or unpopular, he became a glutton for lectures, wouldn't miss one of them. Pearls of wisdom didn't fall from the lecturer's lips every moment, but they *might* and so he had to be ready and wideawake—to be prepared!

For a whole month he was indefatigable and attended every lecture. He filled book after book with his notes, chafing at not knowing shorthand. Gradually he developed a home-made stenography of his own whereby he only wrote the first few letters of every word, but then he had to interpret his notes and write them out immediately after each lecture, otherwise there was no deciphering them. Let them just become an hour old and not even God himself could read them. He discovered that this method cost him double work, first taking the notes, then writing them out, and he was doubly exasperated. In the end he suggested to the others that they adopt a work-saving shift system of taking notes, so that only one was taking down what the lecturer said. From the rationalistic, or efficiency expert's point of view it was an intolerable idea that fifty people should be sitting there writing out the same thing. That was as bad as the monks in the Middle Ages.

They tried his suggestion and for a while the system worked well, but then one note-taker failed to get the most important things down and another's handwriting proved illegible—no, in this world one could rely only on oneself and scarcely that.

Ash, that uncrowned king of the impatient-hearted, buried himself in papers, notes, textbooks, note-books, loose sheets. The more he read, the more seemed left to be read. In the end, the curriculum, that bugbear, became for him another Saerimne, that fabulous boar of Old Nordic mythology which every day was slaughtered, cooked and eaten by the bearded warriors in Valhalla, yet the next morning there it was again running about with its curly tail, as gay and alive as ever. Ash's forefathers, the old Vikings, must have considered a never-ending mountain of food a heavenly idea; but young Ash in the twentieth century, just desperately wanted to be able to eat his way through his Saerimne as quickly as possible and be done with it for ever.

His one solace, and that a real one, he found in the language classes. One of the three world languages, English, German and French, was obligatory. Thirty had chosen English, twelve Ger-

man and eight French. Ash had unhesitatingly chosen French
in which he had already achieved a considerable fluency.
According to the curriculum, one foreign language was regarded
as a necessary element in 'the young businessman's education' and Ash found that he was expected to read French
literature as well as textbooks of correspondence and books
about French economic life. He licked his lips when he saw
names like Zola, Anatole France, Voltaire, Proust, Mauriac,
Stendahl, Balzac, Cocteau—each student had to choose at least
six works of literature and prepare himself to be examined in
them. Not only were they *allowed* to read these books—it was
actually *meritorious* to do so.

It was incredible, too good to be true, and Ash reeled with
happiness.

He had been brought up in a home where his father, a streetcar driver, had always denounced literature as nonsense in a
voice that was full of contempt and condemnation. All that
gave Ash the greatest pleasure in his childhood and youth was
pronounced nonsense. It was newspapers and encyclopedias
that you ought to read, for you learned *facts* from them, knowledge that could be *useful* to you in life. That his own reading of
newspapers and facts had not been of any use to him or brought
him promotion, seemed to have escaped his father's notice entirely. Ash never dared admit it to himself, but in his heart of
hearts he could almost wish that, when he was grown up, his
life should consist of nothing but nonsense: just music, love,
literature, carefree friendship, a life brimming with glorious,
intoxicating Olympian nonsense. Nonsense for breakfast, nonsense for lunch, nonsense for dinner, nonsense all night, a life of
nonsense, of the most glorious nonsense, and he would be the
greatest nonsense-maker of them all, nonsense and ambrosia,
nonsense and nectar, in all nonsensity, amen.

He thought: at least I'll get a good mark in French; I don't
care so much about the other subjects. The lecturer in French
was very good, a first-class philologist; he was apt to be dry,
slightly pedantic, embarrassed and reserved; once or twice Ash
noticed how little beads of sweat appeared on his upper lip
when some explanation or other was causing him difficulty;
when he saw that, Ash looked down, for he knew what a person

feels, whose upper lip becomes beaded with sweat. This lecturer
was completely master of his subject; his lectures were always
well prepared and part of a careful plan; Ash felt happy during
the man's lectures, even though he quaked at the thought of
being heard; you couldn't bluff that man! And Ash was heard
every time, for there were only eight of them sitting round the
table in the small lecture-room. From the pedagogic point of
view it was an ideal class and they just could not help learning
French, especially with such a teacher. After a month, Ash had
become the best in the class. A secret understanding had grown
up between him and the lecturer and every class was a friendly
duel in which they tested each other out. Ash was scared and
attracted by the other's dryness, objectivity and modesty, while
the lecturer secretly admired and was scared of this quivering,
sensitive elk with corn-coloured hair and drumming fingers, who
always rushed in where angels feared to tread.

After only two months Ash had become so good at French
that he would lie on the sofa in his room reading Corneille's *Le
Cid* and enjoying it. 'Almighty God!' he exclaimed rapturously
as he lay wallowing in French culture, then the next moment
his conscience began to prick him at the thought of the other
subjects he ought also to be reading, and heavily and reluctantly he got up, muttering one of Don Diegue's sorrowful
remarks:

> *Jamais nous ne goûtons de parfaite allégresse:*
> *Nos plus heureux succès sont mêlés de tristesse.*

Daniel, who was taking English, looked up from his book.
He was sitting on the other side of the big table that stood in
the middle of their room. Tilting his head on one side, he said:
'Eh?'

Ash, still in Corneille's world, flung out his hand and said
sententiously:

> *Au milieu du bonheur mon âme en sent l'atteinte:*
> *Je nage dans la joie, et je tremble de crainte.*

'Translate,' said Daniel.

'I wallow in joy and I tremble with fear.'

'And I'm going to the pictures,' said Daniel. 'Coming?'

'Can't afford it,' Ash said.

'For once I'll stand you,' Daniel said.

'*Laisse-moi prendre haleine afin de te louer,*'* said Ash and bowed, sweeping the floor with an imaginary plumed hat.

During his first year at The College Ash taught himself to take a siesta. At first it was just a mere forty winks; he lay down on the sofa in his clothes, closed his eyes and dozed off for five minutes. Gradually the five minutes expanded till they had become thirty, and then he took off his jacket and stretched out properly. This siesta became a habit and a vice, for he could never indulge in what was pleasant and did him good without his conscience pricking him. A Norwegian feels he is being moral provided he is seated uncomfortably. Reason told him that this after-lunch nap was a good thing; in return for the half-hour that it stole from his every afternoon, it gave him an extra hour's endurance in the evening and as a result he often worked till two in the morning before tumbling into bed. Emotionally, however, he found this nap indefensible; sentiment told him that it was the act of a petit bourgeois, a sign of inner rottenness and lack of character; who had ever heard of a socialist, a revolutionary, one who fought at the barricades, having an *afternoon nap?*

He half-expected to feel the heavy, black-gloved hand of authority that he had learned to dread descending on his shoulder for his misdemeanour. 'Hullo there! Yes, you. Don't you know this is forbidden in Norway? Your name, please! Address! Dependants? Previous convictions?'

One day he jerked out of his afternoon sleep in nameless terror.

He and Daniel had taken a room in the house of an elderly widow with a middle-aged, unmarried daughter. The old mother brought them their breakfast in the morning: weak coffee, a glass of milk, sliced bread and butter with goat's milk cheese, red whortleberry jam and veal loaf, a thoroughly unimaginative breakfast that every morning made Ash's inside feel dry with disappointment and bitterness. (They had their main meal out.)

---

* 'Let me get my breath back, so that I may praise you.'

It was the middle-aged daughter who had the honour of bringing them their supper. She was tall, pale-complexioned, had a sunken chest and worked in the Inland Revenue office. She suffered from stomach ulcers. When she came home from the office, she cooked dinner for her mother and herself, spreading an intolerably appetizing smell of food through the house, especially intolerable on the days when Ash had decided to skip lunch and had stayed in his room eating dry Ryvita and drinking water. To get to the lavatory you had to go through the kitchen, and while on that errand Ash sometimes found the daughter there bent over a frying pan in which sizzled fragrant rissoles and onions that she was cooking for her mother; she herself was on a permanent diet; there she stood with her nose over the frying pan inhaling the fragrance and groaning hungrily: 'Oh God! Oh God!' And Ash would rush on and, in the lavatory, lean his famished body against the wall and think how strange life is: his stomach would gladly have digested all those rissoles, but they were not his; she owned them all, yet could not eat them. 'Oh God,' he groaned. 'Oh God!'

The supper that this daughter brought them on a tray at about seven or eight o'clock in the evening consisted of a pot of tea, plus, as you may guess, sliced bread and butter with goat's milk cheese, red whortleberry jam and veal loaf, a thoroughly unimaginative supper that every evening turned Ash's inside dry with disappointment and bitterness.

On the day that he woke up with a start, he had overslept and it was half past seven. Daniel was out. What woke him was a crash like the Day of Judgment. Sitting up, Ash saw the middle-aged daughter of the house standing a couple of paces away, grey in the face and looking as though she had just seen Satan in person; the tray lay on the floor at her feet with cups and plates smashed to smithereens, the slices of bread floating in a pool of light brown tea, while a gently bubbling sound came from the melting sugar. She gasped as he sat up, put her hand to her throat and fell backwards out of the door.

Ash rubbed his eyes: for a minute he sat there heavily, bemused with sleep, then leaning forward, he unemotionally surveyed the havoc on the floor. When nothing happened and the daughter didn't come back to sweep it all up, he got up and buttoned his fly.

As he did up the first button, his face flushed scarlet. His fly had been wide open. His many bad habits included one that had often made Daniel laugh at him. Some people sleep with a finger in their mouths, others clasp a pillow in their arms; Ash slept with his hand clasped round the emblem of his manhood. It cannot have been easy for a middle-aged spinster with stomach ulcers, accustomed to nothing but income-tax returns and a very occasional rissole, to see such a sight.

Ash waited a quarter of an hour until his blushes had subsided, then with his clothes in perfect order he went resolutely to the kitchen in search of a broom and another supper. The ghastly embarrassment that comes from knowing that involuntarily you have hurt another person's feelings was great and almost paralysing, but his hunger was greater still.

From that day on he always pulled a blanket over him during his afternoon nap.

Tananarivo?

And now about love.

When Ash had been three weeks in the new town he was suddenly overcome by a feeling of profound loneliness and an equally profound need of tenderness. After all he had come there to find (or create) the red ruby; he did not believe that this, life's finest and loveliest treasure, was to be found in a woman; but on the other hand he believed that if he could find the right woman, he and she together could find the philosopher's stone; partnership with a woman became his greatest longing. He had been with women, but he had never experienced the mutual belonging of true partnership. Ash had never had a sister to give his flowers to, so now in his thoughts he gave them to Her, the one, the only one who would not laugh at him when he got carried away by something lovely, who would not mock at him when he suffered over another's misfortune, who would not punish him when he spoke the truth.

Her.

He looked about him, in the streets and alleyways, in the parks, in the cinema and in the concert hall, in cafés and shops.

He did not see her anywhere.

He knew that she must be out of the ordinary and yet thoroughly human. He knew that the moment he saw her, he would love her. He knew with absolute certainty that already he had her picture in his heart, the negative of her picture. The light from her eyes would make the print so that she would be there in the flesh, conceived by his fierce yearning and born of his burning hope; they would walk towards each other across a long beach and they would meet and he would see her face, and he would know, for he had known since the beginning of eternity; he would see her face, her tender flower-like face, and there would be birds playing in the depths of her eyes, and love would stand quivering at his side, like a spear thrown from on high, like a spear in the sand; and he would sacrifice the proud inviolability of his youth the moment he saw her, he would let her into his heart for ever, he would know her the second he saw her, and calmly—with face wet with the warm tears of fulfilment and thankfulness—he would say: 'Set me as a seal on your heart, as a seal upon your arm,' and calmly she would take his hand; the blind desperate roamings of his youth would be at an end, he would see her face and her eyes, and he would know.

But he did not see her anywhere.

All the same two women came into his life now, hurriedly, taking him by surprise; one remained remote, all too remote; the other became intimate, all too intimate. Which came first, the nameless girl, or the girl with the name? Afterwards he could not remember. There is something timeless about this tale of the two girls, the one all too distant and the other all too close; not only do they illustrate the strange limits within which a young man's need of tenderness oscillates and can be swung; they are equally a symbol of youth's hopeless impotence and bitter helplessness.

Which was strongest in the young man Ash, the romantic or
the sensualist? He did not know. One day he dreamed of the
elf with tiny feet and transparent wings, the unreal being who
was so graceful and tiny that he stood her on his hand and did
not dare breathe on her; the next day he dreamed of the woman
of flesh and blood, the expert courtesan, in whose naked shoulders he set his teeth. These two dreams confused his mind; he
never thought of the possibility that a decent person could look
for both: go with a butterfly and a down-to-earth whore *at the
same time*; he imagined that honour would be satisfied only if
he found the elf and the whore in one and the same person; but
how could he ever esteem an elf if the elf was a whore?—and
tumble in groaning voluptuousness with a whore, if the whore
was an elf? Such problems would strike him—and most forcibly
—just when he was sitting with his tables of logarithms working
out the repurchase value of a discarded closing machine in a
shoe-factory.

He was naturally shy and here, in this strange town, he felt
rootless and homeless into the bargain. It seemed to him that
people in this strange town had their own, secret rules of behaviour that he did not know. He entered on a period when he
had no self-confidence at all. He wanted to talk, but he had no
words; he wanted to stretch out his hand, but his arm was paralysed. He wanted a girl, but he shuddered at the thought of
having to accost a person of the female sex. He saw girls in the
streets, he saw girls in shops, he saw a girl two seats in front of
him in the bus, he stood beside an unknown girl on the platform
of a streetcar. He felt that his anguish would be at an end if
he could just find a word, the word. This horror of making advances, of feeling utterly powerless, will be familiar to most
young men all over the world; these young men lie at night
thinking: 'We ought to have a word. A magic word that will
relieve us of all the torment. The poets have all made words, but
none of them has made *the word*. Why?
And at night Ash lay muttering words to himself. Once he
thought of the word Tananarivo. 'Yes,' he whispered delightedly.
Where had he got that from? Now he remembered: from a

sentence in one of Knut Hamsun's books: 'There streamed into me a meaningless string of wild and tender names of places from which she might come: Uganda, Tananarivo, Honolulu, Venezuela, Atacama. Was it verse? Was it colour? I did not know what to do with them.'

Yes, he whispered. That's the way to use a writer's words in real life. I take two words from Hamsun and out of them I make an introductory conversation between a boy and a girl; that will save the young, lonely man all heartbreaking torment, all waiting, all doubt, all apprehension; a poetic operation that will decide the matter on the spot; I, with Hamsun's help, shall be a benefactor of mankind! I shall introduce a simple technique of erotic contact into world history; I shall sunder the gloom of fear that for centuries has lain upon all meetings between man and woman. I shall let the sunlight flood in upon suffering humanity! I shall give mankind the formula of life in two words! I shall be giving it ten hundred thousand times more than Edison did with his incandescent bulb!

THUS (when they are standing beside each other on the platform of a streetcar; their eyes have met and they have looked away again):

He (casually, tenderly, deferentially, one word): *'Tananarivo?'*
She (looks up, smiles, gives a slight shake of her head meaning that she is not free, that indeed unfortunately she is in love with another. She thanks him though for his attentions and hopes she has not made him too unhappy.)
He (bows slightly, respectfully; of course he is not offended; he sighs; such is life.)

OR

He (tenderly, deferentially, casually, one word): *'Tananarivo?'*
She (looks up, appraises him swiftly and not without interest; turns her head half away, looks out through the window of the streetcar, lowers her eyelids, swallows and says in a low, almost inaudible voice, meaning that she could envisage the possibility of getting to know him better): *'Atacama.*
Both (get off together at the next stop.)

Like that.

Just two words would be enough to give happiness and smiling freedom to all mankind.

'Tananarivo?'

'Atacama.'

Two words.

Were two words too much to ask for?

The fifty young nordic wolves, as has already been mentioned, occasionally threw a casual glance at a school playground some way down the hill from the fenced-in space with tall deciduous trees in which they stood between lectures, chewing buns, smoking and listening for someone to give himself away. This playground belonged to a girls' school. The girls were between twelve and sixteen. They were nothing to look at, indeed they were quite outside the young students' field of interest. They played hopscotch, skipped, stood in shivering groups under a lean-to roof eating the food they had brought with them, or walked in elliptical procession round the playground four abreast, three abreast, or two together, usually arm in arm, chattering, whispering, putting their heads together, now and again one of them exploding with mysterious laughter into a friend's hair. The girls were so far away that you could not distinguish their individuality with the naked eye; they were a mass. It sometimes happened that one of the students waved to them; then their laughter stopped, very occasionally a daring girl waved back, but even then with a violent giggle (the giggle could not be heard at that distance, only seen); usually the girls turned away, dismayed, and hung their heads: the young grown men in white coats up there were *undergraduates*!

The straggly little schoolgirls were just a mass, a grey mass, until, one day, Ash suddenly realized that he had singled one out. He looked down, surprised at himself and momentarily afraid lest the other white-clad young men round about had noticed it and his confusion. He was thoughtful as he went in to the next lecture.

In the days that followed he always went and stood at a point from which he had a full view of the yard of the girls' school. He developed a sort of binocular gaze and could immediately single her out from the others. The girls were small, undeveloped, flat children; were it not for their hair they could just as well have been boys. But this girl to whom his gaze returned again and again, was beginning to be a woman; under her school tunic he could see her womanly curves and shape. She was a quarter of a head taller than her friends and held herself erect. Already there was a hint of woman's sweetness and softness about her. He sensed that she was very pretty. It sounds surprising, perhaps, that at a distance of a hundred yards and without using field-glasses a man could decide whether or not a girl was pretty. But it was true. The beauty was there in the girl's gait, in her carriage, in his awareness of her lissomness, the beauty was there in the way in which she carried her head, in her gestures, in the way in which she bent towards a friend when speaking to her.

After a week Ash had begun to find reasons for strolling down to the end of the grounds during break; the grounds were lovely, having been laid out by a wealthy patrician merchant. Ash was six foot four in his stockinged feet; and when he stood on tiptoe down there he could see over the wall and get a glimpse of the schoolgirls, but alas! only those at the far end of their yard. One day in his need he climbed the six-foot high bronze statue of the departed patrician; that happened to be a day when the girls were playing handball dressed in gym-shoes, blue knickers and blouses. When he climbed down again, he was trembling, bewildered and afraid, though not surprised. He was very silent after that and had to swallow a lump in his throat. The girl was as pretty as a picture.

Afterwards he could not get her out of his mind, he was fascinated and she became an obsession. From the first moment he had a dull, almost nauseating feeling that this was a perilous idea, the whole thing impossible and monstrous. What sort of school was it? He did not dare ask, afraid both to betray his interest and have his fears put into words. If one kind, the girls must be between thirteen and sixteen. If the other, they could be between thirteen and nineteen. In his heart he knew that it was the former. (The three or four friends with whom she went and who must be her classmates were thin and short, like thirteen-year-olds.) He thought: she might have been ill and away

for a year, she could be seventeen. In his heart he knew: she was
fifteen. Then he smiled with embarrassment and there was
sorrow in his heart.

He came to be persecuted by the image of her; she was always
in his thoughts when he fell asleep at night. Then they were in
a flowery meadow together, he stroked her hair, she smiled to
him, they did not speak, he could just smell the fragrance of her
hair and of the flowers she had picked. Only in brief snatches
did he think of her as a woman; it was the girl in her of whom
he dreamed, he may have dreamed of a kiss, but it was a chaste
kiss; his cup of happiness would be full if he could just walk
hand in hand with her. He would wake from such dreams with
a jerk: this is morbid, he told himself, it's perverse; the whole
thing must be connected with my never having had a sister,
that I never had a fine relationship with a girl of my own age
while I was still a boy. It must be a reaction after many nights
with very adult women; now the pendulum has swung the other
way, away from a woman of thirty-seven and another of twenty-
seven, away from their very adult and slightly rancid bodies.
But there must be moderation in this reaction, there are limits
to everything and the limit here—according to the law of
Norway and my own conscience—lies at the sixteenth year.
She is a bud of fifteen, I am an old man of twenty-three. One
does not do such things. Such things don't happen.

And yet there was something in him that would not accept
defeat. It is not true, said an obstinate and bold voice within
him, it is not true that the finest relationship in the world cannot
be one between a girl of fifteen and a man of twenty-three. That
is a difference of eight years. There are seven years' difference
between me and Gunnhild, and seventeen between me and
Siv; that did not matter to me, it was not that which broke it up.
When I think of it, I have read tales from the olden days of how
the beauty was adored at fourteen, wooed at fifteen and led
to the altar when she was sixteen. How old was Juliet when
Romeo laid his heart at her feet? Was she thirty? Most certainly
not. There's nothing wrong with the age of fifteen, but only with
our attitude to it. Naturally, from both a social and a humani-
tarian point of view it is a serious matter to make a girl of fifteen
pregnant, but when have I thought of that? I have dreamed

of holding her hand, that was my dream. And even if we both should be carried away and love in the flesh, she is ripe for that too, as I have seen and felt. She is a rose in bud, but a rose! My being in love with her is *not* abnormal, I am *not* mad. My world has stuffed itself with erroneous ideas, that is what it is! To-morrow I shall see that I meet her; there is honey and tears in my heart and she is my little beloved, fifteen summers old.

But what will the others say if I turn up with a sweetheart of fifteen? 'Have you started your second childhood?' they will ask; 'Have you taken to playing with dolls?'

He twisted and turned in bed and could not get to sleep. The whole thing is crazy, he muttered, and a thunderous snore came from Daniel's bed as though in confirmation.

But a couple of days later he set about it in earnest; he was going to try and meet the girl in the street! He had studied life in the playground of the girls' school long enough to know that their last lesson ended at a quarter past two. At ten minutes past two he was in the street in which the school stood; for almost a quarter of an hour he walked up and down glancing stealthily at the girls as they came out through the school gate. He could not see her. Had she been kept back? Was she ill? Was she a phantom that only existed in his own diseased mind?

On the second day he did see her. He saw the direction she took when she came out of the gate and that was enough for that day; he could not 'run into' her just outside the school gate, right under the teachers' windows!

All was now ready; he had selected the street corner where the encounter was to take place, and he was most horribly afraid.

She was always with friends. How was he going to spirit the friends away? For, surely he must speak with her alone? He flushed, then paled at the idea of his advances being met with giggles and cruel sniggers from a pack of malicious little school-girls.

But, if he did come across her alone, what was he going to *say*? When he thought of that, the eternal, unsolved problem, he felt his guts contract in terror.

Several days passed: every day he cut the last lecture so that
he was out in plenty of time before the school gate opened and
the girls poured out into the street. By then he was in his hiding
place, and as soon as he saw his beloved, he emerged and
walked along slowly and casually in the direction of the school
as if he were an ordinary person out for a stroll. Usually he met
the girl half-way; then he trembled inside and prayed a silent
prayer for strength to stop and speak to her, but each time was
a failure: he walked on in his direction, she in hers. He always
took the opportunity to glance at her: she was wonderful in her
youthful freshness; her hair was dark and curly and quite short;
she usually went bare-headed and had to keep jerking her head
to throw the hair off her forehead; her cheeks were soft and
round, her mat skin had a lovely colour; her eyes were brown
and merry and mostly childishly inquisitive; there was a gentleness about her that set him quivering; her smile was a revelation,
her teeth regular and white, the top ones slightly protruberant,
she was the sweetest thing he had ever seen, her walk was supple
and young-womanly, she wore a coat of light coloured gabardine
with a belt round the waist; in the opening of its neck he caught
a glimpse of a high-necked sweater of black, thin wool;
she wore light-brown low-heeled shoes of some strange
leather, llama skin perhaps. She was well-dressed in a discreet
way and stood out from the other boisterous schoolgirls who
were carelessly dressed and shod. He thought: her parents are
well-to-do, but neither they nor she like to show off. Through
her overcoat he could see that she was shapely, with a soft,
strong body, like a gymnast or a ballet dancer.

Every day—and he patrolled the street for a fortnight—he
said to himself: now I am going to speak to her. But he never
did. He thought: surely I can ask her something that does not
matter, the way to The College or the Zoological Museum?
But he never did.

White with despair and helplessness he thought: if only
something would happen. If a horse would bolt, then in the
commotion I could . . . If she would only stumble and fall, then
I could . . . I could buy a bag of oranges, he thought, and let
them fall out as I pass her and her friends so that they roll all
over the place. That would make them laugh and want to help

pick them up; do please let me, I would say. . . . At the corner
where he stood waiting, he glanced up at the houses, on the third
storey of one was a balcony with flower-pots on it. Why, he
thought, is it only in books that flower-pots drop from the third
storey enabling a young man to run and save a girl from death
by catching the pot at the risk of his own life?

He prayed to God for a miracle, something that could *prod*
him across to the young girl. Once or twice as he walked past
(and there can have been no hiding his burning, desperate gaze)
she had given him a hurried glance. He had not been able to
read anything definite in her eyes, neither astonishment nor
indifference nor dislike nor playfulness. She looked at him as at
any other man in the street. He was a pedestrian, that was all
he was, a pedestrian.

In his dire need it occurred to him that he might ask one of
the others to help. What he wanted was to be introduced (that
most dreadful of all words). Perhaps Daniel? Daniel was a
stranger, Daniel was not stricken with the dumbness that comes
from being in love; he would be able to go up, freely and easily,
to anyone in the street and ask the way to the railway station;
Daniel was free and had the gift of speech. Let us see now:
Daniel could go straight up to her and say: 'Excuse me, I know
this is a little irregular, but I have a friend who very much wants
to make your acquaintance. Here he is. His name is Ash Burlefoot, undergraduate at The College; I'm his friend and can
vouch for his pre-eminent qualities. He is a splendid person:
poet and musician, and he would very much like to be
introduced.' No, good heavens, no. It would be better to feign a
fight with Daniel. No, Daniel should drop his umbrella so that it
fell on her, then he would rave at Daniel, ask him in a firm reproachful voice if he could not be more careful in the street;
then he could turn to her and ask if she were hurt in any way
and then . . . The whole thing must end in laughter and while
they were laughing he could introduce Daniel and *Daniel introduce him*. . . .

But then he became afraid, afraid that he would just stand
dumb and helpless even so. And what would happen then? Then
Daniel would talk with the lovely one, *Daniel* would be
free and easy and amusing (for you can talk when you meet a

girl unprepared; it is when you have lain awake for the best part of a month thinking out plans of attack that you lose both spontaneity and courage!), *Daniel* would make her smile and arouse her interest, while he—Ash—stood there dead like a telegraph pole listening to their conversation; it would be *Daniel* who would get her name and address and possibly invite her to the cinema; in fact *Daniel* would go off with the girl.

If that were so it would be better not to try anything.

Then came the day when Ash, fagged with waiting and exhausted by being unable to do anything, stamped his foot and said to himself: Now stop this! He had looked beyond a possible introduction and seen what the inevitable consequences must be: he had been to see the girl's parents and been met by her father's and her mother's polite, appraising looks. He imagined the father as a doctor, probably a surgeon. He had been there in the house, in the drawing-room, sitting on a pouffe balancing a cup of tea with lemon in his left hand, while her father asked what his intentions were; he had dropped his cup, because he did not know what his intentions were and such a lack of intentions would rightly be interpreted as evidence of criminal, sexually criminal tendencies in him; the atmosphere was chilly, so chilly that he stumbled over a rug when he got up to go and in falling broke a tall flower vase. (And what was he, a father of illegitimate children, a rebel and a red socialist, doing in the house of a respected surgeon? They had other plans for their daughter than to throw her, child as she still was, into the arms of the first adventurer to come along.)

He stamped his foot on the pavement and said aloud: 'Now stop this!'

And he did; sometimes of course his gaze went sorrowfully and longingly across the wall and down to the schoolgirls in their playground, but he never again cut his lectures in order to be in a certain street at a certain time, so as to catch a glimpse of a lovely, young girl's face with merry brown eyes and white, slightly protruding top teeth.

Young girl, little sister, where are you now?
Come back, you whom we never met, back to the street where

*we waited for you, back to a smiling street, young sweetheart
of ours.*

*Childish cheeks peach-curved, eyes clear and hair rebellious,
what were the palms of your hands like? Were your fingers ones
to nibble and your ears for whispering into? And your fine-
textured maiden's hair? We would have blown gently on the
short hair at the nape of your neck and seen it quiver in the
wind of our breath. Shall we ever forget the enchantment, can
we ever in this faithless world betray the song, the secret path,
and the wild strawberries?*

*We would have gone up into the mountains hand in hand,
and from the mountain we could have reached up to heaven
with our hands, you our little sweetheart. Will you come back,
little sister, or are you a ghost that the wind mourns? Quick is
earth's mouth and swift the teeth that gorge on loveliness, and
have we lost you for ever? Lost for ever, little sister?*

Come back, young sweetheart of ours.

Gradually, as the feeling of loneliness gripped him again, he
thought more and more often of the pink Rubens girl with whom
he had had that hasty adventure in the mail-steamer. She
haunted his mind, assumed immense proportions. Now and
again he cursed himself for not having asked her name and
address. Now of course she had vanished in that big town, without trace. He could have given only the most general description
of her; in reality he did not remember her features. Once or
twice he had started in the street, thinking: that's her! But then
it was not her. Or he could not be sure that it was. This last was
the worst.

Now and again he studied his own hands. Why do they not
dare grasp? he thought; that is what they were made to do!
They hold the neck of a violin most excellently, do not tremble
when laid on the keys of a piano, nor when they pick up a fountain pen or take the cover off a typewriter; yet my hand hesi-
tates and cannot act when I want to stretch it out towards a
girl's hand. Everyone on earth is a prisoner of this longing for
the palm of a hand. I feel the longing more strongly than anyone, he thought, because I hesitate when I am standing in front
of the mystery. I *can* speak; but I feel that if I do, I shall break

the spell. My God, he would whisper into the night, spare me the most fearful thing of all, spare me from being in love! And then the next moment: Oh, God, let me have the experience of love! Dear God, let it be like a spear in the sand!

What is Honour?

One evening Ash and Daniel had been out and had a beer at a café. It was eleven o'clock as they got off the trolley and began walking down the side street to their place. They were both thinking of girls. Two girls came along behind them. Ash and Daniel slowed down so that the girls should pass them. It was a dark evening and drizzling. Someone must have made a jesting remark, it could just as well have been one of the girls as one of the students. It could hardly have been Ash. It was almost certainly not he who said the first word. But it was certainly he who said the second. And the third and fourth. The four young people walked together down the street, in a loose group.

And, in fact, the girls went up with them. They wouldn't mind seeing how undergraduates lived! There was even a drop left in a bottle of port. The girls wouldn't take their coats off. Only one of them took a cautious sip from the glass that was handed her. They chatted together for an hour. The two girls were sisters. Ash switched out the ceiling light and sat down with one of the sisters on his bed. Daniel put out the standard lamp, he seemed to have come to some sort of agreement with the other. Now it was quite dark in the room; it also became quite silent; only now and again a wire in a mattress sang as someone shifted; when that happened the girl Ash was sitting with laughed; she was the jollier of the two. At one o'clock she whispered into his ear: 'Not while my sister's here, you understand?' Ash understood. Almost immediately after that they switched on the lights and took the girls home; they lived in the same street; Ash now had a date for the following evening at nine o'clock. Daniel grumbled when he heard that he must go to the pictures, but Ash was adamant, he wanted the room to himself.

And the girl came and she was called Molly, and she was short and she was twenty-two and she served in a Co-operative store, and she had brown, slightly frightened eyes, but was merry and giggled as she talked, and her teeth were small and white and irregular, and Ash felt no love for her; she was a girl; he wondered more than desired. He thought: strange that my heart isn't hammering. He switched out the ceiling light and she had a good smell about her and there was a slight taste of tallow in her lipstick and her mouth was strangely unresponsive. He laid her down on the bed and her eyes grew large and frightened, but she didn't tell him to stop and he tried to be ardent with her and there was the electric tingle in his hand that comes when it slides over a girl's silk-stockinged knee and she was calm but frightened, and he was amazed when she stopped him. He had thought they were agreed. She wouldn't say why he must not. He asked her, but she wouldn't say, he asked and tried and asked and tried and all the time he was edging up and all the time she was moving back, and in the end she had gone as far as the bed would allow, was sitting half leaning against the foot, and in that position he could get no further. They had been struggling quietly and gently for half an hour and he was streaming with sweat and his heart was pounding like a steam-hammer. He tried to talk with her, but his voice was too woolly, then he asked again and she said that it was because it was so sore, and at that his whole body went limp and he lay quiet and still, out of sympathy.

He cleared his throat and asked in low, scared tones if she was a virgin; he had never been with a virgin and was stricken with sudden fear, but she was not a virgin, she said, it was just that it hurt so, and he lay panting thinking this over; he couldn't understand it, couldn't understand how it could hurt, but because he was lying still, she put her arms round him and confided to him that it had never been nice for her, only sore, a real pain; then he said that he would help her and he began to caress her; he was not so very knowledgeable, but he had experienced a thing or two, and he was sorry for the girl and honestly wanted to help her, it seemed to him an awful pity and a shame that a

girl should not enjoy the sweetest of all delights, for a moment
he shuddered at the ghastliness of it being a *torment* for her,
for what is life worth *then?*—it seemed to him more awful than
being blind, or deaf, or crippled; he redoubled his efforts and
his tenderness and heard her say something that he did not at
first catch, then he did, sat up in bed and looked at her wild-
eyed: did she feel anything? did she feel a thing when he
caressed her?—did she mean to say that she was quite without
feeling? She smiled a wry smile and giggled and brightened
up: no, she didn't feel a thing. 'But'—the world stood still for
him—'why then had she come to him, why had she let him
begin, yes, why had she been with others before?' She said:
'Well, it's exciting.'—'Exciting?' 'Yes, exciting, a bit dangerous,
so exciting.' He sat and looked at her thoughtfully. Now he
didn't know what to make of her.

Finally he lay down exhausted beside her. Then she put her
arms round him and he felt a great and genuine happiness because it was not *just* because it was exciting that she had come
to him; they lay in each other's arms and he kissed her gently on
the cheek. Then desire mounted in him again and she noticed
it and did not draw away and a great lump came into his throat
and she kissed him and there was a taste of tallow from her
lipstick and she whispered that he mustn't go on too long and
he could only nod and she trembled, but lay still, and then she
whispered that now it was so sore that he must not go any
further; and then it was over and he collapsed on her and she
whispered a question and he nodded and she was so pleased, so
sparkingly relieved that it was over; she took his head and kissed
him so happily and thankfully, she laughed and chattered and
giggled and he had to laugh too, it was the oddest thing. She
sat up in bed (she had kept her dress on all the time), sat with
her legs crossed, nudging him and chattering away about all
and sundry: chores at home, her sister who had fallen for
Daniel, the raisins she sold in the shop, dried apricots. . . . He
had never seen anyone so relieved in his life, it was as if she had
escaped the fate that is worse than death. . . .

After that she came to him a couple of times a week; Daniel
could not be prevailed upon to go out more often.

His association with the little brown-eyed, squirrel-like girl Molly, whose lack of feeling contrasted so strangely with her friendly, restless, giggling, hysterically-jolly person, caused Ash many a stab of conscience. He felt that he was just making use of her. And then from the very first, from the first time the two sisters had gone up to their room, he had known that this could only be an acquaintanceship, never a love affair. Molly did not belong to his world of ideas, not even to his world of longings; they had nothing in common except the most primitive instincts and scarcely that. They could smile to each other, lie together, they could pant together, she could gasp and he groan; he thought: She doesn't really need even to be able to speak Norwegian. We never exchange ideas; I am quite unable to take an interest in the technique of serving customers in a Co-operative store or in the problems connected with weighing out currants; I smile when she tells me of the little events of her day, but I am not really listening to what she is saying, just to the resonance and melody of her voice; my mind is elsewhere. She is just as little able to take an interest in my concerns: I don't know if I have ever mentioned Bach to her, or spoken of Cassel's theory of economics, of Corneille's works, I don't know that I have ever discussed with her the scientific and historical background of the Co-operative movement, the Rochdale principles, or told her how I am gasping over Anatole France's *Crainquebille*; I only know that on the rare occasions when I have ever touched on any of the things that mean so much to me, on anything intellectual, she has just blinked and giggled, both embarrassed and indifferent, and talked about some romantic film she has seen or how her heel came off the other morning when she was late and had to run for the streetcar.

She was a funny and amusing little creature, but he knew only too well that it was not with her he was going to spend his life; no glow from the red ruby fell over his relations with her. Now and then, he felt ashamed of never doing anything for her, of not giving anything in return. Not that she ever suggested it, it was his own idea: just to take her out one evening, to give her a little of that outside pleasure that everyone needs, to go to the pictures at the very least. But he couldn't, he knew that it was because he had nothing to talk to her about, nothing that linked him with her mentally; but when he was feeling emotional, he would sometimes think that it was because he perhaps despised her socially and would be ashamed to be seen with her in public (and he did shudder at the mere thought of taking her to a College dance; she would discourse on apricots and laddered silk stockings; and for all their inconceivable lack of culture the blond wolves had at least got their matriculation. It would just be painful for her, for him, for everyone; they would only laugh at her: tell us more about currants, Molly! about loose raisins.) And so he told himself that his hesitation— in which there was much sympathy for her—was moral coward-ice. He even said to himself at times: I am just using her as a whore, she comes to me when it is dark, like a creature of the night. . . . Thoughts such as these are capable of poisoning one's existence. The whole thing was shameful, he told himself, there was nothing honourable anywhere in it, he exploited her, it was pure sex. And every evening when he had her up in the room, was he not rather relieved when she got up to go and he could take her home? So that he could get back and fling himself over his books or play his violin, so that he could return to his alchemy, to his trembling search for the philosopher's stone? Wasn't he? Yes. Well then, did that make it a relationship with-out honour, sheer swinishness and filth? And at once the fretful expostulation: Who gave us the concept of honour? Where was it written that life is to be based on honour? And, what, in heaven's name, *was* honour? Perhaps it was just another of the illusions that people never stop to consider properly. Why did we bow unprotestingly to this concept of honour? The incontest-able fact was that Molly was good and nice; he had moments of great enjoyment with her and did not even need to ask her if she liked him, she giggled with joy and, heaven help him, with pride, when she knocked on his door in the evening and walked in. They enjoyed themselves together; he knew that he aimed higher than that, but he wouldn't admit that there was anything dishonourable in enjoying oneself like that. One was allowed to *exist*, while waiting for the miracle.

And, besides, there were his visions. They defeated him and because of them he had to ask Molly to come to him again and again. These visions of Molly half undressed came to him often and most disturbingly during lectures. The lecturers could seldom hold his interest and attention for long at a time; soon his thoughts began to stray, he began to recall the previous evening, and while the lecturer was speaking haltingly of the most efficient method of arranging assets in a balance-sheet, Ash would see a mental picture of Molly's loins. He closed his eyes, but the wild sweetness mounted within him and he did not know what to do, prayed a silent prayer to an unknown God that the lecturer should not take it into his head to call him up to the blackboard while he was in that ungodly state. He glanced round at the other forty-nine to see if any of them looked as though they suffered from similar visions, that would have been a relief, for companionship in adversity is most welcome; but they were all sitting most correctly in their beautiful white coats making notes, and obviously had their whole minds on this, the finest product of double-entry book-keeping, the apotheosis of accountancy: the balance-sheet. They were thinking of columns of figures, he of girls. He was twenty-three and at such moments he was firmly convinced that he was a monster, a devil in human shape, and that his whole life was going to be one long ghastly Walpurgis night.

The Wages of Sin is Death

And the punishment for his unbridled sexual life?

One day he caught a cold, a bad cold, and had to spend two days in bed. The landlady's middle-aged daughter who suffered from stomach ulcers brought him hot lemon drinks. When she spoke to him now, it was with face half averted, and he for his part, was careful to see that he had the eiderdown well over him when she came in. Daniel went to the lectures and in the evening gave Ash a resumé, so that he kept more or less up to date. On the second evening, when Daniel had gone to the pictures by himself and Ash was lying in bed reading, there was a knock at the door. Ash said 'Come in' in a thick, clogged voice, and in walked Molly in raincoat and hat, cautious, giggling, embarrassed, yet with something calm and quiet about her. Ash gulped. She shut the door and came across to the bed and was meek and didn't quite know what to say: her sister had heard from Daniel and told her that Ash was ill and in bed, and so she had only come up for a moment, just to see the invalid, and then she thought that perhaps he ... She opened her bag and produced a packet of biscuits, sweet biscuits of the kind women eat when they forgather. Ash looked at the packet in her hand. She had got it from the store, she said; they were very good biscuits, she said, she had some herself most days. His heart or something inside him began to bleed. It was partly a feeling of shame, because he had the vanity of the male and did not want a woman to see him when he had a cold and was unwell and had a scarf round his neck; she could have warned him that she was coming, anyway she had no business walking in unannounced! And partly it was a feeling of poverty, mostly of her poverty: she had wanted to give him a present, but she had not the money or the imagination to give him anything he would prize; she could have given him anything, a magazine, a packet of pipe-cleaners, some cigarettes, a bottle of beer—but biscuits! He did not like biscuits in any form, he liked bread, fragrant bread, rye bread, oatcakes and *knekkebroed*, but sweet biscuits! And partly—and not least—it was the suspicion that her visit and her packet of biscuits were an embarrassed expression of affection and goodness; perhaps she was even in love with him? The thought horrified him and, sitting up in bed with the packet of biscuits in his hand, he swallowed; as long as it was only sex play between them, that was all right; but if she was now going to exhibit more tender feelings as well! He was filled with shame and despair, wished he could hide under the bedclothes, sink through the floor, weep; if only he could be alone, alone with his dishonour and the poverty of his heart, for he did not love her and never would, the packet of biscuits in his hand made that glaringly obvious to him. Oh Molly, Molly, you should not have come and shown me kindness, he thought. But he kept a hold on himself, retained his friendly smile the whole time; and some way or other he must thank her. 'Thanks,' he said and gulped, 'that's . . .' Embarrassed, she sat down on a chair beside the bed and giggled: she just thought she would pop in; she wasn't going to disturb him. And Ash was crushed (for to be able to receive a gift is one of the most difficult things in life; everybody can give, but it is only the strong who can receive), he felt the gift such an oppressive burden that he had to give her something *in return*, only in that way could they be quits; hurriedly his gaze flitted round the room, but he could see nothing; he had a French book he was reading, on the bedside table was his tobacco and pipe and matches and ashtray and a packet of cough pastilles; in his distress he stretched out his hand (though that was just what he didn't want!), carefully he touched her hand, intending that to be a sort of thanks, and she blushed slightly and blinked squirrel-like and giggled, and he couldn't very well take his hand away at once and it occurred to him dimly that he had really only the one way to thank her, a queer way, but an expression of thanks nonetheless, and though his mind writhed in revolt he squeezed her hand, and she giggled and squeezed his back, and her hand was still a bit cold and a little wet from the rain outside, and she said roguishly, trying to play the social caller: 'And I thought I was visiting an invalid!' and when she had taken off her raincoat: 'I don't need to take off my dress, do I?' And he lifted up the bedclothes for her and pulled her down to him and said heavily and most unhappily: 'No, you don't n-n-need to take off your dress.'

The next morning he was intending to get up and go back to College. Their old landlady had been in with their breakfast tray and Daniel was standing beside the common washstand shaving. Daniel's teeth always looked so amazingly yellow on the few occasions you caught sight of them in the middle of the chalk-white lather. Ash sat up in bed, swung his legs over the edge, stuffed his feet into his slippers—and went dead.

A strange sort of cramp had attacked him in the stomach and belly; he sat rigid, not daring to breathe, he felt cold perspiration break out on his forehead, he closed his eyes and clasped his stomach; he was going to faint of course, such pain was not to be borne. He must have gasped, or perhaps it was his deathly whiteness that attracted Daniel's attention. Daniel came across to him, looked at him, shook his head:

'Is there anything wrong with you?'

Ash managed to nod.

'What is it?'

'D-d-don't know. Something with my stomach. It feels as if I'm,' he couldn't hold his head up any more, 'done for.'

Daniel gulped.

With difficulty Ash said:

'You'll have to help me . . .'

'Of course,' said Daniel.

'Send for a doctor,' said Ash. It had spread down a bit and he could now feel it in his groin too. 'And hurry . . .' Then he couldn't say any more.

'Yes,' Daniel said. He was quite bewildered, wiped the soap off his face with a towel and looked round for his tie and jacket and waistcoat. 'There isn't a phone in the house,' he said.

'There's a call box out in the street,' Ash groaned. 'And tell him to come quickly.'

Daniel rushed out. His parting look at Ash made the latter shudder; it was as if Daniel had looked at someone who was mortally ill, a hopeless case, given up. And there he sat with the most dreadful pain he had ever known; he didn't dare lie down in case he never woke up again; he sat there with his arms clasped round his belly. Colic? On the few occasions in his youth when he had had slight attacks of colic it had always been accompanied by an urge to evacuate his bowels, but he didn't feel that, just a bursting, steady, unshakeable pain; he got to his feet and stood for a moment, but that was just as intolerable and he sank down again. And now he was afraid into the bargain; he had never known that such pain existed and felt certain that he was going to die. Appendicitis? Peritonitis? Something to do with his kidneys? VD? Molly? But she was so clean and newly washed and tidy! The Rubens girl in the boat? And then according to what he had read, VD came sneaking over you, not like a bolt from the blue, didn't it? Oh, God, it must be something to do with sex, this was the punishment for his ungodly life; just the evening before, despite a temperature and a bunged up nose he had done it twice with Molly, and whether it was due to his cold or to his shame it had been unashamedly good both times; of course, only a sex-ridden fool could hazard his

health like that, when one was supposed to be weak from a cold!
He had squandered his life, that's what he had done!—oh God,
never again would he do it when he had a cold, he wouldn't do
it again anyway, from now on he was going to be a well-behaved
decent person; if only he could get over this, he would never
again think of girls, just balance-sheets, from now on just
balance-sheets.

Daniel had spoken to a doctor and the man would come 'as
soon as he could'. There was nothing more Daniel could do, so
he went to his lecture. Ash was alone again; half an hour passed,
an hour. Two hours passed. A doctor, Ash thought; if I ever get
over this, I'll shoot every doctor in the world; the only thing a
doctor can do is to ask when you were born and are you a private
patient or not; a doctor is a fox sitting in his consulting room
twiddling his fingers, sitting with drooping eyelids staring into
space and thinking how pleasantly his income is going up from
year to year, while his waiting room is full of hastily bandaged
patients streaming with blood, and all over the town people lie
dying, as he was.

Ash was wild with pain; it was like having a fractured
stomach; he caught a glimpse of himself in the mirror and nearly
collapsed: his face was as white as a sheet, contorted, unrecognizable. In the end the pain was so great that he felt that the
only way of stopping himself fainting was to provide some
counter-irritant, so he reeled the few paces across the floor to
the table and draped himself over the back of a chair, head
down. The doctor came three hours after he had been sent for.
Ash had no revolver and besides he was now almost unconscious
and beyond caring whether he was alive or dead. He whispered:

'Can you operate here?'

The doctor raised a fair eyebrow, helped him back into bed
and laid him on his back. Although semi-conscious, Ash felt all
his old distaste of being undressed by a stranger, especially
when this stranger then laid cold hands on the bare skin of his
stomach. Where does it hurt most? Here? Yes. Here? Yes. Here?
Yes. Here? Yes. It hurts madly everywhere, seems to be somewhere inside my stomach. Can it be appendicitis, Doctor? No,
it would hurt *here*, if it was. What do you think it is, then?

Can't say for certain (of all ignoramuses doctors are the worst, worse than lecturers in business administration) but I can at least give you something to stop the pain (some sense at last!). The doctor rummaged in his bag, produced a small box, took out a pill, it was conical, about three-quarters of an inch long and gleamed as though made of paraffin wax, it reminded Ash of a suppository and for a moment he thought that the doctor was going to stuff that monstrous pain-killer up his urethra and was so terrified that he felt he was falling through space; then the doctor asked him to turn over on his stomach and Ash was allowed to insert it himself and it slipped in without difficulty, but even so he didn't like having to lie with his backside up in front of a stranger and, groaning, he hastened to turn over again. Then the doctor gathered up his things, told Ash to ring him up in a couple of days and went out, leaving Ash lying there alone, trembling and forlorn and feeling mortally sick again.

He woke.

It was such a strange awakening, so quiet, so imperceptible, like slow birth. At first he could not understand why he was in bed. Daniel was standing by the table setting out books and pencils and rulers. Ash stole a glance at his wrist-watch: four o'clock. So he had been asleep since twelve, had slept for four hours. And hadn't there been something about a doctor? Suddenly he remembered the senseless pain and equally suddenly discovered that it had gone. He lay there, limp and still, like a woman after giving birth; he scarcely dared believe it, but then a wonderful sense of relief and gratitude swept through him: the pain was gone, *completely* gone, it had been washed out of his belly; he felt as clean as a whistle. Doctors are God's blessed emissaries on earth; oh, how he loved all doctors! he would write a cantata in their praise, at once; no, an overture, dedicated to the old god of doctoring, the Aesculapius Overture. But, as though fearing reprisals if he let his joy become too great, he stifled it and tried to placate the god of pain by making himself small before him: I know, he said, that this is just a temporary relief, the pain will be back again in a moment, I don't know what I was talking about, of course I shall be heart-rendingly ill again in no time. He lay for a long time with his eyes closed.

When he thought that he had fawned on the god of pain long enough, he opened his eyes and cautiously turned on his side. Would the pain come back when he turned over? No. Slowly he sat up. Would it come back now? No. Would it come back if he smiled? No. He sat right up. Coming? No. Groaning, he asked Daniel for a cigarette and was given it and a light. Would the pain come back now, as he inhaled the blue smoke with sinful delight? No, most remarkable, but it didn't. Then slowly he swung his legs out over the side and sat listening to his whole being, to his belly, and he smiled a wan and still uncertain smile at Daniel, and in a small little voice he said: 'I do believe I'm all right.'

When he got up, he felt limp from the pain and the drug, but he was perfectly well. The pain never returned, neither that day nor the next, nor the next week, nor the next month, nor in the years to come; he never had such an attack again.

But he was never to forget the morning he spent hanging over the back of a chair, crazed with pain, and there remained lurking within him a secret fear for his belly; he knew that he was going to die, and die young, of some ailment of the belly; the wages of sin is death; he was an exceedingly sinful person and death would strike him in the seat of sin, the source of gratification; he remembered the story of Eugene Gant's old father (at this period he considered Thomas Wolfe the greatest writer in the world), drunkard and fornicator, who died in hospital of cancer. Yes, Ash thought, that's how I too shall die, and it won't be so very long either. Ah, well!

But how swift in life is the transition from grief to joy. Only the stars in the heavens are constant; *they* always show the same face whether two lovers have found each other or an unhappy woman has killed her newborn child by stuffing it into a sewer; Goethe said: 'One does not desire the stars, one delights in their splendour.' Oh, Goethe, there's nothing in the world so devilish as the stars!

The day after this business with the doctor, Ash and Daniel were talking sex. Men talk sex, women talk sex; behind the stories about sex that people tell each other lies a need as eternal as that of eternity; all peoples have stories about sex, and all

peoples have stories about God. To talk about God is a deliverance, and to talk about sex is a deliverance. Without the one or
the other people would burst from suppressed desire to know
and impart; risqué stories and Christ's parables—the latter
make the mind devout, the former make our laughter peal out
—let us to all eternity bless the Scriptures, but let us also bless
risqué stories.

Daniel was sulky, reserved and moody; glum, melancholy
and often indifferent, there was something about him that Ash
could never fathom. He was never lucky with girls; as often as
not he just shrugged his shoulders over them and smiled a wry
smile. Ash knew very little about him, just that his father was
a librarian and over sixty, a small man and a humpback; Daniel
was the first child, so his father must have been over forty
when he was born; and there was something melancholy and
old-mannish about Daniel; when Daniel was eighteen, his
parents had had another child, a daughter. So Daniel had a
little sister of five; one or two of his letters from home also contained strange scribbly drawings and, rather shamefacedly,
Daniel had stuck one of them up on the wall with drawing pins;
Ash had looked down, but not protested; he didn't know why,
but he had shuddered.

That first evening when Molly and her sister came up to their
room, Daniel and the sister had had a long whispered conversation on Daniel's bed. Later, Daniel once or twice had the
room to himself in the evening, and Ash presumed that something or other must have happened; Molly, too, had hinted that
her sister was very taken with Daniel. Ash now asked him outright if anything had come of it. Hm, said Daniel, and shrugged
his shoulders. (A strange person this Daniel, Ash thought; I
have never seen him glad, never seen him jump for joy or laugh
really heartily; he's a depressing person to live with and I think
I shall have to look for a room on my own.) How old do you
think the sister is? Daniel suddenly asked. About nineteen, Ash
thought and recalled her white, unhappy face. Twenty-seven,
said Daniel, glumly. Ash was too astounded to speak and there
was a long pause.

'She's a virgin,' said Daniel.

'Was, you mean?' . . . 'Is.' . . . 'Doesn't she want to?'

'There's nothing she would like better.' . . . 'Well—?' . . . 'It can't be done.'

'Rubbish.'

'It's God's own truth. I've spent three evenings trying. Sheer waste of effort.' . . . 'Rubbish.' . . . 'She gets so het up she lies there weeping, and she helps as much as she can, but I've given up.'

'Don't try to kid me!'

'She's had lots of boy friends before—and they've *all* had to give up!'

'But the girl must go to a doctor!'

'That's what I've told her. But she funks it.'

'What—er—what do you do then, when you're together?'

'She does the handcart with me.'

'Is that anything?'

'Well, not much. I lie there and give my orders: faster, half speed, steady, slow, slow . . .'

'Good God! You'll have to try a dynamite cartridge.'

Again Ash found the world chock full of the surprising, the incomprehensible and the horrible. Molly open and quite insensitive; her sister hermetically sealed and as hot as a stove. A highly peculiar family. And then when he thought of the Rubens girl and her never-ending orgasm, he was filled with abysmal wonder at the variations among woman: why didn't God create all women alike? For all men are alike, in that way, aren't they?

Then one day something happened. Molly, about whom there had been something soft and gentle ever since her visit to the invalid (a new departure that filled Ash with nameless terror), asked if he and Daniel would not go with her and her sister to a mountain hut the following Saturday and spend the night there. Now Ash had reached the stage where he would have preferred to end his friendship with Molly: it was time to put a stop to it. But somehow or other, despite his strong inner objection to her plan (what, in the intervals of being in bed with them, were he and Daniel going to *talk* about with these two? After all there are limits to the time one can spend in bed, and what then?) in the end he reluctantly agreed. Perhaps this was because of his old horror of hurting anyone, perhaps because of his great need for a woman's tenderness, perhaps because of his

dread of loneliness. For if he were to make a swift break with
Molly now, where was the new woman for him?

He was silent and broody as they sat in the bus on the way
out. Bitter, ashamed, unsociable. When they arrived, his mood
became even worse. The hut was so un-lovely, so cold, so devoid
of any hint of beauty or imaginativeness, its bareness was evidence of the profoundest spiritual poverty. He shuddered with
horror. He was beside himself at the thought of having to spend
a whole Saturday evening, a whole Saturday night, a whole
Sunday forenoon and a whole Sunday afternoon with these two
imbecile girls in that hut. He was overcome by a sudden crazy
terror, a sort of claustrophobia: he was imprisoned and could
not escape. When one of the girls wound up a gramophone, put
on a record of *A Little Golden Ring* and suggested that they
should dance, he gasped: to him it was a convict's tango. They
had brought some liquor with them and he filled a tumbler with
aquavit and poured it down his throat. He became drunk at
once, unhappily, nastily drunk; he sang and danced about like
a tree in a storm, and after a while he dragged Molly off into the
bedroom and there they stayed. She was little and frightened
and willing, and he was neither gay nor happy. Some time in
the night he withdrew gasping for the third time and looked
down at his naked body and saw that the condom had burst and
became stone sober, and the world tumbled round his ears and
he fell through seven hells and she felt his terror and was a
little afraid herself, but she giggled and said that if things went
wrong she would see to it, he shouldn't suffer; wondering, he
asked what she meant by that, and she shook her head and said
that there were people who could help, and she said it as though
she knew all about it, or as if she had had it done herself, and
he felt a secret revulsion and horror, for to him that was the
cruellest thing in the world, a sin for which there was no name,
but she put her arms round him and reassured him, and inside
he felt tremendously grateful, perhaps mostly because he had
been spared hating her. He knew that that was the most primitive and ignoble reaction in the world, to hate the woman the
moment it looked as though things had gone wrong, but he
knew that was what happened, he had experienced it before,
he couldn't help it: at such a moment one can feel a fierce desire

to kill the woman, because without her it would not have happened! His tensed muscles slowly relaxed, calm returned to him at her side and as he fell asleep he had such a queer thought: now her magnanimity has given her a fresh hold over me. First that packet of biscuits, now this. His last thought was a very decided one: in future I shall never be content with just one condom, I shall use three, one on top of the other; no, I shall go to a vulcanizing place and get them to make a special one of tyre rubber a good inch thick; *that* won't burst. He had bad dreams that night.

A week later when Molly told him, one evening when she was up in his room, that he mustn't do it that evening, he was almost beside himself with joy. He was ready to do anything for her, to buy her a necklace of Canadian river pearls, to take her to the most fashionable restaurant, anything. . . . He gasped with senseless delight and heedless generosity, went to his jacket and looked in his pocket-book.

There was just enough for a film—if she paid for herself.

It was shortly after this that, one evening, Molly came forward with a new suggestion. She and her sister with escorts (Ash shuddered) were invited to a big dance not in the town, but at the house of an acquaintance at a factory estate a dozen miles away. Awfully nice people, manager of the ready-made clothes factory, big house and plenty of money; it was his daughter giving the dance: there were to be eight couples, all young people; the others had heard of Ash and Daniel and thought it would be great fun to have a couple of undergraduates. No, Ash thought, no, no, no; I won't go in among a crowd of Molly's acquaintances; they will be ghastly; and she will present me as her 'escort' and I can't stand that. But, on the other hand, there might be something in the idea: he had been in the town nearly two months and apart from the first night, when he had stayed with his mother's horrible relatives, he had not set foot inside a private house, a home. Lecture-hall, club-rooms, cafés, picture houses, students' rooms, yes, but never a home. Big house and plenty of money? Surely that would mean not just dancing and gin and painful conversation with people you did not know, but perhaps an atmosphere of warmth and abundance, of good food and drink, perhaps Rhine wine in tall, narrow, sea-green chilled bottles and a loaded cold table, perhaps bowls of fragrant lobster meat and mayonnaise? Poor Ash found himself suddenly drooling and tremendously hungry. The vision of so much food made his head swim. And was there not something else? Eight couples? That meant eight girls. Subtract Molly and her sister, the known, that left six unknown girls; he had to turn his face away from Molly as the thought struck him. He was trembling inside. Six unknown girls. Would he find Her there?

'Yes,' he said, 'I'll talk to Daniel about it.'

A Hand of Friendship from Mexico

They hired a car to take them on that Saturday evening; Molly and her sister paid. At the last moment Daniel had taken half a bottle of whisky and he passed this round in the car. Thinking of how ghastly the people there might be, Ash took a swig. He had a strange feeling sitting there with Molly on his lap: you don't know it, Molly, he thought, but this is the last time you will sit on my knees. The thought filled him with a queer melancholy and he had to force himself to smile at the girl's excited chattering. Now and then he glanced at Molly's sister, that queer pale girl, but dropped his eyes as soon as she looked at him. He felt a great compassion for her: twenty-seven, virgin, sealed, living a life of constant despair, terror, inferiority, grief and shame. Shame on her own account, shame on the men's account, double shame. Then came a surprising thought: perhaps I should try? I am much more experienced than Daniel, Daniel is a dreary sulky quitter; I should be doing her the greatest imaginable service and I should be helping Daniel too.

They were offered a cocktail the moment they arrived. As a result, and because Ash was always scared to death in the company of strangers, there was little he remembered afterwards of the interior of the house, and not much of the guests either. He couldn't even remember what food there had been, or if there had been Rhine wine; he must have made a great effort to be charming. And young Ash had quite a lot of social charm which is synonymous with being afraid of strangers; the effect of charm is both to keep people away from the especially tender spots in one's own soul and to create an atmosphere of warmth and friendliness.

After the cocktail, they had a couple of whiskies and soda. Ash could remember that it was very good whisky, and all evening he played the gay undergraduate. There were two men in the company whom he intuitively disliked and therefore avoided. Ash had only to shake hands with a man to know at once whether he was a decent person or a slimy brute; it was as though he had a sixth sense in his skin for judging men, a sort of telepathy. But he was hopeless at judging women and their characters; perhaps his sexual sensitivity blinded him to the other sides of their natures; he registered instantaneously when there was sympathetic contact between him and a woman, but he could never tell straight off whether she was a Florence Nightingale or a Lucretia Borgia.

To one of the men there, a swarthy pharmacist with rimless glasses and white teeth, Ash's antipathy was so strong that his skin tingled every time he walked or danced past him. For Ash, the evening was a tremendous release after almost two months' duress, a liberation from his textbooks and lecture-notes and the weight of his bank-loan. For a while he forgot; he sang, and he was a good ballad-singer, he played jazz on the piano, he was a useful pianist, gave them *Tiger Rag* and *The Sheik of Araby;* and he danced with the girls and the devil was in his body. But he never danced with Molly. Now and again he caught a glimpse of her, sitting in a corner, and he felt her small brown doglike eyes on him, perhaps there was a streak of green in them as well, but he couldn't help it, he danced only with the others.

The six unknown girls.
They were all well-dressed, bourgeois, with an air of having

a modest permanent job in an office or shop, a job to which they went every day and which they performed diligently and conscientiously, but without real interest, for they all hoped that they would not spend too many years of their young lives in business, hoped for wedding bells and a bride's bouquet and bridesmaids and a honeymoon and a home with a bathroom and a bedroom with a double-bed of birchwood and a dressing table with a triple mirror and a taffeta housecoat, a place where they could entertain their former girl-friends and offer them sherry and home-made biscuits and sponge-cake, sit on their own modern armchairs with big fat bellies and heavy gold rings on their fingers knitting tiny garments of pink angora wool, and their friends would all be loud in their admiration and jealous witnesses of their riches and good fortune.

Fleetingly the gay student was aware of all this and of the future that awaited them, and momentarily he felt sorry for them and sad at the thought of their future happiness, the stagnation of the duck pond. They have no daring, these girls, he thought despairingly; they never risk anything, they have no imagination, no dreams, no courage (for poetry is courage). My God, he prayed in that second, show me a girl who dares. Let me for once in my life see a girl who *dares*. Who does not take a job in an office, but builds her own business, who puts out a mimographed magazine, who has a small market garden, or a workshop for making wooden ornaments (ebony, rosewood, teak, heavens, how lovely things are in lovely wood!) who has a mail order business for rubber goods, who fights for a cause—O God, let me once see a young woman who is not just thinking of a ring and Mendelssohn's wedding march and cakes baked in her own oven!

But this gloomy feeling of despair lasted only a second. He was the gay undergraduate, the witty dog and the jazzing elk.

Already over that first cocktail he had had a good look at the girls.

Four were obviously of no interest, their voices flat, their faces devoid of sorrow. All the same he danced once or twice with each of them; they were inert, like sacks of flour and as difficult to shift; some of them had shaved off their eyebrows and blacked in a new line; the lipstick on their lips was uneven.

Of the other two, one had attracted his notice at once. She was tall and slim, with dark-blond gleaming hair; indeed it was her lovely, slightly wavy hair that he had first noticed, there was something quietly elegant about the way it was done and then the gloss of it. She wore a semi-long silk dress, the material rustled, so perhaps it was taffeta; the skirt was close-fitting; it was a black dress and that and the close-fitting skirt made her stand out from the others who wore gaily coloured frocks with wide puffed-out skirts. She was very shapely and had the supple bodily grace of a little girl; she looked a quiet and careful person; she could have been about twenty-one; there was something elegantly sweet-natured about her; she wore no rings. When Ash was introduced to her she smiled slightly and held out her hand; it was small and warm; her eyes were grey and very beautiful; there was uncertainty in her smile and something in her nature made her press her lips together as though she were afraid to smile and open out; a line or two round her mouth could have been evidence of sorrow and as a result Ash was instantly captivated by her; with a slight nervous thumping of his heart he tried to converse with her. She did not mix so much with the others, preferred to keep herself to herself. After their dances she and Ash often went and sat by themselves on the window-sill. The window stood open and outside was the mild autumnal evening. She was head girl in a beauty salon, she told him; he looked at her hands, she had good hands, but they were hesitant, unfinished. Their proportions were right for dancing together, she was lithe and calm, easy to dance with, like a fairy. There was no provocation in her body, but it had a warm and very feminine fragrance. She was far too nice, far too much of a *good* girl, for Ash to dare make intimate advances; he felt that she would shrink from that; he sat there in the window and talked with her; he sighed, he desired her, but his main feeling was of being in love; outside was the mild autumn night.

His hostess, the manager's daughter, a girl of about twenty-five, came and clapped him on the shoulder; now she was going to have a dance with him. She was half German and her name was Wilhelmine; Ash had to smile when he heard it and asked if she were called after *der Kaiser*. She was not actually good-looking; she had a slight stoop; her shoulders were very slightly raised, as though she felt an inner urge to hide her head; her brown face was not really pretty either; she gave the impression of being rather dull and heavy; her jaw was slightly underhung too. When she got out of a chair the movement was sluggish, reluctant, perhaps nonchalant; she went about among her guests with shoulders raised and hands thrust into the pockets of her skirt; there was something manly about her and for a moment Ash thought of a shy ship's engineer on shore leave. Even so she appealed to him; she was the second of the two girls Ash had noticed at the very start. She wore a dress of thin flowered material, semi-long, with a full skirt, her legs were strong and shapely, her ankles very neat. She was reserved and almost gruff as she talked with Ash; but when he got her to smile, she lost all her unhappy bulldog look; when her dark face broke into a rare smile, it was like the sun rising, her teeth were white and healthy and particularly beautiful; when she smiled, you could see that she was capable of great tenderness.

Now she had come across to the window where Ash had entrenched himself with the lovely Constance (that was the name of the girl in the black taffeta dress) had given him a mannish and slightly reproachful clap on the shoulder to claim him for a dance. They danced. Her hair was dark, very dark, and it had a sweet smell. She kept close to him as they danced; at first she held herself slightly away, but when he cautiously drew her towards him, she came, and now she was close. Could he have danced with her before? He didn't know; only he was so amazed to feel her body: it was strong, muscular, supple. Her slouch brought her pelvis forward strongly and he could feel that she could have no underclothes on to speak of.

He danced away and all at once he could feel her pressed against his thigh. He glanced down at her, saw the black hair of her head, a little of the skin of her neck, some of the skin on her lower arm, and at that moment he knew that this gruff girl was a soft sensual woman, knew that her skin was like brown warm silk; then the music stopped and they walked across to put on another record, and he took his handkerchief and mopped his forehead, and it was hot, and he said so, and he (or she) said that they could go out for a breath of air, and outside it was dark, suddenly pitch dark after all the light inside, and he had to take her hand, and they walked down the garden along a gravel path.

It was a large garden with many trees; he turned for an instant towards the house, Constance was still in her place in the window, now she was sitting talking with another man. He walked on down the path with Wilhelmine. It was a late autumn evening and only slightly chilly; autumnal night, dew on the grass, a moist velvety darkness, and then a warm scent of fruit. Then he could see the trees still covered with apples; it was such a heavy smell, a smell of abundance and ripening decay. He felt her tremble slightly and he put his hand on her waist and drew her to him. For a second he felt her hip roll against his thigh, as his arm was round her waist, and then he had his hand under her breast and it was so heavy, heavy as a ripe apple that she could only have had the thin muslin frock on and nothing underneath, he could feel the shape and fashion of her breast and the shape of the nipple more distinctly than if he had had her breast bare in his hand, and, quivering, he turned her towards him, and his kiss must have been hard, because her lips were hard and slightly curled in over her teeth; he took hold of her head so that he could get her tongue, then he set her against a tree and her thin frock made her seem doubly naked, he set his hand trembling on her, she whispered no and thrust her pelvis forward, she whispered no and he scrabbled her skirt up, she was not wearing a suspender belt and only silk panties so small they were a joke. Without transition or fight he had his hand on her nakedness; now his hands were rough and his heart was pounding, 'No' she said and her belly was working madly, she clung to him and whispered 'No, no' and for a brief instant he stopped, hurt and disappointed, not knowing if she meant it; 'No' she said as he let go of her with one hand and made himself ready, and now he was smiling and felt the male animal's exasperation at being delayed, he twined his fingers in her hair and dragged her head back and kissed her, now the giddy moment was at hand when the man knows that the power and the glory are his, 'No' she whispered, and he parted her thighs and thrust strongly into her, he was so tall compared to her that he had to stand with bent knees. Now she had forgotten everything except to say 'No': for a brief moment he had a glimpse of her closed eyes and ecstatic expression, then it was she blindly working on him, her belly was wonderfully supple and strong, two panting people beneath a tree, and gasping he had to ask her, 'Slower,' but she worked on blindly, her last 'No' was a convulsive groan and her head jerked back against the trunk and some apples fell with heavy dull thuds, on to the grass, and he gave at the knees, had to withdraw in a hurry, stood gasping with her in his arms.

His damned preventatives were in the house, in his coat, she whispered a question and said that he must be careful not to get any on himself, and she fumbled over his body, avid to give requital, and he was filled with an immeasurable sweetness and it happened for him in her hand. He searched in his pocket for a handkerchief and handed it to her and he could not speak for his pounding heart and gasping breath. Through the trees he could see the lighted windows of the house, and in one of them the lovely Constance, and he knew that there was no other place where such strange things happen as in this world.

They straightened their clothes and she asked if he had a comb, and they stood in the dark and listened for a moment, but all was quiet, except for the music up in the house and the pounding of their blood, and they smiled awkwardly and happily to each other, and he whispered 'Thank you' and she nodded; he was so grateful to God that he could have plucked the apple trees up by their roots, a cry swelled in his throat and he laid his hand round her neck, the first tender caress he had given her, and she took his hand and laid it against her cheek. Then they really had to get back to the house. He tried to hold her back, but she dragged him with her. He asked when she could get to the town and she told him that she worked in her father's office, but she could come on Friday, Friday evening, and he wondered if Friday was a day when Daniel could be bundled off to a film, and it was; he gave her his address: Friday at nine o'clock, nine o'clock sharp, and they parted with a handclasp on the steps and walked in without looking at each other, without exchanging another glance, and he went and sat with the lovely Constance and her smile was good and free of suspicion, and he asked her if he could go out with her one evening, to a film, or a concert, and sitting there he knew that he was going to have Constance too, not now, perhaps not for months, for she was not

like that, with her he was groping his way and rather timid and
not at all brutal, but he knew that she was his, and he asked if
she was free on Saturday and she was, and their heads came a
little closer together and their voices dropped a little as he asked
where he could phone her, and they thought they would go to
a film, and they danced a last dance together and her dark
golden glossy fragrant hair was so close that it tickled his chin,
and he felt that her body was not afraid and that one day he
would know her, and for a moment as they danced the palms of
their hands spoke to each other, and when he said goodnight to
her there was a shy smile on their faces; he said goodnight to
Constance and a formal goodbye to Wilhelmine and so it was
Wilhelmine on Friday and Constance on Saturday, he had a
moment of megalomania, he had struck gold, it couldn't be true,
but when he was sitting in the car driving back with Daniel and
Molly and Molly's sister, he saw from Molly's little face that it
was true, for Molly had considered herself his girl and she must
have sensed something of what had been happening, and she
knew that she had lost, she had crept up into one corner of the
back seat and her freckled face was white and her eyes green,
and when in a moment of overwhelmingly bad conscience, he
tried to put his arm round her shoulders, she shook it off. Not
many words were spoken on that drive home and the silence got
on his nerves most horribly; all at once he found himself hating
Molly as only a man can hate who has met with nothing but
goodness from a girl and been most unfair to her right under
her nose.

After that he never invited Molly to his room again. He had
known that evening in the car that it was over.

He met her once by chance two years later. (The Second
World War had broken out, the Germans had occupied Norway
and much had changed in his own life.) He was in a side street
and went into a grocer's to buy a bottle of vinegar. He had not
noticed that there was CO-OPERATIVE written up outside or
else he might have been to some extent prepared. All at
once, there was little Molly behind the counter, smiling, eyes

screwed up, face freckled, giggling, just the same as before, only shy and a little agitated at seeing him again. She was wearing white shop-overalls with a belt. He looked at her hand as she rolled his bottle of vinegar in some paper. She had no ring. He swallowed hard, paid, and went out quickly. He discovered that she had given him too much change. He did not go back.

That was how he was to remember her for the rest of his life: the girl who gave him more than he should have had.

Workers of the World Unite!

At the beginning of November, Ash had a conversation with one of the other students at The College that was to bring about a decisive change in the course of his life and which he was to remember with exceptional vividness in later years.

This student was called Erik. They had noticed each other at the lectures, where Erik's quiet, sober, clever arguments in support of the Co-operative movement, trade unions and state control finally left Ash in no doubt but that the other also held socialistic views. Thus, in that stronghold of liberalism, there were not just one, but two socialists. It almost smacked of conspiracy. Perhaps, if he delved a bit deeper he would find *many* socialists beneath the white coats the students wore? The thought staggered him. But he did not investigate.

It is said that opposites attract each other. If so, the attraction comes about in shyness and with concealed mutual admiration. These two were as different as they could be. Erik appeared to admire Ash for his physical size, for his artistic turn of mind, his recklessness, his bold tongue; to Erik he seemed wild and not a little crazy; Erik admired him for his vast, hilarious, unstoppable laughter when anything amusing was said or done; for his cheerful activities as conductor of the undergraduates' choir and little orchestra (an *unselfish* man, Erik thought, one

who dispenses joy and song; and how does he find the *time!*)
and finally for his frequently and clearly expressed contempt
for the commonplace, for hypocrisy and bigotry. To Erik,
Ash was the Adventurer, the Poet and, most exciting of all,
the *Bohemian!*

Little did Erik know to what degree Ash admired and respected *him.*

There were, it is true, certain comical, even outright ridiculous
things about Erik Floden, but they could not overshadow his
intelligence and serenity. He was a short, thin, slightly-
built man with a big head and hands like a peasant's. He had
a coarse but kindly face, which was sprinkled with little warts
—probably subterranean pimples—and these made shaving
difficult, so that often he had tiny pieces of newspaper on his
chin, while here and there about his face inaccessible tufts of
bristles protruded like bleached mountain grass. Seen from in
front, his face looked rectangular, and that gave the beholder
the impression of confronting a quiet, good-natured carthorse.
His hair was very fair and thin, and a lock of it was con-
tinually falling over his forehead, and when this happened he
would stroke it back into place with a rather feminine gesture.
Undoubtedly he was of peasant stock, but a simple and un-
complicated soul, and that made it doubly curious that a
young fellow with such a rugged horsy face should have such
feminine elements in his character. This may have been due to
lack of social assurance; at all events it was a source of amazement to Ash to see this horsy person behaving like a dandy,
and waggling his hips coquettishly when he walked. Also there
was something of the snob and the eminently respectable citizen
about him; his tie was beautifully tied and he always had a
white handkerchief in his breastpocket and often a flower in
his buttonhole. This peasant lad wore galoshes and an Anthony
Eden hat and carried a slender silk umbrella (which he either
swung very elegantly or leaned on). One day—it was some
special occasion at The College—our rustic socialist turned up
in black coat, white shirt, grey tie and striped trousers, looking
like an English aristocrat on his way to the club. Never had
anything approaching such elegance been observed at or near
The College. Correct, irreproachable, but also with a taste for

whispered, feminine confidences about the private affairs of the professors, lecturers and readers, and those of the local bigwigs as well. He knew which of the local magnates had changed their names, who was syphilitic and who had stomach ulcers, whose wife was a dypsomaniac and whose children imbecile; he knew everyone's income and fortune and the boards they sat on; he was the Readers' Postbag, a Banker's Reference and Who's Who rolled into one. Ash listened to him round-eyed, but forgot all he was told the next moment, for he had no interest whatever in such things.

After this, it will be no surprise to learn that Erik Floden smoked cigars, small cigarillos which he produced with the utmost elegance from a cardboard box. He did not inhale, using his cigars to demonstrate what a distinguished person he was; he tapped the ash off with his index finger and looked to see where it fell with slightly raised eyebrows and an expression of slight, tired interest. It may be a surprise, however, to learn that Erik Floden was engaged and so had a love life. The real surprise, though, came when you saw the girl of his choice. One would have expected a snob like Erik Floden to have got himself a girl of good family, if not one of noble birth; but his fiancée was a mountain of flesh, twice his size and weight, and the daughter of a cobbler. She was one of the fattest, reddest-cheeked, biggest bosomed women Ash had ever seen, but Erik loved her most devotedly and surrounded her with every possible affectionate attention; he called her 'little Thea'. At the evening functions in the Club it was always: 'Are you all right, little Thea? Are you cold, little Thea? Shall I fetch your cardigan, little Thea?' But the really fantastic sight was when Erik invited his enormous Thea to dance: happy, tender, perspiring, hair falling over his forehead, he trundled his mountain round the floor, sometimes disappearing altogether in her skirts. At such moments one could not help wondering whether there was any sexual relationship between them; the thought made Ash think of a miniature poodle dog trying in an access of love to reach the charms of a St. Bernard bitch, but being able to do no more than clasp its beloved's knee.

Yes, Erik Floden was both comical and ridiculous, but there wasn't a drop of evil in him, and for all his foppishness Ash had to admire him. There was a stability about him that made a deep impression on Ash; Erik had a clear brain, a fantastic memory and a rare ability to argue temperately, objectively and convincingly; he quickly attracted the lecturers' attention for he knew his subjects, was never at a loss and always had figures and facts to back up his arguments. Once or twice Ash had thought delightedly: the professors are a bit afraid of Floden! And it also occurred to him that the way Erik preached socialism, so calmly, convincingly, dispassionately and without giving offence, he ought to be able to turn The College into a socialist university in no time at all.

Such, then, were the two socialists at The College. Erik was the realist; he was the son—so Ash discovered—not of a peasant, but of a trade unionist and editor of a provincial labour newspaper; Erik had grown up in an atmosphere of socialism which to him was an everyday affair. To Ash socialism was a vision he had seen in a dream and almost sacred. Erik wanted to build factories in the valleys and plough up the low-lying areas; Ash wanted to build beacons on mountaintops and beat the big drum.

Two young socialists, as different as day and night, yet in those surroundings the complement of each other; they had a shy, unexpressed respect—and perhaps also envy—for each other.

One day in November they were in a café to which they had gone after lectures to discuss some problem of economics together. Ash had ordered a glass of beer; Erik drank nothing alcoholic because, he said, of a stomach ailment, but in his heart Ash knew that Erik was a teetotaller as well as a trade unionist and he felt a sudden distaste for his beer.

'Have you never thought of coming to one of the meetings?' Erik asked all at once.

'Meetings?'

'I've spoken about you. They wonder why you don't come.'

'Come? Where to? Who are they?'

He was seized by a nameless excitement, by a sense of swelling promise, as was always the case when he heard that others had been speaking of him. So Erik had told them about him, *what* had he told them? The others had *talked* about him. They had sat and *spoken* about him! *What* had they said? He was wringing his hands in his lap with burning, newly aroused longing for fellowship and recognition; somewhere in this town were people who were talking about him, about *him*; who wanted him to come to *them*, merciful heavens!

'Who are they?' he howled.

'The Socialist Students' Group,' said Erik, blinking at the vehemence of the other's outburst.

Ash sat for a moment open-mouthed. He felt a sudden sweet warm languor in his body, a giddiness, as though, having tramped and begged his way across the world, now at last . . . he gulped and said in a thick voice:

'Do you mean to say that—er—that here in this town—there's —er—a set, an executive committee—I mean an *organised group* of socialist students?'

'Of course,' said Erik. 'I'll tell you the next time there's a meeting.'

'C-can anyone go to the meetings?'

'Oh, no!' said Erik, pursing his lips; then he leaned towards Ash and poked a finger into his side, confidential, mysterious: 'But I have told them about *you*.' Grinning, he got to his feet and walked out, leaving the paralysed Ash to his own devices. What had Erik told them? About the time Ash took off his trousers and jumped into the pond in the grounds to try and see whether the lonely fish in it was male or female; or when he hiccoughed in an economics lecture when the rector said unctuously: 'I believe in liberalism,' or when at a dance in the club he had become ecstatically tight and had swung from the chandelier uttering gorilla-like cries? Was that the sort of thing Erik had told them? If so, what sort of socialist would they think him? Or—the line of his jaw went white—did Erik who knew everything about everyone, who was worse than any woman in his curiosity about family relationships, a specialist in scandal, did he perhaps also know a bit about Ash's private life? About what he had tried to keep a deep secret? (When Ash had applied for a free place and a student's loan, he had had to fill up a form and the secretary had asked: 'Have you anyone dependent on you?' Ash had hesitated for a second that was

as long as a century, looked away, gulped and said: 'No.' He
was remitted half the fees, but he knew that he need not have
paid anything; however, the secret of his past was his alone, no
one was to know about his skeletons.) Perhaps Erik had been
making inquiries? Perhaps Erik knew *everything* about him?
Perhaps the Socialist Students' Group was at that moment sitting sniggering over his disgrace and wretchedness?

Slowly that senseless fear subsided, only to have its place
taken by another. The quiver of delight, the fierce feeling of
warm pleasure he had felt at the thought of meeting the group,
was still there, but ... This, of course, was what he had longed
for, a group of socialists, a brotherhood welded together, a
secret band of rebels, defiant, strong solidarity, the fellowship,
the door, the hand. ... But what did they *require* of him, what
were they like, what jobs would be given him, what ability or
knowledge had he to offer them, how could *he* serve so noble
a cause? He did not know what this revolutionary group did,
nor what their underground activities consisted of; for a brief
second he saw himself standing making an incendiary speech
in a cellar with discoloured walls and only a smoky paraffin
lamp to read his notes by, or did he have to speak *without notes!*
He saw the fifty workers who were his audience, their faces
turned up to him like white flowers in the night, and away at the
basement door a guard standing ready to whistle if the police
made a raid; for that fleeting second he was fighting in the streets
and at barricades, smelling the smell of asphalt and petrol
and falling plaster, hearing the shriek of tyres skidding on
corners and the jingle of falling glass from broken window
panes, hearing cries and groans, smelling the smell of blood and
gun oil from revolvers, the smell of smoke and gunpowder, his
heart pounding, his hand bandaged, himself kneeling in the
shelter of a cement stairway, the whine of bullets and the crackle
of shots, he had never held a pistol before, good lord! He
thought of the cool head and organizing talent they expected
of him, the map carried in his head, the plan of the streets,
bridges, factories and barracks, the tactics and strategy, exact
knowledge of who was a friend and who an enemy, the cool
head and stout heart. Take the cross from your flag and hoist
it clean and red—Yes! The WAY FORWARD, TOWARDS THE DAY,

give me the proud and the pure of heart—Yes! Workers of the world unite!—Yes! and the smell of gun oil from his hot, steel-blue revolver, and the assumption of power, ASSUMPTION OF POWER, now it is dawning, brothers! Pale and with quivering jaw this son of the revolution got up from the table. He had been giddily up in the clouds, the blood-red clouds of freedom and his heart had ceased to beat.

In that stillness he heard a sneeze from one of the waitresses out in the kitchen.

The Colonel

Wilhelmine was to come on Friday.

By Thursday Ash was seeing visions and that evening he had to go to the pictures, for if he had tried to read *Industrial Accountancy, Technique and Method* he would only have seen a bed with two naked bodies in it, on every page himself and Wilhelmine, Wilhelmine stark naked, he knew how her silky skin would feel; the picture of her was all the more exciting because she hid her strong sexuality beneath that gruff face and slouched shoulders. He forgot her while he was watching Gary Cooper, remembered her the moment the lights went up and then the only thing he could do was to trudge the silent streets till he was dog-tired; it would have helped if he could have gone back and played the violin, but Daniel had no taste for lying in bed at midnight listening to Ash's playing, even if Ash put the mute on. Ash understood that: it is one thing to hear Mischa Elman at a concert, and quite another to listen to an indifferent player scraping out studies and sonatas solo, in confined space, only six feet from one's eardrums.

On Friday Ash didn't know what to do with himself. He spent the morning prodding a pocket-knife into the palm of his hand, a manœuvre intended to distract his thoughts. In the restaurant where a number of undergraduates had lunch, he was nearly sick when he tried to eat what was normally one of his favourite dishes. The afternoon was as long as the Dark Ages; he had to go out and walk the streets; he did not dare close his eyes, for then he could feel her breast again beneath her muslin dress, did not dare open his eyes, for everything he saw became an image of what awaited him; he tramped about the streets with set jaw and hands clenched in the pockets of his overcoat.

He was panic-stricken when he returned to his room and saw that Daniel had already gone. He was alone. He looked at his watch: eighteen minutes to nine. At the same time he felt exhausted with waiting, dull, a weak fever-patient; he drank a glass of water and began absently to tidy the room, putting books back in their place and smoothing the beds. A sort of bitterness welled up inside him: all this blood-coursing excitement for something that in itself was so brief, two working days gone to blazes for 'a bit of fun'; was life synonymous with belly? He felt a gust of hatred, first of her who was to come, then of the dark powers that seize control of our dreams and make us defenceless. Loins and heart, he thought suddenly. This is only loins. But peace and honour presumably lie in uniting the two? Is that the eternal, is that God, is that the love that all have sung, but no one seen?

And with sudden fear: but what if the voice of the heart becomes stronger than the throbbing of the loins, if a man loves a girl with an unselfish pure love (what *are* unselfish and pure?) —then perhaps the sexual act will become gentler and calmer? Perhaps you don't take your heart's beloved up against an apple tree so that apples shower to the ground? But if real love is a gentle, quiet emotion, soul to soul, that must mean that one loses the clamour of the flesh? And isn't hot-blooded adventure good? Was not his experience with Wilhelmine in the mild apple-scented night one of the most wonderful he had had? Was it wrong? In what way was it wrong? Both had been set gasping by the happiness of their senses, at that moment Norway had been Tahiti.

Dull, dead from waiting, he greeted her with a touch of animosity. That might also have been due to her wearing a gabardine coat with a belt; it had a sort of military air about it; she had a little hat perched on the side of her head and that too was rather like a soldier's cap. She had her hands in her pockets

as she walked in and for a moment he felt that she was like a
colonel stomping across the floor. Is she unsure of herself, he
thought; or has she really got a militaristic soul?

To begin with he did not recognize her; of course it had been
dark in the garden. With trembling hands he took her coat and
hung it up; she at once sat down on one of the chairs by the
table. He thought: why doesn't she take off her galoshes? He
looked at her dress; it did not suit her very well. Does she dress
unimaginatively on purpose, he wondered? Is there some mechanism in her that makes her hide and perhaps despise her
feminity? For, being the daughter of a manager with his own
house, she must be able to *afford* to make herself attractive?
Or is she disappointed, bitter, has life out there at the trading
centre knocked many of her yearnings on the head, does she
now cold shoulder them, just to be on the safe side? All at once
he could see—she was sitting in the circle of light from the ceiling lamp above the table—that she was not so young. Twenty-
five? Most women are married by then. Well, he was not going
to lead her to the altar. Did she know that?

'Aren't you going to take off your galoshes?' he said.

'Oh, yes,' she said slowly, almost indifferently; she got up and
walked over to the door, supported herself with one hand on
the wall while she thrust them off with the other. When she
straightened up again and was walking back to the table, he
noticed a heaviness in her body and he knew what she was
feeling and why she was so sulky. He met her half-way and she
was heavy with dark shame and dark lust, he tilted her face up
towards him, she had a bluish swelling on one side of her lower
lip, her voice was deep and slightly husky as she smiled and
said: 'The book-keeper asked if it was a wasp sting.' He stood
with her black-haired head in his hands and looked down into
her good unlovely face, at the mouth that carried the memento
of his bite. Trembling he kissed her eyes.

And it was so different from what he had envisaged in his
over-excited visions. After a while they sat down on his bed
and held hands; then her other hand came and thrust in under
his shirt-cuff. He felt her warm little hand slide up his bare forearm, right up to the elbow. It was as though she wanted to be
with him, creep into him, and that made him more tender than

lustful. He patted her head and stroked her cautiously. Then after a while they undressed, calmly, without a word, with just an occasional shy glance at each other, she was naked and got quickly under the bedclothes, he was naked and it was chilly in the room and he dived in after her. Just a moment later he was out of bed again, on his way to the chest of drawers for the necessary. But there was an air of cool composure, frightened composure, about them as they turned to each other under the bedclothes. He lay on his back holding her to him, lay with his arm under her neck. For a second he thought: we could let it be. Secretly he smiled at himself, rather wanly and surprised; he could feel that he was limp, and yet for the last two days he had gone about like a redhot gun barrel! It was still a bit cold in the bed and he rolled over towards her and rubbed her, massaged her, made her skin glow, her silky skin, and she crept close to him, he saw her face and suddenly he kissed her, hungrily; she took hold of his head and drew his tongue into her mouth and milled it, his head swimming he lifted up the bedclothes and saw her naked for the first time. Trembling, he set his mouth at her breast and opened his eyes, her breast was so heavy and beautiful. She groaned and quivered and he could feel that she was ashamed of her own violent hunger and so, instead, he kissed her eyes, closed her eyes with kisses, his mouth was over her chin and her neck and her shoulder, the skin of her belly and her silky side and for an instant he saw her hand clenched on the sheet, then she raised it and struck him on the nape of the neck; a sob was squeezed from her throat; he sank over her and her hand grabbed blindly.

Slowly consciousness returned, first of breathing; then of seeing, then breathing again; he was lying heavily on her and felt her limbs go limp; she was smiling but whimpered as he drew himself free. She would have liked him to dwell in her for always of course; they lay quivering and naked side by side and smiled when they saw that the bedclothes were all on the floor; the storm was stilled, they lay quietly beside each other and breathed quietly into each other's faces, there was silence and he was able to think once more, pulled up the bedclothes and there was a long stillness; she refused the cigarette he offered her and as he lay on his back smoking, he felt her hand slip

quietly under the bedclothes and on to his chest and play with
the little forest of hair there, all was quiet, and just as he was
wondering what the time was, she said calmly, so calmly that
he felt a stab of apprehension:

'I wasn't sure whether I ought to come this evening.'

He stopped breathing. He raised himself on his elbow in
order to flick the ash off his cigarette and to have his face
averted:

'Why?" he asked.

He knew already what would be implicit in her reply. He did
not know what words she would use, but he knew what she was
going to say. And his apprehension was deep and heavy, he took
extra good time over flicking off the ash, he must have his back
turned when her reply came.

Quietly, calmly, as though addressing the ceiling, she said:

'Because I could fall in love with you.'

Slowly, in a succession of little jerks, he slipped down on to his
back again. He pulled the bedclothes over them, up to their
chins.

He made no reply.

A long time afterwards he realized with queer surprise that at
that moment he had thought of God.

But he had to say something, do something. Cautiously he
turned his head towards her, pursed his lips, smiled. He managed to make it a convincing smile. She also smiled, a dry
wondering smile, her gaze moved appraisingly across his
face, he felt her eyes like finger-tips exploring his features.
Then she drew her gaze in again. He could not tell for certain
what she had read there, but she seemed to be calm and quite
composed.

He breathed again with relief as he thought of the time.
Blessed be the man who invented the clock.

'Daniel will be here in twenty minutes,' he said.

'Mhm,' she said, almost indifferently.

He half rose up and bent over her, nibbled her ear and stroked
her bare body. He rolled her over and took her hurriedly. He
did not want to look her in the face.

After that they dressed. He asked her when she could get
into town again. She was doing nothing tomorrow, she said, was

he free on Saturday evenings? He became very busy tidying the bed. Bending over it he said that unfortunately he was engaged tomorrow. Perhaps Monday instead? She pondered, she could manage Thursday. Thursday suited him perfectly. He added that he was getting himself another room, going to be on his own, but that would not be by Thursday.

A minute afterwards Daniel came. He greeted Wilhelmine politely and thanked her again for the dance. Ash had to smile, *he* had forgotten to do that. He did so as he walked with her to the bus. 'Thank you too,' she said with a grim smile. She was exactly like a colonel in a trenchcoat.

A *Girl who Trusts You*

The following day was Saturday, Constance day. He rang her up during a break and her voice sounded different on the telephone, she was busy with a customer and asked him not to keep her long, her voice hinted at pressure of work, at crossness and tiredness, and also at a sort of veiled hysteria. He had noticed a pent-up-ness about her at the dance and remembered a tightness about her mouth, how her upper lip seemed afraid to slide up when she smiled, had been heavy and frightened, and at that moment he felt compassion and a sort of affection for her, but at the same time he was a little scared of the relationship that might one day develop between them. For a moment he felt that she must be in need of a doctor and a husband. He could only be her lover. Why was it that, even with Constance, he could only be a lover? Was it because his was a shallow nature, was he at heart frivolous, did he always shrink from the burdensome, the things that entailed duties, that smacked of conflict and pain?

They agreed to go to a film at nine o'clock that evening. Would he come and fetch her from home? He excused himself, saying he had such a lot to do; could they not meet outside the cinema ten minutes earlier, instead? Her suggestion that he should go to her home had made him shudder. If he had a horror of anything, it was of a girl's home, of her father, her mother, their dining-room, their parlour. Above anything in the world (except his own mother) he dreaded a girl's home and meeting her family: the mere suggestion made him hear the clink of prison-chains, feel that the door of the cell might shut behind him at any moment. And yet he had a wild, burning desire for a home, for a door and a hand!

Their eyes were slightly embarrassed when they met. They greeted each other, smiled, liked each other. During the performance he took her hand, she let him hold it, but he could not feel any life in her palm. Afterwards they were a bit shy with each other; he said that unfortunately he could not afford to invite her to a restaurant; would she like to go for a bit of a walk with him, or would she like to come to his room for a while? Daniel was at a party, a somewhat mysterious party at the house of some people to whom Molly's sister had introduced him, it was to go on very late. 'Is that all right?' said Constance and looked at him, her face frank and open. He swallowed. 'Quite all right." It struck him that perhaps she had never been in an undergraduate's room before. And there had been something else too, a serenity in her face. She trusted him. He writhed inwardly; there is something horrible about taking a girl who trusts you up to your room.

But once there he was gay and free, he joked with her, teased her, admired her dress and the way she had done her hair (he took a quick look at her hands, her fingers; her nails were prettily and discreetly manicured), he showed her some of his music, but refused to play for her; another time' he said. He had a couple of bottles of beer and was pleasantly surprised to hear that she liked beer; he went to the cupboard and fetched bread and butter and a tomato and some smoked mutton, he carved some dark indigo-coloured slices of meat and it was a real feast, even though he was highly surprised at how little food a girl eats and what tiny pieces she puts in her mouth and what tiny sips she takes at her glass. Sitting opposite this lovely, assured, elegant, bourgeois girl with the tiny appetite, he was ashamed of his own vast hunger, felt like some Moloch or Saturn stuffing mountains and villages and churches and trees and people and little live children into his vast mouth and then licking his lips and looking round for more.

When, almost two hours later, he was helping her on with her coat, he suddenly kissed her. It was a spontaneous, deferential kiss. She answered it cautiously and her eyes became very deep: for a moment he was aware of her slender waist and the warm fragrance of her body; it was a heavy scent like that of hot tears and it made him gulp; but then slowly she withdrew from his embrace and smiled: there was a little surprise and a little reproach and a little panic and a little pleasure in her smile, but mostly it was sorrow and he could not understand it and looked down at the floor. He took her home and she lived right on the other side of the town. There was a grocer's shop beside her house and he looked at the name and asked and she said that it was her father and mother who had the shop, and he kissed her again and she said that one day he must come to her home, and he said thanks, he would love to, and she went up the steps and got out her key and they waved to each other in the night and she opened the door quietly and slipped in and he could see her no longer and stood there a moment—a little bit happy and a little bit apprehensive—then he turned and walked away; a little way up the street he turned and looked back at Constance's house and the grocer's shop and shuddered.

And in those silent streets he began to think of yet another girl, a young clerk in the rector's office. He had gone there that morning and she had given him the information he wanted. She was strong, plump, short-bodied, soft and luxuriant, slightly pigeon-toed and had good strong legs; she was fair-haired and had a face like a freckled apple, pretty grey eyes, a short upper lip and a sweet square snub nose; her mouth was red and full and wide, her teeth were small and white with gaps between them, her hair ash-blond and thin; she was like a poster for healthy carefree Norway. She had smiled to Ash as he stood at the desk, she had leaned over it and rested her full bosom on it, they had looked at each other and inside him he had felt that sweet sensation like marzipan. He had begun to breathe heavily, had picked up his papers and was gone. But once outside he had swallowed hard, he knew.

And now, the day after Wilhelmine, and with every prospect of Constance, he must needs think of that ash-blond apple girl.

I'm abnormal, he thought, and felt like weeping.

And the next second, hard, determined: Now I must *work*.

And the second after that, soft, head-swimming: On Thursday evening Wilhelmine is coming. A gentle encounter between cannibals. We shall devour each other between the sheets. Merciful heavens. Colonel Wilhelmine!

The Socialist Students' Group

On the day of the meeting he was in a state of extreme, most humble excitement. A young recruit to Freemasonry going to the decisive ceremony of acceptance, a young Catholic given audience in Rome and knowing that he is going to kiss the Pope's toe, the missionary travelling into the jungle to meet heathens and martyrdom, none of these could have felt more devotion and readiness to serve than young Ash did the day he went to the socialists. His hands shook every time he thought of his having been *invited* (for a young man whose destiny is loneliness, there is nothing greater or more full of promise of rich wonderful fellowship than an invitation!), his heart thumped in awe and humility when he thought that this was going to be his initiation. He gave himself a deep cut on the chin as he shaved.

This was what he had longed for so wildly and sorrowfully: these upright ones, the pure, the strong, would they accept him, would he be allowed to become one of them, would they bother about the hand he held out?—they could cut it off if they wished, but would they have a use for it?

He walked through the streets, the evening streets, he was early and walked round the block many times, then he could delay no longer, he had to hang on to the banister as he walked up the stairs, it was on the fourth floor, he looked at the name plate on the door and stared like one hypnotized at the white ivory door bell; three times he stretched out a trembling index finger towards the bell-push, he gasped when he heard that he had touched it, a terrible bell rang in the hall, he ran his hand over his damp face, quaked, prayed. He heard voices in the hall, loud metallic voices, he gave at the knees and half fell inside when the door was opened.

It was a woman with grey hair and brown, confident eyes who let him in and showed him where he could hang his things. 'A considerable acquisition,' she said, her voice drily humorous, as her eyes travelled up him. Ash smiled back wanly; how he envied people who were not always looked at as though they were giraffes. With clammy hands and his bowels ready to turn to water, he walked on through the hall and stopped at a double portière over the living-room door; he put his hand to his throat, this was the veil before the holy of holies, quivering with religious devotion he drew the curtain aside, an avalanche of light struck him and he heard the voice of the high priest inside, saying:

'Devil take the entire Farmers' Party.'

Later, Ash remembered nothing of that meeting, the whole memory of it was vague, as though those present had been shadowy ghosts without faces.

It was a big room, rather ugly and bare, there were twelve or fourteen people there. Some were sitting on chairs, others had curled up on a divan, some were on leather pouffes on the floor, others again on the bare floor itself, one stood leaning against a window-sill. As Ash walked in, they were conversing in half humorous, half fretful tones; the conversation stopped instantly and so did Ash's heart. The silence and stillness were massive. He did not know whom to shake hands with first; he had no idea of the etiquette of dynamiters; he straddled past people and chairs and pouffes, stumbled, almost fell headlong over two beings resembling women, a pretty girl with nut-brown hair said, smiling: 'Norway, land of giant feet' and she had meant *him*, which made him madly embarrassed, he blushed, sweated, turned deadly pale, twisted the folds of his face into something that was meant to be a pleasant grin, shook hands and said 'pleased to meet you' and again 'pleased to meet you', though it pleased him so very little that it really pained him considerably; it was a dreadfully bourgeois thing for him to say, but what did socialists say when they shook hands?—he had mumbled his name, but so quietly that of course they did not hear, and he was asked to repeat it, but again it was inaudible; then lots of them seemed to want to know it and he *shouted* 'Ash Burlefoot', and they thought that an amusing name and he cordially agreed with them, he had suffered a lot in his youth because of it; he hadn't chosen it, but he couldn't point that out to them; he just had to stand like a dummy among them and be called Ash Burlefoot and most cordially wish that he was Lars Olsen.

A young, black-haired student of meteorology with piercing eyes—he seemed to be chairman of that evening's meeting—turned to Erik Floden who was sitting in a chair thoroughly at home, smoking one of his cigars, and asked him a question in a loud whisper. Quickly and smiling Erik gave him a little lecture on The College and the new arrival, Ash Burlefoot. You see, growled the black-haired man, he had not asked just to be impertinent but that evening they had in their midst a refugee from Hitler's Germany, a man who had fled from the concentration camps and had now come to Norway on a Nansen passport (Ash looked across at the refugee in awe); this Wolfgang was going to tell them about Nazism and feelings among the workers in Germany, and what he had to say was not to be broadcast. . . . Ash of course would understand that they must ask a few questions when a new face appeared among them—to say nothing of a student from the shipowners' own college—Ash smiled wanly.

'Don't worry,' said Erik in a calm paternal voice and flicked the ash off his cigar, 'he's our man.' He winked at Ash.

A feeling of profound, warm, wonderful pride coursed through Ash. *He's our man.* That was the nicest thing that had ever been said of him, he felt tears of gratitude come into his eyes; he belonged, he was our man. And simultaneously with this wonderful sense of fellowship came a stab of dismay and involuntarily he took a short step back. *Our man?* Had he at last found the door, only to discover that there was no handle on the inside? A secret fear assailed him and he went white from a sudden urge to defend himself; did they need him just to destroy him? Did one have to sign on the dotted line that one's heart could be roasted and the ash used as scouring powder by the charwomen in the People's House? In a fleeting moment he knew with piercing certainty that he could never be anyone's man, neither God's nor Satan's, unto death he must insist on his right to be his own. And as this dreadful thought passed through his mind, he felt that he was deceiving and failing the group. I am no use, he thought. I am a traitor. I had better leave now.

Not everyone was yet there, so the black-haired meteorologist had time to devote to Ash. He wanted to know why Ash had gone to The College. If Ash was interested in economics why was he not studying it at Oslo University? They did it seriously there. Was this shopkeepers' school anything but a place for those born with silver spoons in their mouths, a hatchery for coupon clippers? What did they actually do there? Lecture on pink Manchester liberalism? Dinner jacket parties? Raffles to provide funds for the widows and by-blows of commercial travellers?

The questions were fired at him in a hot barking voice; there was a certain element of humour in them and the others sniggered, but Ash was numbed, he found it revolting and disgraceful, he opened and shut his mouth like a fish out of water and could not stammer out a single sound that seemed human, he had to make do with a polite sickly smile. Besides they were sitting so far apart; the meteorologist was on his own territory and did not seem to mind having to shout across ten yards of floor.

He relapsed into profound, angry silence. He had to clutch at the seat of his chair to keep from blubbing. Priggish and cheap, that was what the meteorologist had been; would anyone kindly tell Ash why it should be more honourable from the socialistic point of view to study meteorology than business economy? If a newcomer to that august gathering might be permitted to ask a question, he would very much like to know whether there was more honour and socialism among the clouds in a meteorologist's mackerel sky than in a mechanic's workshop down on earth? Well? And as far as professional competence went—if a newcomer to that august gathering might graciously be allowed to ask a question—when had any meteorologist foretold the next day's weather with the same accuracy as an economist judged a business's profitability? Possibly he was being a trifle too outspoken but, was it impertinent to ask what use a meteorologist was to society? For all the lofty talk of scientific investigation, was not a meteorologist really just a fortune-teller in disguise? What did a socialist society want meteorologists for, what benefit did society derive from these modern astrologers, medicine-men and cabbalists? Was it not in every way better, more sensible and above all a far prettier sight to watch the flight of swallows above the field? Well, wasn't it?

That is what Ash said.

Only he said it to himself and not till he had got back home to his room.

Every night all over the world millions of people lie on their backs unable to sleep; lying there in bed, their lips frame the words of the fine, striking things they should have said, but did not. In the darkness of the night they grind their teeth and clench their fists and think of the wonderful, apt retort that would have squashed the other person flat. Every night millions of people lie on their backs practising the perfect retort that they are going to use *next time*. Only that next time is quite different when it comes and the retort is no longer apt.

The best retorts in the world are never heard; they are born in the night and they die from lack of suitable occasions.

Ash stayed till the end of the meeting, however. Without being able to put it into words—for it is the tragedy of youth that it cannot express its feelings, as it is age's tragedy no longer to have feelings to give substance to its utterances—Ash knew —and it was so obvious—that you did not need to be a capitalist at heart because you were at The College. Surely the socialist society as well—in fact first and foremost—ought to be governed in accordance with a plan and insight and calculation? Even a Co-operative shop can surely afford to use double-entry book-keeping?

What hampered him most, however, and made him as dumb as an oyster that first evening, was his secret awareness of the duality in his own self. He felt like a witness at a trial, a witness who knew the truth and wanted to tell it to the judge, but who for some mysterious, dangerous reason is in such a position that if he tells the truth, he will not be believed, *cannot* be believed.

The thing was that Ash had gone a step further than amusing himself with the little student choir and still smaller orchestra. As though he did not already have enough to do, as though the reading he had to do was not immense enough and indigestible enough, he had gone one day to the *Conservatory* and had asked for a *programme of tuition*. He had sat up all one night studying the little brochure and making wonderful, enchanting plans. Here he was in a strange town—no parental eye was on him—so could he not contrive to get a bit of musical education alongside his studies at The College? Kill two birds, at any rate one and a half, with one stone? No one need know about it. And the work at The College, was it really so infernally difficult that he could not take a couple of subjects in music at the same time? Musical theory, orchestration, counterpoint? The only awkward thing about the plan was that each subject at the Conservatory would mean an additional outlay of twenty-five crowns a month. He had begun with the theory of harmony; he had already done several exercises, his heart glowed with a wonderful happiness as so much of what he had previously only felt and sensed now became visible on the music lines and with specific technical names attached to it; he had been swept straight into a dangerous, exciting, fabulous world, an enchanted forest in which he picked flowers and made lovely bouquets of them: tonic, dominant seventh, inverted triad (oh!) binary chord, the disappointing resolution, organ-point, plagal ending, suspension, reciprocal anticipation, the unrehearsed modulations of Wagner, the pure *tremolo* (a musical devil, that Wagner, he was beginning reluctantly to admire *Tannhäuser* and *Lohengrin*), studies and themes from Bach, Grieg, Beethoven; and where in music could you find such a *pearl* of *false relation* as at the beginning of Mozart's C-major quartet?

Of all composers he loved Haydn best. God, he could pray,

give me Haydn's repose. Whatever becomes of me, let me be like Haydn, let me be *pure* like Haydn.

(One day he had come running back to the world of man out of his enchanted forest bringing a little bunch of its flowers. Bashfully he had laid a little composition on the table in front of his teacher in the theory of harmony, an old, grey-haired organist; it was a tiny little waltz, he had called it *The Gallion Girl*, the old man had looked at it, played it through, had said 'Hm' and with a fat hairy finger pointed out a couple of errors in harmonizing. He said nothing else. To Ash that 'Hm' was the most precious sound any person had ever uttered since the world began.)

But there he now sat—in the Socialist Students' Group—in the midst of the technicians and engineers of the future, the clear-headed politicians of days to come, in among a group of twentieth-century dark angels, being interrogated by a yapping meteorologist about his *purpose* in studying at The College.

But he had no purpose!

He was a fraudulent criminal, he was defrauding his parents, defrauding the bank that had lent him money, defrauding Gunnhild and the child, defrauding The College that had re-mitted half its fees in the hope of gaining another economist for society, and now too he was deceiving the members of the Socialist Students' Group!

He did not dare confess to any living soul that he was to be-come . . . oh, he did not dare name it, but he hoped to . . . at any rate he was going to try to become—his private most secret longing was that one day he would be able to write music, to create music. (Hurriedly he fished out his handkerchief and blew his nose to hide his blushes; he was attending his first meet-ing of a Socialist Students' Group and knew that his real yearn-ing was to be able one day—to *compose*.)

And if he gave himself away here, if he told them that he had chosen The College in order to be able to study *music*—who would understand him? They would look at him as though he were a lunatic, a whirligig, a fantastic idiot, they would giggle hysterically and ask him to take himself off somewhere else— this was a place where people took things seriously.

Ash felt crushed. He had *liquidated himself* the first time he came among the socialists. And he realized that you can tell the world's judges everything except truth.

Through a haze he listened to Wolfgang the German. Wolfgang of course was a pseudonym, the man had managed to escape from Germany through Poland, from there to Denmark and so to Norway. He was a short, stocky, rather fat man with Slavonic features, his eyes sparkled behind their glasses, and radiated strength. He spoke quickly and with assurance, ingratiating and magnetically persuasive. 'Comrades,' he said, and Ash quivered devoutly when he heard it, so they were all comrades, were they? After a while, however, he began to find the conversation slightly boring, perhaps because of the man's German thoroughness.

As he walked home from that first meeting with the socialists, he felt as though he had been put through a mangle. Never had he felt such a failure, so incompetent, so bitterly alone.

He had gone to them, honest and upright, with outstretched hand and the humblest wish to serve. Calmly they had let the black-haired meteorologist knock him out in the first round; then they had left him sitting punch-drunk on a chair and never addressed one friendly word to him; they had regarded him as of no interest, had continued their discussions over his head as though he had not existed; he felt bitter and discouraged, all the more bitter because he felt that he could have taken the initiative and himself made friends instead of sitting there full of hate and self-pity.

But all the same, any clergyman's wife will tell you that you must welcome a newcomer with a smile, take him round and introduce him to the others, take a little interest in him, ask him about himself, create a little circle of warmth and snugness round him, offer him a Danish pastry and a glass of fruit juice and water—any idiot knows that. You don't win adherents to a cause by spitting in the face of neophytes. These socialists lacked even the most *elementary* idea of how to organize groups and institutions. Ash had heard of their battle cry 'Dynamite in the bore-holes', but these socialists had dynamite in their dimples!

Very well, excellent. If they thought people were *queuing up* to join the Socialist Students' Group! Excellent. They would have to *ask* him before he went there again. That perhaps would teach them a lesson. And they thought they were going to organize the entire community! Excellent.

He wept with anger and ignominy when he got back to his rooms.

Then he blew his nose and washed his face and then he thought of the meteorologist, that black-haired devil. He would pay him back at the next opportunity. He kicked at a chair to confirm this. Where would a meteorologist place the Marxian concept of 'surplus value'? In a hail squall observed over the Dogger Bank?

He would tell the meteorologist where to get off.

At the very next meeting.

Solomon and Hitler

He moved out of the room he had been sharing with Daniel. They parted good friends, both agreeing that it would be quite pleasant to be on their own.

He found a nice room in the flat of an elderly, small, swarthy, very fat woman called Mrs. Abrahamsen who ran her dead husband's clothing shop. She had only one young son living at home, a schoolboy; Mrs. Abrahamsen was a find. After a couple of days, various impressions suddenly fell into place and Ash realized that Mrs. Abrahamsen was a Jewess. That rather impressed him. He had read and heard so much about the persecution of the Jews in Germany; he never mentioned this to Mrs. Abrahamsen, but he went out of his way to be nice to her, always tiptoed quietly along the corridor, made his own bed, behaved as a gentleman in every respect and one day came home with a little bunch of flowers for her. She was fearfully pleased and blushed, hugged him, smiling delightedly (she was so short that her arms went round his hips), pirouetted and laughed fatly: 'Fancy bringing flowers to an old woman!' He was so timid where people's personal affairs were concerned that he never liked to ask if she had relatives in Germany, and so he never got to know anything about her; as a Jewish woman's lodger he felt vaguely guilty; the least he could do was to be courteous and considerate; that was his little private revenge on Hitler.

And the bitter sadness, the bitter pathos of youth, of knowing that one's contribution to help avert approaching world tragedy, to stop the concentration camps, the madness, the roaring and that bestial man—that one's entire contribution was a certain amount of shy kindliness shown to an old Jewess, that all one could do to save the world was to buy a shilling's worth of flowers.

Wilhelmine came once a week. All Mrs. Abrahamsen's furniture was good and solid with the single exception of the sofa and that creaked. Wilhelmine and he always had to use the bed. And he was beginning to have a certain aversion to that. In the bed, he felt, they were like man and wife, and this was such an oppressive thought that once it even rendered him impotent. Since the sofa creaked so loudly that the noise could probably be heard in Mrs. Abrahamsen's room, he tried other ways, on the floor, against the table, in the armchair.

Once Wilhelmine stayed all night: after all she lived twelve miles outside the town and never got from the office till late in the afternoon, and she felt that it made their time together so short when she had to take the bus in and out again the same evening. Ash was a little doubtful about her idea of staying all night with him, he did not know what nice old Mrs. Abrahamsen would say, even though she had always been cheerful, kindly and cultured. Once he had thought: I will become a Jew. I have resigned from the Church of Norway and it does not matter to me if I have to learn a few Mosaic articles of faith of no importance and make a Jewish promise: I will gladly do so, if only I can share in that rich, cordial, wonderful community and fellowship that these Jews have. But will they accept a boy with corn-coloured hair? I would not mind finding a Jewish girl to marry; what don't the Jews know about love?

the most wonderful poem in the world about love-making is the Song of Solomon!

He was certain that a woman like Mrs. Abrahamsen would never pass remarks if Wilhelmine did spend the night with him. If she ever noticed it, she would look at him the next day with a mysterious, merry smile in her brown eyes, a secretly bene-volent understanding smile. And yet—he was apprehensive—he knew that of all sex-haters, landladies are the worst. He was slightly nervous when Wilhelmine came to stay the night. He talked in an especially low, hushed voice, but then he forgot all his caution as soon as they were between the sheets. Bless you, he gasped, hot and happy. He did not say that however, later on that night, at three in the morning, when Wilhelmine whispered to him that she must pee. The bathroom and lavatory was right at the end of the long corridor, which meant that Wilhelmine would have to walk ten yards through a hushed house and perhaps wake Mrs. Abrahamsen. Suppose the two met in the narrow corridor, Wilhelmine in the nightdress she had brought and Mrs. Abrahamsen in her flowered kimono! What an encounter! He shuddered: to himself he cursed all girls, why could Nature not have equipped them with bladders that could last a whole night? He sat up in bed and looked round; there was no pot in his room; there was the small wash basin, but he did not like that idea; on the table stood two wine glasses and an almost empty half-bottle of port, a man might have managed, but not a woman; his gaze alighted on the black coke stove in the corner, perhaps in there?—he was seized with a fit of painful hysterical laughter. If only one had a flower-pot, he thought desperately, and that gave him an idea. Outside his room was a balcony; the balcony had a little fence, fastened on the inside of the fence up at the rail, were long wooden flower boxes; when he moved in, the boxes had still been full of flower-ing nasturtiums, but now the flowers had faded; a flower-box is just as good as a flower-pot; the balcony looked towards a church and it was night-time; one could not imagine there being a clergyman or verger sitting up in that tall church tower with field-glasses at that hour; he told Wilhelmine of his stroke of genius; she looked at him wide-eyed, but smiled and got up. He sat on the bed and watched her as barefoot and in her lemon

yellow chiffon nightie she opened the door on to the balcony
and, gasping with the cold, stepped like a fairy into the dark
night; Ash was always embarrassed by this side of woman's
nature, he wanted to leave her on her own, but it was only a
second or two before Wilhelmine came in again with a comical
and half-ashamed expression on her face and said apologetically: 'I can't reach!' 'Do it on the balcony floor,' said Ash. 'Are
you crazy?' she said. 'All right,' said Ash, stood up, took a chair
and followed her out on to the balcony. He trembled with the
cold, it was the beginning of December and he had only
pyjamas on. She got up on to the chair, he had to hold her hand
as she squatted over the flower-box, she was afraid of falling
over, it was the third floor and there was a paved street far beneath them. There he stood in the night holding the shivering
Wilhelmine by the hand and staring fixedly at the church clock,
it was like a glowing tiger's eye in the night. Then she had
finished, gave herself a shake, stepped down and they went in
shivering, taking the chair and locking the door behind them.

As they lay in bed again, rubbing each other warm, he began
to laugh and had to hide his head under the bedclothes. Then
she began to laugh too, and they lay together gasping under
the bedclothes. Then she came with her searching hands, they
always slid up his arms as though she wanted to come closer.
There was an element of childish longing about Wilhelmine's
hands, she wanted to creep up to him, as though to a mother,
and for a moment he was profoundly moved by this need of
tenderness in her, a need that always seemed to excite him tremendously. There is something knowing about a woman hungrily searching a man's body with her hands; they had been
laughing there under the bedclothes, but were laughing no
more, now he was biting her and she let herself be bitten, and
all at once her firm body became loose and supple, she was lying
still and limp under him, her breasts soft and collapsed, lying
as though asleep, dead, ready and ripe to be possessed, her
mouth half open.

Wilhelmine was reserved, gloomy, shy, somewhat gruff. Sometimes he felt almost as if she were uncomfortable in his
company. Once she had let slip that she envied people who had

matriculated; in her family it was only her brother who had so good an education; she herself had had to be content with a business school and a shorthand course; now she was a clerk in her father's office, she could see no future in that, but did not know what else she could do. No, said Ash, that's just it.

It was not till many years later that Ash realized that there are people—surprisingly many people—who regard a university student as a being set above his fellows, surrounded with a mysterious aura, a person endowed with rare intelligence and dangerous knowledge, a demi-god with golden, winged helmet. That, in his own student days, he regarded himself as the lowest of the low, an insect, an ignorant poor devil with frayed coat sleeves and holes in the soles of his shoes, a creature of the back streets only permitted to exist because society graciously disregarded him (if it had discovered him, it would have put its heel on him), that he had this dreadfully humiliating opinion of himself is merely another example of that eternal tragedy: the discrepancy between reality and imagination. Wilhelmine suffered because she thought she was not good enough for him, while he suffered because he believed he was not good enough for anyone. And to each other they never dared mention it, never dared confess their fears.

None the less Ash was curious to know her, as long as he did not come too near the deep craters in her; one day he asked her about Germany, for her mother was originally German. Oh, Germany was a lovely country, she said; different from Norway; people were more polite there (she had once told him about her first experience of love-making and he had a feeling that it had taken place in Germany). Germany a lovely country? Had she been there lately? Yes, she went almost every summer to her mother's relatives and stayed with them for three weeks or so. And so Germany was lovely? Yes, she would like to live in Germany. With Hitler at the helm? She understood so little of politics; but anyway she thought what Hitler was doing was right and splendid and grand; business was going full-steam ahead, no unemployment, the autobahns—he should see the fantastic autobahns, what a difference to Norway's dirt roads where you got your kidneys jolted out of you in the bus; she couldn't see that Hitler had done anything wrong; on the contrary he had created order, put the Communists and mischief-makers in their place, forbidden strikes. . . . Ash swallowed when he heard her pronounce the word *order*. He realized suddenly that that was the most dangerous of all concepts and that he would fight against it all his life; the idea of order concealed a desire for despotic, tyrannical power, behind it were death and blood and terror, behind it the cadaverous horses of the Apocalypse were lined up ready to trample life underfoot.

(And yet: had not Goethe himself said that he thought disorder even worse than injustice?)

And the Jews? he said with averted face. The Jews? she said lightly, with a shrug of her shoulders, it was their fault, they were only getting what they deserved.

This side of her appalled him. He went deathly pale when he heard from her lips this old falsehood of the Jews' guilt; he knew so perfectly well that, morally, Hitler's régime had made Germany go back a thousand years in time, when they said that the Jews ate babies and under cover of this medieval accusation themselves murdered the Jews and hung them on iron hooks; he knew so well . . . a ghastly feeling of helplessness came over him; he had to lie on the bed and bury his face in his hands; how was he to explain to Wilhelmine what Nazism really was?

How did he himself know what Nazism was? He had read books. He had read Langhoff's *A Year in Hell* and Hermynia zur Mühlen's *They Took our Daughters*; he knew that writers never lied. He knew that it was possible to hold a book in your hand, listen to the message that comes from its pages and say: 'This book does not lie.'

Was it *Das grosse Vaterland* that captured Wilhelmine's imagination? He had heard that patriotism was the last refuge of a scoundrel. And now, sitting on his bed beside his mistress, he knew that it was so. At that instant he also realized why he was a socialist: because socialism was international, it transcended frontiers, a socialist had comrades in all countries. And he realized too that he had more in common with all the Negroes and Jews whom he had never even seen, than with any nationalistic Norwegian or nationalistic German. *Deutsch-*

land über alles? Oh, there was something higher than Germany! Something! Could he say what it was? No. But it existed! It *must.* He would discover it, some time, and hold it up for the world to see.

He ought to marry a Negro girl, that's what he should do; that would be the first step on the way; have five lovely mulatto children who would go about on skis—and he would show every living Norwegian and every living German that mulatto children could be as good skiers as any Aryan!—yes and one of his mulatto sons would become world ski-jumping champion and another slalom champion, just to show them that this talk of *race* was stuff and nonsense, and one of his mulatto daughters would become president of the Storting, another an eminent scientist, the third the most brilliant concert pianist Norway had ever had! Negroes! Were there any finer or more beautiful people in the whole world than Negroes?

He sat beside Wilhelmine exhausted and unable to speak.

Swiftly and with a stab of horror he glanced at Wilhelmine: did she know that at that moment she was sitting on a Jewish woman's bed? Did she know that she had drunk from a Jewish woman's wine glass?

He did not dare ask her questions, he dared not talk politics with her. He sat there shaking; he was such a passionate opponent of Nazism that he became nauseated at the mere thought of it; he sat there knowing that if he so much as opened his mouth to say one word about the Nazis' shameful deeds, he would lose his self-control, would shout, rave, break the furniture, one word would lead to another and before he knew it he would have heaped both Hitler and Wilhelmine with names that never could and never would be expunged from her memory; it would not matter to Hitler, since he wasn't there; but to Wilhelmine it would mean everything; again he had the cruel knowledge that because he was so uncontrolled and vehement there was always a risk of merely destroying and achieving nothing positive. He was no diplomat, no healer of souls. If he had had his feelings in hand he could have given her one factual, objective explanation of Nazism one day, another the next day, with continual gentle tutoring got her to see what Nazism was and what Germany was under the Nazi régime. . . . But he knew that he could not do it. He did not have the patience, the calmness, the composure, the love. She was his mistress and he had a profound affection for her, but he did not love her. Did she know what he knew? That he would never become her husband, was never going to give her a home and children?

Besides, latterly he had become involved with Constance too.

8 *December* 1938

Constance had been up to his room several times, and each time there had been the same shy, cautious tone between them. Constance was so grave, so frightened; her grey eyes were always so open and pure when they rested on him. 'Are you scared of me?' he whispered one evening, as he sat with his arm round her waist. She shook her head and smiled. 'Well, but . . .?' he said interrogatively, vehement, it was as though a warm tropical wind were blowing through his body, now he desired her passionately, there was such a warm, moist smell of body coming from her, her waist was so slight and supple, God! how he desired her. But the whole time there was something about her that made him apprehensive, she was such a grave, serious person, she would never be able to take an affair with him light-heartedly. She could laugh, but he had never heard her give a resounding, whole-hearted laugh. What can be wrong with a girl, he thought, who can never forget herself so far as to surrender to laughter? She did not need to leap up on to a table and dance the can-can with her skirt drawn up, she did not need to be a whirlwind of senseless laughter and *joie de vivre*. . . . It would have been quite enough if she had once sat in a chair clasping her stomach and rocking with laughter. But she never did. Her upper lip was too heavy for her. Her lips were pressed too tightly together; in fact they had acquired a few old woman's wrinkles from being kept so incessantly and carefully in place. He thought: Her lips tremble when I kiss her, her body is just as ardent for mine as mine for hers; yet she always breaks off the kiss, puts a hand between us and looks away. Why?

They had known each other for nearly two months. They had been out together many times, to films, to concerts (it was usually she who paid); once they had been for a Sunday ramble. He could never make her out; he just felt that she was very fond of him; he heard that in her voice, felt it in her handclasp, saw it in the slight, hurried, restrained smile she gave him every time they met. And now, here with her, *he* felt a little afraid of falling in love with her. She was so good, so upright.

Did she know that he was carrying on with Wilhelmine?

There was no indication that she did.

She had been to his rooms many times. On the last few occasions he had tried more intimate caresses: she had just shaken her head, and slowly he had let go of her. 'Are you angry with me?' he could not help exclaiming once, his hands trembling. 'Am I doing anything that is wrong or ugly, when I search your body, when I want union between our bodies?' She gave him a melancholy look; then she smiled and shook her head. He was almost going mad; but he was too fond of her to insist. If she did not want to, she did not; if it were to come, it would come; he hoped most fervently that it would be soon. And he trembled, for he felt desire in her body too.

They were going to his room one evening in December and met Mrs. Abrahamsen in the hall; she smiled at them; Ash hesitated a second, did not know how to deal with such a situation, then he took the plunge and introduced Constance. He did not know why, but he felt that the situation was deeply significant. 'How do you do,' said Mrs. Abrahamsen and took Constance's hand; she looked merrily up at Ash as though to say 'You've got yourself a nice, pretty girl, hold on to her.' Ash gulped at this unspoken advice. Mrs. Abrahamsen watched them go, when they were a couple of steps further across the hall she remarked: 'Listen, Mr. Burlefoot, if you would like to make yourself coffee, or tea, by all means use the kitchen.' Ash swallowed and bowed. As long as she did not also invite them in to her.

'She's awfully sweet, your landlady,' said Constance in his room, and let Ash take off her coat.

'She is,' said Ash. He pursed his lips and could not make out why his heart sank.

However, after a little while, he did go to the kitchen and make tea. It was so queer going through Mrs. Abrahamsen's cupboards: he usually made his breakfast and evening meal in his room: milk and bread and something to put on it; it tasted good, it was simple and cheap as well as nourishing; and it made him independent and free. Every day, on his way back from the students' canteen he went into a dairy and bought a bottle of milk; on the first few occasions he had hidden it in his brief-case or under his overcoat; then he had become more courageous and in the end carried it openly and shamelessly in his hand; then he had thought: I'm beginning to grow up. There he was now in Mrs. Abrahamsen's kitchen for the first time; he had permission to go to her cupboard for tea-pot and tea and sugar and cups. As he opened the cupboard a wonderfully familiar smell struck him, such a homely smell, the smell of childhood, of preserves and anchovies and green cheese and butter and cinnamon; for a moment it was like standing on holy ground—a kitchen is as personal and private as a bedroom—and it gave him such a queer feeling. There stood the Bohemian with a lump in his throat, the stove, the sink, the draining board, the jars on the shelves. . . .

As he came wobbling down the corridor with the tray, he had to kick on the door instead of knocking, for he had no free hand. Constance opened and took the tray.

'You've been a long time,' she said with a smile.

'It takes a while to boil water,' he said. 'Have you been frantic?'

She looked down, and he was sorry he had teased her.

They stood side by side laying the table; he went to a drawer in his chest-of-drawers, took out bread, butter, cold meat and carried them to the table. When he had put the things down and was about to tell her that supper was served, she suddenly came up close to him. She put her arms round his neck and gave him a hurried kiss, shyly and timidly. He took her round the waist and looked down at her.

'That's the first time you've kissed me,' he said.

'One must begin some time,' she said. Then she looked at him: 'It wasn't wrong was it, for me to do it?'

'No,' he said, 'bless you, no.'

He had no great appetite, nor had she. They soon went and sat on the sofa.

'It's so strong, that ceiling light,' she said.

He stood up and went to the door, where the switch was. As he turned again, he saw her by the door to the balcony; she drew the curtain across it. Her body was so lovely as she stood with one arm raised to the curtain; but all at once he saw that there was something girlish about her, undeveloped; he had had an impression of tallness and firmness, of something elegantly womanly about her, now all at once he saw that her body was slight, she was a girl. And it had become quite quiet in the room.

She came back. Hurriedly he lit a cigarette.

'Will you have a cigarette?' he asked, he felt his head swimming.

She had sat down on the sofa. Slowly she shook her head, her deep golden hair rippled slightly.

'I can share yours,' she said.

And so he went across to her and sat down and held out the cigarette, and she took a pull, and he took the cigarette back, and he happened to touch her hand and he stubbed out the cigarette in the ashtray.

Slowly he laid his cheek against her hair, he put his hand on her shoulder. Then felt her free herself and sink backwards, slowly she lay back on the sofa. He slipped to his knees on the floor. Slowly he took her legs and lifted them up on to the sofa. He cast a hurried, confused look at her face, she was lying with her face turned to the wall.

He knelt beside her, laid his cheek on her stomach; lay like that for a long while. Her hand came and stroked his hair and his ear, finally she let it lie still on his cheek.

She was wearing a thin woollen dress; he lay with his cheek against the material, with his cheek against the harder woollen belt; her little stomach rose and sank beneath his cheek. He raised his head and brushed her breast with his nose; she jerked her head. He set his mouth against her neck, under her chin; he did not kiss, he lay with his lips against the skin of her neck.

'How you're trembling,' she whispered.

'Am I to get you now?' he asked into her neck.

She did not answer.

She patted his hair.

He put his arms round her and burrowed his face into the hollow of her neck; he had to hide; and there he lay. She stroked his cheek; he turned his face away, but she had felt the tears.

'Why?' she whispered.

'I have waited so long,' he said.

She took hold of his head and let him find her mouth. She was so warm, he felt as if he were sinking into her.

'I believe I'm going to shake to death,' he whispered, and indeed he was shaking all over, his teeth chattering. He hugged her to try and stop it, laid his head against her stomach, under her breast, clasped her round the waist, below her hips.

'Can I ask one thing of you,' she whispered.

'Yes?' he said.

'Don't be rough with me,' she whispered quietly.

He raised his head, but she turned her face away.

'Am I being rough?' he asked, surprised.

She shook her head.

He had to bend low over her face to hear what she said, so soft was her voice.

'Not now,' she said.

'No,' he said heavily, huskily, 'I shan't be rough with you.'

He must have swooned, so profound was his joy, so fierce his gratitude, at least he was not conscious for several seconds. For a long while he was unable to speak. Slowly he traversed her body with his hands, they only just touched the material of her dress, she quivered as his hand slid over her groin, slowly he took off her shoes and put them on the floor.

"You have a h-hole in your big toe,' he said happily.

She raised her head slightly, but let it fall back. He had seen that she had smiled. But then the trembling and seriousness returned to him, he did not know how to use his hands, not with Constance. To start feeling up her legs seemed to him at that moment the height of coarse indecency.

He had been kneeling the whole time. Now he laid his head
up beside hers, whispered:

'Will you lift up a bit?'

'Why?'

'You have a long, narrow hampering envelope of cloth round
you.'

She shook her head.

'Won't you take off your dress?' he whispered.

She shook her head.

'It will get crumpled,' he pleaded.

She shook her head.

So he was alone again, with no one to help him; cautiously he
caressed her ankles, but could not bring himself to go further.
Something in his hands and in his mind held him back, he shuddered at the thought of his hands sliding up over Constance's
small round silk-clad knees. He could not say why, but he felt
that that way of approach would be profoundly undignified,
shameful, swinish, lewd, like a drunk in a café with his hand
under the table, fumbling at the waitress's legs, a way for snakes
and prowlers. . . . For a brief moment the idea filled him with
numbing, fierce anger; at that same instant too he caught a
glimpse of Constance's legs, she had such dreadfully sweet legs;
not lovely, they were sweet; a girl's legs, heavens above; he lay
powerless and to himself he said: Constance, you won't understand this, it just is so; afterwards, when we have been together,
then I can stroke your legs and play with your skin, but not
now, not beforehand.

Again he laid his head on her stomach; her eyes shut he took
hold of the hem of her skirt and slowly pulled it up her,
in little jerks. He could feel that a hot, silent struggle was going
on inside her; she raised her body the tiniest bit to help him,
at the same time as she took hold of his hands to hinder him.
Her resistance he found wonderfully welcome; then the intolerable pressure burst in him, in one thrust he had put his hand
up and laid it on her groin, he felt its softness and warmth beneath his hand, he let his hand lie there, his hand was firm when
hers came to remove it; then he was clasping her in his spread
hand.

She half rose up and clutched him; her lips were quivering,

her burning eyes looked into his as though she were searching for a brother, a defender, she said:

'Ash?'

'Yes?'

Then her head fell back, and she turned her face to the wall and lay still, and he felt her, and slowly he pulled off her little silk pants and the smell of her was warm and moist and strong, a hothouse smell and she put her hands over her face in bashfulness now that he could see how shamelessly ready she was; and despite her resistance he put his mouth on her bare stomach and kissed her little navel. 'No,' she whispered. 'Yes,' he stammered, 'don't be afraid, it is beautiful, beautiful,' and he came to her and she trembled: 'You will be careful with me, won't you?' And he, gasping: 'Yes, yes, I will be careful.' He did not know what it could be, for a moment he thought the worst: that she might be a virgin; at that second he almost got up from her, he was so full of tenderness and devotion that if she had insisted, he could have gone without, but then he found her mouth, their tongues met, and he took her without hindrance.

Gasping with happiness and clasping her head, he stammered: 'Doesn't hurt?' She gave a faint shake of her head; slowly he became bolder in her, slowly grew stronger, got a horrible fright when, after a while, she braced her hands against his chest and asked him to wait, she wanted him to withdraw and in frantic self-reproach he asked: 'Was it hurting?' her mouth was half-open, she shook her head, 'What is it then?' she just lay still with her eyes shut; blood racing, he bent over her, 'What *is* it, then?' She whispered, 'I just want you to wait a bit,' and he couldn't see why he should have to wait, then a dizzy thought came to him and he shuddered. 'Has it happened?' he whispered and she turned her face away and he repeated his question and she gave a slight nod, hands in front of her face, and he tumbled down beside her, choked with happiness and throbbing with expectation, he lay there breathing into her hair, he would wait, he could wait all right, slowly he set his hand on her breast, slowly he turned her towards him, she hid her face, but there was no resistance now, he slid into her again, again without difficulty, she was made to receive a man, to receive him. But now he couldn't hold it back any longer and it was the sweetest he had ever had, and he had to let it come, and afterwards he slid gasping off her and tumbled over on the floor, and there he lay, gasping with happiness, lay on the floor as though dead; blindly he reached up a hand, hers came and laid itself in it.

They were very silent, as they walked together through the quiet streets. There was a chill in the air and he put his arm round her waist and drew her to him. Now and again he shot a careful, imperceptible glance down at her face. Was she happy? Was she happy?

They reached her house, stood and whispered together for a while on her steps. Shyly she stroked his cheek, then she turned her face up towards him. 'Thank you for being so kind,' she whispered. He gulped. He could not take praise. If anyone praised him, there must be something wrong with him. He did not know what to say. 'Next time I shan't be quite so kind,' he said. She smiled, but there was melancholy in her smile, a burden, and then she transferred the burden to him when she said, slowly: 'Next time?' An oppressive emotion to which he could not put a name made him frantic. She said: 'Are you going to invite me up again then?' And he could not understand what she meant by that; she did not mean to be outrageous, but it was outrageous; did she feel that she was the sort of person he would not want to have anything more to do with, or was she feeling inferior, did she too suffer from a feeling of not being good enough? And now he could not answer her, he did not know what his intentions with her were, and he could only smile and falter, now she had knocked him out, now he ought to go on his knees to her and *assure* her of his affection and adoration, he could not do that and would not do that, and he felt profoundly ashamed and afraid because he could not tell her that he loved her. She was a most wonderful girl, but he did not know if he *loved* her, he gave her a hurried, reluctant kiss and watched her go into the hall and shut the door behind her carefully so as not to wake her parents, and he walked away and turned and saw the little house and grocer's shop and shuddered, and he got back to his room and drank a cup of ice-cold tea and knew that it had all been perfect, but that even so there was an element about their relationship that made it incomplete, and he shivered in the night at the thought that perhaps it was he who was incomplete, that there was some love sense that was not developed in him, an all-important faculty that constituted the difference between man and devil; he shivered with horror and self-reproach, wandered about his room in the night, stroked the backs of the books on the shelves, happened to feel soft leather under his fingers and looked up. He had touched a book bound in red leather, an unusual book of blank pages, a journal he had been sent as a birthday present by his young brother, Balder, a handsome red book with a lock on it and a little key; he had never written in it, for the events of every day seemed so heart-rending that there was no reason to record them into the bargain. He stood there with the limp, handsome book in his hand, unlocked it with a stony face, got out his fountain pen and sat down at the table. He bit his lip, this would be his first poetic communication to the white paper, he was alone in the night and he had to seek refuge in cynicism, he wrote the following poem:

8 December 1938. Constance.

I Forgive You, Old Man

December.

Never snow in this town; never the metallic, refreshing, animal pleasure of fresh frosty air penetrating astringently into your nostrils and settling as hoarfrost on the small hairs there, never the sight of people's breath like little clouds issuing from their mouths. Rain. Cold rain. Now and again sleet. His feet were always cold.

Rain. Pouring rain. Later in life, it was the rain he was to remember best of this town, the rain that soaked through the brim of his hat and dripped down his neck, inside his collar, the umbrella that he closed with a wet smack every time he

entered a door, the water that ran off the umbrella, the smell
of the umbrella, the drips that came from its ferrule, the trail of
water he left behind him, that watery trail.

Il pleure dans mon coeur
Comme il pleut sur la ville.

I'll go to France in the summer, he thought. You have to be
an idiot not to see that there's going to be a bust-up with Hitler
sooner or later. If I go this summer, I shall still manage to see
Paris.

Paris. Ye gods.

Perhaps I can get a job over the New Year, teaching at a commercial college or something, an hour or two a day, earn a
little money; in Paris I shall live on just bread and water and
grace and light and radishes (red wine is so cheap there, it's like
water), if necessary I shall go down on all fours in the Tuileries
and *graze*, if a horse can live off just grass, so can I.

He walked through the streets, shivered and was wet, he
wiped the wet from his cheeks, did not know whether it was
rain or tears.

There were a few end-of-term exams in December. He was
cheerful and happy as he sat down to do the French paper, but
not so confident about the other subjects. In economics he got
lost: he knew the thing, but suddenly he couldn't see the light.
It was like being in a labyrinth. He wrote four pages, but had
a sickening feeling that what he had answered was not the
question he was asked. But then, he forgot about it; he had so
much else to think about, his music, his finances, Wilhelmine,
Constance. Then, one day, their papers were returned; the old,
grey-haired professor in economics handed them out with a
smile. Pretty well everyone had passed, he said, not that it was
a difficult test, mostly to see that the students had been keeping
up; there was only one student he must ask to come to his office
for an oral exam, this student's paper was very weak and quite
unconnected with the question. Mr. Burlefoot.

Forty-nine faces looked at him, they had thought him quite
a gifted chap, but this was really the same as being ploughed.

And for Ash's self-confidence it was a tremendous blow, it filled him with terror; of all the students there, he was the one who *must* pass all exams; the others could fail and try again, they could take forty years over it, go on for ever, he alone *must* pass and get it behind him.

Deeply hurt, angry and wild with dismay, he sat down for two days and nights and crammed economics. The third day he went to the professor's office, where he had never been before. He was white with apprehension; he had considered himself an idiot and a spineless ignoramus in most fields of life, but he had thought that he could *learn*, had told himself that at least he could *read a book* and answer questions on paper—now even this poor comfort was perhaps going to be taken from him!

Ash was never able to remember what question the professor asked him. It must have been about marginal productivity or the theory of reinvestment. For the first few seconds after hearing the question, he sat paralysed with examination horror, then with a frantic effort he brought himself back to life, his eyes flitted round the room to find an object to fix on, and then he made a discovery that saved him. A hurried glance round showed him that the professor's office had nice modern furniture; a little writing table of polished oak, with a telephone on it; otherwise just a revolving chair in which the professor sat, an ordinary chair for visitors in which Ash sat, and a wall covered with bookshelves. The room was surprisingly bare, so bare that you could not help noticing the only striking thing. There were six bookshelves on the wall one above the other; they could have held a couple of hundred books; yet they were quite empty except for one small plain-looking book. Ash looked at its spine. It was a textbook written by the professor himself, his only book. *It* was in the bookcase!

As Ash made the discovery, he swallowed hard. The next instant he was mentally rubbing his hands, having grasped the old professor's ignominy and poverty. In the profoundest thankfulness he thought: I have never seen such academic folly. He asked the professor to repeat the question. A quarter of an hour later Ash walked out again with a bow to the old man; he had passed.

But later in life, much later, he thought differently of the old professor, when he remembered that solitary book in the bookcase. Erik Floden once whispered to him that in his young days the seventy-year-old professor had composed a few short romances and songs. ('This mustn't be mentioned; the professor does not like to be reminded of the sins of his youth.')

So the man had begun life as a composer. He had ended as an economist. In his young days he had had a dream of the highest realm of all, that of the spirit; later he had had to turn back to the material world. Now he ate from the outstretched hand of big business and regurgitated conservative truths.

When Ash thought of it in that way, his memory of that visit to the old professor's office was not that of a person's folly, but a sad memory of a man's fall. And then in his heart he forgave the old man.

The Feast of Bad Conscience

December.

One day the word *Christmas* cut into his consciousness. Frantically he looked at his watch, though it was a calendar he needed. Wasn't the Post Office overloaded at Christmas and didn't you have to post parcels early when they had to go far? It was the fifteenth. His teeth began to chatter. Perhaps he was already too late.

He set off at a run, stopped in front of a toy shop. Out in the world he had a daughter, a little girl of one and a half, a child he had never seen. A little girl. She was called Astrid. Her mother had given her the name. Gunnhild had taken the child to church and let a clergyman pour water over its head. That, perhaps, had been a triumph for her; she knew that Ash had resigned from the church. But now he was just thinking of the child, Astrid, a child without a father: had she started talking— had she begun to ask questions? When does a little girl begin to ask: 'Mummy, why haven't I a daddy?'

He stood outside the toyshop, white-faced, peering through the glass: there were dolls, fret-saw sets, cars and trucks, Christmas tree decorations, rocking horses, tin soldiers, doll's furniture, even a little sewing box, and all at once he knew that he couldn't do it. He did not know why, but he couldn't, couldn't go in and ask for a sleeping doll. His guilt was too great. He could take anything in his hand, but not a sleeping doll for a little girl of one and a half.

For a moment the tall young Scandinavian had to lean against the toyshop window, then he turned and walked heavily through the streets, his eyes blinded. Eventually he found the post office, there was an intolerable damp heat like a hot-house inside and it was full of people who had come in dripping with rain. His face was pale and tense as he filled out the form for a telegraphic remittance of forty crowns.

The next day he ordered a book for his thirteen year-old brother, Balder. The shop assistant promised to send it letter post. It was a thriller, one he had himself read in his green youth, a book by Hugo called *The Laughing Man*. The hero was a man who had been kidnapped by gipsies in his childhood; the gipsies had slit the corners of his mouth with a knife and then exhibited him at fairs, where people paid to see him; the moment they saw the boy's face, they roared with laughter.

A letter from his mother: 'Are you coming home for Christmas?'

'No.'

A letter from Balder: 'I'm so hoping you will come home for Christmas.'

'No. Must stay here and work.'

Wilhelmine: 'If you're not doing anything else, perhaps you would come out to us for Christmas?'

'Thanks awfully, but . . .'

And Constance, bashful, low-voiced: 'If you could bear being with my parents, if you would—for Christmas—?'

'Thanks awfully, but . . .'

And Mrs. Abrahamsen: 'If you aren't doing anything over Christmas and are feeling lonely, just come in to us. There'll be just the two of us, my son and I.'

'Thanks awfully, but . . .'

And Daniel, good old Daniel: 'Two or three of us are thinking of a little get-together at my place over Christmas. A stag party. Crab and beer and a schnapps.'

'Crab? At this time of the year?'

'Yes. My landlady has said she'll cook them for us. Two each. One of the lads knows how to pick them. Good, big crabs. Will you join us?'

He gasped with relief and gratitude and crab-hunger. Juicy white meat from the claws, brown inside meat, red roe from the shell. Cold schnapps. Beer.

He swallowed hard: 'But you must get your landlady to make toast too. We must have toast and butter with them.'

'That will be all right. And you must cough up five crowns for schnapps.'

'Do you want it now?'

And Christmas came and they stuffed themselves and got rather tight, and there were candles on the table and cigar smoke drifted about the room, and they were loud-voiced and sang songs, but not Christmas songs, for which Ash was thankful, for Christmas is the feast of bad conscience and the most heart-rending institution man has ever invented, but unfortunately all shopkeepers will violently resist its abolition.

Clean Bodies and Factory Concerts
_____

Not till the New Year did Ash go back to the socialists.

He went in fear and trembling, thinking of the black-haired meteorologist and muttering brilliant repartee to himself as he walked along. But the meteorologist was not at that meeting; there was another young socialist who slapped Ash delightedly on the shoulder when he saw him and cried:

'The shipowners' hope is with us again!'

For a fraction of a second Ash considered, then he decided to answer in the same coin: he smiled, pulled out his right-hand

brace with his thumb, put a Napoleonic foot forward, let the
elastic brace snap back and said:

'The Prince of Wall Street, if you please.'

Everyone laughed.

Ash had become a member of the Socialist Students' Group.

He had once imagined that these people were all supermen,
heroes, gods. He did not know why, but he had thought that all
young socialists had been in the Spanish Civil War, had spent a
year or two in prison for their beliefs, had fought at barricades
and been taken bandaged and bleeding to hospitals singing the
Internationale as they lay on the stretchers, that they had been
driven from home by their parents and condemned by their
teachers, that they had publicly spat on patriotism, religion and
morals, that they were a noble lot, successors to Robin Hood,
stealing from the rich and giving to the poor, that by night they
were gentlemen thieves and avengers, that they were the finest
outlaws there had ever been.

Gradually he came to see that they were human. Some
appealed to him immediately, others seemed materialistic op-
portunists, others were nail-biters. And he heard only of one
who had been in Spain. None the less he had a boundless admiration for them. They had not only their beliefs, they also had
knowledge and understanding. Most were young, not much
older than Ash—though the leaders of the group were middle-
aged—yet it was the most natural thing in the world for them
to get to their feet and, hands gripping the back of their chairs,
speak fluently, unhesitatingly, clearly, logically and *convincingly* for fifteen minutes. (At school Ash had won a couple of
prizes for eloquence; that had been an oratorical feat, playing
with words, and his audience had consisted of contemporaries
who roared with grateful laughter if he just mentioned the word
fig-leaf. They thought he was a genius. And if he remembered
aright, he had won these prizes after first drinking a quarter
bottle of port, having discovered that that made your tongue
work on its own; then you could hardly help becoming elo-
quent.)

Ash had begun to feel fellowship with them, he thought that
he could see pleasure in their faces when he came. He found

himself in an atmosphere of friendliness, but that did not make him feel any less uncertain or inadequate. On the contrary! They turned to him over questions of business and economics, they took him to be an expert in these fields. That made Ash gasp with horror and embarrassment; he writhed like a worm; how did they expect him to get up and tell them straight off about the proportional decline in the peasant-farmer class in Norway since 1920? If he had even had the Statistical Year-book on him. But who went about with that ghastly book in his pocket?

In most other fields, too, he felt quite lost. If only they had let him just sit and listen, but they forced him to express an opinion. Among these intellectuals scarcely a minute passed without words or expressions being used that Ash had never heard and which he did not understand. Often he caught himself sitting with his mouth open, and shut it quickly and looked round stealthily, for no one ever looks more of an idiot than when sitting with his mouth open. It seemed to him that he had a duty to himself to make good his lack of knowledge, that he must make himself worthy of this socialist comradeship. To crown it all, a card framed in glass hung on the wall bearing the brutal lines from Rudolf Nilsen's poem *The Voice of the Revolution*:

> *More than many who say 'I believe'*
> *We need one who will say 'I know!'*

All his life he was to shudder when he saw those words. He must be one who knew. He must know all that was going on in science, art, politics; during his latter schooldays and until now he had lived in the unreal world of novels (for him to be really interested in a book, it had to be about people and human des-tinies); as a member of a political group he must now aim at comprehensive knowledge, universality. He could not sit there dumb when the others were talking of the Mendelian Law, the Oedipus complex, Picasso, the budget, defence, Montessori, old age pensions, the Willendorf Venus, banana flies, Léon Blum, sun spots, Darwin, multiple genes, dadaism, chromosomes or the sexual life of the Maoris.

Once in reply to a casual question, he said:
'Stravinsky seems to me amusing.'

'It seems to me.'
When at last the world is able to look at socialism from a distance, history books will record that the worst thing you could say among socialist intellectuals was 'it seems to me'. At those words, the clock of the universe stopped, the cosmos froze to ice, everyone's face was turned mercilessly towards the culprit, and God laughed a sneering laugh through breathless space:

> *More than many who say 'I believe'*
> *We need one who will say 'it seems to me'!*

For are there in the whole language four other words more revealing of the speaker's ignorance and lack of information? '*It seems to me.*' It is youth's intolerable shame: he realizes it the moment the phrase slips out; it reeks and stinks of flabby-mindedness and loose thinking, he lacks even the most elementary knowledge of the subject, yes, that's the word: *elementary!* he could have bitten off his tongue the moment these four disgraceful words passed his lips, but it was already too late. There is always someone there to raise his eyebrows and ask:

'It seems to you? What do you mean by that?'
And there is no worse punishment for the young man trying to be grown-up than to be put back at a school desk by the cutting question: 'What do you mean by that?'
And as if that wasn't enough, there follows the second phase of the punishment, that of complete humiliation:

'Stravinsky amusing? *Amusing*, Stravinsky? *How* do you mean, amusing?'
Then the young man can only bow his head and clasp his hands. The word just slipped out. But he knows now that that is just what words mustn't do. They must be thought out. Of course he hadn't meant that Stravinsky was a *diverting* composer, a musical master of revels, the Charlie Chaplin of music, no, of course not, not in any way, he hadn't meant *amusing*, just

'amusing', oh, how was he to put it!—he had really meant the exact opposite of amusing!—boring, in fact?—no, no, for God's sake, not boring, he had meant, he had meant—he sits there and doesn't know what he had meant. In his despair he belches, he has no words.

People learn to solve their conflicts differently. Some will stop associating with people who have the insufferably bad habit of requiring that one always gives one's reasons for what one thinks. Some develop an answering-technique which consists in replying to a question different from that asked. 'Stravinsky? My knowledge of his work is pretty limited.' (Said in the right tone that can sound as if, unfortunately, one knew only his five ballet suites and two operas.) 'But Bela Bartok, now, I find him more interesting.' (The word 'interesting' is harmless and sexless compared with 'amusing' which is dangerous and compromising and anyway in the surprise occasioned by this impudent switch from Stravinsky to Bartok it will be quite overlooked.)

And some take to a pipe.

A pipe lies so well in the hand, sits so nicely between one's teeth. Let us consider the pipe-smoker.

A pipe provides the smoker with a smoke-screen for his face, gives him the right to strike up to three matches before he replies, and lends him an air of composure and unfathomable calm. Now let us consider those who regard the pipe-smoker.

There is something mysterious about the pipe-smoker; he is a Tibetan lama, the oracle in Delphi and the sacred cat of Ancient Egypt in one and the same person; everyone lets himself be impressed and fascinated by a man smoking a pipe; his wordless puffs of smoke and smacking noises (like those of a deaf-mute) give him an aura of wisdom and magical knowledge beyond all conception.

Ash took to a pipe.

It was only later in life, when he came to think back on those days, that he realized with considerable surprise that many of the others had done the same.

When the social democratic idea later triumphed in Norway, its victory was said to have been founded on the solidarity of the working classes and their readiness to fight, on the spread of the labour press, on its pamphlets, the zeal of its agitators, the enthusiasm of its poets and on the threat of strikes. Have people forgotten the pipe? The pipe that the representatives of the party and trade unions clenched between their teeth, with which they walked, sat, talked and slept?

Ash had been accepted into the company of the young socialists, had been given a seat at their fraternal table. It was no longer they who owed him anything, it was he who owed them everything. As a socialist he must not bring shame over them, he must get on, it was his duty to become a universal genius.

He had heard of Nygaardsvold, because he was one of his country's ministers of state; but he had never heard of Jaurès, the Frenchman, and his assassination. He became furious over these gaps in his education; as far as knowledge was concerned he was like a picture-frame without a picture. In this state of mind he began going to the public library; he went there every day and almost every day he went home from there so laden with heavy books that one day he got a crick in his back (that made him frantic and terrified, he thought he was about to die because of his erotic sins). All evening and half the night he sat reading till his eyelids swelled and his eyes became bloodshot.

He read books as a horse eats oats, but much less systematically. In the course of the next two months he read over twenty thousand printed pages. He ploughed through the whole of Marx's *Das Kapital*, first what was available in Norwegian translation, then the rest in German. He worked out a reading technique of his own, he fixed his eyes in the middle of the first line and then let his gaze slide steadily down the page without moving either to right or left; in this way he drew the stuff into the middle and absorbed it into his brain; he didn't *read* a page, he *cut* down it. Sometimes he timed himself with his wrist-watch: Twenty seconds for that page, I must do better than that. Jesse Owens runs a hundred metres in 10.2! That's better, sixteen seconds isn't too bad, but I must get a bit lower! Fifteen? Even I've done the hundred metres in 11.4—What? Up to *seventeen*? Good God, I've got to get down to eight seconds, down to *two*, one day I'll have to construct a reading machine ... !

There was a desperate raging hunger in him, he had utterly wasted two years of his life, he had fornicated and produced a couple of bastards (a thing that any idiot of a man can do without any difficulty). Two years had just run out into the sand, two years, seven hundred and thirty days; seventeen thousand, five hundred and twenty hours. He panted as he flung himself like an animal over the books to devour them and make up for lost time. He read Engels, H. G. Wells, Julian Huxley and Krapotkin, the whole *Arbeiderbladet* for 1932, the twelve volumes of Frazer's *The Golden Bough*; he read a popular account of Einstein's theory of relativity and his head swam; he read Johan Vogt's *The Collapse of Dogma in the Face of Economics* and exulted; he read Lenin's *Religion*, Freud's *Totem and Taboo*, Trygve Braaty's *Beyond Freud* (he had a moment of vision; it struck him how much more interesting it would be to be able to see into a writer's mind during the process of creating, than it is to read the finished work, whether scientific or artistic; reading Goethe's *Faust* is far less fascinating than it would have been if he could have seen into Goethe's mind from the moment the idea occurred to him till he had written the last full stop. He thought: the process is more exciting than the result!)—he read two volumes of Lund's *Daily Life in the North in the Seventeenth Century*, Hitler's *Mein Kampf*, the murdered Rosa Luxembourg's *Marxism versus Dictatorship* (it surprised him immeasurably and gave him a warm, languid feeling to discover that socialism did not need to be inhuman, had no need to be absolute, that it wasn't in any way synonymous with terror and NKVD and dictatorship; and immediately he thought of a girl who belonged to the Socialist Students' Society; before, he had had eyes and ears for nothing but the debates and had thought of nothing but his own ignorance; this young girl had a soft smile and nutbrown hair and the biggest blue eyes he had ever seen—and at that moment he could see her); he came across a recently published book by a Swedish philosopher, Rud. Holmö, called *The Ethic of Socialism*, and that was a revelation to him, at the same time as it made him feel thoroughly uncertain, for, of course, it was an attack on most of the tenets of socialism; it spoke straight to his heart and armed him with the strongest of arguments, ones

that, strangely enough, he could use against the Marxists in
the Socialist Students' Society!—he read an English brochure
on Marxism and Poetry, he read *Ecclesiastes* in the Bible,
Lenin's *Ueber die Frauenfrage*, the Norwegian Labour Party's
election programme, Bernard Shaw's *Man and Superman* (and
after that he knew that the writer is greater than the politician,
knew once and for all that Arnulf Øverland was greater than
Erling Falk), he read *Schools for the People* published by the
Norwegian Socialist Teachers' Association and he had just
brought back from the library the first two volumes of Speng-
ler's *Untergang des Abendlandes*—one afternoon in February
—when he vomited blood and collapsed with a violent attack of
influenza.

He had to keep to his bed for over two weeks; Mrs. Abrahamsen was very kind, got him a doctor and brought him lunch
every day. When eventually he was on his feet again, he was
emaciated and hollow-cheeked, grey-faced, dull-eyed and had
a thin reddish beard; his protruding cheekbones and half-moon
shaped drooping moustache made him look like an Asiatic, an
asylum patient out of one of Dostoevsky's novels, an escaped
convict from Siberia. He shrank back with a gasp from the fear-
some image in the looking-glass above his chest-of-drawers; he
had to sit down on the bed, weak and dull. He felt as though his
whole body was made of wet flour. What should he tackle now?
Two weeks lost, fourteen days, three hundred and thirty six
hours that *would never come back*!

He had to support himself against the house-walls as he staggered through the town at about two o'clock. Some of the undergraduates lunched at a boarding-house in the centre of the town
where they got a vast meal for one crown twenty-five. They
ate at long tables in two large rooms. There was an adjoining
billiards-room where they could play for as long as they liked
after lunch without charge. Ash had a horror of gambling, especially at cards, partly because he nearly always lost, partly
because he could not understand how people could spend the
only precious life they had sitting arranging fifty-two pieces of
coloured paste-board in different groupings.

He had never even played billiards, but that afternoon he
spent three hours in the billiards-room. In the end they had to

drag him out; he thought he had never come across such a noble, exciting, exacting occupation as that. His delight and enthusiasm were boundless. The green cloth, the ivory balls, the slim cues, the hair-fine calculation, aiming, the accurate cueing, the easy, non-committal, gloriously superficial friendship that can arise among a group of men engaged in a game. He played billiards for a whole week, never touched a book, telephoned neither Wilhelmine nor Constance, went for walks by himself in the surrounding country, drank two whole bottles of milk and slept ten hours every day.

Then, one day Ash felt recovered and well, and he went back to his brothers, the socialists.

Wonderingly, he noticed the friendliness and frankness and solidarity there was between them. He, with his past and his future, sat apart; was he made of different stuff from other people —or must a Judas always be outside, in the darkness? They never dissembled to each other, often they bared their hearts to the others. One told of his money difficulties and at once there was an eager warm-hearted discussion about who might be able to lend him five crowns; another, a temporary schoolteacher, told of how he had called one of the children names in front of the others and now did not know how to get out of it, could anyone suggest what he should do?—another told of a love affair that had gone wrong, making his world intolerably dreary and would anyone come out on a binge with him and see that he got roaring drunk and drowned himself in the fjord?

The path, the door, the hand.

One evening there was a new fellow there; quite young, strong, stocky, with a huge full beard. At first glance he looked like a young skipper of an arctic trawler, but he turned out to be a student of meteorology (there were eight of them in the group, a phenomenon Ash could never explain) who had been wintering in Greenland and had just got back.

Ash could never discover anything remarkable or unique in the man. On the contrary, in a brief access of irritable envy he had told himself that it could only be a sign of lack of intelli-

gence when a young man voluntarily spent six months of his
life in a desert of ice, in a sleeping bag; that going out into the
winter storm twice a day to take readings from instruments
that recorded temperature and the strength of the wind was an
occupation for inferiors. But there was something warm-
hearted about him, and Ash found himself strangely moved by
the way he was immediately among friends again, how they
immediately recognized him despite his beard and told him how
much had not been done recently because he had not been
there, but that now there would be a change for the better. Oh
no, he must not try to make his exams an excuse, they all had
those! They chuckled and laughed, everyone had to go up and
pull his beard to see if it were genuine, and the girls, shuddering,
wanted a kiss. He was thrust into the best chair and offered
cigarettes. Twelve packs were held out simultaneously, but
perhaps—ha, ha!—he only chewed tobacco now? They all
drew their chairs up to him, all wanted to feel the warmth from
him, the girls wanted to make tea for him, if he still drank it,
and unfortunately they had no blubber, ha-ha, nor fresh walrus
blood, and he could have a bit of fat pork to chew if that would
do.

A lump came into Ash's throat. It was so fine. The others'
touching pleasure at seeing the man again. And the man himself: his eyes shone with gay serenity.

That's what coming home is like, thought Ash.

Home.

At other times he would be violently irritated by them, especially by a couple of the younger ones. It was not that there was
anything bad in them, but they lisped (out of contempt for all
form), their hair was uncombed and hung over their foreheads,
their fingers were brown with nicotine and had long dirty nails
and they always wore high-necked sweaters of black wool. They
wore them as though that were a sort of proletarian uniform.
When he sat near them, he could smell their acrid unwashed
bodies. He knew that they were so-called poor students; but he
also knew that one of them had a rich businessman for an uncle,
who could have lent him the money for his education if he had
been willing to demean himself to ask. Ash had not the least
sympathy with the fellow for refusing to go to his capitalist

uncle. Besides, a hot shower at the public baths cost only forty øre. There was no one in all Norway who could not afford that.

After those meetings Ash went home boiling with anger, undressed, carefully put his trousers between the mattress and the sheet and cautiously lay down on top. He never moved all night for fear of crumpling his trousers. If those two young students had to be demonstratively unkempt to be good socialists, he intended to demonstrate the opposite. He would very much like to be informed where Marx said that to keep one's body and clothes decent was capitalistic behaviour. He, Ash, would turn up at the next meeting with a sharp crease in his trousers, a *new-lain* crease, and he would like to see the socialist who would dare to propose having him turned out of the group on that account.

For some reason or other Ash could feel an hysterical hatred of people who made life more ugly and nasty than it *had* to be. He had hated the girl in the mail-steamer, the Rubens girl's friend, who had stopped her own teeth with blue-white filling; he hated humility in workers, wives and servants, he hated lines of resignation in a face and bowed heads; he was young and proud; if one cannot live with one's head held high, he thought, one can have recourse to flight or to the proud expedient of suicide; he hated preachers and chapel-goers, those who strewed sour ashes over the song and the apple, and the dance and the wine; and especially he hated young socialists in black sweaters who did not wash.

Lenin told the Russian people: 'Socialism is workers' councils and electrification.'

Ash Burlefoot said to himself: 'Socialism is clean bodies and symphony concerts in factories.'

A Night on the Rack

He got on to a slightly more intimate footing with the other members of the group, the leaders, the veterans.

One evening he had an experience that he was never to forget. Leaving a meeting of the group, he walked downstairs in company with a journalist on the workers' paper, Anders Taraldsen, and an elderly spinster called Poppi. Taraldsen seemed relieved the meeting was over and to have a hankering for some serious drinking. 'Come on,' he said to Ash, 'you and Poppi come along up to my flat, I have a few bottles of beer.' Ash felt as though a red-hot spear had been driven through him; he was quite faint with pleasure at this invitation; he felt so honoured that he hiccoughed, no one in the group had ever invited him home; and now Anders and Poppi were wanting *his* company! Were they really going to sit in Anders's flat drinking beer and conversing, those two and *he*? His head swam with happiness and he stammered yes; he was petrified at the thought of what it was going to be like; they were sharp as razors, both of them, hyper-intelligent, they specialized in the use of that gruesome question: 'What exactly do you mean by ... ?' Overawed by their superior knowledge, he had never ventured any intelligent exchange with them, but now apparently they had discovered that he was worth having up to the flat. He felt fearfully honoured. He trotted along behind them feeling almost ready to cry, like a cat wanting to rub itself against a person's leg; he said: 'Poppi, would you like me to carry your umbrella?' Poppi was angrily discussing James M. Cain's *Serenade* with Taraldsen and did not hear him. He did not dare ask again; he tried to keep as close to them as possible, for he wanted to snap up every word they had to say about Cain. 'Watch out where you're stepping, man!' said Poppi irritably, turning round; he had stepped on her heel; Ash went as red as a peony.

Poppi and Anders walked up the stairs together; Ash followed. They hung up their things in the hall. It was a modern one-roomed flat.

Ash was beside himself with excitement and agitation; he had to say something; he said:

'*Serenade* ...'

'Bad book,' said Poppi. 'Second-rate author.'

Ash stood there gaping, slowly he bowed his head: of course. He was an idiot; he had read the book, had thought it one of the best books he had ever read; but of course. If Poppi said so ... He was an idiot.

According to the little he had heard about her, Poppi was a quite ordinary woman without a university education. But all the same she was unusually well read and now and again she revealed an unusual understanding of music. She was a woman of over fifty, thin, with a short and very unlovely grey shingle. She had an unhealthy reddish complexion as though she suffered from high blood pressure or some nervous complaint; her eyes were a metallic grey and utterly without compassion, the lids without lashes; her nose was big and fat and bluish red, its skin pitted with holes, despite the fact that she never drank anything stronger than beer. She had big buck-teeth flecked with brown, and her thin, pale, spinsterish lips had been hastily smeared with sickly yellow-coloured lipstick. She had travelled and been about the world, earning her living teaching or as a governess; she knew an astounding number of languages and now had a job as private secretary and foreign correspondent in the managing director's office of an engineering firm. Ash was never clear about her membership of the Socialist Students' Group. She was a phenomenon and a phantom; she did not appear at many of the meetings, then all at once she popped up again like a ghost, was suddenly standing there among them, her grey birdlike head on one side and eyes fixed on the ceiling as though she despised them (or envied them?), her contribution to the debate would be one word, a killing word of correction, they were sorry for her and terrified of her and admired her for her trenchant wit. She was the most unwomanly woman Ash had seen; one of the elder members, a bon-vivant and old academician who went by the name of Fiffolo, was once asked

at a dance by one of the other women if he would not dance
with Poppi. Fiffolo had given himself a shake and replied in a
low, but determined whisper:

'I am not a homo.'

Taraldsen, the journalist, was a youngish man, about thirty,
stocky, broad-shouldered, strong, like a mountain. His face was
broad with coarse-hewn features and a deep furrow in the skin
on either side of his nose; when you saw him from the front it
was like runes carved in rock, the nose like an inverted V. There
was something soft and lustreless about his skin and he was a
well-mannered fellow; he had a force of his own and an easy,
jocular way of talking; his manner was a bit patronizing. He
was the son of a member of the Storting and belonged as it
were to the socialist aristocracy; Ash was not altogether sure
he liked him; Taraldsen had that stockiness that can turn to
fat before too many years have passed; there was something
practical and efficient and smooth about him. Once Ash
had thought: Taraldsen will end as a bigwig.

So now Ash was sitting with these two redoubtable coryphaei.

He did not know why he was so madly excited at having been
invited to a glass of beer and a talk with these two. Later in life
he was to realize why: it was the poor young tramp's besetting
yearning for cultured conversation, to be present at cultured
conversation, to take part in cultured conversation. Does that
sound strange? That was Ash's inner poverty; he had only read
in books of people who could conduct a cultured conversation.
His father and mother, his school-fellows and their families,
his entire circle of acquaintances, his teachers, his pupils, his
mistresses—they had all been able to talk self-centredly about
food and clothes and the cost of living and money and the
weather, but never had he taken part in a cultured conversation,
the conversation that is stamped by gracefulness and ease, style
and knowledge, generosity and open-minded curiosity. . . .

His excitement that evening was so great that he sat the whole
time secretly rubbing his hands. He kept uttering incomprehensible little sounds, hoping fervently that Poppi was not angry
with him because of her heel; this was a sacred initiation; he
jolted his glass and an effervescent pool of beer spread across

the varnished table top, he could have been as wild and ecstatic
as a puppy in its first snowdrift, except that he was in a narrow
space ten feet by ten and himself an ungainly beanpole of over
six feet.

He felt the mystery of the situation and its attraction, sensed
the adventure of the mind and the full warm song of the heart;
but as always the foretaste of pleasure was mixed with a strange
fear lest all should not turn out as he had imagined, lest the
good fortune should dissolve into thin air, lest he should stretch
out his hand towards the door and there would be no door. It
was frightening and inexplicable, but it seemed that all the
houses he had approached had been ghost-houses, astral houses;
he could walk into them, right through them, and then they
were not there any longer; he was left standing in mortal terror
and mortal loneliness, fumbling for something that did not exist,
groping in evasive smoke, and always there was a cutting note
of eternal mockery in the echoes that answered his despairing
cries.

The three sat in a semicircle at a small sofa-table, Ash and
Poppi side by side on a divan, Taraldsen facing them in an armchair, near Ash. Three people could scarcely have been gathered
in a more intimate group.

All at once it was just Poppi and Taraldsen talking together.
All at once it was just those two. All at once Ash was excluded.
The discovery was all the more cruel because there he sat, aban-
doned and superfluous, *between* the two talkers. Since he was
so tall, they did not talk over his head, they talked across his
chest.

They talked quickly, in passionate, confident voices. Ash had
the feeling that the one talked to examine the extent of the
other's knowledge and understanding; it was as though at first
they had used Ash as a listening dummy, bent at the joints and
seated on the sofa. Later, they forgot that he was there.

To begin with he coughed a few times, cleared his throat,
tried to get a word in. They looked at him with raised eyebrows,
smiled condescendingly and continued their display. For half
an hour they talked about painting. The discussion was started
by a painting Taraldsen had hanging on the wall facing the
divan, it depicted a naked woman. The woman was standing on

the floor, naked, one hand resting on a chair; Ash made the sickening discovery that despite all his gigantic reading during the last few months he had not read a word about painting. The other two spoke of brushwork, colour, tone, composition, light and shade, impressionism, expressionism, cubism, realism, brushwork, colour, tone, composition, depth, plastic representation. Ash sat white-faced and rigid, listening; he took a sip of beer and said 'skaal', the others did not hear; he looked down into his glass and thought bitterly: That girl in the painting is an ordinary naked woman. She is not nearly so well-made as Constance. She's a naked woman and that's all there is to it. Taraldsen lives alone, his fiancée in a different town altogether. Taraldsen has hung the naked girl up on his wall not for aesthetic reasons or because he is interested in art, but so that he can lie at night looking at her, when he is feeling so inclined. He might be honest enough to say as much to Poppi and me, then we wouldn't have to listen to any more about composition and brushwork and depth. If he and Poppi happened to be painters themselves, it would be different. There are no more dreadful people than the amateur-experts who can reel off a whole thesis at the mere sight of a naked woman. If only she had been alive. Then she and I could have slipped out into the passage, while they talked.

Horrified and repentant, he hastened to contradict himself: Tomorrow I must go to the library and find a history of art. I must. Tomorrow without fail. Perhaps I ought to start painting too. The Academy of Arts. Water-colour, oil, gouache, goulash. He giggled convulsively at the word 'goulash'. They looked at him uncomprehendingly. Went on talking. After that he did not laugh, did not say a word; they sat for four hours talking, talked incessantly across him, the faint beery smell of their breath billowing under his nose. They went from painting to newspapers, from newspapers to local education, from that to students (and that was the only time that Ash pricked his ears). Taraldsen criticized a girl in the Group for having turned up that evening with green-varnished nails; this was the pretty girl with the soft face and the incredibly blue eyes and nut-brown hair. Taraldsen thought she went a bit far in more than one direction, but they must make her give up green nails. Ash would

have liked to have heard more about her, would have very
much liked to, but no more was said and he thought: Are green
nails irreconcilable with socialism? Can't they attend to their
own affairs? Is the yellow lipstick on Poppi's lips any better?
From the Group back to newspapers, from newspapers to educational policy, from educational policy to painting! The whole
time interpolating little knowing remarks about people's private
lives and ramifications of influence.

Not only had Poppi and Taraldsen—as though by magic—
concentrated exclusively upon subjects of which Ash knew
nothing—but they talked the whole night of things of which
Ash *wished* to know nothing. He was utterly indifferent to the
fact that the secretary of some trade union or other had
begun to drink too much, that it was rumoured that he had put
his typist in the family way, and that the treasurer of the same
union was trying to get him turned out and to take his place.
Ash could not work up any interest in either of them. Let them
both fall into a sewer and drown.

Have you ever, as a shy youth, sat all night in a confined room
just listening? Straining to listen politely, to pay attention, to
follow, for of course a question *might* come your way, all the
while smiling and polite, sat for four hours with a Buddha smirk
glued to your face? Have you sat in dense cigarette smoke and
fog feeling stiffness coming over you? The growing headache?
The iron band round your forehead? The naked despair? The
cramp? (And by cramp we mean cramp; when all muscles,
sinews, guts and nerves knit themselves into the tightest, most
inextricable knot; do you know what complete cramp is?) Do
you remember how it felt like toothache all over your body?
How you wanted to stand up and bellow with the pain of it,
how you wished you could roll over on the divan where you sat
and sleep, sleep, sleep, get away from that ghastly conversation
that had become so intolerably sterile; do you remember how
your greatest wish was to be able to get to your feet and say
goodnight, get out in the silent streets and fill your lungs with
God's free night air and be alone, singly alone, not a thousand-
times alone as here because you are sitting in the same room as
two others, with two people who are supposed to be your

friends! Do you remember the night that never ended? Do you?

At four o'clock Taraldsen heaved a deep sigh, got heavily to his feet and said that he must go and pump ship. Poppi turned her head and looked at Ash, blinked her lashless eyes as if she had difficulty in remembering who this individual was, sighed and said: 'Ah, yes.'

Taraldsen came in again buttoning up his fly.

'Ah,' he said, 'when you've been drinking beer for hours, there's nothing so good as a pee.' He rubbed his hands with a far-away look on his face and said: 'It's a sheer orgasm.'

Ash was to remember that comparison in later life for several reasons, but most perhaps because the man's entrance and pronouncement at such a moment came as an immeasurable deliverance. It was as much of a surprise as a warder coming in to a prisoner who has been fettered in solitary confinement for thirty years and saying 'You have been pardoned by a special decree of the government. You are free.'

Ash came to life, yawned, stretched out his long limbs with a creaking noise, felt the blood stream back into them, staggered to his feet and had a hysterical feeling as his knees gave, he had to stand for a moment massaging the feeling back into his thigh; then he was restored to life again, to liberty, for if Taraldsen could go out, so could he. And once out in the hall, he had an excuse, he could without embarrassment say that, unfortunately, it had been a very pleasant evening, but it's past four o'clock and I have a lecture to attend at half past eight. . . .

He stormed out into the hall and into the lavatory. In the ecstasy of his release he kissed the wall of the little room; he took hold of the metal chain above the pan and kissed the handle, he went on his knees and pressed his lips to the chromium-plated paper-holder in real ecstasy.

He was never to forget those four hours he spent imprisoned on Taraldsen's divan, between him and Poppi, four hours during which he had sat mute and embarrassed and appallingly lonely; it was the most painful and humiliating experience he had ever had. He had not had strength or brutality enough to leave after ten minutes, to ask them to move aside and let him out, for by the end of ten minutes he had sensed their kind and their pettiness. He had been so weak, so incredibly hungry for the possibility of a friendly word, of a cultured conversation, of a glint of understanding and a breath of tenderness, a token of solidarity, like a masterless dog he would have licked their shoes for a kind word. That night was profoundly shaming, evidence that he was unable on his own to conduct a conversation and direct people where he wanted. And all the time, as though he had been walking on invisible stilts or his mind had been soaring high up above like a hawk, he had watched and let the shameful scene imprint itself upon his mind for ever: the three in that little room: Poppi, Ash and Taraldsen.

The Chiefs

Some other older members of the group were splendid people. There were three men for whom he felt boundless admiration, for very different reasons.

The first was the undisputed leader of the group, though he often left the various tasks to the younger members partly out of modesty, partly because his own time was very limited, partly to allow the younger ones to develop through having practical tasks to perform. This Francis Stabell, mathematics master at the Cathedral School, was spare of build and insignificant-looking, a mouse. He dressed modestly, almost poorly, he did not appear to think of the material side of life; his salary as a schoolmaster was meagre, but he used his own (and other people's) money to support political refugees, the Group's finances and anyone in need of help. He was married, but had no children. He was the most unselfish and genial person Ash had met, a spontaneous, ecstatic person with a soul as clear as crystal; he laughed often and at the most unexpected times, a neighing laugh like a young stallion's. His laugh could come as a revelation in situations where from anyone else laughter would have seemed highly indecent.

A mouse? Yes, but not when you were in the same room with Francis Stabell, not when you felt the radiation of his dynamic being, not when you saw his face and his head. He was bald, his skull so well polished that it seemed to belong to the basalt statue of an old Pharaoh. He wore glasses, his forehead was high, broad and bulging, his nose long and pointed; when he was out of earshot the others in genuine admiration used to call him Lenin Minor. His head was so powerful that it seemed too big for his thin, little body; when he shook his head, Ash felt that he wanted to rush up and stand ready to catch it as it fell.

Stabell came from an old family of government officials; there was always something cultured about him, his worn grey suit could never hide the intellectual aristocrat; there was to come a time when Ash understood Stabell's secret sorrow : that he was never to be able to talk to the socialist workers in their own language. Stabell wanted to, there was nothing he wanted more than to be one of the people, for that was the only way that he, with his gift for political leadership, could build up socialism on a broad basis. But his polished, elegant speech always bore the stamp of the scholar, it was and remained beautiful literary language and he could not change that. Nor, in his heart of hearts, did he wish to; in his heart of hearts he despised the type of politician who twists his individuality—if he has any— so as to be what he thinks people 'want him to be'. Perhaps his lack of success as a politician could be traced to his sense of style, his uprightness and honesty, his incorruptibility, his personal modesty and his elegant speech. To Ash he was the embodiment of all that was strong, straight, courageous and loyal; he was a skilful theorist and a fantastic debater.

At one meeting of the young socialists—they were discussing a lecture on 'youth and morality' Stabell had given outside the town and which had been met with fierce condemnation in the town's bourgeois and Christian newspapers—Stabell said : 'A socialist is a foreign body under the skin of society. A socialist's first task is to scandalize.'

Ash folded his hands in the deepest awe. He had never heard a man utter such a truth.

Nevertheless, there was something childish and touching about this man who became young Ash's hero and model. He

neither smoked nor drank; on the rare occasions when, out of
politeness, he had to accept a glass of beer, he blinked discon-
certedly and set his head on one side as though listening; then
he took a cautious sip of the yellow liquid and held the glass
out away from him with every sign of terror; he was then like a
small boy who has seen a snake and doesn't know whether it is
a slow-worm or an adder. (Years later Ash was to discover that
Francis Stabell belonged to an old family of eminent judges,
scientists and high officials, that his father had been the first to
go into business, and that he had ruined his business through
drinking and had spent the last years of his life in a home for
alcoholics. This shed a new light on Stabell's suspicion and
caution where drink was concerned, and Ash thought that he
also understood better why Francis Stabell had become a rebel
and a socialist; why he was an aristocratic socialist.)

It would have been simpler and more friendly to have called
him by his Christian name, but when they did, they noticed that,
for all his democratic convictions, he didn't like it. 'Stabell' he
would say angrily, 'Mr. Stabell'. He felt it a breach of conven-
tions, and he was himself very particular, almost touchy, where
names and titles were concerned.

He was incredibly generous; no one ever asked for assistance
or financial help in vain. It was a sight to see this proud rebel,
scandalizer, socialist and aristocrat with his purse. It was a
great leather purse, the sort of thing horse-traders used to carry,
which he drew from his pocket slowly and reverentially. He
opened it with a devout click, put his head on one side and
peered down into it; pursing his lips as though in prayer, he
slowly took a silver crown from one of the compartments, held
it between thumb and forefinger while he squinted at it,
stretched his hand out to the recipient, drew it back again for a
last look at this mysterious and wonderful coin, then slowly
laid it in the recipient's palm with a significant and grave little
downward thrust.

And once or twice Ash had seen another thing, which had
made the deepest impression on him. This was on the rare occasions when Francis Stabell had to remove his spectacles, either
because he had been laughing so loudly and violently that
tears were streaming from his eyes, or simply because they

needed cleaning. Ash had seen then that this fearless warrior's eyes were light-blue and innocent, like a child's; he had caught a fleeting glimpse of something fearfully gentle, almost helpless, something naked and defenceless that had brought a lump into his throat and made him look away.

Fiffolo on the other hand bore his nickname with pleasure and elegant composure. He was an ingratiating, kindly man of about fifty. He was high up in the Customs Office and the only one in the circle who had a well-salaried position. He was a rather stocky man of athletic build; his somewhat reddish face made one think at first glance of sunbathing and the open-air life, at the second one realized that the skin of the face was cracked and sapped by alcohol. He always went with his chest thrust out and in so dapper, elegant a person this manly posture was faintly comical. In pleasing contrast to his rather asinine ways his bearing was always very dignified. For from the time he came till he went, he cracked jokes in a low voice and with imperturbable calm. He had a classical and a legal education; there was an aura of the scholar and the man-of-the-world about him; he smelt of after-shaving lotion and wine. His shirt cuffs, which were immaculately white, always protruded a quarter of an inch below the sleeve of his jacket and emphasized his beautiful, small, hairy hands; his tie was always perfectly tied; he carried a dazzling white handkerchief in his breast pocket. His hair was slightly grizzled at the temples, cut short and glossy with brilliantine; he reminded one of a Spanish nobleman, on occasion he wore a flower in his buttonhole. Ash did not properly understand Fiffolo's attachment to the socialist camp: the man never made a political speech, never took part in a debate or attended a study circle; he just sat in a corner in a comfortable armchair with a drink on the arm, while his lips soundlessly shaped words; these soundless words were without doubt indecent and doubly so because they were mute. He only had to wrinkle his forehead for the young socialists to burst out laughing. It was only when the debate was over that he came to life and began to recruit volunteers for a carry-on party. Then he became a fount of low-voiced gaiety, he turned and twisted everything that was said, bon mots, witticisms and quo-

tations flowed from him in an easy stream; and the whole time
he looked at his audience with an unruffled smile in his grey,
somewhat faded eyes; he was the Group's master of revels, its
uncle, a unique and delightful person.

Once, in a confidential moment, Ash had asked what his
position in the socialist camp was; with a twinkle in his eye
Fiffolo had held up a hairy jocular finger and said: 'I am an
agnostic. I bring to the socialists the wisdom of the excise man
and the folly of the smuggler. When I die, the Norwegian
socialists will erect a temple to my memory, and my last will and
testament will contain a request that this temple be designed
and run as a wine parlour.' He smiled, pointed in invitation at a
bottle of whisky and some glasses standing on a table and said:
'Please help yourself.'

Fiffolo had a younger brother who occasionally popped his
head in at the meetings. Ash could scarcely believe that they
were brothers; the other was a tall, fair, elegant hawk-like man,
an architect with twinkling rimless spectacles; he had never
seen people so different as these two. When he discovered that
they were half-brothers, it became a bit more understandable.
They were often together. Architect Smith-Hermansen (the
latter was Fiffolo's surname as well) had been trained in
Germany and loved German drinking songs, which he sang in
a powerful metallic tenor. When he popped his head round the
door and gave the study group a wave of his hand and a smile of
pearly white teeth, his elegance was startling in such surroundings; dark well-cut coat, dark well-cut suit, a dazzling glint of
white from a long silk scarf. Both brothers were prominent
members of the Students' Choral Society, and one evening, at
the Society, Smith-Hermansen came up to Ash, smiling and
polite: would Ash give him the pleasure of coming out to his
house one evening, so that they could have a chat over dinner
and a bottle of Moselle? Ash, Fiffolo and he, just the three of
them; a little stag party? Yes, thank you very much, but ... ?
They had heard that he had started a choir at The College,
which they thought a splendid thing to have done, and they
would like to hear a bit more about it and perhaps discuss the
possibility of Ash's choir and the Students' Choral Society
collaborating. . . .

Ash did not remember much of that evening at Smith-Hermansen's house. He just remembered the atmosphere: a very nicely furnished place with paintings on the walls, good paintings and they would have been even better if the man had omitted to tell you how much he had paid for them. It was perhaps this that first chilled Ash and made him feel a secret repugnance for the other; a moment came when he began to take a dislike to the architect; he found him a self-important braggart, a young snob with a richly furnished house and an empty mind, who became thoroughly loathsome when he sat down at the piano and sang arias, face suddenly greasy with self-glorification, for to Ash there was nothing worse than the amateur singer who turned up his eyes in enjoyment of his own voice. A quick glance at the dinner table gave Ash a glimpse of something below the surface that momentarily reconciled him to the other's brassy nature. The table was unusually beautifully and richly laid with a battery of flashing silver forks, spoons and knives; there was an array of at least four different wine glasses beside each place; there were lighted candles; Ash felt it slightly embarrassing; he hoped they wouldn't eat off gold plate; they were waited on by an elderly woman in a dark dress, starched white apron and starched lace cap, a gentle smiling old woman. And when she first came in Ash scrambled to his feet and bowed and held out his hand, though she didn't notice that. She went out again almost at once and Smith-Hermansen said:

'That was just my housekeeper.'

Having been guilty of a *faux pas* he didn't understand, having stood up and tried to shake hands with an elderly woman, with whom according to rules of this higher society he should not shake hands, and since he considered an elderly housekeeper just as much a human being as a young architect and couldn't kill that miserable architect whose guest he was, Ash had to content himself with blushing. He took his seat at table, glad that the electric light had been switched off. He was so furious that he didn't notice what he was eating, didn't notice what they drank, and he was a person who had hunger-phantasies every day. After a while, when they had *skaal*-ed together, he allowed himself to ask his host who had just been expatiating

on the size of his home and its many rooms—whether the architect was married?

Young Smith-Hermansen held his wine glass up level with
the candles to admire the colour of the wine; he looked at Ash
and said:

'I was.' Ash noticed a slight flicker of his eyes behind his
glasses; he made a slight sweeping gesture with the glass and
in a forcedly supercilious voice, said: 'That's finished. I don't
talk about it. *Skaal!*'

Ash swallowed and looked at the man's ringless hand; he
had not meant to be inquisitive; the question had just tumbled
out of him; Smith-Hermansen was a good bit over thirty and
with a home like that . . . Well!

During dinner they talked about the choir. Would the members of Ash's little choir consider joining the Students' Choral
Society? Ash stroked his cheek and didn't know, but he would
certainly ask them at the next rehearsal. To himself he thought:
I'm not joining any choir that includes Mr. Architect Smith-
Hermansen among its members, not till he allows people
to shake hands with elderly housekeepers. After dinner he
was particularly careful to praise the excellence of the meal
so that the housekeeper heard him, and the tension relaxed
inside him when he noticed a faint flush of pleasure on
her cheeks.

'The whisky's there on the sideboard,' Smith-Hermansen said
to Fiffolo. 'Would you fetch it?'

'*Stante pene,*' said Fiffolo getting up briskly.

'What?' Ash said.

Fiffolo had kept rather in the background during the meal,
leaving the essentials of the discussion about the choir to the
other two.

'Are you a Latin scholar?' Fiffolo asked. Now that they
were switching to whisky and lighter matters, he was in his
element.

'Yes and no,' said Ash. 'I read it for the Oslo University entrance, that was when I thought of becoming a philologist, but
then I gave it up. I was' (he had to think quickly in order to
avoid becoming involved in further questions about his past)
'afraid of staying a schoolmaster all my life.'

Fiffolo pursed his lips. He had put the bottles on the table and now stood pressing the tips of his fingers together, which was an unfailing sign that a jest was coming.

'Perhaps you know the Latin expression *stante pede*?' he said.

'Yes,' Ash said. 'It means "on the spot". But that wasn't what you said.'

At that moment Ash felt that the architect's eyes were on him. He looked up, the architect was smiling to himself. He looked at Fiffolo, he too seemed to be enjoying what was coming.

Fiffolo said:

'And you know the Latin word *penis*?'

'I've a vague idea that I have heard of it.'

'Well then, in good dog Latin: *stante pene*.'

Ash was sitting between the two brothers at the point of inter- section of their smiles. He didn't look at them, because he was aware of their shaggy solidarity; he just smiled politely at the joke and felt that he was flushing slightly; for one reason or another he didn't think the joke was so funny. He never went to the architect's again and probably he would have forgotten that little Latin lesson, if, some years later, he had not heard that same expression used by a young woman of whom he was very fond. It recalled the scene in Smith-Hermansen's rich but empty house. When he heard it, he glanced up at the young woman's rich and smiling face and felt a little stab of inexpres- sible terror in his heart.

No one could help admiring and liking Fiffolo. Ash had heard it mentioned casually that he and his wife did not get on as well as they might (they had three children) and he had noticed that Fiffolo did not wear a ring, but he had merely thought it a gay and rather smart thing for a married man not to wear a ring. Late one evening Fiffolo invited four or five of the Group back to his house. Was it all right to go to his home at that hour, they wondered. What about his wife and children? Wouldn't it be better to go somewhere else? Fiffolo brushed their objections aside and bundled them into a taxi. It was well after twelve, when they got there. They seated themselves in the sitting-room, feeling rather uneasy, and Fiffolo produced drinks, humming

to himself and in the best of spirits; the company of young people
was obviously something he needed, in the same way as he
needed spirits.

When they had been sitting for ten minutes or so chatting and
drinking, a sudden paralysing silence fell over the little group.
Ash turned his head. In the doorway stood a middle-aged, sleep-
bemused woman in dressing-gown and bedroom slippers; her
face was hard and unhappy and small varicose veins were visible on her bare legs; her hair was dark and tousled and the
flickering light from the fire made it appear shiny and greasy.
She looked at the group sitting round the table, her face grey
and tired, moistening her dry colourless lips, she said in a rough,
joyless voice:

'So *this* you can afford!'

Fiffolo was opening a bottle of soda water. He said:

'Go back to bed. And put out the light in the passage. You
look best in the dark.'

Ash tried to stay on a bit after the woman had shuffled out.
He did not dare look at Fiffolo, who went on telling his gay,
rather risqué stories. Fiffolo wanted them to *skaal*, but Ash was
numbed by nameless despair, he sat there, deathly pale and
trembling, wishing he could sink through the floor and die; he
had seen two people's ignominy and dishonour laid bare and
felt that it had taken possession of his own heart—for ever; husband and wife! Good lord! Husband and wife! He knew that
he would never be able to forget that shameful, dreadful scene
and he had to fight to stop himself sobbing aloud. He turned his
face away to hide his fierce grief, his sorrow, then he stood up,
stammered some meaningless excuse, that he had to go, be up
early for a lecture, and stuttered:

'Where can I phone for a t-taxi?'

At the time of this episode, Fiffolo had already begun to irri-
tate Ash. He still admired his easy, smart, man-of-the-world-
ways, but he had begun to find his flow of jokes rather tedious.
He had noticed that Fiffolo was not always the cultured man
with a fine palate he had thought him to be, for he sometimes
smelt of methylated and surgical spirit, and that made Ash
boundlessly unhappy, reducing Fiffolo to the ranks of the Nor-

wegian barbarians who drank for the sake of drinking, drank just in order to become intoxicated and to obtain or borrow a weak and shameful strength.

(There was nothing about his fellow countrymen that caused him more grief and apprehension than this urge to engage in joyless drinking that he so often noticed. It was largely because of this that he was cautious about associating with the ordinary working man, and that, in the country, he never achieved real contact with the farmers; he had a terror of the brutish in people; he could never hide his abhorrence and despair when, in the dark, on a stair or outside a youth centre, someone proffered a bottle of hootch with a shaggy menacing neigh; he always refused the offer and it had happened that he had even taken to his heels, hearing behind him the ghastly words: 'Think yourself too good for us, eh?' The apprehension and sense of inferiority and nightmare unhappiness in the words had made him desperately sad, yet the words had stung, stung most horribly, and he thought it the most dreadful thing in the world that they should think he felt himself too good for them.)

What Ash now saw in Fiffolo's faded eyes, when he laid a hand on a girl's shoulder and suggested a late party, was as often dread as joy. And it now seemed as though he only told his risqué stories in order to get a secondhand waft of sex. Once a poem was recited in the Group which contained the expression 'my favourite hunt'. Fiffolo's nose twitched and he leaned forward to a girl's ear. The mere movement had been enough to tell the others that in his whisper he had changed the first letter of the last word. Ash smiled, but it was a polite, wry smile.

The third of the group and the man who was to mean more than any other to him in that lonely year, was a middle-aged assistant master at the same school where Francis Stabell taught. He was nice, kindly, clever; he had an ugly bloated face, thin straggling sandy hair, protruberant eyes, crooked teeth, freckled spongy hands and a laugh like a sick camel's. He was the most glorious man Ash had ever met.

He was fat and very heavily built, his shoulders drooped and his hips were wide; his was the stature of a ruined pyramid.

He was well over thirty, perhaps nearer forty, married, had two children; there was something flippant and casual about him, something gloomily jolly both in the way he dressed and in the way he talked. He was a schoolmaster teaching languages and history in a secondary school; he had never taken the second examination that would have enabled him to gain promotion from badly paid master in a secondary school to slightly less badly paid master in a high school; he had always been intending to do so, but his life's balloon seemed to have been pricked and he never even got as far as buying a ticket to Oslo. His schoolwork took so much of his energy, even though he would tell you with his neighing laugh that he had invented his own method of correcting English and Norwegian essays at lightning speed (he mumbled something about taking out a patent for it, but never said what the system was; Ash suspected that it was just setting his pupils an essay once a month instead of once a week); he had a wife and two children, he had his work with the young members of the Socialist Students' Group, he had so much on his hands, alas and alack.

The only purpose of life was to fill space with sighs, life was children having mumps, when they weren't having measles; life was pupils unable to learn the difference between *two* and *too*; life was unpaid bills and wasted opportunities, and now he was writing a broadcast talk, had spent three weeks on it, and did Ash know what fee you were paid for a twenty-minute talk? Twenty crowns. Twenty crowns for three weeks' work. He looked at Ash, twisted his flabby mouth into a despairing grimace and rumbled: 'May I die!' His voice was always tired and mock peevish, his lids drooping and his body slumped; when you met him and asked how he was, he covered his eyes with a spongy hand, uttered a despairing sigh that ran all through his great pyramid of fat and groaned: 'May I die.'

Then he took the hand away and you saw that his eyes were full of laughter; he was a man who made fun of himself and was loved unreservedly. He went by the name of Doff and Ash heard that even the schoolchildren called him that.

Doff was an inveterate lover of cafés, beer and conversation. Every day after school-hours he was to be found in a certain restaurant at a certain table with a tall glass of beer in front of him and a fat satchel on the chair beside him. He had an insatiable hunger for company and gay conversation and he was a wonderful raconteur, a pyramid of wit.

The first time Ash met him in this restaurant, he had stretched out a waving, inviting hand and called out in a stentorian voice: 'Come and sit here!' And when Ash had come and sat down, Doff groaned: 'I must have someone decent to talk to. I've just read the leader in the *Worker's News*. The world is populated entirely by schoolchildren and wheelwrights. May I die! Have you any tobacco?' He was fingering an empty pipe. He had had to choose, he said, between tobacco and a beer and had thought: if I have my beer in the restaurant as usual, I may meet some kind soul who will trickle a few grains of tobacco into my pipe; but if I buy tobacco and stand outside on the pavement, will anyone come and pour a beer down my throat? Didn't Ash agree with that reasoning? Groaning with laughter, Ash agreed most heartily, and watched admiringly as Doff, instead of just filling his pipe, pulled off a great wadge of tobacco and stuffed it into his waistcoat pocket. 'You have a good heart,' he said. Ash sat open-mouthed and delighted at having his tobacco taken in such a noble way.

If you went by people's opinion of him, Doff ought to have become something great—professor of art history, or of music, or literature . . . but it was as if he had seen beyond all that and knew that it wasn't diplomas and sealing wax and gold-braided uniforms and pompous visiting cards that gave you the greatest thing of all: freedom; that it wasn't in high, strained office that people enjoyed the greatest opportunity for free development as human beings. ('Idleness is the root of all good,' he said and looked at Ash severely. 'You should remember that.' And Ash did, all his life.) Therefore it seemed that in a way he was content with his threadbare existence as a schoolmaster and a permanent job that enabled him to pay his rent and gave him a home for his beloved books, his piano, his children, his beloved gramophone records and his wife, without his being high enough up the ladder to be fettered by the need to consider his position. A professor was a sacred cow that had to watch its step, but people could look through their fingers at the doings of an obscure assistant master. People would be more

amused than scandalized if, late one night, Doff were seen drunk
in the street, dancing ecstatically with a policeman. Did Ash
comprehend how valuable it was that a grown man should have
the right once in a way, when excessively drunk, to dance in the
street with a policeman without having to answer to the nation
for it the next day? Ash thought that he did, and at that moment
the fat, spongy, ugly person in front of him became transformed
into a philosopher, a Diogenes, a Socrates, and Ash sat gaping at
his immeasurable wisdom.

As a mere schoolmaster with his own patent method of correcting essays he was able to cultivate all his many interests; he
had time to read every important book that came out (he had
of course read all the classics from Aeschylus to Söderberg), he
went to all the concerts and saw all the plays, and exhibitions
of paintings and sculpture, he knew all the actors, painters,
writers and musicians in the town, he associated and was intimate with every person there who was worth knowing (here he
pressed an enormous spongy finger into student Burlefoot's ribs
and his eyes twinkled, and Ash blushed faintly). He was more
or less leader of the finest band of young socialists in the world,
Norway's future brains trust (another delighted twinkle at Ash,
who again blushed); he had time for ten minutes in a restaurant
every day and usually he had a few grains of tobacco in his
pipe, and if he hadn't, well he hadn't, but there was usually
someone else who had.

Ash came to admire Doff as sincerely as he was devoted to
him. For Doff, unlike other eminent beings, was interested in
Ash and enjoyed being with him; Doff often made Ash blush
by touching on secrets that Ash kept bashfully hidden, but there
was always a flapping, rumbling cordiality about him that Ash
never forgot. Doff talked to him. To *him*. Doff talked with him.
With *him*. For usually it was Doff who did the talking, he was
a born talker; the ability to give a whole lecture in a quarter of
an hour in a café seemed to be in his blood; his hurried, panting,
slap-dash monologues were masterpieces, cultural lectures in
cabaret form; he was a wonder, he was beyond all conception.
When Ash had to leave the café after sitting for a while with
Doff, when he saw Doff stumble off homewards heavily laden,
irritable, tired, home to wife and children and papers he must

correct—when Doff disappeared it was the sun going down, the rest of the day was flat and empty.

One day Doff was talking about education; he looked at Ash and said: 'With the education you will have had, you could go into the foreign service.' He didn't say any more and Ash nearly died of curiosity to know why Doff thought he would make a good diplomat, but he didn't dare ask.

Instead, Doff went on to speak of the kind of job one ought to have in order to be able to retain a certain surplus of intellectual curiosity and delight in living. He gave an inspired lecture on France (where he had never been) and how there the state, more or less clandestinely, gives sinecures to people with talent; not ostentatious positions with responsibilities and duties and telephones and secretaries, but obscure jobs as under-secretaries in some department or other, where they are given a little office tucked away under the eaves in some old building, an office to which they go in the morning, but where there are never any documents lying on the desk waiting for them, or if there are, only such as can perfectly well wait a couple of years; and no one inspects their work, so they sit and write their poetry, the best lyrics in the world, they have a small salary and a small office and no duties. That was how life ought to be arranged for people with talent (his eyes twinkled as he gave Ash a nudge, and Ash gulped and looked down), in that way the state kept culture alive. And what did they do in Nor-way? Was it even conceivable that a Norwegian government department would give a job to a man who *didn't do anything*? Well, was it? If such a thing should be discovered, there would be a flood of the most bloodthirsty protests from all the farmers' organizations, trade unions, housewives' associations and mis-sionary societies in the country, the government would have to resign, he who doesn't do something useful mustn't eat! To write poetry is a sin! Provided, that is, that you aren't working yourself to death during the day, as a schoolmaster for example, and in your spare time write a couple of lines of poetry instead of playing patience.

'You must never become a schoolmaster,' Doff said severely.

'No.'

'Not in primary, secondary or high school.'

'No.'

'Even if you have a wife and children.'

'No.'

'If you become a schoolmaster you turn yourself into an intellectual whore.'

'Yes.'

'And so you do, if you become a journalist.'

'Yes.'

'You must send your wife and children into the street to beg for you.'

'Yes.'

'Have you any tobacco?'

Ash shuddered and admiringly held out his pouch.

'That's good tobacco you have,' Doff said. 'Do you know,' he went on pressing the glowing tobacco down with the flat of his index finger, while Ash sat spell-bound looking at it, it was a biblical miracle that his finger could remain so long on that red glow without becoming charred, 'do you know, what I would have liked to have been?'

'No,' Ash said, he knew something funny was coming and was intrigued.

Doff blew out a vast cloud of smoke, replaced his pipe and said slowly and dreamily :

'An actor—being paid to rest.'

He looked at Ash through the cloud of smoke, then his eyes filled with tears of laughter, he tried to restrain his delight at his own joke, put his hand to his throat to choke back his triumphant laughter, but it was too much for him. He clasped his hands round his enormous stomach, he shook like a mountain of jelly, his fat bloated face became pink, then mauve, he tried to bite his lip with his pointed front teeth, but then he lost his grip on his lip as well and sat there with bared teeth shrieking with laughter, he was like an enormous rabbit, a gigantic pink and mauve rabbit, no, like a pink camel (camels also belong to the rodent family don't they?), a sick mauve camel, he gasped for breath and roared : Heee—heehee ! The mouths of the pedestrians and drivers of milkcarts and taxis in the street began to twitch, the traffic stopped.

Now and again Doff invited Ash home. Those were the golden hours of that year, even though Doff was not quite the same wound-up wonder at home as he was in the café. He was a bit bashful as he stood in the hall welcoming Ash; it was as though he wanted to say: you must excuse it being a bit untidy and all that here; but I'm afraid I don't live quite as I ought. On each occasion Ash had gone so late in the evening that the children were already in bed, but he met Doff's wife, Maia, a small woman with tranquil brown eyes, obviously a nice and good person, but with a hint of nervousness and tiredness between her eyes. While Doff was huge and fat and easily moved to laughter and liked to put his feet on the table, Maia was small and neat and finicky; when she looked round the room, she seemed to have a dust-pan in her gaze.

'Sit properly when we have visitors,' she said to Doff.

'May I die,' said Doff removing his feet from the table with a groan.

Ash had to look away; he had never heard a husband and wife talk like that.

While Doff had no idea of money, Maia was a strict accountant and Ash noticed that she kept watch on how much he ate. The next time Ash went to them, he took some sliced ham and Italian salad with him; Maia was genuinely moved. It could not have been easy keeping a home going with the money she got from Doff. If she got any.

At home Doff put on a pair of slippers so aged and worn that there were only the uppers left. He called them his 'cothurnus'. Then he jettisoned his jacket, undid the top button of his trousers, groaning with the pleasure of the relief, and put on the strangest dressing-gown Ash had ever seen. It was a cross between a piece of drapery and a moth-eaten tent; it had no sleeves and its colour was indeterminate, a faded dirty yellow, and it proved to have a woollen lining from some trenchcoat long since defunct. This garment Doff called his 'Goethe coat' and every time he put it on, he felt genius enter into him. He loved then to sit down at the piano, the wretched stool creaking beneath his enormous weight, and let his long, bloated, freckled fingers stray about the keys, preferably playing Tchaikovsky. He played well and once Ash told him so.

'Well?' said Doff and looked at Ash with a heavy smile; he seemed suddenly so tired. 'Well?' Ash gulped, he had had a feeling of both terror and grief, it was as though he were sinking, as though for a brief second he had looked into something he should not have seen, a cosmic grief, a gifted man's despair at never being able to perform what was perfect.

Doff also had a gramophone. Once when Doff and Maia were in the kitchen, Ash began looking through the records. Then he heard Maia scolding Doff for eating the ham off the open sandwiches she had gone to such trouble to make. 'Ash brought that. That's Ash's ham. Will you leave it alone!' Doff came in chewing and shaking with laughter and thievish delight. The next moment he had sneaked back into the kitchen; there was a crash and little Maia kicked him into the sitting-room; the delighted Doff landed on the piano stool, where he sat avidly licking his fingers; it was obvious that this time he had liberated a lump of Italian salad. Doff and Maia were the finest people Ash had met. If I ever become rich, he thought, I shall send them a case of champagne, a barrel of oysters and a jar of Russian caviare. Yes, and some cakes for the children, and a Persian lamb coat for Maia, so that she need not feel ashamed when she goes out.

Ash had chosen Paganini's violin concerto No. 2 played by Mischa Elman. When it was finished, Ash was breathing heavily.

'He has used a fiddle before, that Mr. Elman,' said Doff.

Ash had to smile. After a while he said:

'It's a fantastic concerto. Paganini has got everything into it. Everything conceivable for a violin solo. Into the last movement.'

'How do you mean?' said Doff.

'From the point of view of technique,' said Ash. 'Everything. He jumps from the highest position of the E string down to loose G string. He has all the harmonics and they take five years to learn if you are talented and have sufficiently sensitive fingers and the ear. He even has *double harmonics*! He has octave-grip. To play a pure octave-grip on the violin takes ten years to learn provided you have the ear; the stretch for an octave is greater in the lower register than in the high; it is not like the piano where an octave is always an octave; with a violin your

fingers have to listen their way to an octave. Then he has pizzi-
cato. There's not much more you can do with a violin.'

'You can drum on it with your nails,' said Doff.

'Yes,' said Ash.

'And you can chuck it against the wall,' said Doff. 'That too
will produce a sound.'

Ash said nothing.

Those were golden hours, starry hours. Dangerous, sparkling
hours in which a star might die or its light go out. That poor
apartment, Maia crotcheting, rumbling Doff wrapped in his
Goethe coat and the young student with the hungry face listening.

'Culture?' Doff said on one occasion. 'I heard you at the last
meeting; you were talking fervently about the socialistic culture
of the future; if I understood you aright, you meant that every
child in the country should be equipped with palette and
brushes, every child have its piano, its rhyming dictionary, its
puppet theatre, in order that the world shall become a creative
world—to have the whole people creating. Good lord!'

He took a pinch of tobacco from Ash's pouch, ignoring his
wife's reproachful look and went on:

'Culture is the art of *not* creating. Naturally we shall always
have those crazy people who cannot live without creating. They
are the artists. Art and culture are not the same. Artistic genius
is usually quite independent of milieu. Michelangelo was born
and brought up in the high civilization of Italy; Henrik Ibsen
grew up in a barbarous country that has never yet held out a
friendly hand to any artist. The creative artist sprouts up and
reaches the light—even if he is lying stifled under a glacier.
But culture doesn't mean creating. Culture means enjoying.
Culture doesn't mean giving, but receiving. We need not, cannot bother about the creative geniuses. A society cannot create
a genius. What we can do is to create a cultured society, educate
people to listen and to see, create a milieu that can receive a
genius when one comes, people who have the ability to distinguish between the good and the bad, people who can enjoy.
That is culture.'

He put his great feet up on the table; a glance from Maia made
him take them down again.

'You,' he said to Ash, 'are a barbarian.'

Ash swallowed hard.

'You would rather create than enjoy.'

'How d-do you know that?' Ash whispered, not daring to look at the other.

'Have you ever seen yourself in a mirror?' Doff asked mildly, teasingly.

'No,' said Ash. 'Yes, of course I have. I mean . . .'

'Sooner or later you will create something. You will probably break your neck, but you will not give up before you've got there. I don't know what it will be. Nor do you probably. You have a devil in your body. You're so uneducated that you cannot sit quietly when you listen to music. I've watched you. You sit hiding your hands in your trouser pockets, you're conducting inside your pockets, I have seen it. You mark time with your feet. You are so barbarous that you even sit there singing the obligato or bass in a loud voice. You harmonize beautifully, by the way. You can never sit quiet and just enjoy it. You're a hooligan. Blushing won't help you. I have more compliments yet to pay you. You will never be satisfied to lay hold half way up the trunk, you will try to climb higher. You are a barbarian. I see it: you harbour plans of *creating*.'

He looked at the quivering Ash, who was red in the face.

'Never satisfied with the common run, never satisfied with what is ordinary. "Lips that save themselves hungry and bite blessed bread." That's an American, Léonie Adams. Devil take it,' he said, suddenly thoughtful, 'how well the poets sometimes put things.'

There was a pause. In the silence Ash could hear his own heart thumping right up in his throat. Doff had said such strange things, dangerous things. . . .

'Well,' said Doff, 'go off and create something. You'll be madly unhappy, because no one has ever managed to make anything quite as they wanted it to be. But make a start. Take the plunge. As long as you don't first fail in your art and then switch to politics. There's nothing in the world more dangerous than an artist who has failed. Did you know that Hitler began as a serious painter?'

He sighed and his great body quivered.

"The police ought to keep an eye on all politicians who once practised one of the arts. Look out for them, I say. Now I'm going to turn you out. It's two o'clock and I must get some sleep.'

He rose from his armchair in all his might, yawned, shuddered:

'Oh God, I've to be at school early. Do you know that not a single person ever learned anything of value at a school? You could shut down all our schools and nothing would be lost. The only thing a reasonably intelligent person needs to be taught is the alphabet; the rest he can manage himself. Every day year in, year out, I go and work at an institution that is utterly useless, both for me and my pupils. May I die!'

Another golden hour some weeks later. A dangerous hour. They had been discussing composers. Ash had said that he thought Beethoven greater than Rossini. Doff had smiled at that:

'Of course.'

Ash bit his lip; he did not like being caught saying the obvious. Doff saw his irritation and was amused. He said:

'Do you consider the *Coriolanus* overture greater music than the overture to *The Barber of Seville*?'

Ash wriggled; it was not right of Doff to ask questions like that; he said:

'Yes. But I should have been in some doubt if you had said the overture to *The Thieving Magpie*.'

That answer seemed to please Doff immeasurably. He got up, laid a heavy hand on Ash's shoulder and stepped out on to the floor.

'There is hope for you,' he said.

He rubbed his unshaven chin with a rasping sound, then said ecstatically:

'There's hope for you, my son! You have not only a sense for the heroic, the dark, the cannibal, but also for the frivolous!'

All at once he became serious. He pointed an enormous, menacing finger at Ash and said:

'Do you know that the socialists of all countries will celebrate

Beethoven's birthday, but that no socialist in any country will celebrate Rossini's? *The Thieving Magpie* smacks of rococo and boudoirs and the erotic and frivolous, Rossini's magpie is an upper-class magpie, she has no solidarity with the ordinary working people, she's not an *organized* magpie!'

He glowed and rubbed his hands with pleasure at the phrase. Then he became serious again:

'As a socialist I say to you: *Beware of socialism!*'

Ash sat for a long time open-mouthed. That was difficult for a believer to swallow: in his heart of hearts he did not like Doff poking fun at the working class. He understood the joke, he understood the intention, and the worst was that he also realized the truth in what Doff had just said—but he did not like it. No, he did not like it.

About this time Doff managed to persuade Ash to play the piano for him. It had taken Doff a long time. Ash was dreadfully bashful and diffident in that house. It had been no help Doff telling him that Maia was quite unmusical and did not know the difference between the song *Gubben Noa*—'Old Man Noah'—and the Jupiter Symphony ('Thank God,' Doff had said, 'what would it have been like if I'd had a musical wife and she too had wanted to sit swooning at the piano! It would have been intolerable. But you're a guest. I'll listen to you for ten minutes. Now begin.') Ash finally gave in. His whole body was wet with sweat as he began. He considered Doff the best, soundest and greatest judge of music that had ever lived. Just a word from him ... He did not for the life of him dare play anything he had composed; with trembling hands he played a paraphrase of a folk song from Baden, the student song: *Hark, what enters from without?* a thing he had arranged for the students' choir:

> The one I love, I cannot get,
> hollahi, hollaho,
> and no other do I want,
> holla hia ho!

He had set the last verse in a minor key:

When once I am dead,
carry me to the grave,
set no tombstone over me,
but plant violets and forget-me-nots,
holla hia ho!

and made the last stanza ecclesiastical in mode.

'Doric,' said Doff.

'Phrygian,' said Ash.

'Doric,' said Doff sure of himself.

'Phrygian,' said Ash firmly.

'Doric!' said Doff and stamped his foot.

'*Phrygian!*' said Ash and slapped the table top with his hand.

Doff looked at him, blinked. Heavily and menacingly he got to his feet, went to a bookshelf, took out an enormous dictionary of music, spat on a finger, turned some pages, read. He stood for a long while reading. Ash was aware of a sneaking feeling. . . . Doff put the book back in the shelf, turned, twisted his mouth:

'The devil! You were right.'

When Ash left that evening Doff came down to the outer door with him. He wrapped his vast Goethe coat round him, for it was cold in the outer corridor. He halted, stood chewing at his ugly lips, it was as though he were labouring to overcome something inside himself. He said in a low voice, his face half turned away:

'You see, I, too, was once one of those who wanted to accomplish something, to create something original. I still have a locked drawer full of trash from my youth: poems, essays, ballads and piano pieces. There's even the draft of an operetta there.'

Ash opened his eyes wide: he had not known this. And the thought of what might be lying there in the cupboard overwhelmed him; it was not just curiosity, a desire to see into the other's being, it was far more the thought of what the contents of that drawer might mean to the world, Doff's poems, Doff's essays. . . . He gasped. 'But . . . ?' he said, tremendously excited.

Swiftly Doff turned his face towards him and averted it again. Ash had seen something in his face, a paleness, a heavy grief, a weariness, a resignation, and he began to tremble.

'But it wasn't any good,' Doff said quietly, 'none of it. Not good. That little bit of harmonizing you played for me this evening, you old devil, was more original than the whole lot of what I did in twenty years. Only don't think . . .'

He unwound a weary, spongy hand from the folds of his jacket and raised it warningly.

'. . . don't think that what you played me is outstanding. It's really quite ordinary, I'm sure. A thing any schoolboy or wheelwright who'd had two lessons at a Conservatoire could have done. The only thing I can tell you, you old devil, is that it's better than anything I've ever done.'

Ash blushed, paled, the blood came and went in his cheeks; he was shivering, chiefly with inexplicable, nameless sorrow at the bitterness that lay hidden beneath the other's assumed bluff, jovial manner. He did not know what to say or do; in his despair he took a packet of cigarettes from his pocket, lit one and held the packet out to Doff. Doff took a cigarette, surveyed that strange way of consuming tobacco, tore it open, gathered the tobacco in the palm of his hand, rolled it into a ball and popped it into his mouth, between his teeth and lower lip, like a quid. Ash had never seen anything like it. But the other's wild grief tore at him; he felt that what Doff had just told him had never been told to anyone before, it was as though Doff had opened a door a little way and let Ash see into his soul, and it must have been hard to open that door. . . .

'Perhaps I was too fine, too educated, too burdened with background,' said Doff, his enormous body heaving up in a sigh. 'My father was a lawyer, a puisne-judge. Perhaps I have judge-blood in me. Perhaps I am so critical of myself that I shall never be able to present anything I produce to the world. No,' he said quietly, reflectively, 'it's not that. It is simply that it's not good. Not good. And . . .' he looked at Ash and his eyes were so full of resignation and weariness that Ash caught his breath in a strange sort of terror, even before he had heard the end of the sentence '. . . and *if* it had been "good", what would have been the point? What would I have had to show for it?'

'No!' Ash exclaimed, his lips quivering. He had cried out aloud and heard the echo from the smooth wall of the stairs.

'Hm,' said Doff with a strange, almost disordered look. 'In the world there are at the most five plays, five paintings, five musical works, five poems that perhaps deserve to be called perfect works of art and which I should be proud to be the author of. All the other hundreds and thousands are merely works ... and as I know that I shall never be able to do what is perfect, why should I torment and lash myself just to add another miserable stone to the mountains of bad works of art that have been created already? Why this crazy striving, why this unprofitable aspiration? The things that are great and immortal, for which we would give our whole lives and eternity to create, are so impossible, so infernally, desperately impossible! And when we can't make the best, why should we make anything at all?'

'No,' said Ash, he had gone close up to Doff and at this moment noticed that he was taller than the lecturer. 'No.' He stared into his friend's fat, ugly, fine, spongy face and seized him by the arm. He was wild with horror at the discovery of this cancer of doom and resignation gnawing at his friend's heart; he took hold of Doff, his teacher, the man he valued most on earth, seized his youth's Diogenes, his lonely youth's Socrates, seized him by the arm and banged him against the wall as though it were a question of knocking a spark of life into him, as if the pain of the jolt could wake him to life; for a moment he felt as though he could *kill* Doff in order to bring life back into him, in a menacing voice he said: 'It *is* of use.'

He threw Doff back against the wall. He was deathly pale, beside himself with his secret grief and horror; he said: 'It is of use. Do you hear? It is of use. It *must* be.'

A movement in the other's enormous body made Ash think for a moment that Doff was going to retaliate, that he was going to hit out at him, and a blow from Doff's ham-sized fist could have killed him. But Doff stood where he was, head hanging, slowly gathering his Goethe coat round him. Ash stood shaking with a strange feeling of repulsion in his hands from having taken hold of Doff's thick, soft, spongy arm; he was abysmally unhappy over having let his agitation run away with him.

'Listen,' he said in a thick voice.

There was a long silence between them.

'You old devil,' said Doff. There was a sorrowful smile round
his mouth. Then his face darkened, he looked at Ash with a
remarkably bitter, hard expression, took a step towards him
and said in a whisper:

'You are a barbarian. You are the greenest person I have ever
met, as naïve as a young girl, you believe in art, and love and
socialism, and God. Yes, I think that you even believe in God.
I don't know your background, you have never told me about
your parents. I only know that you are a barbarian, a moon-sick
centaur, a hungry gipsy; if joy lay at the bottom of the sea, as
Strindberg says, you would drink the sea empty to reach it;
you have no education, no fine feelings, you are an idiot, you
have nothing but your boundless unappeasable hunger. And
do you know . . .' here he lowered his voice still further and
came so close that Ash could feel his hot, acrid breath, 'do you
know how evil a man's soul can be? I am so wicked that from
the depths of my old, useless heart I envy you. I wish that
you . . .'

Ash had buried his face in his hands; a moment later when
Doff laid a hand on his shoulder he became frantic, he did not
want Doff to see his humiliation and his tears; he shook the
hand off.

'Perhaps I did not mean as much as I said,' said Doff. 'But
don't come back for a bit. You have been too much for me. Go
now.' And in an almost inaudible whisper: 'Go now.'

The Hero

It was at a meeting of the Socialist Students' Group. This was
held at a place that went by the name of 'The Stable', their
usual meeting place. Before the lecture, while they were still
sitting round the table talking, one of them clicked his fingers
as if he had suddenly remembered something; then he leant forward over the table, looked at Ash and said:

'I know something about you.'

Ash went deathly pale. He felt fear sprout like an ice-flower within him. He could feel that the eyes of all the others were on him.

The boy shoved his chair back and stood up: it was as though he intended to make a speech.

'Comrades,' he said and Ash was aware of an undertone of warmth and merriment in the other's voice and his fear receded slightly, only to return paralysingly. 'Here we have all been regarding our Ash as an ordinary mortal, gifted, of course, like every socialist, ahem, and pleasant and nice, with a great talent for making unsuitable remarks at the most suitable times, with a great and brilliant future ahead of him ("Where else would he have it? Behind him?"—"Sssh!") a good brother, but —an ordinary mortal.'

He made a little pause: he had the others' attention now; in his despair Ash could only stare at the boy's face, smiling fixedly; perhaps he could hypnotize him into sitting down.

'However,' said the boy. 'I find myself under the necessity of telling this gathering that our good Ash has been keeping something from us.'

Ash felt as though he were sinking through the floor.

'Like the Ash-Lad in the fairytale, he has been going about with something in his bag that we didn't know about. You see he is not an ordinary mortal, he is one of the elect, one of the few. Comrades, our Ash-Lad is a hero! Yes, I know, we all are, only Ash-Lad has it in black and white. He even has a medal!'

Ash gulped; his head was swimming. What luck! It could have been much much worse. Not that this wasn't bad enough: ghastly, appalling. He could not deal with situations, at any rate not one where fifteen young people sat round a table smiling and looking at his white face.

'Comrades,' said the boy, rubbing his hands, 'Comrade Ash Burlefoot holds a medal for life-saving. I happened to be going through some old newspapers of two years ago and found mention of a student, Ash Burlefoot, aged twenty-one, having received a reward from the Carnegie Hero Fund. He had—I hope I am quoting correctly—saved a woman and child from drowning and in doing so had shown unusual daring. Ash, my boy, you do us honour. Comrades, let's give him a hand.'

And, of course, no one there knew how it all happened, no one knew that at the time Ash did not care whether he lived or died, that he had just read a telegram from Gunnhild and that before he read it he had prayed that the child might be still-born, perhaps even, that Gunnhild might die in giving birth to it, and that then he had read that it was a girl and all was well with both mother and child, except that the baby had a birth-mark on one cheek, and that he had been frantic with horror and guilt because he knew that it was he and his wishing it dead that had seared the child's cheek for all time, and so he had fled, flung himself on to his bicycle and fled and then there had been a bridge and people on it and they had stopped him and pointed and gesticulated ... but he couldn't tell anyone about that, at any rate not his brethren, the socialists, and he smiled desperately, did not know what to say, said hysterically:

'It was nothing. Anyone would have done the same.'

And then embarrassment fell over the little gathering, he noticed it and knew why they felt embarrassed, but he could not help them, he could not help himself.

He would have liked to have left then, but he forced himself to sit through the meeting.

After the lecture one of the girls came up to him. She asked if he would join a new study circle for child psychology.

Ash looked down.

This girl had such a calm, soft smile. She had nut-brown hair and big, big blue eyes, sometimes she wore glasses. He had never really dared look at her.

On Being Good

'Let me kiss your breasts,' he asked with a catch in his breath. He was lying beside her. 'Why won't you let me take your things off?' Constance, lying with head averted, did not reply. 'Why shouldn't we be naked together?' She shook her head; it was as though she had shuddered. His trembling hands fumbled at her breasts; her hands came and wanted to stop him, but the opposition in them was not great; he began unbuttoning the top of her dress and she lay still, and he saw the skin of her neck and smelt the warm damp smell of her, and there were what seemed to be tears in her eyes, a prayer in her eyes, as he pulled the dress off her shoulders (why tears? why a prayer?); her torso was bare, except that she still had a brassière on; he put his mouth to it and took hold of her nipple between his lips, 'it's perfectly all right, my darling,' she was trembling, and he undid the fastening of her brassière, and she covered her naked breasts with her hands and he took her hands away, 'look,' he said, 'how beautiful they are,' and she was breathing heavily and raised her head and looked at his mouth and she gave a low frightened groan. After a while he had to look up at her, because of a movement in her body. 'Why are you crying?' he whispered. 'Don't know,' she whispered. Then he waited, scared and wondering. 'Can't you take off your dress?' he whispered. 'Oh, no,' she said with a frightened jerk of her head.

He wanted so badly to have her naked, to feel her body against his, live skin on live skin, the big naked embrace. What was it held her back? She who was so lovely and well-made and smelled so nicely, a good, warm moist smell? Strong, moist, bitter smell, but good good good ... Slowly he drew up the skirt of her dress and she lay quiet, she helped him imperceptibly as he searched for the elastic in her little pants, he pulled them off and she accepted that, though she did pull her skirt down a little so that it covered her loins; he struggled with the suspenders of her belt, got them undone and shoved her stupid belt up, that tight elastic uniform, but of course women must have something to fasten their stockings to; there she lay with bare torso and bare underneath; it seemed strange to him that she should lie with her dress in a roll round her stomach, a queer illusion of being dressed. He pulled her to her feet and she was standing on the floor at his side. He began to take her dress off and she let it happen, then they were standing naked on the floor and her dress lay at her feet, and he drew her to him, the whole of her body against the whole of his, their two whole bodies, and he saw that she had the soul of a little girl and gulped, and he put his arms round her and pressed himself into her as they stood clasped, and he put her on the sofa, on the very edge, so that her hips were on the edge and her feet on the floor, and he swooned and was completely unconscious for two seconds, she was so wonderfully good.

Late that night she whispered to him :
'You are so good.'
'It is you who are good. You are the most good thing I've ever had to do with.'
'Nice, then.'
'What do you mean by nice?' he said. He was a Judas, and she didn't know it; and besides no man likes to hear a woman tell him that he's *nice*, a man wants to hear that he's . . . well, lots of things, but not nice. No, definitely not nice.
'You know,' she said quietly, without transition, 'the first time it didn't hurt me in the least, not in that way. Isn't it queer? There wasn't a drop of blood. I thought that all went together.'
'Hm,' he said. He didn't know why she had embarked on this. And it gave him a slightly uncomfortable feeling in his heart, or his midriff. . . .
'Have you been with many before?' he asked. He hadn't meant to ask, but somehow the question was forced out of him.
'One,' she said. 'We were engaged for almost a year.'
He lay on his back and looked up at the ceiling.
'He has just got engaged to someone else,' she said. 'We're still quite good friends.'
'It was I who broke it off. He . . .' she paused and her voice became different, 'he was so . . .' He heard her gulp. 'He wanted to have me, when I didn't want to. He used force. And in the end I couldn't.' She raised her head and looked at him; the gravity of her face was that of a little girl, her eyes were burning and nervous, it was as though she had to have his approbation : 'It was rather difficult, because I couldn't tell my parents why I broke it off. They liked him : good family, good position, you know. A pharmacist. But I couldn't. Now could I?'
'No,' he whispered.
Carefully she stroked his arm.
'But you are different,' she said.

A lump came into his throat. He felt dread and an emptiness, and was there not also a touch of bitterness? He could feel it as a slight pressure on his jaws.

'You are good,' she said.

A tortured groan escaped him. He got up on one elbow and searched for cigarettes. He smoked the cigarette to the end. Then their hands met. Slowly he turned towards her and looked at her face. She smiled. She wanted to keep hold of the eiderdown, but he took it off. He looked at her, she was lying naked, he felt a quivering in her because he was looking at her. He had not touched her. He said:

'You are going to be angry with me.'

'Why should I?'

'Because—now I want you.'

Quiet. Just her chest rising and falling. She looked at him and her nostrils quivered.

'Take me,' she said.

As he was walking home with her that night, she said:

'You've even met him once.'

'Him?'

'My ex-fiancé.'

'Have I?'

'That first evening at Wilhelmine's. He's Wilhelmine's second cousin. That's how I know her.'

Had there been a hint of iciness in her voice at the word *her*? He didn't dare turn his face to look.

'I can't remember him.'

'He was there with his new fiancée,' she said.

'Hm,' he said. 'What's she like.'

'Oh, well.'

'What's—er—he like?'

'Fairly ordinary, quite good looking. Bit swarthy. Glasses.'

Ash gulped.

'Those rimless things?'

'Mmm.'

Ash remembered the peculiar feeling he had had that evening every time he danced or walked past one of the men, a chill on his skin.

'I believe I do remember him,' he said, 'just.'

She was very vehement in her embrace when they parted on her stairs. Heavy. Vehement. Happy.

Little Constance, he thought. But he couldn't say a word.

The Stable

The academic year is like a pregnancy. This is not because it lasts nine months (September, October, November, December —January, February, March, April, May)—that is fortuitous and superficial—but because the young participant carries within him a mysterious weight, a pressure, something of which he has to be delivered. Thinking back in later life to such an academic year, a person will recall that it must have been about the fourth or fifth month that he felt something happening inside, a slight kick, a sign of life. The first time, he did not pay attention to it, didn't think about it; later it took possession of almost all his thoughts and he was unable to escape what was coming. We all carry our destiny within us; its fecundation is a miracle. We are blind in our searching youth, yet in our blindness we are wise; our destiny leads us on and fulfils us, and one day everyone on earth will know inside himself : 'It has been fulfilled.'

The Stable was an old-fashioned building on the outskirts of the town. Originally it must have been a real stable, but a painter with a sense of the possibilities of tumbledown houses had restored it and turned it into a cross between a studio and a bedsitter. Now he had gone abroad for a couple of years and a young girl, a member of the Group, had rented it while he was away.

The ground floor had log walls and a low ceiling; Ash had to duck to keep his head from brushing against the rectangular white-washed beams. In one corner were a couple of broken-springed sofas, in the middle of the floor a long farmhouse table;

there was a corner cupboard, a seat along one wall and in another corner a curtain; behind the curtain was a gas ring and some shelves, in other words a kitchen. There was one deep and unusually comfortable wing-chair; this was always reserved for the evening's guest of honour, usually the speaker opening the evening's debate. The others sat round the table on high, exceptionally uncomfortable straight-backed wooden chairs with seats of woven string and the front legs protruding two inches above the seat. This made great difficulties for the occupant's legs. If you sat with your legs together, squeezed between the two tall wooden knobs, you soon got cramps. You could of course raise your legs and have each thigh resting on a knob, but that soon became intolerably painful. Or you could spread your legs wide so that they were on the outside of the knobs, but the muscles on the inside of your thighs will soon get cramp. Thus the inevitable end was that you swivelled the chair round and sat with one leg between the knobs and one outside; that meant that you had a knob almost in your groin, but with the exercise of a little caution it was possible to avoid being impaled. Strangely enough no one ever protested against those chairs, no one ever sawed the senseless knobs off; which just shows what dumb, suffering humanity will let fashion-designers and interior decorators inflict upon it. As well as the chairs' seats being dreadful, the backs were straight up and down—so straight that they almost inclined inwards. There was no possible restful position on these chairs, they were instruments of torture. To remain upright on them, you either had to exert your stomach muscles or stretch your arms out and twine them round the back of the chair. Either way, you gave up sooner or later and leaned forward with your hands, or your elbows, resting on your knees, or you just folded up. A stranger chancing to come in during a meeting would have thought that he had come upon the world's most dejected gathering, all bowed in mute contrition. But the occupants of those chairs felt no contrition; it was just that their backs ached; in that bowed attitude their eyes were on the floor and they noticed to their amazement that it was made of cement. It had plenty of rag rugs on it, but it was of cement none the less. You could just imagine the place having been a stable.

For several months Ash's mouth watered for the huge wing-

chair. It was upholstered in blue, the material had a rough surface, almost like towelling; yet it was soft and pleasant to the
touch. Ash had run his hand across the arm once or twice.

That blue armchair.

And he was always to remember the atmosphere of the room.
It had a good smell. Not the clean smell you get when you come
into a room in the morning and the floor is freshly-washed and
the windows wide open and crisp winter outside, when the room
still has a faint smell of soft soap and you hesitate to step on the
washed boards—this was a stuffy smell, a smell of dust and
old bedclothes, of oil, turpentine, masonry and food; Ash felt
that if he lifted up the cover of one of the rickety sofas he would
find a torn old mattress with a mouse's nest in it and the old
blue-striped ticking covered with spots of rust, of oil-paint, of
tar. He did not know why, he just knew that that was what the
mattresses were like.

In a queer way it was a good and pleasant atmosphere. It
was not evidence of human indifference and apathy; quite the
reverse, it bore triumphant witness to the fact that there was
one person whose whole energies were directed on other things,
on sparkling creative work. A person to whom washing floors
and beating mattresses were of secondary importance, things
you did when one day you woke up, rubbed your eyes and saw
that the place looked *too* ghastly. Thus there was a fine old
spider's web to be seen on the beams, fine old dust on your
fingers when you ran your hand over the corner cupboard, fine
old grease on the unwashed plates behind the kitchen-curtain,
fine old dirt trodden into the rugs on the floor. (The fine young
person concerned happened to be slightly short-sighted, occasionally wore glasses and thus could not discover every little
fault.)

In the farthest corner of the room was a wooden spiral stair-
case leading to the next floor. You had to use this when you made
a trip to the lavatory. The steps creaked most abominably. The
little bathroom smelled clean and warm; it had a feminine smell;
at the far end was a ceiling shower with a curtain of thin oilcloth. On the shelf under the window were jars of face cream

and boxes of powder and small mysterious bottles, a lipstick in a brass container, a big lump of cottonwool which—you could see by the colour—had been used as a powder-puff.

On the shelf there was also a razor.

Ash had only once peeped in through the door on the first floor that led into the pottery workshop. The studio it was called. He had caught a glimpse of big glass windows in a sloping roof, of work-tables and chairs, of unfinished clay objects on wooden pedestals; there was a thing that looked like an oven (doesn't pottery have to be baked like cakes?); there were shelves on the walls covered with bowls and dishes and other things; a shaded ceiling lamp that could be moved up or down, and he had caught a smell of chalk and oil and clay and woman. Here worked and slept the girl who was socialist and potter, hostess and Bohemian, whose person lent serenity and colour to their meetings, who in so many ways was the one who held the Group together and gave it a place in which to exist.

The pottery studio was her own little business and she had two employees, a middle-aged woman and a young girl. These two never took part in the meetings; they were only occasionally to be seen tiptoeing through the sitting-room on their way out, when presumably they had been working overtime.

The girl herself was a student and a year or two over twenty, so young and merry that she might have been no more than twenty, so independent and poised that she could have been twenty-five. It was some time before Ash discovered her; she was sweet-natured, quiet, almost meek, at all events that is how she appeared in that gathering of self-opinionated, loud-voiced reformers of the world. She had nut-brown hair and the biggest blue eyes Ash had ever seen; her gentle blue eyes were enormous, she was like a figure from a book of fairytales, her eyelids were heavy with a womanly fullness and drooped very slightly over her eyes; this lent her an air of tranquillity and wisdom, but also added a touch of something indolently sensual and unfathomable; one day when she was not wearing glasses Ash had glimpsed a darker tinge to the skin round her eyes, on her eyelids and in the hollows under her eyes; and fleetingly this brownish hue had reminded him of something sexual, it was the same brown tinge as round a woman's nipples, a tinge that immediately strikes a note in a man's mind, a tint that has no name, it is the dark tint of conception and suckling, the dangerous hue of lust and death, a hasty glimpse of which makes a man's heart stop, it is the womanliness of womanliness; before it a man drops his gaze in secret awe, it makes him feel as though he had seen something that only God and children should see. For an instant he had looked into her enormous, smilingly cordial, half-closed Mediterranean-eyes, then quickly he had looked away. That hurried glimpse had been strange and wonderful; all at once he had looked in upon something dark and mature in her; and yet was she not just a young girl?

But that was not the first thing about her to have impressed him. The very first had been her hands. Now and then when he happened to be sitting near her at the long table during a meeting, he could see her hands. They were brown and small, soft yet strong; the skin was transparent so that he could almost see the bones beneath; they were a refined, miniature edition of the hands of a craftsman; the fingers were strong, their tips thick and not really pretty, but they told of sensory inquiry and undaunted power; this girl was not afraid to take *hold* of things. The nails themselves were thick and strong; she usually varnished them red (only once had she appeared with green nails); the blood-red lacquer was laid on very carefully, leaving a tiny strip unpainted between the lacquer and the cuticle up either side of the nail; it struck him that this could have been done to make the nails appear narrower and longer than they were (they were kept cut short). She uses optical illusion, he thought, and was impressed to find such inventiveness and thought in a girl. When the study circle was in session round the table, she always had something in her hands. She might have some lumps of clay on a little board on the table in front of her, and now and again she would take a piece and shape it under the table, almost absentmindedly, yet all the time following what was being said and discussed; her hands seemed to work on their own, then they emerged from the depths under the table and set a figure on the board. Or she would bend little pieces of black wire into amusing shapes, or she rolled cigarettes with a machine, or she knitted, using enormous brown varnished

wooden needles ('snoozing-rug for an aged aunt' she explained
apologetically, vehemently blinking her great eyelids; it was so
comical when she blinked like that, hurriedly and repeatedly,
that they all had to laugh; she was like a sleeping-doll whose
eyes had gone mad), or she broke matches and arranged the
pieces in patterns in front of her, or she appliquéd bits of coloured material on to a cloth using glue from a tube (when she
wiped her fingers on the seat of her trousers, she looked up
quickly at the others with an apologetic smile), or she sat drawing on the block they each had in front of them. Ash was intrigued to see that she did not hold her pencil between her thumb
and index finger as other people do, using her second finger
to hold it in place; with her it was only her little finger that was
not used; she held her pencil between her thumb and first
three fingers, which showed what a strange, strong, intimate
and dominating relationship to the pencil hers was. Ash did
not know much about her and for some reason or other he
always found an excuse to change the subject when the ever-
knowledgeable Erik Floden dropped his voice to impart some
item of information about her. He only knew that after leaving
school she had been a year in Oslo and taken a course at a handi-
crafts school; then she had spent a year in Paris studying cera-
mics, had then come back and started her own studio at the
Stable. They were all proud of her and secretly admired her;
it was the admiration that the intellectual feels for those who
do things with their hands; she intended to take a degree later,
of course, but first she had to work up her business and get it
on its feet.

     She smoked a lot. When, after inhaling, she blew the smoke
out, it gave her an ugly look, for she thrust her lower lip and
jaw forward to make the smoke go straight up into the air.
(This was at a time when it was not usual to find young ladies
who were inveterate smokers.) Did she just smoke like that,
Ash wondered, to appear dashing? Does a girl make herself
appear dashing in order to overcome some internal or external
opposition? Sometimes she let her cigarette dangle from one
corner of her mouth while she worked away at something, and
then she kept her head tilted so as not to get the smoke in her
eyes; but usually she just took a long pull and put the cigarette

down, on a matchbox, or the edge of a table, so as to have her
hands free; all the table-edges, window-sills, cornices and box-
lids in the room had brown scorchmarks on them, showing
where she had left a cigarette too long. Ash admired her for her
smoking. A girl who smoked was a rebel against the established
order.

Was she good-looking? Perhaps. But her looks were more the
radiance of an inner light and inner grace, than outward per-
fection of proportion. Occasionally, when Ash was alone and
thinking about her, he would close his eyes and try to conjure
up her face, but he could never see it. There was something
impersonal about her good looks, as with a doll. There were
moments when he was reminded of a childhood's crush he had
had on a film star, Mary Pickford, 'the world's sweetheart', but
he dismissed this as silly, even insulting to this socialist comrade.
Her face was very slightly lop-sided, a wryness that only became apparent when she smiled or laughed; perhaps her nose
was a shade too big and her chin a shade too weak for her face
to be called really beautiful or classical; but that was not a thing
one thought of when in the same room with her. Then one only
felt a quiet pleasure at being together with someone so pretty
and charming; if you noticed anything special about her face,
it was her amazingly large blue eyes and the merry, happy
serenity that they radiated. If you sat close beside her, you could
also sense that her softness in some mysterious way was physical,
that it came from her *skin*; like that on her hands and fingers,
the skin on her face was also supple, soft and transparent. When
she was frightened or gay she could contort the skin of her face
into the strangest and most comical folds; when she thought
herself unobserved she could make the loose skin under her
chin jump about like that of a croaking frog; she played with
the supple skin of her face as other people, in moments of dis-
traction, pick their nose or teeth, or scratch their ears. The essence of her being seemed to be suppleness. You became
warmed and happy in her presence; when for one reason or
another the Group had to hold a meeting elsewhere than in the
Stable, they felt chilled and forlorn; the walls of the hall in the
People's House seemed grey and unattractive; there they sat

in their overcoats with the collars turned up and tended to snap at each other.

At the meeting in the Stable she usually wore a jumper, long trousers and rope sandals. When you saw her in slacks, you could see that the rest of her otherwise shapely body was not entirely in accordance with the accepted formula either, for her hips began a quarter of an inch lower down her body than those of the Venus de Milo. As a result people found *her* amusing and interesting, while the Venus de Milo is correct and banal. She attached importance to her appearance, and Ash liked her for that, not only because she was a good-looking young girl, but because some young socialists tried to make themselves and others believe that socialism was synonymous with being unkempt. Her nails, eyebrows, lips, hair, clothes all looked as though despite her many duties and her work, she took some minutes every day to attend to her femininity, that she was not ashamed of being pretty and feminine, but took a quiet pleasure in it. Ash was convinced that every time she made up her lips, she did so with the same natural careful craftsman's delight as when she designed or shaped a piece of ceramic jewellery or an ashtray. In fact, once or twice he had actually seen her make her lips up; it had been an entrancing sight: she had done it in front of everybody, quite without embarrassment; it had not been a hasty, imperfect dabbing with her lipstick, there had been no question of bashfulness or bad conscience over doing something she really ought not to do: openly, freely, with lips thrust forward she had made them up carefully, surely, wielding her lipstick with the same assurance and ease as a carpenter his plane or a violinist his bow; only, once she had stuffed the lipstick back into her hand-bag, she blinked her enormous eyelids at them hurriedly and comically, as though to turn any possible disapproval into friendly, understanding laughter. Are the wages of sin death? The wages of her sin were always a friendly understanding mumble from those present. In ancient Rome the gladiators used to greet Caesar with 'We who are dedicated to death, salute you.' This young girl's silent greeting to her friends was: 'I, who am dedicated to life, salute you.'

Once in the heat of a debate one of the men had banged his

fist on the table and Ash had seen her face and little mouth at
that moment; in that instant he had realized that beneath her
dashing, laughing, strong exterior she had the heart of a little
bird; in that brief moment he had been able to read in her eyes
that she feared violence and hated boisterousness.

There were things about her face that told him that she
worked hard and intensely, that she did not always get the
sleep she needed. Was there anything, or anyone, gnawing at
her heart? All that he knew about her was that she was the
daughter of a respected economist, belonged to a 'good' family,
that her ancestors included poets, sculptors, physicians, judges,
nationalist priests and more doctors—but that she had shaken
off her entire family, got herself a practical training and gone to
live on her own. More than all things which Ash admired in her,
was her breaking with her family and all that that implied. To
him it was a revelation. But—he thought, wondering and
anxious—having all the cultural background anyone could
want, having her own studio and freedom and friends, what
can be the cause of her occasionally looking pale and drawn,
and having the shadow of a hollow in her cheek? Can the others
see the shadow of grief in her sweet face, or am I the only one?

Her face was usually framed in her nut-brown hair; when
she sat with her cigarette in the corner of her mouth, her
face pale from too little sleep, there was a look of a French
demimonde about her, she reminded him of a picture of Mistinguette he had once seen. But on the next occasion she had done
her hair differently, pulled it tight and fastened it in a little bun
on top of her head; then you saw that she had a small, beautiful,
well-bred head; you were reminded of a picture of Nofretete,
daughter of ancient Egyptian kings, and Ash had had to look
away. He preferred Nofretete to Mistinguette. (Someone—was
it Erik?— said once that she went on the spree a bit too much?
Spree? She? How? When? With whom? Go on the spree, did
that just mean going to bed late?)

Ash did not know when he had first noticed her. She was
so quiet and amiable, never pushed herself forward. At a distance there was nothing so remarkable about her. But she loved
colour and you could not help—sooner or later—noticing her
skirts or blouses or pullovers, there was always something amus-

ing, fresh and original about them; once she had appeared in a skirt, an ordinary black skirt except that the seam was not sewn, the vertical join was made with a row of gleaming copper rivets driven through the material and hammered flat on the inside (she said, half jokingly, half apologetically, eyelids blinking: 'Felt I wanted a new skirt and had only five minutes to make one, so I took some copper rivets and a steak-hammer,' and Ash had never seen a prettier skirt in his life); she wore strange necklaces of stones, corals, cubes, she had ear-clips of pottery, metal, wood. But her hands were bare, he never saw her wear a ring.

She usually had her forearms bare too. That was because of her craft—she always had to have her sleeves rolled up—though it may have been unconsciousness. Pretty and good as was the rest of her, her arms were as perfect and beautiful as anything Ash had seen. When she was speaking, she also talked with her hands. Ash could not take his eyes off them, sometimes he became quite bewitched by them; they laughed, joked, hummed, sang; they were a party, a ball, a ballet. And when she put words to this graceful hand-rhapsody it was a low-voiced chatter that quivered with repressed roguishness, it was like watching the bubbles rise in a glass of champagne; when she began to speak, the others gradually stopped, till all were turned to her; in a smaller gathering she had a smiling, irresistible talent as a *raconteur*; yet if she were up on a rostrum and had to be serious, she became stiff and pedantic. She couldn't very well use graceful finger-flutterings when starting a discussion on chapter eight of Erling Falk's book on Marxism. She always refused, most definitely and with vehement blinking, to let her name be included in the list of members of the Socialist Group taking part in the public debates that were held in the Students' Society.

It would be as well to explain about these debates in the Students' Society. The Students' Society was the open, common forum for all those in the town with an academic training, old and young, conservative and radical, white, black, brown or red. The Socialist Students' Group, under the leadership of Francis Stabell (who had been trained in the Socialist Group, 'Towards the Day' in Oslo), considered one of its primary tasks to be to spread the ideas of socialism in the Students' Society and, if possible, to conquer the Society. Winning university people for socialism was at least as important as winning the workers. Numerically the former were a small group in the community, but because of the positions they held, they were very important. There was more rejoicing in Francis Stabell's heaven over one university convert to socialism than over two hundred plumbers joining a union. The battle was for the young student members of the Society, those who in a few years' time would be schoolmasters, lawyers, doctors, zoologists, psychologists, architects, engineers, managers. If you got them on your side, then you would get the socialist society from above, while the trade unions did the same from below; it was like driving a vertical tunnel through a mountain; one day the two teams would meet inside the mountain, the last blows would be struck with the pick and then the way would be free and they would look straight into the clear blue sky of freedom.

And how were these students to be won over? By appealing partly to their intelligence, partly to their sentiment and generosity; but the debates must also be made dramatic, an element of sport must be introduced; speaking figuratively, each debate must be made a boxing match at which the defeated opponent was always knocked out and the winner, he whose hand was held up, always the socialist.

Thus each appearance of the socialists in the Students' Society was prepared most thoroughly. The lecturer was studied and weighed; all possible information was obtained about his person, political convictions and past, and the whole subject carefully analysed. Then Francis Stabell drew up a plan of attack; ten socialists were to hold themselves in readiness; one was to keep himself up-to-date in this, the next in that, together they were to provide a conspectus of the problem far more comprehensive than the wretched speaker's; the ten were to speak in turn in the debate following the lecture, and what they had to say would effectively and mercilessly pull the speaker's arguments to pieces; if they didn't leave him a corpse, he must at least be plucked like a fowl.

For one reason or another Ash did not relish this procedure; in the first place it seemed obvious to him that even a bourgeois speaker could have sensible things to say, then he could never properly take in what the 'enemy' speaker said when he had to be thinking out counter arguments the whole time. And even though Stabell's tactics often brought them victory, they did not by any means always do so. In fact the bourgeois speakers and conservative students won the bout surprisingly often. This was probably due to the fact that the socialist students had been far too thorough in their preparation, they were stale; when they mounted the rostrum in the Students' Society they had none of the fire and spontaneity and elasticity of thought that are required to convince an audience. Stabell had carefully spread a net, but all too often his own disciples were caught in it.

Ash refused to take part in the debates in the Students' Society. His excuse was that he had too much to do at the College and so could not prepare himself. The real cause was his dread of speaking in public, at least when there were socialists present. At the College he was a keen speaker and liked to get up on his hind legs; the students there were wolves to whom he owed no respect. Among socialists Ash was like an oyster. He knew that after the debates in the Students' Society the socialist speakers were summoned to Francis Stabell, who then criticized what each had said. And Stabell was not merciful. Lenin Minor was not always fair.

And Ash was never happy, never fearless, never convinced of any truth, unless he was riding on the crest of an inner wave.

The Red Knight

One day Ash and Doff were sitting in a restaurant drinking beer; for a change Doff had his own tobacco and even offered some to Ash. Ash had been saying how surprised he was that the women in the Socialist Group so seldom took part in the debates: had they joined for social reasons, or because they wanted to listen, or—here Ash hesitated a moment—were they *stupid*?

'Women as debaters?' said Doff. 'It's only practice they lack.
Practice and some assurance that they will have a *use* for public
speaking in later life. That would give them a spur, and once
women *can* speak in public, they will knock any man into a
cocked hat. As they do in all fields. Where is the man who can
outdo a woman in erotic endurance? Have you thought of that,
you old devil?'

No, Ash had not thought about that.

'There is a woman to beat even the most enduring male erotic
athlete in the world. When he has wrung the absolutely last
drop out of himself, she will lie there smiling and able to take
more. That is why the Christians won't have women clergy.
Women are unbeatable. Ah, brother, wait till you're married. . . .
May I die.'

He raised his glass and took a gulp of beer. It was as though
he were at his own wake.

'Woman as a debater? Good heavens, no one can beat her
when she's really trying. I remember a story . . .'

He lit his pipe, his fat face seemed to become a shade fatter
Ash knew what sort of story was coming and chewed hard at
his pipe to keep his teeth together.

'It was the first woman student in the medical faculty at Oslo.
Must have been around 1908 or thereabouts. The idea of
women's emancipation naturally aroused no enthusiasm among
the professors of medicine. Women in medicine! The professor
in surgery felt his male dignity wounded. One day in his anat-
omy lecture he asked the girl to come up to the blackboard. He was going to teach her a lesson. You can picture her,
twenty years old, bashful, hair done on top of her head, wasp-
waisted and lace blouse buttoned up to her chin and skirt down
to her heels and high button-boots; you must also imagine the
hall crowded with male medical students wearing full beards;
in those days young men looked like their own grandfathers.
Modest and with downcast eyes the young girl stood there on
the cathedra; the male audience got a jolt when the professor
asked her to be good enough to take the chalk and draw on the
blackboard an outline of the male genitalia in profile.'

Doff turned away and looked through the café window. His
face had grown very puffy.

'The professor turned his back on the girl while she scraped away with the chalk. A strange commotion in the hall made the professor turn. He opened his eyes wide and saw that the maiden had drawn the male organ in the position of erection! He recovered himself more or less, told her that her drawing was highly unconventional.'

Doff cleared his throat and pursed his lips. Then he turned to Ash:

'Do you know what the lass replied?'

Ash did not dare say a word; he was clutching the edge of the table.

Doff yawned, a dark colour mantled his cheeks:

' "I am sorry if I have drawn it wrong, Professor, but that is the only way *I* have seen it," she said.'

When the traffic in the street started up again and Ash had pulled himself together (he was always to remember Doff's story-telling as the only utterly rewarding and liberating moments of that year), Doff became serious.

As serious as that night on the stairs, but this time not on his own account, but another's.

'Have you noticed how they all hang round her, the whole lot of them? And she is the kindest person in the world, she is—excuse the expression, you old heathen—she is a *saintly* person. The only one I have found among the whole crowd of wheelwrights and Stalinists.'

He looked menacingly at Ash.

'I have told them often that they must not abuse her hospitality; you would think they could see that the girl is overworked; but no, if anything turns up that has to be done, it is shoved on to her. They of course are too busy with their precious soulful, expensive studies; *they* haven't time to run round collecting subscriptions; *they* can't very well arrange accommodation at a youth hostel for these refugees from Spain, *they* can't go round with the refugees from the police to the immigration authorities, find them lodgings and work, give them clothes and shoes, how can *they* do all the dirty work? They who are so importantly occupied working out equations for cyclones or compiling statistics of the incidence of lice on Norwegian cows or mapping the bottom of the dead end of a fjord or writing an unreadable treatise on the symbolism of Ibsen's *The Wild Duck.*' He looked angrily at Ash. 'She's always there, she never says no. Because she's such a saint she always has the honour of doing all the work for the rest of you.'

Ash gulped.

'I've told them, time and again, that when a meeting is over, it's over. She happens to run a *business* too. But do you think that prevents them sitting on into the small hours killing her with their talk of the difference between tactics and strategy and the right time to assume power? They crash in on her at any old time in the forenoon, in the afternoon, they ring her up in the middle of the night and ask if they can come along and bring a bottle with them.'

Doff looked really angry, the veins in his forehead were swollen.

'You people use her as a doormat, message boy, washer-woman, you blow your noses on her towels and piss in her bath-room, you drink her tea and eat her cakes. Do any of you ever think what it must cost her? Do you think her parents are million-aires? Let me tell you, the girl has had an overdraft at the bank since she started the workshop; at Christmas she had to borrow another two hundred crowns to pay her grocer's bill! Which of you thinks of money? Money? A concept for grocers and petit bourgeois! A genuine socialist is only concerned with theory and pure science; he leaves it to the women to get the money.

Doff spat; he was tremendously worked up:

'Unless someone teaches that girl how to say no, don't be sur-prised if the next time she gets up at a meeting to say anything, she spews blood all over the table. To me she was ripe for hos-pital long ago—Department of Internal Medicine.'

Ash felt like a whipped dog. Doff realized his feeling and laid a huge, ponderous hand on his arm.

'Let me do as the Danish clergyman did when he saw that he had frightened his congregation out of their wits with his brim-stone sermon on hell, and say: "Don't take it too much to heart, dear parishioners, it isn't necessarily true." '

Nevertheless, at the next meeting Ash proposed with a firmness that surprised himself, that they should all leave the meeting in a body, he was sure she needed a good night's sleep like anybody else.

She smiled and protested, but the others took the hint. As they went, he noticed how they had muddied the floor, should he . . . ? Well, perhaps it would be misunderstood. One of them had already remarked that Ash-Lad seemed to be setting himself up as her knight.

'Red Knight' he had said, quite fatuously, quite pointlessly; and instantly Ash's cheeks had assumed the colour of that fatuous fairytale knight.

As they walked back through the streets Ash had a strange feeling that when they parted company one of them would sneak back and knock on her door and tell her how forlorn he was and ask if he might not come in and sit for a while, and he could distinctly hear her good, warm voice: 'But you know you can!'

He looked round at the others, with narrowed eyes. Which of them could it be? He felt sure that there was a sneak and snake-in-the-grass among them; but he saw nothing in any of their faces to support his suspicions.

The girl at the Stable.
The blue armchair.

When Ash was the one giving the introductory talk that preceded the evening's discussion, he would be stiff with fright when he came to the meeting. He would have read miles of print, made thousands of notes, written a whole treatise; if he had read all that he had written, they would have had to sit listening for four hours, whereas the introductory talk was supposed to last fifteen minutes at the most.

He placed his enormous bundle of notes on the table beside him, gulped, realized the impossibility of reading even a bit of the elephantine opus he had produced and threw up the sponge. He could feel nervous perspiration eating at his armpits like formic acid. Dejectedly he picked up Erling Falk's *What is Marxism?*, found his chapter and read straight from the book. He read in a hard, cold voice, hoping most profoundly that he was the only one who could smell the hot smell of formic acid. Some of them no doubt thought him a bit supercilious.

What a relief it was to be able to listen to the girl with the nut-brown hair and the azure eyes. When she gave the talk, she created an atmosphere of warmth and ease from the very beginning. She excused herself for being so badly prepared, but one of her girls in the studio had tripped when carrying a stack of wet clay figures and had gone flat on her face on the floor, like this; she stretched her arms out in front of her and spread her fingers like a frog putting on the brake in the water and at the same time thrust her head upwards and back, let her jaw drop and said 'Flop!' and it was so ridiculously life-like that they all laughed till they cried, and so did she; with tears streaming down her face she told them it had taken them two hours to clear up, the studio had looked as though a fire ball had done a war dance there, teehee (she pressed her handkerchief to her eyes, teehee, biting her lips and quite helpless with laughter), they were all lying across the table sobbing with laughter. So they would understand that she wasn't as well prepared as she might have been. But if they would help her to get going...

She was a wonder.

Her hands spoke for her. Often she did not complete a sentence, as though to do so would have been trite; the premises having been given, the conclusion must follow, one wasn't an idiot. She said: 'Like that, you know' and gestured with her hand out into space, letting her fingers trip up the ladder of thought; it reminded you of a squirrel flashing up a branch and disappearing with a light bound into the next tree, it was comic and unbelievably illustrative. In that way lists of kings and zoological epochs and series of arguments and whole sections of Marx went rolling wordlessly off her fingers into the air, and they sat staring at the words she had conjured up. She was a wonder, a quiet, smiling wonder, she had a gospel in her forearms.

There were a couple of other girls in the Group and he had gone for them first. One was fair and had a smile so pure and clean that she seemed to be freshly scrubbed; there was nothing to her. The other was dark and tall; she had a Tahitian face

and used a deep pink lipstick; she was heavy to dance with and
difficult to talk to; he never managed to get a sensible word
out of her and quickly lost interest in her too. Then there were
two elderly women schoolmistresses, who were serious and sober
and grey-haired, and there was Poppi. Then there were the
wives of the zoologists and meteorologists and philologists and
Doff's wife and Stabell's wife; but they had the embarrassing
habit of talking of broth and baby powder while their husbands
discussed ground-rent in the capitalist society. If the husbands'
voices were raised, you could not hear what the wives were
whispering. If there was a pause in the debate, the women lowered their voices further. But there was one memorable occasion
when a speaker stopped after quoting figures to show how the
value of a site in a city increased even if the owner slept; in
this chance pause one of the knitting wives was heard to say in
a clear voice:

'To knit stockings for children costs you *twenty* øre a yard.'

The gathering sat as though turned into stone, looking at the
woman who had spoken. It was the most painful and oppressive
pause in the history of the Group and heaven only knows what
the end would have been, if the Girl of the Stable had not mur-
mured in a gentle, conciliatory voice:

'As Storm Petersen said: it takes strength of character to sell
elastic by the yard.'

Her enormous eyes gave a succession of frightened blinks;
she and what she had said were incredibly comical and there
was a roar of laughter, you could hear Ash the elk, Doff the
camel and Stabell the shrill stallion, the Socialist Student's Group
roared and roared so that whitewash and cobweb and dust
trickled down from the beams in the roof.

Ash was calm, quiet and respectful in her presence. She had
become for him the epitome of warmheartedness, goodness, self-
sacrifice, fair play, grace, culture, grit; she was remote and belonged to another world. It was as belonging to this other world
that he wanted to think of her, and he felt a gust of inexplicable
irritation every time he was aware of her as a young woman
and a very shapely one at that. There were moments when he
did not like the lipstick on her lips, the varnish on her nails, her
bare forearms, her necklaces, ear-clips. Of course: it was so

right and pretty, but it was just that at such times it was so difficult for him to think clearly and properly about the abstract
socialistic future of the world. His mind was most at ease when
she was wearing a frock or a blouse and skirt; unfortunately
she loved pullovers and sweaters. Sometimes she sat next to him
at the long table; and then if she happened to bend forward over
the table to draw something on her block and her mature,
pretty bosom touched the table-top a slight, confusing electric
thrill would go through Ash. Angrily he composed an instruction
book: 'ABC for socialist girls wishing to dress intelligently.'

She attracted him, but in an unreal, tender way. To him and
to all men she was so open, so disarmingly open. He remembered
one of the first times he had spoken to her properly and
been aware of her. He had come to a meeting at the Stable and
arrived rather early. She came to the door and greeted him, her
hand was small, but strong in his, her face wonderfully open,
cool and warm at the same time: 'Hullo, it's you, Ash! Come in,
come in and get yourself a cushion!' For a second they had
stood and looked each other in the face, smiling, for a fleeting
moment he had felt—without seeing—that her shirt-blouse was
open at the neck, that she had big collar-bones, that the skin on
her neck and chest and arms was browner and more healthy
than that on her flowerlike face, he had sensed the cleft in her
bosom beneath the V of her blouse and had thought: she is so
indecently ingenuous, so indecently pure, she feels neither fear
nor guilt: if I was as open as she, I could this moment lay my
hand on her bare collar-bone; I could; if she were not so open
and so pure.

She made him restless. That nettled him. It annoyed him
that he was annoyed when any of the other men spoke to her
in low intimate tones, pulled her hair, clapped her on the backside; after one meeting, one of them, in a rush of enthusiasm,
had thrust her down on one of the creaking sofas in the living-
room and said: 'Now you're jolly well going to have a kiss!'
They all laughed, she did too, so did Ash, but he had to look
away when the kiss was given. It irritated him too to see how
Fiffolo hovered round her. Once Fiffolo put his hand on her arm,
spoke smilingly and persuasively to her, perhaps suggesting

going on somewhere for a party; she smiled and shook her head, but he continued his persuasions, must have said something irresistibly funny, for she burst out laughing; then Fiffolo went up close and whispered into her ear, and Ash knew the sort of thing Fiffolo whispered into people's ears, he saw her face inflate with delighted laughter; Fiffolo took a short step back to observe the effect of what he had said, she bit her lip and had to wipe the tears from her eyes; of course, Fiffolo was a tremendously amusing person, but there are things one does not say to a saint. And—this figures in every young person's philosophy—there are things at which a saint does not laugh.

The first time he thought about her name it was like a mysterious, incomprehensible little kick in his belly.

He told himself that he was not superstitious. When he was sixteen he had bet that he would spend a whole night in the cathedral, the old Gothic cathedral, in a sleeping bag on the high altar. He had demanded fifty crowns for this, but none of his school friends had been able to raise such an enormous sum. So Ash did not know what it was like to lie alone in an empty church on the altar listening to the clock striking twelve.

This, however, had nothing to do with Christianity. It was the story of the creation such as the heathen Vikings had imagined it that suddenly came back to him. The heat of the streams of air from Muspellsheim melted the ice in Nivlheim; out of that fecund stream arose the first being, the giant Yme; he had a cow, Audhumbla, whose milk he drank. Audhumbla conjured up more life by licking the ice-covered salt-stones; thus Borr was born and his sons who became the gods Odin, Vilje and Ve. The gods killed the giant Yme and made the world out of his corpse; thus Yme's body became the earth, his bones its mountains and stones, his hair became trees and grass, his skull the vault of the heavens, his blood the sea, his brain the clouds and the maggots in his body the little dwarfs that lived underground.

Then the gods created the first two people.

Were they made out of two trees? Perhaps. But they were found on the sea shore, lying lifeless in the wet sand, without breath, without soul and without blood. Odin gave them breath, Vilje gave them souls, and Ve gave them blood and colour. Did the cow Audhumbla lift her muzzle from the salt-stones and low when the first people sat up newborn in the sand and rubbed their eyes?

Those two on the shore.

The first two people: their names were Ash and Embla.

A Gay Deceiver

Afterwards, it was impossible for him to remember how he had started it, or perhaps it was she who had done so. He must have smiled to her when he was in the rector's ante-room, and she must have smiled back; perhaps it was he who invited her to a film, or she who happened to have two tickets for a concert. There had been a little tingling of the skin with both of them, at any rate with him; this chubby office girl with tiny freckles on the chin of her healthy face and her incredibly Norwegian tip-tilted nose, this chubby, rather knock-kneed Synnoeve with her square mouth and white Norwegian teeth, was like a ripe apple on a branch: smiling, the apple asked: 'Will you pick me?' After the film (or the concert) they were walking along and he stopped by chance and pointed to a house, 'That's where I live,' said he and they walked on, and they were standing on the steps and she looked at him with grey, expressionless eyes, and said: 'I know that you are a decent person,' and he said 'Of course,' and she said: 'If I come up with you, can I trust you?' and he 'of course' and they went up to his room and he took off her overcoat and there was a smell of apples from her soft, chubby body, and he stood her against the edge of the writing table, and all the while he was unbuttoning her blouse, she kept her gaze fixed on a point below his left eye, unwaveringly; he took off her blouse and her bra; she kept her eyes fixed intently on the point under his left eye, while he stood and with spread fingers stroked her big, lovely milk-white breasts; her nipples were very small and sweet and the colour of a kitten's tongue.

Later he was to think back with wonder to Synnoeve and

the short time they were together. She was the first woman with whom he had felt utterly free. This was because from the very first moment each deceived the other!

If ever Ash had been with a complete bourgeoise it was her. All she thought of or talked about was nice furniture, nice behaviour, marriage with a nice white wedding in church; her only reading was *Every Woman's Own* and *Love Story Magazine*; when—towards the end of their acquaintance—he happened to let slip that he belonged to the Students' Socialist Group she gasped in horror; her own belief was in mahogany for the dining-room. (She told him once that her father was a clerk at the Town Hall. 'In what department?' Ash asked. 'Refuse,' she said and looked at him angrily.)

Just as Ash was after her marzipan body, she was only after a future head of department, manager, director or banker. There was never any shy whispering between them; never a tender caress. He understood that there would be no reproaches if he did not propose and lead her to the altar; it would be quite enough for her if he introduced her to the great world; actually she would be satisfied if he would take her as his partner to one of the dances or balls at the College; she had never been there, that was her great dream. 'Yes,' said Ash, 'I'll take you one Saturday.' He lied to her, openly and frankly.

He had never met anyone with such duality of character. The two halves of her mind acted quite independently of each other. She was puritanical and easily offended where other girls were concerned, spoke with tight lips of those who led immoral Bohemian lives and thus undermined social morality; and as she was actually saying this, she undressed and stretched out naked on Ash's divan; like a gust from her other world came an earnest request not to gossip about her to the others at the College. Then she closed her eyes and let herself be covered. Always it was as though in some strange way she got herself to believe that it was not happening, or that it was happening in an *Every Woman's Own* world, that she was on her nuptial couch with a university professor; Ash had never come across such self-deception; he enjoyed her enormously while it lasted, there was no timidity about her.

If she did not undress herself, he did it for her; she was stark

naked every time. He had never seen anything so soft and milk-
white and chubby. The sexual act gave her a glow, but apparently no release; he could be slow or quick just as it suited him;
and it made his enjoyment even greater to know that when she
was sitting she was gazing the whole time with veiled eyes at
the calendar on the wall counting how many days there were
to the next College dance. But mostly they lay on the divan.
She was milky-white and chubby and even when lying with
expressionless eyes and her mind firmly anchored in her *Every
Woman's Own* world, she was efficient and orderly; she took
hold of him with her right hand, herself with her left, like a typist
carefully putting the sheets into a typewriter, then settled
herself contentedly and during the rest of the proceedings lay
with a faint smile on her face dreaming that Sir John was wooing
the young office girl Gladys; when it was over, she came to life,
raised her head and looked to see that there had been no acci-
dent, then satisfied, nodding like an accountant who has just
checked the list of assets and found it correct, let her head sink
back, smiled an absent, satisfied smile and muttered:

'Will you take me to the College dance on Saturday?'

And he, still in the shaking afterpains of desire:

'S-s-sure I will.'

But he never took her to any dance, and finally a sort of chilli-
ness came over her, as though she sensed that she was wasting
her time. Their affair lasted a good two weeks. On the last Saturday, when they were up in his room instead of at the College
dance, they agreed to go for a tramp in the mountains together
the next day. They were to meet at a certain street corner at
ten o'clock the next morning. When he was back in his own
bed, alone, he picked up his alarm clock to set it. First he put the
pointer to nine; then a thoughtful expression came over his
face, turned into a smile, and he moved the pointer on till it
was at eleven. He knew that he slept like a stone and never woke
before the alarm went off. Gaily, his heart smilingly serene and
his conscience at peace, he turned over, put out the light and
fell asleep like a child that has spent a long and happy day in
its sand pit.

He was awakened on Sunday morning by a peculiar, noisy,
crackling rain of sparks falling over his bed. Dazed, bewildered,

his heart thumping, he sat up, hair tousled and eyes bricked up with sleep. The rain of sparks had come from the door. He rubbed his eyes, the room was in semi-darkness, it was only after a while that he saw that the door was half open and in the opening—on the threshold—stood Synnoeve.

'Is that y-you? Well, good morning! How—er—who let you in?'

'The landlady's son. I said I wanted to see you. He told me I could go in. *Do you know what the time is?*'

'No. What is it?'

'I have been standing there for over half an hour, three-quarters of an hour, waiting for you! Is that nice of you, do you think?'

'No, indeed no. I must have overslept. Come in. Don't stand there in the doorway.'

'With you lying in bed? What do you think I am? I shall wait in the hall till you're dressed.'

'In the hall? Good heavens, why there? I must have ten minutes, or a quarter of an hour, and I haven't eaten yet. And you want to stand out there in the hall!'

'You know perfectly well that I am not the sort of girl who goes into a student's room.'

'What? Yes, of course. I must have overslept.'

Then the alarm clock on his bedside table went off. Never had the ring of an alarm clock been more piercing or more of a give-away. He heaved himself over it and stuffed it under the bedclothes, but it was too late.

'Did you say you had overslept?'

He did not reply.

'You are not the gentleman I took you to be.'

He did not reply.

'You don't imagine we can carry on together after this?'

He did not reply. He turned his head towards her, got a last glimpse of her thick Norwegian lips that he had so often run his tongue over and her Norwegian freckled apple-face now red with irritation. She was standing there in long ski trousers and an anorak and had a kerchief round her head; the nostrils of her square turned-up Norwegian nose were white; for an instant he had an urge to jump out in his pyjamas and pull her into bed, but he let her go; this young man who otherwise was so sensitive and tender where women were concerned, so attached to the feminine, so mortally dependent on women, so afraid of hurting a woman that in none of his affairs had he been able to say stop, let Synnoeve go; she slammed the door behind her with such force and indignation that his violin banged against the wall and an ashtray fell to the floor. He heard her stump down the corridor and his only thought was: I wonder if dear Mrs. Abrahamsen witnessed all that; as far as Synnoeve was concerned, he was free and guiltless; one deceiver had gone, another was left lying in bed; he was so relieved, so gracelessly, heathenly relieved that he curled up and pulled the bedclothes over his head and laughed and laughed and laughed.

Does God Reckon People's Days or their Nights?

His affair with Wilhelmine came to an end too. It was one evening in March. She had come to his room as arranged. He was restless and gloomy, finding it difficult to talk with her. That evening, for some reason or other, she had not wanted to take off her raincoat; she sat down in it on the divan. He seated himself beside her. He took her hand, did not rightly know what to say, probably asked her what things had been like at the office the last week. Then, well of course, they were old friends and he sat with his arm round her shoulder, and he played a bit with the hair at her ear, and she curled up and snuggled into him and once again her hand came and tried to make its way in under his shirt-cuff. He would always remember that hand of hers, that evening the sensation was strong, like when a puppy blindly bores its nose into a person, wants to get into his clothes, into his armpit, into his lap, into his heart. He tried to take her coat off. She stopped him.

'I have the curse,' she said. She glanced up at him quickly, apologetically. 'Got it this morning. And you don't have a phone.'

'I see,' he said and took his hand away.

'That's why I didn't want to take my coat off,' she said.

'I see,' he said and swallowed.

'I didn't know if it made any difference to you,' she said, softly.

'I see,' he said, softly.

'Does it?'

'No,' he said. 'That is . . .' He did not know what to say. He did not feel any exaggerated aversion, it had happened before that his emotion had been so strong that it had not mattered to him; but—No, not with Wilhelmine. There had been so much already in their relationship that had jarred, things that he had not been able to tell her. And now, the curse, no.

'No,' he said.

Her hand came towards him, a puppy's nuzzling muzzle. She sank against him, beseeching:

'But you could, couldn't you?'

'No.' He felt like a drowning man, he had to clutch at something, he looked at his watch, twenty to nine, they could still get there if they ran. 'We'll go to a film.'

'It's so long since the last time.'

'No, we'll go to a film.'

'I want to so badly.' She had hidden her face and her voice was almost inaudible.

'We're going to a film.'

'But can't you—make it right for me?'

'No, I can't. Forgive me. Come, we'll go to a film.'

And that was the last time they talked together in his room, the last time. He telephoned to her once or twice after that, but they never met again.

And later, whenever he thought of Wilhelmine it was with a feeling that with her there was something that had been left unfinished and incomplete; he had had tenderness for her, they had been good to each other, and where sex was concerned they had been mute and honest; their first love-making in the autumn night beneath that apple tree had been spontaneous and without deceit, neither had asked about the other's intentions and two people cannot be franker with each other than that. But then there had been all the other things, her mute prayer that he rescue her from her grey life in her father's office, her mute prayer for recognition (in the form of marriage?), her tacit sympathy for Germany, Hitler's Germany. He had not been able to help her and he was always to feel that there he had failed her. All the more so as on their last evening he had repulsed her. Dimly he sensed that in having to beg him for sexual satisfaction, she had suffered a cruel defeat. A man who is repulsed by a woman suffers a defeat, but defeat is part of the hazard, he is grieved as a person, but not humiliated as a man. For a woman who asks for physical love and is refused, it must seem far more serious. She is not only grieved as a person, she is degraded as a woman. He came to think, with horror: she was wounded to the quick of her womanhood; she must have thought that I found her repulsive as a woman! He would have made up for it later, but the occasion never came.

Some years later, when war had long since come to the country and Norway was occupied by German troops, he ran into her in the street. They almost bumped into each other as she came out of a house. He looked up at the house and felt afraid. It was a large office building that had been requisitioned by the Germans. They greeted each other with a little smile, he asked how she was, what she was doing. Working in the office here, she said. Here? he said. She jerked her head slightly in the direction of the building and said: 'Security Police.' Well, did she like it there? Yes, she must say she did. Well, so long then, and so long, and there they parted, and when he got round the next corner he had a shivering fit, it was guilt and it was terror, for 'Security Police' was a fine way of saying Gestapo wasn't it? And he remembered her face when she told him where she worked, it had not been hard or superior, there had been something apologetic about her, as with a dog, it had been something in her brown eyes, and he was never able to decide where a person's guilt begins and where it ends.

Wilhelmine, who had sat one night on his balcony and watered the flowers. So submissive she had been afterwards. Those good nights with Wilhelmine. (Does God who is in heaven count people's days or their nights?)

The Boy who Hung from the Gutter

One sunny day in March he bumped into a man on the pavement. Ash was walking fast to get to a lecture on time. The collision was so violent that both their jaws shut with a painful snap, their hats jerked over their eyes and neither could see.

Norwegians have a word and incantation for such occasions which vents their anguish and puts the blame on the other person. It is a well-known and well-loved word, it can be barked out curtly or rendered drawn-out and beautiful. You can also keep it to yourself. The first thing Ash noticed about the other was his amazing ability to suppress that word, swiftly and neatly; as he stood with his eyes on the other's face he saw the desire to say that word drain away as though it had never existed in the other's heart; the man was all human kindness and gentle smile; Ash was amazed by the other's feat: was it piety or play-acting? Because for a moment he *had* seen the dark shadow of cursing fury in the man's eyes. Hadn't he?

All this took place in less than a second. And when, instead of hitting him, the man laid firm and affectionate hold of him, Ash felt alarm and sickening repugnance.

The man held him gently and gaily by the upper part of the arm, held him a little way off, looked at him with smiling, cordial, brown eyes and said with a mixture of genuine surprise and profound joy: '*Ash!*'

In that first instant Ash did not recognize him, though he knew that he had seen that firm, calm, ruddy, sunburned face before, knew that once earlier in his life he had looked into those deep, brown, knowing, persuasive eyes.

Then he remembered.

He felt a stab of profound and sickening repulsion. He wished most heartily that he could just raise his hat and walk on, but that would have been discourteous, and besides it would give the man the triumph of assuming that he—Ash—was a coward.

The man into whom he had barged was from the Oxford Group. He had met him at a house-party in his native town a few years before, while he was still at school. This busy, healthy, energetic man had in some mysterious way been after Ash the whole time, that at least is what Ash had felt; the man had kept trying to draw Ash aside, had chatted with him in a quiet and friendly way, praised his intelligence, there had been one moment when they were standing alone together in an entrance hall and Ash could remember how his shoes had sunk into a soft and expensive carpet, there had been a silence and the man, smiling, had asked in a low, calm voice: 'And you, Ash, how do *you* stand with God?'

Suddenly it all came back to him, he saw the hall, the performance, the people. He remembered the faces of the young men who stood up in front and confessed their sins, they were Norwegians and Americans, mostly young. There was something stuffy and frightening and comical about this memory; the faces of the youths as they stood up and confessed, their shining faces, they all threw back a lock or two of fair hair, and they trotted out their confessions like a lesson learned off by heart; they all began with the phrase: 'When I first came in contact with the Oxford Group . . .' Was it all carefully stage-managed? 'When I first came in contact with the Oxford Group . . .' Ash could not remember what followed, but it was probably '. . . I was a sinner.' He only remembered the way the youths got to their feet, half proud, half ingratiating, all the time smiling a bright, good-boy, slightly wry smile. What had these young sinners done? It was their deeds more than anything else that gave Ash the feeling of having got on to the wrong planet. One had stolen apples from his neighbour's garden when he was a boy (had even filled his baggy plus-fours with them!—a proud half-horrified smile slid across the faces of the audience); one had borrowed a stamp collection from a friend and 'forgotten' (subdued, satisfied laughter from the other members of the Group) to give it back; another had hardened his heart against a friend and hated him, until he was 'changed'; then in the quiet hour one morning God had told him to go and see his friend and ask his forgiveness, and he had done this (the members nodded and smiled happily); another had stolen money from his father's pocket-book and used it to go on the spree, but now he had told his father about it. (And this was so exciting that the leader of the meeting interrupted):

'Tell them, Bill, tell them how your father reacted!'

'Well, of course the old man got terribly mad, you know, and threatened to beat the living daylights out of me. . . .'

Subdued, satisfied laughter in the hall.

'That is (translating to the company) Bill's father was dreadfully angry and threatened to give him a good thrashing. But now both Bill and his father are changed.' (To Bill): 'But now your father is changed too, isn't he, Bill? Tell them!'

'Yes.'

'And most of the workers at your father's plant are changed, too, aren't they, Bill? Tell them!'

'Yes.'

'And no strikes any more? No more disputes about wages? Everybody is content? Tell them, Bill!'

'Yes.'

'And all because Bill and his father found the way to God, because they have learned to live in absolute love, absolute honesty, absolute unselfishness and absolute purity. Thank you, Bill.'

And Ash remembered the man (Robert Seeberg was his name), this stocky, energetic, mild, good man with the athletic bearing and frank, affectionate eyes, the man with the pocket New Testament in English; he remembered, too, something Seeberg had told them at that house-party about some young people from the Workers' Youth Movement whom he had been meeting; he had talked with these young socialists and he said: 'Unfortunately I have to tell you that there my words had no effect; they are uncomfortably intelligent these young socialists, we must realize that. Also we must arm ourselves with arguments, we must become as clever and sharp as they!'

And now, as they stood facing each other in the street two years later, Ash had himself become a member of a socialist organization, was one of the 'uncomfortably intelligent', and Robert Seeberg did not know it. There was something strongly and ingratiatingly masculine about this Robert Seeberg; he might have been about thirty, he reminded you of an athletic member of the carefree upper classes. He always looked as though he had just come back from riding or playing tennis, well-dressed, jovial, robust, glowing with health and cleanliness, yet with an undertone of something deep, fascinating yet over-bearing. Ash had a moment's recollection of something bestial from his boyhood, of a setter they used to play with; this setter had a habit of making mating movements on the boys' knees; queer and amusing at first, it became frightening when the dog would not let itself be shooed away; the clasp of the fore-legs, the movements of the dog's body, its panting breath, the impos-sibility of getting rid of it, the game that had turned into its loathsome opposite, and he had never known when the trans-formation took place or the reason for it, and that is the dark unfathomable secret of all relationships, even those between people and animals; the transition that none can comprehend.

'Ash!' said the man, and his handsome face radiated cordi-ality. 'Ash! Fancy meeting you!'

The man took a step back to get a better look at the younger man. Ash could have died of relief when the other let go of him.

'I've thought about you such a lot! Of all those I met that time, there is no one I've thought so much about as you. I wonder how Ash is, I've thought, what he's doing. But I didn't have your address, you know. And besides, I've spent over a year in America.'

Ash writhed. Instantly and with searing intensity he had seen through the technique. He had himself read Dale Carnegie's *How to win Friends and Influence People*—it was required reading for the theory of advertising—success in all friend-winning is based on emphasizing to the other that he means something, that he is the one person you have been looking forward to seeing; that of all the people in the world he is the one in whom you have the most burning interest, the only one in the world on whom you can rely, the only one who can carry out the most noble mission in the world. . . . Ash's intelligence told him all that as he stood facing the other; with his intelli-gence he saw right through Robert Seeberg and his American way of fishing for men; and yet . . . there was no doubt that the man was upright and genuine, against his will he could not help feeling a waft of genuine warmth. No other person had spoken to him in this way all that year; he had been alone, mortally alone, in this strange town, bitterly alone. . . .

'Each time I've thought of you, I've said to myself: There was something in Ash. You were one of the best, Ash. You're one of those who will do great things. I have really missed you, Ash.'

And as Ash heard that a wild glow coursed through him. There was vast promise in those words, the unfading dream of greatness and fame, he had to clutch at his throat to keep himself from crying out, a wave of warm, wonderful, thankful triumph rose up in him. . . .

'I know what we'll do,' Robert said, laying one hand on Ash's arm. 'I'm staying at the Grand. You and I will have lunch together there today. You're my guest.'

Ash had never been inside the Grand. He was dimly aware that Robert had an ulterior motive, that this was not just an invitation to lunch, but he hadn't had a decent meal for several days and he was still borne along by the warm wonderful wave of hope and belief; at this moment he was triumphantly on the crest and it fitted in perfectly with his picture of himself in the future that he should now be going to dine at the Grand: chicken, browned roast chicken; a man who was Oxford Group and who could stay at the Grand could obviously also afford to stand him a majestic meal: soup first, strong soup, oxtail soup, yes, ye gods, and then golden-skinned tender chicken and vegetables, asparagus, heavens above, perhaps a place like the Grand could also produce a salad even if it was March; and then for dessert, let me see, that had better be caramel pudding with whipped cream; he was reeling with under-nourishment and hunger, he couldn't talk for saliva, was almost choked by his own spittle, blessed be the Oxford Group; for such a dinner he would say and promise all that Robert wanted, he would gladly believe in all the four absolutes, he would swear his soul away to four hundred absolutes. . . .

So they walked on, strolled on down the street and Ash had long since written off the lecture he was supposed to be attending, and then Robert asked him where he lived and Ash told him, and Robert asked if he would show him his room, and Ash did not like the idea, but could think of no excuse, there was something about Robert that alarmed him, Robert was a mysterious lie-detector or rather alarm-detector. The only thing was to pretend to be unconcerned and they walked up the stairs and into Mrs. Abrahamsen's long hall and into Ash's room, and Robert looked round and said, smiling:

'What a nice place you have!'

Ash could not deny that. Then they took their things off and sat down, and Robert talked about his travels in Norway and America, and declined smilingly when Ash offered him a cigarette; and they sat there for a quarter of an hour or twenty minutes and Ash found it most oppressive and in the end Robert worked round to Ash's personal affairs and then Ash had to get up and take a turn about the floor, and Robert asked in a low, calm voice:

'Ash, do you masturbate?'

Ash halted, a sickening sensation came over him; it was horror and repugnance, but mostly it was a feeling of shame on the other's behalf; good Lord, so it was true, that was the question they fired off sooner or later at every possible convert. For an instant he considered whether just to shrug his shoulders and let the question go unanswered; young boys can ask each other such questions in order to learn about life; but when a grown man does so. . . . All at once he decided to accept the challenge; quietly he turned to Robert and in a clear voice said:

'Of course. *Don't you?*'

Robert gave a start, almost imperceptible, then again he was urbane, benevolent, understanding.

'Ash, you have a wonderfully healthy way of saying it. You know,' he had got to his feet and laid a hand on the younger man's shoulder, 'you know, I have a great liking for you? You are honest. You don't cheat.'

Ash bit his lip. That was a brilliant manœuvre. It had given Robert the upper hand again.

'Do you often go with girls?' he asked, quietly.

Ash sighed, he noticed that his breathing trembled slightly. Ash said:

'As often as I can.'

He took a step towards the divan, put his hand on it and said:

'But unfortunately I have to take my landlady into account. The divan creaks so abominably. Listen.' He pressed the springs up and down and looked at Robert.

'Ash, Ash,' said Robert. 'There's no getting away from it: you're certainly honest.'

'Hm,' said Ash.

'Is there one girl whom you are going to marry?' Robert asked.

Ash shook his head. Without realizing it, he sighed again.

'Do you go with different girls?'

Again Ash sighed; the conversation was no longer funny, he felt tired.

'Well,' he said, 'some three or four thousand.'

Again Robert gave a start, almost imperceptible; then he smiled at Ash. Ash did not like that smile. A preacher ought to condemn sex; there is something dangerous about a preacher who stands and smiles at erotic cock-and-bull stories.

'But,' said Robert, 'does it never occur to you that you are sinning against these girls?'

'Sinning?' This hit Ash in his midriff. Robert was now dangerously near his tender spot.

'Perhaps you don't mean any harm.'

'No,' said Ash, and in a fit of sardonic humour that made him grin with relief, 'I mean well by every single one of them!'

Robert smiled; it was as though he appreciated this smart man-to-man retort; Ash felt suddenly furious. Then changing his voice, Robert said:

'But do you never think of the girls? That they have to go on in life? Does it never strike you that you are just making use of them, and afterwards you don't bother about them. What sort of future is it you are giving your girls? You forget that you have a responsibility, Ash.'

And Robert said that to the young man Ash, this youth who was crushed beneath a mountain of duties and responsibilities; Ash felt how disgraceful it was of the other to say that, but now he was unable to put his thoughts into words; like a drowning man he grasped at a straw; desperate, he counter-attacked:

'But you,' he said to Robert, 'how do you manage? Do *you* never go with women?'

'God helps me, Ash.'

'Hm. Don't you even dream?'

'Not any longer.'

'Have you never been with a girl?'

There was a pause. Ash could see that he had asked a question that the other was going to have to answer, that Robert could not get round his own requirement for honesty, and he was excited, there was no denying it.

'Yes,' Robert said in a low voice.

It became quite quiet in the room. Suddenly Ash felt sorry for the other. Robert's voice came to him as though from far away:

'I was a young student then. I was even studying theology. But I was wicked in my heart. I once did something appalling to a girl. You cannot imagine how I befouled her. I think that I have received forgiveness from God, but I cannot be sure. Oh, Ash . . .' He turned to the young man and Ash was trembling, with excitement and agitation; what dreadful thing could the man have done? He thought that now he was going to hear of one of the most ghastly crimes in world history, he stuttered, clenched his fists to control himself:

'What d-d-did you d-do?'

'Oh, Ash. I was so wicked. I shall never forget it. I . . .'

'Y-yes?'

'Do you know what I did to her?'

'N-n-o!'

'I . . .' He lowered his voice, turned half way, clasped his hands. 'I . . .'

'Yes?'

'I got her to . . . . use her mouth.'

Slowly he turned his head and looked at Ash; his gaze was partly pleading, partly searching to discover the effect his confession had had on the young man.

Ash was paralysed; he had to stamp his foot on the floor to get his breath and circulation back again. Then he was seized by a fit of hysterical sobbing, morbid laughter, and had to sit down on the sofa. He had expected the most revolting act of violence in the world and then this. . . . There was something so childish about Robert's story; good heavens! Ash knew what sin was, but he also knew what sin was not. There had never been any sin in the most intimate and tenderest of caresses a man and woman could give each other, never!—and here was this grown man who had been going about all these years with the most violent sin-complex all because of a caress! Because of something over which he ought to have rejoiced to high heaven! For a moment he stopped his fearful laughter and looked at Robert, a suspicion cut through him : Perhaps Robert had *forced* the girl to do it? That, of course, would be a very different matter. There were worse things; indeed, there were.... He, Ash, knew of worse things. It was not a sin to love a woman, but it could be a sin not to love her. There were things in the world worse than the things one did; the cruellest things in the world were the things a man did *not* do. And he, Ash, knew that. All at once it seemed to him that Robert was the greatest cry-baby he had ever met in his life, mentally Robert was an overgrown baby.

'Come,' he said and got up from the sofa, 'let's go.'

'Where?' Robert said, surprised and rather disappointed.

'Didn't you invite me to lunch? It's nearly two.'

And they came to the Grand and sat down in the big half-empty dining-room, and Ash quivered slightly because it seemed so expensive and smart, and then the waiter came with the menu and Robert looked at it.

'Every time I come to this town,' Robert said, 'I have boiled cod. Won't you have some too? Fresh cod, I know nothing nicer. Freshly caught, you won't get it so fine anywhere else in the country.'

He had handed the menu back to the waiter, and Ash was his guest, and also diffident; of course, cod is a fine fish, a delicacy, especially when it is so fresh that the flesh is chalky white and has white muscle-knots in it, but when you're a student and get cod three times a week at the students' restaurant, and when you've been promising yourself golden-brown roast chicken.... Perhaps it was all nonsense about there being American millionaires behind the Oxford Group, perhaps Robert Seeberg was just an ordinary businessman. . . . Ah, well, goodbye oxtail soup, goodbye caramel pudding.

They had cod, good cod, excellent cod, superb cod. As sweet

they had sago pudding with a red sauce. And the forks and
knives and spoons, of course, were elegant and lay heavily in
one's hand and no doubt were silver. And the tablecloth was
very white and freshly ironed. And there were flowers on the
table too, two carnations in a tall vase. Yes, it was an elegant
meal none the less.

'Would you come up to my room for a bit?' Robert said afterwards.

Ash made excuses, he had things to write, a lot to do.

'Ash,' said Robert looking at him with frank, calm eyes, and
Ash felt secretly afraid and secretly furious, 'you're not afraid,
are you?'

'Afraid?'

'It could be that God has something to say to you.'

A shiver oozed up Ash's spine; he remembered the time he
bet that he could spend a night in the cathedral, sleep on the
high altar; heavy with alarm and hate, he got to his feet and
said:

'For a little while, then.'

The little while in Robert's room became an hour, became
two hours; Ash did not know why, but he could not find a decent
excuse for leaving, for escaping. Robert had been speaking the
whole time in a quiet voice, polite, gentle, persuasive, tireless;
it was as if there were more strength in Robert than in Ash. Ash
felt the need for a nap; he was sitting in a deep leather armchair
but could not relax, he wished most heartily that he could go
and stretch out on the sofa. But he didn't, he didn't want in-
timacy, to start a friendship with Robert; it is only among
friends that you go and lie down on another man's bed. The
feeling of having bits of cod between his teeth contributed to
his drowsiness and slackness, but naturally he could not ask to
borrow the other's toothbrush, that would be to found a friendship for all time. And he was unhappy because he could find no
arguments to counter the other's attack on the times and people;
he sat there locked in the depths of an enormous leather armchair, tired and dispirited. He felt that the other was ringing
him in, yet he could not fight back; his only defence would be
to be downright impertinent—if he could muster up the cour-

age—to curse and bawl, yet all the time there was something profoundly honest, honourable, cordial, genuine about Robert and Ash had never learned the art of hurting people, at any rate not those who take their faith seriously.

At that moment he was pitiably aware that his greatest weakness was weakness, his lack of ability to thrust his own troops forward and take the offensive; he felt a genuine desire to hear what Robert had to say, to try and understand him and his Oxford Group, and his understanding and sympathy made him —as so often before in his life—go much too far; he had already caught himself a number of times nodding at what Robert said, had said that yes, he agreed: no, he had no definite ·beliefs; no, he wasn't entirely happy; no, he had not found himself; yes, it was a wicked world we lived in; yes, there was something he longed for and which he couldn't explain; no, he didn't think that girls and money and success were the road to happiness; yes, he had often felt a rotter. 'You are afraid, Ash,' Robert said in a low voice. 'No,' Ash replied. 'Yes,' said Robert. 'No,' said Ash. (And it was not till many years later that Ash made the discovery, the only one of value in life, that only he who can admit his fear can master it. Had he known that then, he could have said to Robert: 'Yes. I am afraid. I am afraid to continue this discussion with you; everyone is afraid of the unknown; you know that, you can play on one's fear of being afraid, but I am brave because I dare say that I am afraid; I have the courage that is required to take to flight; therefore you cannot hit me; I am already as afraid as you want to make me; we'll stop this conversation; you go to your security with God, I'll go to uncertainty with myself; thanks for the chat and the lunch.')

But he sat there and did not know what to do; on the face of it, all Robert said was correct and incontrovertible, and in the end Ash hid his face in his hands. He felt strangely forlorn, and why should he contradict this nice Robert who had stood him a lunch? He might as well give him the pleasure of listening to his little sermon, especially as Robert was an educated and cultured man, no fire-and-brimstone ranter. And Robert came closer and closer with his God, and Ash felt afraid with a nameless fear, the fear one never experiences when awake, but only in dreams, in nightmares; it was as though deep within his body was a creature with tentacles that now wanted to drag him down, half forgotten fears, a feeling of terror and gloom.

(He did not know it then, but was to remember later, how a woman in his childhood had made God into a dark being who saw everything, everything, and the Devil into one who always stood behind him, behind him, and how the boy went to his mother's dressing table and looked at himself in the mirror, but there was no Devil there then, for the Devil cannot be seen in a mirror yet was always behind him, and the boy spun round, time and again, to get a glimpse of the Devil, but never saw him, and never saw him behind other people's backs either. Hidden, forgotten, half-forgotten, yet the shadows of God and the Devil had followed him, the dark shadow had followed him all his life. Was he not a young man with a fear of the police; did he not often stop short in inexplicable fear that a black-gloved hand was about to be laid on his shoulder from behind? God? This thundercloud of bad conscience and oppressive guilt, of inadequacy and weakness; God who is everything, *sees* everything, especially lust?

And then a dark tentacle emerged from the depths, confirmation; he had not wanted to be confirmed, but had not been able to stand up to his mother's tearful pleading: all decent boys were confirmed, he must do it for her sake, and he must think of his soul; he had even let her threaten and cajole him into taking communion afterwards, he had wept with repugnance and talked wildly about cannibalism, but if he did not go up to the altar she did not know what she would do, he must not shame her, and along with the crowd of the others he had marched up to the altar, knelt on the crescent-shaped stool, he had felt like a circus horse kneeling on the edge of the ring and doing tricks; the clergyman had laid a thin bit of biscuit on his tongue and said that it was Christ's body, and he had filled a little silver beaker with raspberry juice and said that that was Christ's blood, and there had been a far-away, businesslike look in the clergyman's eyes and he asked the young lad absently if he would forswear the Devil and all his works and the boy had contorted his face into a cynical grimace and said that he would, and after that the boy had looked across at the others being confirmed and snickered, but the ceremony had made a greater impression on him than he knew; he had forsworn the Devil, reluctantly but he had done it, and that is no small matter and a tremendous promise and an unfathomable mystery, and that night the boy had promised God that never again would he sinfully abuse himself, for if anything was the Devil, it must be that; he promised God that that night, promised it to God in his fifteenth year, and he managed to keep his promise for two days, and ever afterwards the man Ash had a burning hatred of all promises, of the Boy Scout's promise, the teetotaller's promise, promises at the altar and at a deathbed; the most disgraceful thing in the whole world is to exact a promise, even more disgraceful to give one.)

And it was as if the thirty-year-old, robust, healthy, nice Robert had noticed his fear and uncertainty and was coming nearer and nearer (could he not feel Robert's hot, healthy breath on his face now?), the quiet questions became more and more insistent and burning: these socialists he was with, were they happy?—no; these socialists he knew, were they all good people?—no; Robert had himself heard Francis Stabell speak in the Students' Society, had seen his furrowed brow and blinking eyes as he prepared a retort. Would Ash say that Francis Stabell was a good and happy person, a person without hate?—no. 'Then look round about you, Ash, you who are so clever and have such rare abilities, look at the world, imagine how different everything could be, how true and filled with peace and goodness, if only people could be true and good, if only people were utterly truth-loving and honest, think of that Ash, imagine everyone everywhere being honest and fair to each other, imagine all the world's businessmen, you only need absolute honesty, absolute unselfishness, think of all the workers' leaders, honesty and truth, think of the new world, the wonderful world, think of all the lawyers, think if the law was as simple as absolute fairness, there you have the solution, Ash, I know that you see it now, you have laughed, but now you are there, the solution, Ash, the absolute solution of all torment and all doubt, just give me your hand, Ash. . . .'

And for a second as long as eternity Ash was hanging over the abyss of eternity; he was on the roof of an immensely tall house, he was slipping, he tried to shout but heard no sound, he had become dumb, he slipped down the ice-covered roof, this was the primeval dream, the most horrible of all dreams, he was slipping, had slipped over the edge, it was three hundred feet to the street, with one hand he got hold of the gutter, hung by one hand, beneath him was the emptiness of space, and Robert asked him: 'Do you believe, Ash?' and Ash got hold of the gutter with his other hand too, hung thus, suddenly the world of reality came back to him with cruel, paralysing clarity, the man Robert had slipped to the floor beside the chair where he was sitting, Robert had laid a hand on his knee, Robert asked, quietly persuasively:

'Ash, will you pray with me?'

And then the dream shivered, the boy in the dream made a gigantic effort, heaved himself up on his arms with the strength of a Titan; now he had the gutter under him, he had won, but could not believe it; the abyss was still there at his back. Ash staggered to his feet, his face was white and covered with sweat, 'No,' he said heavily.

And even then when he was on his feet, even when he had won his victory (over what?), even when he was standing looking down at Robert even when he stood feeling such repulsion for this man, a loathing so strong that he could distinctly see how Robert's face would look after his fist had smashed into it, even then he could not be discourteous, even then he could not wound Robert, he could only mutter:

'Not now.'

Robert had got to his feet. He sighed, but did not give up:

'Ring me up tomorrow then?'

'Yes.'

'Tomorrow's Saturday. I shall be here in the hotel all evening. Will you ring me at eight o'clock?'

'Yes.'

'I'm counting on you, you know.'

'Yes.'

And then in some mysterious way he got out of Robert's hotel room, out into the corridor, down in the splendid lift, out into the street, into the fresh air, and he knew that he would rather be drawn and quartered than ring Robert up on Saturday.

But that was a betrayal, for he had promised, yet for the time being he could only fill his lungs brimful with fresh air; heavens above, he had never been so near perdition before, it had been touch and go; what sort of person was he, just a thin membrane over a sea of horror, any idiot could come along and turn all his ideas upside down, where had his remarkable intelligence been those last two hours?

He trembled in alarm; he was so frightened that he did not even dare admit to himself that for one dizzy moment he had been about to sink to his knees and pray to God. He. The Socialist. The man without fear. Later in life he was to think of that moment as the profoundest degradation of his life.

On Monday morning, between lectures, Ash was called to the telephone. He went into the booth, closed the door, picked up the receiver:

'Hullo?'

'Ash? This is Robert.'

'Hullo.'

'Ash, I was counting on you. I stayed in all Saturday evening waiting for you to telephone.'

Pause. Ash hoped that the other could not hear the dreadful guilty pounding of his heart.

'Er. I did phone, about nine I think, but they said you were out.'

Pause.

'And where were you all yesterday, Ash, on Sunday?'

'I was—at home, reading.'

'You're lying, Ash.'

The other's deep, magnetic voice was calm.

'I can tell from your voice that you're lying. Besides, I paid you a visit. Your landlady said that you had gone off with a couple of others and your girl, to a hut for the weekend. You went on Saturday afternoon, she said.'

Pause.

'A night of whoring, wasn't it, Ash?'

Good heavens, yes. Constance. He had wanted to forget everything, with Constance, and never had Constance been so good. It was the first time he had spent a whole night with her. They had had a room to themselves, the other two were a newly married couple. All four had drunk quite hard, and Ash had sung and strummed on a guitar. Constance, so bashful, so lovely, she had had the sweetest nightdress of white cotton material with little dots on it; little blue dots, and there had been a thin sash round it that she had wanted to tie before jumping into bed, but he had taken hold of her and said that he would tie a bow for her, afterwards. She had been quite naked for him and not shy, she had been gay, she had put her arms round his neck and told him he was good. Whoring? No, not whoring. Robert could go to Mount Sinai with his commandment about whoring. Robert could go to the desert, find Moses' stone tablets and bash his own head in with them.

'So you were afraid to come on Saturday, Ash?'

'No.'

'Now you are lying again. You can lie to me, you know, but you can never lie to God.'

'Was there anything more?'

'Yes, Ash. I want to ask you to come to the station this evening before I leave. Then we can say goodbye to each other. There are several of us in the team travelling together. Many of the others have heard about you and they *dreadfully* want to meet you. They are splendid chaps, I can tell you.'

'I'm sorry. I'm awfully busy. So long.'

'Well, well, Ash. We'll meet again some time, for sure. I *know* that God has a purpose for you, Ash.'

And so it was over. He felt horribly afraid that perhaps he might meet the man again later in life, that he would never be rid of him, but the telephone had gone click and he stood there with the receiver in his hand, and when he opened the door of the telephone booth and walked out into the corridor his whole body was shaking with fear and humiliation; he was so full of desperate rage that he could have killed, at that moment he was aware of the immeasurably deep powers cooped up within him; at that moment he knew that one day he could become a killer, he went down the corridor with downcast eyes and not daring to look at the others, for there might be someone there whose face he did not like and he could kill any of them with just one blow, he halted in front of his clothes locker, intending to kick the narrow door in till it looked like a car's fender after a collision, but his safety catch stayed on and he walked on out into the grounds, looked round for a slab of stone he could lift above his head and fling at a wall, but there was none large enough and smashable enough; he walked out into the street, saw a streetcar coming, he could have picked that up and hurled it to the ground, but there were innocent people in it.

He had walked off some of the fury of despair by the time he got back to the lecture-room, but not all; he was still quivering; and this was a lecture in business management and the man lecturing had a mild, gentle face and a boyish lock of hair hanging over his forehead, and that was why Ash Burlefoot, who otherwise was shy and contented himself with little witty asides in class, gave the forty-nine other students and the man on the rostrum no end of a shock. Right in the middle of the lecture he could stand no more, banged the lid of his desk with the flat of his hand and stood up; someone smiled weakly, but no one smiled when Ash, in a voice that made the windows rattle, said:

'To serve mankind? May I ask, sir, that in future you stick to your subject, business management, and kindly (another resounding slap on the lid of the desk) spare us your moral views?'

He stood there, still and quivering, his face as white as a sheet; there was deathly silence in the room; slowly his consciousness returned, he felt the stinging pain in his hand, bowed his head; he did not look at the professor; but gulped, gathered his books together, bowed to the rostrum, said 'Excuse me' in a low voice and walked out.

After a few seconds spent collecting himself in the corridor, he went to the Dean's office, got hold of Synnoeve, also one of God's creatures, asked to see the Dean, was ushered in and related the incident. After the break the professor came along, presumably on the same errand as Ash. Ash excused himself by saying that he was overworked and on edge, and there the matter rested; Mr. Burlefoot was not subjected to disciplinary action.

After that Ash and the professor were better friends. And the professor did not mention the moral task of business as often as he had before.

Where to Find a Stable for a Horse?

About this time Ash developed a day-dream. It came to him no doubt because the summer holidays were approaching, it had to do with freedom.

He spent many days dreaming about a horse. A stallion. A white stallion.

Longing for the white stallion. He was going to saddle it and have two saddle-bags, a sleeping bag and a one-man tent. Then he would ride out. He would ride round the North, it must be fine riding a white stallion in Sweden. When evening fell, he would stop at a farm, ask for stabling for the horse. Or they could spend the night in the forest, the two of them; he would find a stream for the horse, watch it as it thrust its muzzle in and drank; it's good to watch a horse drinking. And in the forests in the North there is green, fresh, fragrant grass. Violets, wood-anemones, clover, harebells, marigolds and small wild pansies. He and the white horse. At night he would hear its breathing and feel the warmth of its body, and he would have the peace of the forest.

Riding his horse, now trotting, now at a slow and comfortable walk, all round the country; he on the horse. He would pat its neck and the white stallion would whinny softly back. And when they stopped to rest, he would take off the saddle and currycomb it, hold its head, stroke its forelock, look into its dark eyes, talk to it; the horse would understand him, he would not stammer with the horse.

And he would sit high up on the horse. Free, in the pure air, high up, powerful in his ability to direct; just a tiny pull on the reins and the white horse would go where he wished.

A dream about a white horse.

He spoke with his French teacher about the possibility of spending the summer in France. Were there summer language

courses for foreigners in France? He was given several bro-
chures. He spent a couple of evenings looking at them. There
was one course that he finally decided was the most interesting,
not because it was for young Scandinavians, not because it cost
three hundred crowns including fees and board and lodging,
not because it lasted six weeks and native teachers gave instruction in French business correspondence, French literature and
French conversation, but because it was held in a small unknown
town in the department of Les Hautes Pyrénées. The High
Pyrenees. He looked it up on the map, discovered that it lay
half-way between the Spanish part of the Bay of Biscay and
the Mediterranean. The Riviera. I should like to have bathed
once in the blue Mediterranean, he thought; it was on that sea's
shores that man's civilization was created. As he thought of the
Mediterranean, he also thought of Embla's eyes.

And then he thought of the immense sum of three hundred
crowns; and he shuddered.

Some days later through a friend he heard of a motor-car
dealer who also dealt in second-hand motor-cycles and who
happened to have a small 250 cc. German machine for eight
hundred crowns. But you could have it on instalments. Two
hundred crowns down and the rest in monthly instalments of a
hundred crowns starting in the autumn.

Ash had not forgotten the white stallion, but he had thought:
when autumn comes, it will be easier to find room for a motor-
cycle than a stable for a white horse.

But he never forgot the white horse. He had many a conversation with the horse and their talks were a great relief to him;
he whispered into the horse's ear all the things which otherwise
he could not put into words, and in the horse's good brown eyes
he read that here was one at last who understood him and
who accepted him as he was, without moral reprobation.

He took stock of his worldly goods, had a look at his bank
book. It was sheer madness, the trip to France would cost him
five hundred crowns cash, three hundred for the course, two
hundred for the motor-cycle. Besides that, he must have

pocket money for tobacco, wine, peaches, grapes. And the motor-cycle had to have something to run on.

Sheer madness.

In his heart he had already made up his mind.

Why do we absolutely have to Love *every time we make Love?*

It was about this time that, during a meeting at the Stable, Erik Floden and Ash Burlefoot met on the creaking, rickety spiral stairs leading from the ground floor up to the first floor.

A matter of urgency had taken them both there. When Ash came out of the bathroom Erik was still on the landing.

'Have you ever been inside the studio?' Erik asked in a low, confidential tone and flicked cigar ash on to the stairs.

'No,' said Ash.

'Come,' said Erik, 'I'll show you something.'

He opened the door to the workshop and went in. There was no one there. The room was in semi-darkness; only a solitary standard lamp in one corner was alight. There was a faint smell of oil, clay, turpentine, chalk. Erik hauled Ash across to the far corner where stood a good modern bed made of some light-coloured wood. A bookshelf was let into the foot that faced them.

'Embla sleeps here,' Erik whispered, his voice full of the desire to impart information.

Ash felt suddenly bashful and awestruck. He wanted to turn and go, but a strange curiosity held him back. He looked down at the thick blanket covering the bed; it appeared to be of African origin, had black and brown arabesques on a white ground. Erik leaned over the bed and pointed eloquently at something on the wall. The light was bad and Ash had to bend forward to see. It was a sort of sign, a white enamel plate almost a foot long and perhaps four inches high. He tried to read the black lettering on it. Erik said:

'Doesn't mince words, does she?'

Ash leaned still further forward; now he could read what was on the plate. For a second he could not see the joke; it must have been a sign-plate that Embla or one of her friends had pinched from a streetcar, in the way young people pinch ash-trays or spoons from restaurants as souvenirs. Embla must have hung it up over her bed in a fit of arrogance. And now he saw the joke.

'They say,' Erik whispered, blowing out a confidential little cloud of cigar smoke, 'that when her parents came to see her here and happened to see the plate, they threatened to disinherit her if she didn't take it down.' Erik rubbed his chin delightedly; he had been able to tell Ash one of the Stable's family secrets.

Ash's first feeling was one of admiration and triumph. Embla had done *that*! The girl with the dimples and the enormous blue eyes! She was not only their angel of saintliness and good-ness, but she also brandished the scourge of offence over the bourgeois attitude and concept of decency! She had told them to their faces: 'My bed is my bed!'

But when he and Erik had rejoined the others and were seated once more at the long table, another emotion flooded through him. He glanced cautiously at her. Her mouth was so small and so soft. He had never heard it say the word no. Un-doubtedly, there were people unscrupulous enough to be cap-able of exploiting her goodness and her soft mouth. And her bed up there, that no doubt could tell tales of other things than abstract idealism? He did not know why, but for a brief moment he felt a piercing, searing wave mounting inside him, a metal-hard cynicism, unsmiling and quivering, he felt himself capable of getting up, walking across to her place at the table, bending over her nut-brown hair and whispering into her ear: 'How much do you charge, Embla?'

When the meeting was over and he was back at home in his room, he struck himself on the mouth for that vile thought. He struck so hard that his lower lip bled.

For he knew that no matter what she had done, no matter what she was doing, it was noble, beautiful, proud and right. He would always defend her.

It was the coolest thing he had ever seen a young girl do: to nail a stolen streetcar notice over her bed, a sign that said:

PLEASE TENDER THE EXACT FARE AND STATE YOUR DESTINATION

There was to be a meeting of the Students' Society just before Easter. The speaker was to be the Norwegian poet of whom Ash thought more highly than any other, the poet *sans peur et sans reproche*. Ash had never heard or seen him before, just read his beautiful poems and his forceful *Scandalous Essays*, and he was almost beside himself with excitement long before the time of the meeting. He wanted to pay homage to this man, but how did you pay homage to a poet? He didn't dare go up and shake hands and address him directly; the man would have regarded that as untimely and presumptuous, and besides Ash would never have got a word out; and to shake a man's hand while you stood as dumb as an oyster could scarcely be called homage. Should he write a poem to him? Ash could find it in him to write poems about all sorts of things and to all sorts of people, but not to the best poet in the world; that would be sheer foolishness. Send him flowers? Flowers to a socialist? The only way would be if, during the subsequent discussion, Ash could get up and give him his warmest support. (Ash didn't need to hear what the man had to say—his talk had the ironic title YOUTH'S IMMORALITY—he was prepared to subscribe to all his views— unseen and unheard.) But there were two things that Ash could not do: give articulate expression to his burning enthusiasms or to his loathings. He was frightened by the violence of his feelings and, fettering the volcano inside him, just sat, his face deathly pale, clenched fists thrust into his trouser pockets.

The time for the meeting came. Ash sat shivering with excitement and happiness. The hall was crowded, feelings were going to run high. He had only seen photographs of the man before, now he was confronted with the man behind the picture and at first, as he was mounting the rostrum to begin his talk, Ash felt a tiny gust of disappointment. A poet, a poet of the people, he had imagined someone like Bjørnson, tall, heavy, brooding, a chieftain with a head of hair like a plumed helmet. This man was short, slightly built, his hair dark and—what was more—brushed forward and cut in a straight line along his forehead making him look like a medieval spearman. But no sooner had he begun to speak than Ash—and the entire audience—felt the power that radiated from him, an invulnerable force that weather-beaten fishermen have or the spare herders of reindeer, men who are all sinew and muscle, without an ounce of superfluous fat on their bodies, who put to sea after fish or go off into the wilds on skis after reindeer, and for whom an empty net or an unsuccessful hunt are as natural as to see their efforts succeed, who lose every day, yet never give up, men whose essence is toughness, who cannot be killed, who never give up. Surprised, Ash turned and looked at the student who sat beside him, a stranger, tall and fair, rather fat, and he thought: this chap could go up and strike that little, middle-aged poet to the floor with a single blow. Yet, if he did, when he was standing over him on the floor, over the dying poet, he would read something in that swarthy weathered face, in those brown eyes, see in that smiling, calm, silent face that there are things that cannot be killed; then the student would realize that the body can be murdered, yet the soul lives on. Ash thought: the writer always wins. That thought made a tremendous impression on him; he had seen a truth of which he had not heard before, and he sat open-mouthed; it was a good while before he could concentrate on the talk.

The man had a low, but strong voice. His technique was to use irony and paradox, and he spoke slowly in what was almost a drawl, every word articulated and distinct, he had a complete mastery of the art of public speaking; he didn't talk, he conjured, he bound them with spells.

Ash remembered this:

'Let me read you, ladies and gentlemen, part of a letter to a daily paper. (Drawling.) Like most letters (a hint of a sigh in his voice) about morals, it is *anonymous*. (Slight snigger from the audience; the speaker's face is unmoved by it; his ability to sway his audience and control himself is fantastic.) I shall read only one sentence: "A stop must be put to so-called free love among young people. Every young person has a moral duty to wait till he or she can enter into legal marriage; by taking love in advance, young people are wasting the power of their love;

love is man's most precious possession, it must not be squandered." '

The speaker made a little pause. His ability to use well-calcu-
lated pauses was fantastic, yet it didn't appear studied or
acquired, but an inherent, part of him. Having intrigued his
audience, he went on:

'When I read this, I wondered greatly. (Sniggers.) We all
know that when athletes go to take part in an Olympiad, they
do not go *unprepared*. (Pause.) *They* have not been *afraid* to *try
out their capabilities* in advance (pause), they have not sat
with their hands in their *laps* feeling their abilities *quietly* growing. (The man's calm grim irony was devastating.) Our athletes
haven't wasted their powers because they trained! (Pause.)
They haven't (diabolical pause) *squandered* their powers.'

An excited buzz passed through the five hundred members of
his audience; half were smiling in delight at this way of scoring
a point, the others had their eyes glued to the floor, angry at
the man's irreverent jesting with eternal values.

The speaker righted his horn-rimmed spectacles, and calmly
went on:

'Having read this letter which was signed Anonymous, my
first impulse was to throw the newspaper into the wastepaper
basket, it was (pause) a mediocre bit of writing like most (slight
sigh) letters to the editor. But then, for some reason or other
I became curious. Who, I wondered, could write that? What
sort of person? I bent over the page. I looked at the printed
letters. First through my spectacles. Then I removed my spectacles. Then I put them on again. I took the paper in my hands
and held it up to my face, looked at that letter with my right eye,
then with my left. (He demonstrated all this. He was a superb
actor.) I *smelt* the letter. Pondered. Then I said to myself.'

He paused. A deathly silence reigned. He ran his tongue over
his lips, bit his lips, cut a diabolical grimace, removed his spectacles, looked at his audience, leaned forward very slightly,
and in a clear, hissing, piercing, triumphant voice, said:

'A *parson!*'

For a tenth of a second the audience sat paralysed, then an
exultant roar burst forth. Ash felt such a surge of delight that
in his enthusiasm he sent his chair over backwards. It went

right over and left him lying, shrieking with delight, his head in the lap of an elderly woman he had never seen before. 'Oh!' he cried and squeezed the woman's hand, 'Oh!' he wiped the wild tears of laughter away and wailed: 'Oh! That was good. Oh, that was *good!*' and the elderly woman thrust his head off her lap and said severely:

'You ought to be ashamed of yourself.'

He was also to remember this:

There was the usual discussion after the talk. For this meeting Stabell had not drawn up any strategic plan of defence, smilingly saying of the speaker: '*He'*ll be able to stand up for himself!' One of the speakers in the discussion was the professor in business management from the College; he spoke gravely and gently and impressively about true love, the unselfish love; this sickened Ash and he thought, with a shudder, this is my chance, now I can stand up and if I catch the chairman's eye I can have the professor on toast and pay homage to the poet, two beautiful birds with one stone. But his jaw began to quiver at the mere thought and he didn't dare.

But then another young fellow leaped up. Ash had noticed him once or twice before at these meetings and once or twice he had also been at the meetings of the Socialist Students' Group. He was just a boy, in his last year at school, his manner was as fresh as a spring day, his face as clear and open and smiling as the sky; he was tall and held himself straight, sparklingly alive, he had gaps between his white teeth and his hair was red and unruly; he was quivering with youth and enthusiasm; now he couldn't get to the rostrum because the people in front of him were packed too tight, so he jumped up and stood on his own chair; he was so eager and exasperated and enthusiastic that he stammered; the words poured from him like a cataract; there he stood up above all the others, his red hair glowing as though the sun were on it, and he laughed and stammered and stammered and laughed, and he wouldn't let himself be pulled down; he completely captivated the audience and he said one thing that the audience applauded and which Ash was never to forget: it went to his heart like a revelation.

Some twenty years later Ash and the red-haired schoolboy

met again. The redhead had recently been made a doctor of philosophy for a thick tome on morality in international politics. Ash had read the book and also attended the discussion of the thesis. The party at which they met that evening was in the other's honour. Late that evening Ash drew the man aside and said:

'You wrote a very good book, but your best philosophy has yet to be printed.'

'Well?' said the other, smiling. He had the same old open smile, the same red hair standing up on end, the same generous gaps between his teeth.

'It was that time in 1939, during a debate in the Students' Society, when you got up and made a fiery speech in support of free love.'

'Did I,' said the redhead pulling at his nose. 'And what did I say?'

'You stood up on your chair and shouted out furiously: "*Why do we absolutely have to LOVE every time we make love?*"'

The other pulled his white tie straight (he was in tails), pursed his lips and considered this. Then he looked at Ash, wide-eyed, and said in a serious voice:

'Did I really say that?'

'Yes,' said Ash.

'But, damn it, that's the best thing I've ever said.'

There was a pause in which neither spoke. Then the redhead looked up at Ash and whispered with a gay, melancholy smile:

'But that was inspired!'

'Yes,' said Ash. 'It was the saying of your life.'

'There's a whole moral revolution contained in that.'

'A Dionysian revolution.'

'It's worth more than my whole thesis!'

'It is.'

'And I had forgotten it!'

'But I remembered it. I—preserved it.'

'Um—how did it go now?'

'You can't use it now. A doctor of philosophy aged forty can't say that. You have to have the smiling persuasiveness of the nineteen-year-old. Let it lie buried along with your youth, the time when we are inspired and nobody knows it.'

The future professor in philosophy had produced notebook and pen in order to write the sentence down, slowly he returned them to the pocket of his tails.

In silence the two men rejoined the others.

Ash also had another memory from that meeting. They were to dance after the discussion, which lasted well over an hour. Ash took a stroll round; he saw some of the leading members of the Socialist Students' Group sitting at the committee's table in friendly, intimate converse with the poet; he didn't dare go up to them, but he dearly wished that one of them would invite him to sit down and have a glass of beer with them. But why should anyone invite him to sit with the poet?

He had seen Embla earlier that evening, but now that dancing had begun, he could no longer see her; she must have gone; why had she gone? With whom had she gone? At that moment his highest aspirations were: to be able to sit and talk with the poet and to dance with Embla.

For a quarter of an hour he walked about looking at the dancers. Then he drew a deep, quivering breath and went home to his room.

He went on an Easter trip that year. Constance had a best friend, Gerda, whom they had once introduced to Daniel. Daniel and Gerda had taken a liking to each other. Two couples going off for Easter. Constance knew of a mountain hut they could rent, four hours in the train, then two hours' going on skis. The farmer would take up their food and baggage; he had a horse and sledge. Ash was not to think of the expense, said Constance. Gerda and she both had good jobs, they would pay. Ash nodded, pale of cheek, he had rather a bad conscience where Constance was concerned. And besides, going off for Easter together was pretty near to announcing an engagement. He was to do many peculiar things in his life, but one thing he would never do: he would never become engaged. He sighed and said that he would go. The four days they spent up in the mountains was a difficult time for him, he felt out of temper and ill at ease, he had to make an effort to be merry and appear happy. At odd brief moments, when they sat by the fire in the hut, or when the two couples said goodnight and went each to their room, he felt as if they were two young married couples. Secretly, and apprehensively, he listened to Constance's voice and observed all her moods.

One evening he had to go outside to visit the little place to which even kings go on foot. He put on his anorak and ski-ing cap; it was a two minutes' walk, dark and the temperature well below freezing, and the place itself one of the draughtiest of its kind.

'Oh,' said Constance, 'may I come with you?'

'What?' he said.

'It's so horrid to go there alone,' she said.

'But c-c-can't you go with Gerda?'

Gerda did not need to. Also she thought it far too cold.

'It's a wonderful phenomenon in girls,' said Ash, 'this not being able to attend to nature without an escort.' He was smiling, yet he was terrified. He had done many things with girls, but never this. It was a two-seater. How did one behave in such a situation?

They walked through the snow, they had a torch, but even so they fell; it was blowing hard and snowing and it took them all their time to get the hook in the hasp on the inside of the door. How *can* she, Ash thought; Constance had already pulled her knickers down and was seated; he could see a glimpse of her white thighs; the torch lay on the wooden floor; the storm was making the rickety little wooden building shake; how *can* she; it's a strange thing with women: they have no inhibitions; they are shamelessly natural.

He gulped, got himself ready, sat down. The next moment he had broken wind into the deep hole. Never had he felt so embarrassed, never had he been involved in anything so indelicate; here sat Constance and he on the same two-seater, it was an impossible situation; he had to give up his errand, stood up and hurriedly pulled up his trousers. He stood with his back to Constance till she was finished. He took her by the hand and led her across and into the house and the warmth and parked her there. Then he went back to the little house and sat down furiously: people should be alone for this sort of thing.

On his way back to the hut, he halted abruptly, paralysed;

he thought: when two people are married and associate intimately and every day, presumably this sort of thing can happen quite often? It can happen not only with the husband, but with the wife too!

'I will never marry,' he thought.

He kicked his shoes against the door-step to knock the snow off; he thought: But usually there are single-seaters indoors; one has to do it *one at a time*; one can lock the door and be safe and spared this. Perhaps marriage is a tolerable institution after all.

They left the hut on the fifth day, sun-burned. The farmer came up with his horse and a sledge, and while Daniel and Gerda swept down on skis, Ash walked on skis beside the sledge. Now and then he took off his mitten and stretched his hand; among the boxes and rucksacks on the sledge, with a fur over her, lay Constance: she had fallen and twisted her ankle the day before when they had come rushing down the mountainside on crust-snow, and now she couldn't walk.

'Is it terribly painful?' Ash said, as he plodded along beside the sledge.

'Don't feel anything, when I'm lying down,' she said; she lay there jolting and looked at him with a kindly smile; she touched his outstretched hand. Good, devoted, dear Constance.

Whom he was not going to marry.

Why should we absolutely be compelled to *Love*, every time we make love?

'A Hug is a Cosy Thing'

The last meeting of the Group was held at the Stable some time at the end of April. So many of the students were taking their exams in May, when it would be difficult to round them up for a political meeting, that it was thought best to wait till September and resume the meetings then.

There was an electric atmosphere about the meeting: the people were gay, excited, nervous. There was a feeling of breaking-up, the last meeting before the holidays. And then there was the faint, distant pressure from Europe. Germany lay far away, but the wireless and newspapers brought Hitler very close; they had him under their skin. Chamberlain had gone to Germany to talk peace with Hitler. Would it not have been more fitting if Hitler had gone to England? What was brewing?

They were all there, Doff and Maia, Taraldsen, Poppi, Erik Floden, Fiffolo, the meteorologists, the other students, Stabell and his wife. The German refugee Wolfgang was there too, with his wife. Doff had had one or two before he came and sat croaking queer songs; he was mad about anything to do with Austria, he sat and sang: 'My Mum was a Viennese.' Afterwards Ash hummed some lines from a German folk song. Wolfgang asked what the words were: Ash did not know; he had only come across the song in a book of verse. But the title? Ash thought, then he remembered. He said, with a smile: 'A *Busserl is a schnuckri Ding.*' Wolfgang smiled, it was the first time Ash had seen him smile. Wolfgang asked what it meant. Ash was dumbfounded: didn't *Wolfgang* know? Wolfgang said that it was dialect, presumably Bavarian; he could guess what 'Busserl' meant, but did not know what 'schnuckri' was. Ash did not know either, he only remembered that in the book of music there had been a sub-title, a translation of the title, into English: 'I love Kisses.' Again Wolfgang smiled; Ash saw the smile in the man's eyes, suddenly got a glimpse of something tender and soft; perhaps it was a folk song, or a children's song; it must have reminded Wolfgang of something that had once been; the political refugee who was now pursued by Hitler's bloodhounds, must have had a childhood once and a youth, he too must have had little moments of happiness, joy, dancing? It gripped Ash so strangely by the heart. Wolfgang went across to Stabell and the others, came back after a while to Ash and said: What was that title again? Ash looked down. He said:

'A *Busserl is a schnuckri Ding.*'

Afterwards he thought: I said to Wolfgang: a hug is a cosy

thing (that's what it means, of course). And the man was glad. It was as if I had given him a gift.

The meeting got under way.
Whose evening was it?
First it was Francis Stabell's, then Wolfgang's, then Embla's. That was how he was to remember that last evening.

Francis Stabell was among them, listening to the young people; he laughed his piercing whinnying laugh, righted his twinkling spectacles, nervously ran his hand over his bald Lenin's head, explained concepts, reduced their flowers of thought to order, slanged them, scored off them, thumped their shoulders; he didn't smoke, he didn't drink, his long thin fingers drummed playfully on the table-top, his brain was as sharp as a new razor blade, 'What exactly do you mean by that?'

Wolfgang, the refugee, and his wife. She was a small, fallen-in, pale, unlovely woman getting on for forty. Her cheeks were sunken and she attempted to make herself look better with rouge; she was blond, but there was an incipient gleam of grey in her thin mat of hair; she was German, unsmart, and Ash felt inexplicably sorry for her. Flowers, he had once thought for one moment, if I dared give her some flowers; I am sure she has never been given flowers. Also she wasn't really Wolfgang's wife; Erik Floden had told him that they were 'together'; she had been Wolfgang's secretary in Germany for many years; they had escaped across the frontier together; they had stuck together, they lived together, they were 'together'. Wolfgang had learned to write and read and understand Norwegian in an amazingly short time, but Hanne, his wife, was hopelessly out of it when the others conversed in Norwegian. She sat with a quiet, pale, polite smile pretending that she enjoyed listening; there was something in her melancholy, slightly red-rimmed eyes that brought a lump into Ash's throat. For one moment the cruel thought struck him: Hanne's position here in Norway is the same as mine; we both smile and listen politely, but our hearts weep. She is a waif without a passport; I a waif with a passport. Hanne, would you like my passport?

Wolfgang insisted on the others speaking Norwegian in his presence; he understood it perfectly, only asked to be allowed to answer in German; speaking Norwegian he found a little difficult. Again Ash had to admire the man for the strength and toughness that lay concealed in his stocky body and broad, short head; there was power even in his thick dark hair; his eyes shone with intelligence and organizing ability; he was a chain-smoker and used the longest cigarette-holder Ash had ever seen, he conducted in the air with it, as it were, when he spoke; everything he said was properly thought out, he never gave a faulty explanation or a loose definition; there was something uncomfortable about him, in fact, at moments he could remind you of an animal, a rat; he had brown eyes and when did a Scandinavian ever feel safe with a person with brown eyes? His voice was clear and low, he spoke as one who belonged (had belonged?) to the inner circle, the inner executive committee for Europe; he knew everything, he had Marx at his finger-tips, quoted long passages from memory without once scratching his head; he knew everything from Marx to the organization of underground resistance groups and the distribution of illegal pamphlets and ammunition (this latter was never said, Ash just read it in the man's face): he had done everything that a twentieth-century socialist can do, and more; thus there was always quiet when Wolfgang cleared his throat and said: 'Comrades, just a few words. I do not contest Comrade Stabell's views, but I should like to enlarge upon one or two points he has raised.' He was not contesting what Stabell had said, just going to amplify a few points (!); in reality he picked what the other said to pieces, but in a kind and courteous way. They all admired him, they all listened to him; he was infallible, at times so infallible, so unspeakably German and thorough, that he became rather irritating. When he noticed that, he changed the subject to the topics of the moment and a veiled passion would come into his voice; then they realized that the man was a demagogue and a giant, that he could stand on a soap box in a factory or on a tribune in a square and rap out his sentences. Here in Norway, among chattering, theorizing young students and socialists he was quieter, but the passion was there. 'Comrades,' he said fervently, insistently, 'at this hour, in this year

we cannot take such a simple view of the question. The Gestapo
do not leave us the peace for that. (Ash thought of Wilhelmine,
fixed his eyes on the table.) 'Comrades, in Germany our comrades are fighting, in Germany, in Austria, in Czecho-Slovakia.
For these comrades every day is a real, literal battle, is blood, is
despair, poverty, oppression. Comrades, I tell you this question
is not an academic one ... you will not find the answer in
books.'

This is not an *academic* question—Ash did not remember
what question it had been; he just remembered Wolfgang's
phrase: the answer was not to be found by reading books. At
that moment he had thought: you cannot find the answer to
any question in any book. Someone ought to tell people that. It
is a hard thing to tell people, but if they knew perhaps we could
stop using the alphabet to kill each other.

But, then, surely not only the Bible, but also Marx's *Capital*,
are dangerous books, false books, as long as there are still people
who believe in the letters they contain and will risk their lives
for them?

Yes, he whispered spontaneously.

This young socialist, sitting among his friends the socialists,
drew his head between his shoulders in terror and looked round
warily at the others. Had anyone heard what he had thought?

All at once he realized that Embla was speaking. For a change
her voice was serious; she looked troubled, sat drawing on her
block.

Someone had asked whether, if the state took over the charge
of children's upbringing, men would not be tempted to be unscrupulous in their behaviour to women.

'I take it we must assume that a woman will be able to have
an abortion if she wants?' said Embla. He could see that she
was slightly nervous at being questioned publicly in this way,
with everyone's attention suddenly directed at her, he could see
the skin of her throat move as she made a number of quick frog-
like gulping movements. Hurriedly she lit a cigarette, inhaled
deeply.

'And even if it resulted in women having more children ...'
He could see she was nervous and he was tremendously im-

pressed: fancy her daring, he thought, here, in the same room as
Stabell and Wolfgang. . . . She swallowed, cleared her throat,
her voice carried better now:

'If the State provides the money for the child's maintenance
and upbringing, that will make women independent at last,
won't it?' She blinked her great eyes and looked round rather
unhappily. As no one contradicted her, she went on: 'As things
are today, women make either tarts or slaves of themselves.
They are dependent on their husband's pleasure; they are either
given, or take the money for their children's maintenance from
his pocket-book. Woman's position is humiliating. She lives on
perpetual poor relief, on private charity.'

They leaned forward a shade, it was so seldom they heard
her speak so quietly and objectively, without smile-wrinkles
round her nose. One of the meteorologists asked her a personal
question: If she should have a child herself, would she accept
help from the man?

She blinked, thought this over.

'As long as two people are in love, that question does not apply,
does it? They will both pay what they can; the man if he has
a job; the woman if she has a job. . . .'

'But love can fade. If you parted company? Would you refuse
to accept maintenance for the child from the man?'

'I don't know. But I think so. I would never accept anything
that was not given freely. The obligation ceases with the love.
(She dares pronounce the word love! Ash thought.) When my
beloved was beloved no longer, how could I accept money from
him without making myself a prostitute? Even if, what a
thought, the man should be my lawful husband.'

'You would support the child yourself, then?'

'Of course.' She drew a breath, added: 'As long as we are not
living in a socialist society.' She had one more thing to say,
cleared her throat: 'The introduction of a socialist society is
bound to have a disintegrating effect on marriage as an institution. But "disintegrating" is a silly word, it smacks of . . .' She
flickered her fingers in the air and immediately they all understood what it smacked of. 'Better say that fewer marriages would
be entered into. Nowadays most women marry in order to get
someone to provide for themselves and their children. In a

socialist society there would be fewer marriages, perhaps none at all. To make up for it, men and women would be able to meet as equals. Less marriage, but more friendship.'

'Bravo,' said Maia, Doff's wife. No one had ever heard her say a word at a meeting before.

'May I die,' said Doff and almost imperceptibly blushed.

After a while, when the murmur of voices had subsided, they heard Wolfgang's low, full, rasping voice:

'Do you know August Bebel's *Woman and Socialism*? How many of you have read it? Only one? Two?'

He would like, he said, to start a study circle in the autumn on woman's place under socialism, if that would interest them. Several greeted the suggestion with pleasure and interest. Embla was voted a life member in view of her brilliant contribution that evening. Ash had been watching Wolfgang, he had addressed himself to Embla, had done so all the time he was speaking; there was something in Wolfgang's face Ash could not interpret; suddenly he felt that he knew: Wolfgang was a Jew. And for one reason or another Ash then turned and cautiously looked at small, pale, anaemic Hanne. She sat there so silent, so colourless, so timid; Ash gulped; it was as though she had yearned all her life for a secure existence, a flat, a home, a kitchen of her own, for children, but that the man's energy and political activity had robbed her of all these possibilities of feminine happiness. At that moment he thought he could read her life's story in her face: she had followed Wolfgang through thick and thin, with her shorthand notebook and her little portable typewriter, her life had been spent in newspaper offices, attics, libraries, cellars, prisons, concentration camps; her life had been a life of continual journeying and of absolute unselfishness; now that she had landed up here, as a refugee, without a future, a baby was the most academic of all questions where she was concerned, for socialism came first, didn't it? (He glanced quickly at Wolfgang as this thought came to him: Wolfgang had given him that nice phrase 'academic question', now he could have it back with interest!) Ash had been able to see in Hanne's face what she had gone through, what she had lost and forfeited, and he was filled with bitterness and a desire to punish Wolfgang and all socialism. He thought angrily: What do we want a study circle on women under socialism for? We have one here. In *practice*. Look at Wolfgang's worn-out Hanne!

No sooner had he thought so nasty a thought, than he hid his face in his hands. Who am I, he thought in despair, to set myself up in judgment over any other man? I? Gunnhild wrote asking me for fifty crowns, for clothes for little Astrid; I sent her thirty, and I am intending to spend over five hundred on myself, on this trip to France!

When the meeting broke up that evening, he took care to be among the last to go. In the end he was the last. He wanted to say goodbye to Embla.

'This isn't the last time I'm going to see your fair face before the summer holidays, is it?' she asked.

'No-o,' said Ash.

'You're welcome, you know.'

'So long then,' said Ash. He didn't know what to say, he had been prepared to make a nice little farewell speech. All at once he said: 'I am thinking of buying a motor-cycle, thinking of taking a trip to France this summer.'

'Oh,' she said, 'that will be splendid for you.'

'If I buy the motor-cycle and when I've got my driving licence, can I ring up one evening and—will you come out for a spin?'

'Me? On a motor-cycle?' She blinked in such frantic horror that Ash's stomach muscles relaxed and he began to laugh. 'I've only been on a motor-cycle once in my life. I thought I should die. I squealed like a stuck pig, and everything went black before my eyes. It wasn't till we got where we were going that I discovered that I had been sitting with my skirt over my face. I shall *never* do that again!'

Ash felt slightly disappointed, but he couldn't help roaring with laughter.

'No,' she said. 'Rather you come here one evening before you go, *on foot*. Then we can have a chat together about Paris. If you would like, that is.'

'Of course I would.'

'You see, one should only do the things one likes,' she said gaily.

He was rather pained. Good heavens, he thought, she can certainly talk. . . . Then he had to gulp, he could not bear it that she should stand there holding his hand. She let go of it.

'As long as I can be sure I won't be disturbing you,' he said, dully.

'You know you won't,' she replied. 'But ring up just to make sure. It does happen that we suddenly get up to our eyes in work and then . . .' She flickered her fingers out into space.

'Mhm,' said he. 'Well, goodnight and . . . thanks for this evening.'

'Goodnight, Ash,' she said.

Something snapped inside him as she said that. He had to glance hurriedly at her face, at her eyes behind her glasses; no, it was just her ordinary sweet nature, nothing special. 'Goodnight, Ash.' It was the most heart-warming thing anyone had ever said to him. What a decent person she is, he thought. She feels kindness towards me, towards everyone.

Then she began to shut the door, waved to him through the last chink, a little flicker with her fingers. Again he glimpsed the doe, the squirrel, the butterfly in her and as he raised his hand to return the greeting, he felt how stiff his own salute was.

He walked off in the direction of home, but could not bring himself to go straight there. His room. Suddenly the thought of his room was violently distasteful.

She was brave, really brave. But, but . . . she should not be so positive. Actually she had not been so positive. But she should not put her arguments to the test. He had filled in a number of money-order forms in his life and mentally had followed them to their destination; he knew and he could feel what life was like for a woman when she was alone and had a child. Viewed from outside, Embla, by the light of theory, it can seem noble for a woman to stand up and declare herself independent of her child's father; but from inside . . . Embla, you should not be so confident. Don't put your arguments to the test. Wait till we have a socialist society. There are more shames in heaven and earth, Embla, than are dreamt of in youth's philosophy. It is so easy to lose the beauty. Economic poverty blisters even love.

She thought too well of the world, thought too well of people. Her own simple-heartedness could trip her up And it's ghastly to see a good girl go . . . she needed someone to look—look af— . . .

He had gone round in a circle.

He was back again, standing on the street between the two concrete office buildings: on one corner was a Co-operative store with a lighted show window: in one window stood a row of cartons of soap powder. 'Persil,' he read, and spoke it aloud in a half-whisper. Slowly he walked into the silent alleyway, came into the open space at the end where the Stable was, an anachronism in the twentieth century. He thought: The best thoughts in this town, perhaps in the whole country, come from the Stable here. The old wooden building lay there in the dark night, he could see no lights in its windows.

He halted some paces from the door, gazed at it. It was a sort of restored barn door with a diagonal bracing board. There was an old lock-cover with a hole for a stable-key, but above this was a modern Yale lock that had been let in. He looked at the door: the Stable, he thought, the good old Stable. He stood still, holding his breath. He thought he might be permitted to stand for a while and look at it.

On the ground, in front of the door, was a broad stone flag. Beside it, close in to the timber wall where the snow had melted, a white snowdrop had grown up out of the dark earth.

He lit a cigarette, threw the match to the ground, stood looking at the light flower. He did not know what he was thinking.

Then he turned and slowly walked across the space and into the alleyway.

It struck him as he rounded the Co-operative store with Persil in the window. Till then he had smothered it. But now he knew.

He walked on down the street, carefully and slowly. He knew that if he tried to hurry or run, he would stumble and fall. His legs were only just carrying him.

He clasped one arm round his stomach as though to prevent his entrails from pouring out.

He knew now. He knew. And his bleeding knowledge was utterly without hope.

She was everything that he had yearned for all his youth.

Here his journey ended: now he knew. The ship. The door. The hand.

Only that she was not for him. And now, because he knew that he loved her, he could never go back to her.

Once he slipped on the ice-encrusted pavement. He fell, remained on his knees in the slush and felt icy water seeping through his trousers. He took his time about getting to his feet. It occurred to him how thoroughly fitting it was, that when he knelt for the first time in his life, it should be in icy water.

Co-dispensers

The centaur had seen his first human. The centaur looked down at its own shaggy animal's body; the centaur did not have the heart of a ravisher and therefore he was without hope.

To take careful hold of her head, hold her beloved head in his hands.

How?

How to look into her big, pure, smiling blue eyes?

But the centaur could whisper her name.

He could stand still in the thicket, so still that no one discovered him and the secret of his heart, so still that he became one with the trees; he could stand like that and quietly whisper her beloved name.

Only she could conjure the shaggy animal's skin off him; only through her love could he become human.

He had moments of frenzy when he sat over his fat tomes and checked off the list of books he must read. I am not even going to manage this, he thought, I am going to fail. I had all the riches in the world and I have squandered my whole inheritance.

Constance had rung him at the College; she had broken her ankle, nothing serious, but she had to have her foot in plaster.

Would he care to come to a party at her home on Saturday evening? She had thought of asking just two other couples. What about her parents? They were to be out, at some friend's silver wedding party, and would not be back till three. Who was she thinking of inviting? Well, Gerda and Daniel, and then her former fiancé, the pharmacist, and his new fiancée. No. Why no? He could not explain properly, but he had an aversion against this business of 'formers' meeting socially. It was only that she had the impression that the pharmacist had a sort of bad conscience about having left her, 'let her down,' and now she wanted to show him that she was merry and bright. . . . It was all so simple, a meeting in all friendship; it wouldn't embarrass Ash to spend an evening with him, would it?

When Ash had put the receiver down, he remained standing there with a thoughtful expression on his face, biting his lip. What actually *was* the purpose of this party? What does a person's mind look like on the inside? Was Constance as quiet and nice and good as was his impression of her, or was there an infamous little devil also inhabiting her? Was she going to sit there with her plastered foot and with secret enjoyment play on two heart strings—a sort of reconciliation feast? Could it not just as easily be intended as a little private feast of jealousy for her? The pleasure of seeing confusion and *embarrassment* in two men's faces? Playing the past lover off against the present, so that the past lover was made bitterly aware of what he had thrown away? Playing the present lover off against the past, so that the present lover was made to see what she had previously possessed and enjoyed? If that was it, how did it tally with the story she told him about the pharmacist having used violence on her? Ash loathed violence and crimes of violence; he also loathed the thought of this man having been intimate with her; all at once a series of crystal-clear sexual pictures came to him, so distinct that he went white in the face; I do not love Constance, he thought. Why then do I have such a violent aversion to the idea that he and I have shared her? Then he forgot the thought, found it comical. Ha-ha, he said cynically, now we shall have a look at the pharmacist's *present* fiancée, perhaps she'll let herself be taken out for a bit, into the hall, or down to the basement; out into the dark silent street, perhaps there's a dark backyard;

we shall do it with despatch and discretion, my dear pharmacist; it's a simple prescription: three decigrammes hot breath
in the face, two decigrammes right hand, two decigrammes
fierce clutch, one decigramme of ignoring the word no, making
up to one gramme with muscular motion; shake the girl well, to
be taken standing. We're experienced co-dispensers, aren't we,
Mr. Pharmacist?

Constance, who are you?

When Ash arrived on Saturday evening he was welcomed in
the hall by Constance. He stared at her plastered foot. In less
than a second he had got the smell of the hall, glanced in through
a door and caught the atmosphere of the living-room, a niceish
room, rather over-furnished, standard lamps with big shades
with drooping silk fringes (and a plush armchair), niceish and
fairly cosy and redolent of honest, stuffy family life, and it made
him go stiff with horror. He didn't hear what Constance said,
but asked her to give him a drink—What? Even *before* he went
in?—and she limped off to the kitchen with him and poured
him out a glass of brandy; and he almost swooned with horror
when he saw the oilcloth on the dresser. There's nothing in the
world that says so much about a family as worn oilcloth on a
kitchen dresser. He spluttered the brandy all over the floor and
had to ask for another glass. He was given it. Then he felt the
alcohol tingling and warming in his veins, he looked hard at
Constance so as not to say anything about the kitchen, and
asked gaily: 'Do you think in your state you can stand a pat on
the bottom?' She could. Covertly he tried to read her thoughts
from her face. 'Does your foot hurt?'—'Not in the least. It just
itches a bit under the plaster.'—'When will you be able to have
that off?'—'In two or three days.'
When he entered the room and greeted the others, Ash was
slightly drunk, and fortunately he became a little more so during
the evening. To his surprise he did not feel the old shivering
in his skin when he found himself near the pharmacist. He took
a squint at the man's new fiancée. Heavens, she looked dumb!
The pharmacist could have her to himself, *all his life.* He sat
down feeling that this was the most majestic revenge he had

ever had. He rubbed his hands, became really gay, walked across and slapped the pharmacist delightedly on the shoulder. 'Real sweet girl, your fiancée,' Ash said, in a low voice. 'Not so bad,' said the pharmacist and gave a little bow. Ash bowed back. He was thoroughly on top.

A little later that evening the pharmacist sang for them. He had been trained in Germany, in Munich where he had also studied music. Ash became icily sober. Germany, Wilhelmine, singing, his thoughts came into focus; the pharmacist was a tenor, he sang like—who was he so horribly like?—yes, the architect, Smith-Hermansen; the pharmacist sat at the small, well-worn piano with yellowed keys and sang Schubert's *The Shepherd on the Rocks*, his new fiancée sat beside him, enraptured, staring at him as he sang; Ash stared too and saw the man's nostrils go white and the nape of his neck red from the effort of producing his screeches; the man had turned up his face and sang with unseeing eyes, open mouth and bared teeth. He was in a trance of self-glorification; if he doesn't look out, Ash thought, he'll shoot off. He became filled with a violent hatred of singers, of men who sang, amateurs who thought themselves something; it suddenly struck him, like a profound scientific truth, that mediocre singers are the stupidest people on earth; a man who can screech like that and think he is entertaining anyone but himself and his hen of a fiancée *must* be a colossal idiot. At the same time another thought struck him with heavy violence: I have had the impossible idea of becoming a composer. Or a poet. Here is the most glaring example of the use to which the works of an artist can be put. At this moment Schubert must be writhing in his grave, he must be spinning round wishing he had never composed *The Shepherd on the Rocks*, he will be prepared to give all eternity for it to have been unwritten. *An artist must protect himself.* How is he to do it? By never writing anything so light and tuneful that it becomes popular, by never writing anything that can be sung by any ignoramus. So, never a poem so metrical, rhythmical and dramatic that anybody at all can recite it. (Suddenly he remembered Ibsen's *Terje Vigen* and shuddered as he thought of all the times he had heard it recited, groaned, sobbed, trotted out, and murdered. Never in my life as much as two lines that scan, he thought.) Dramas, novels, yes, but only prose; things no architect or pharmacist would ever read a line of aloud. Excellent. And as far as music went, would he never write a song, never a ballad, never anything a person could sing? He thought this over. Opera, he thought, arias for operas, but then they must be arias of the same degree of difficulty as those in *The Barber of Seville*—let me see, Basilio's aria, Figaro's cavatina—they shall be so difficult where breathing is concerned that they rule themselves out. Even that self-glorifying pharmacist wouldn't dare embark on Figaro's cavatina, would he? Or would he? Good lord, just look at his bellowing face, the veins in forehead and neck are all swollen; dear God, kill all singing pharmacists!

At twelve o'clock the pharmacist and his fiancée got up to go. Gerda and Daniel and Ash also stood up. There was a strange and painful moment when the pharmacist came in again from the hall in hat and coat. Only Ash and Constance were left in the room and Ash had just said that he had better go too. 'Never heard such nonsense,' said the pharmacist, ecstatic, exuberant, blustering, his nose quivering with human kindness beneath his gleaming rimless glasses, '*You* don't have to just because we do!' Ash gulped. The pharmacist shoved him back into the room. 'Constance, I'm sure, won't want you to go immediately.' Ash looked down, felt himself blushing slightly. He did not dare look at Constance. He had not the least desire to stay. But having been given an open invitation with Constance listening . . . from the pharmacist! He had felt the profoundest distaste for the hasty glint of something salacious in the man's eyes. 'Stay on a bit longer,' said the pharmacist in a low warm voice. I should have to take his specs off before I hit him, Ash thought.

When the other four had gone, Ash said nothing for a long while.

'Would you like some more coffee?' Constance said cautiously; she was sitting at the little sofa table that had the coffee things on it.

'Perhaps half a cup,' Ash said and sat down.

He sat staring at the floor. He was angry and taciturn, out of his depth. What had been the point of the evening? Why had he come? He sighed heavily; then he raised his head and looked sadly at Constance.

'Didn't you enjoy yourself?' she asked.

He shook his head. He felt sad, a strange melancholy that seemed to be centred in his jaws. He went across and sat beside Constance on the divan, sat with his arm round her waist. 'No,' he said and sighed, 'now I must go.'

She held on to his hand a bit as he drew it away. 'My parents won't be back till three,' she said gently, 'it's only one now.'

He looked down. 'You know,' he said heavily, 'I want to be with you, but . . .'

'Is it my foot you are thinking of?' she said.

'Yes,' he said.

She turned her head away, said softly: 'I would love to.'

He gulped. He looked at her back, at her lovely, girlish back, beneath the close-fitting dress of dove-grey woollen material. He said: 'But won't it hurt your foot?'

She shook her head, her dark golden gleaming hair billowed slightly.

He put his hand on her shoulder, she was trembling slightly. Neither said anything, carefully he laid her down. He had become tremendously excited: the sight of the plaster on her leg was so strange, it created an atmosphere of hospital. And despite his excitement, he was hard, businesslike; he did not kiss her, gave no preliminary caresses. He placed her on the outside edge of the divan so that her feet were on the floor; firmly he pulled her dress up, firmly drew her panties off; she tried to draw her dress down, but he pulled it up again; firm and determined. She submitted and lay there; he looked at her face and she looked away, unable to meet his gaze and that was what he had wanted; he got to his feet and undid his own buttons; he who was always so blushingly embarrassed to let a girl see him in that state, who always tried to cover it up with his hand and dive under the bedclothes to hide — now took Constance's hand, Constance's hand was to do the rest, for a moment it refused, then she obeyed, opened her eyes an instant and saw what she was doing, and that was what he had wanted; then he went on, shaking with ardent desire, but also with hot vengeance, and never had she been so good. He supported himself on outstretched arms so that there was a couple of feet between their faces; after a while she wiped one of her eyes and looked up, a drop of sweat from Ash's forehead had fallen on her; lovingly and almost unconsciously she put up a hand and wiped his forehead, he whispered 'Thanks'; it was hot in the room; then he got up and wiped his forehead and neck with his handkerchief; then he had armed himself with what would prevent pregnancy, went back to her and bent over her, whispered: 'It will be almost at once now,' and she whispered: 'Yes.'

Then he had made his excuses, was ready to go (for a moment he felt a senseless terror lest her parents came back earlier than expected; not because of their being caught in any situation, but because he shuddered at the very thought of having to shake hands with Constance's parents) they parted with a word or two, he gave her a light kiss on the cheek, yes, he would ring her on Friday.

Then he was walking home through the streets. It was night. He was going home to his room. He was not happy. He lifted his hands up and smelled them. It was the loveliest smell in the world. But he was not happy.

And then he was back in his room and was undressing, slowly taking off his things. Constance, Constance. He was filled with despair, his heart was so young, and so impossible; he would so much like to be nice to everyone in the world, but he only seemed to be bad.

The young man sank to his knees on the floor, filled with a despair that shook him, but he could not make Constance happy; he knelt thus and hammered his fist on the floor, he was trembling with helplessness: I don't love her. I do *not* love her. I do NOT love her.'

The Driving Examiner and the Cosmos

In the middle of reading for the exams he got a letter from Gunnhild. He had had many letters that year; every single one of them had driven him into dark, hopeless depression; their language was that of a fishwife, each letter consisting almost exclusively of threats and curses. When they used to meet, she had often stunk of cheap alcohol when she came in the evenings; that last night, the night when he had made her pregnant, she had drunk neat whisky from a tumbler; he had tried to take the tumbler from her and she had struck him on the forehead with a piece of firewood; this woman was his daughter's mother; her letters always gave him the numbing feeling that they had been written when she was half drunk (and where was the little child then, when its mother sat at the table, half drunk, writing letters of hate?); the very sight of her irregular, faltering handwriting on an envelope was enough to make him collapse in helpless despair.

This letter, however, contained an item of information that made him open his eyes wide. Since he never gave her enough money, she wrote, she had kept the child and herself for the last year by taking odd jobs here and there; for a short time she had been a waitress in a hotel, then she had worked in a shop. Now she had arranged to park the baby with her brother and his wife, who had no children, and was going to try and find a job on a boat, as stewardess or waitress, and so get away for a bit. That wasn't a bad idea, he thought; damn me if I haven't been mistaken in her.

The next moment his teeth were chattering with fear: If she gets a job in a boat, he thought, it may be a mail-boat. That means she'll come here! Once every fortnight! And the mail-boat puts in here for three days. She will come and see me. She might come to my room, she might come to the Students' Group, she might walk into the rector's office and ask to speak to Mr. Burlefoot!

Heavens above! Am I *never* going to get away from the woman?

They had been out on a trial run. Everything seemed in perfect order.

'Couldn't you let it go for seven-fifty?' Ash asked.

'Hm, no,' said the man.

'Take seven-fifty for it and I'll sign the form now.'

'Hm,' said the man and scratched the back of his neck. 'But I must have two hundred cash down.'

'I have the money here,' said Ash. 'And the next instalment on September the fifteenth.'

There was a pause. Ash lit a cigarette, offered the man one. 'All right,' said the man. 'But you're getting it darned cheap.'

'The customer's always right,' said Ash.

'They seem to teach you most things at the College, don't they?' The man was smiling.

'You know,' Ash said, 'you don't need a university education to knock a bit off the price of a motor-bike.'

'No,' said the man, 'perhaps not.'

'Here,' said Ash, producing his fountain-pen.

Afterwards he felt quite dizzy. He had paid out two hundred crowns. Two red hundred crown notes!

And he had become the owner of a motorcycle.

But not quite that. According to the law of hire-purchase, the object remains the property of the vendor until all the instalments have been paid.

But I *feel* as though it were mine, Ash thought; that's what matters.

The motorcycle had to stay with the dealer till Ash had passed his driving test. A week later he found himself on the street outside the police station, having spent all night cramming a pamphlet called *ABC of the Driving Test*. His head was buzzing with terms like carburettor, cam, internal combustion engine, sparking plug, chassis, gearbox, universal joint, differential, and he had spent the early hours trying to identify these wonders on his motorcycle and been unable to find even one; the damned pamphlet had been written for people who drove great huge *motor-cars*, there wasn't a word in it to help a poor devil who had got himself a motor*cycle*! What did a motorcyclist want all that knowledge for? You only had to stamp on the self-starter, engage gear, give a twist to the hand-grip and accelerate, and you were off and away! While laboriously searching for the universal joint on his little motorcycle he had become hysterical; in the end he had come to the remarkable conclusion that there wasn't one. He had decided that he would ask the examiner about this : perhaps the dealer had swindled him? Circles and triangles were dancing in front of his eyes, red and yellow and white and blue, the signs for One Way Street, No Entry, No Parking, Major Road Ahead, Crossing, Level Crossing; standing there outside the police station he suddenly couldn't remember a thing, didn't even know which was the front and which the back of his machine.

At last the examiner emerged and walked slowly down the steps as though deep in thought. He was quite a young man, scarcely thirty, wearing a raincoat with a belt and a hat. He stopped on the pavement, lit a cigarette. Ash thought: has he forgotten me? He cleared his throat. The man didn't look at him. Ah, thought Ash, suddenly calm and alert, it's a sort of war of nerves, they do this to drive candidates off their heads with nervousness. They get double fees if a person fails and has to take the test a second time. It may even be a business racket. Well, we'll see. Ash had become perfectly cool, and now he remembered every one of the traffic signs. If he can smoke, Ash thought, so can I. He lit a cigarette. Waited. We'll see. What was that advice the dealer gave him? Close turn when you're turning to the right, wide turn when you turn to the left. Always give a hand-signal when you turn; it makes a good impression on the examiner if you hold your arm well out to the side. Well out. All right. Let him come now. He's not going to be able to plough me. I'll drive as beautifully as though I were God himself.

The man walked up to Ash.

'Well,' he said.

'That's it,' said Ash and raised his hat. Best be polite. That at least didn't cost anything.

'Motorcycle?' the man said and looked at the motorcycle.

'That's it,' said Ash. He couldn't very well deny what they could both see with their own eyes.

'You want a test, do you?'

'That's the idea,' said Ash.

The man looked at him coldly and Ash at once expunged the little smile from his face.

'Well, start up and let me see you ride round a bit.'

'You're not going to get up behind then?' Ash asked.

'No, I'm staying here,' said the man. 'You ride round the block once or twice.'

'All right,' Ash said.

He walked towards the motorcycle that he had parked at the edge of the pavement.

He swung his leg across and sat down, jerked up the stand with a little click, settled himself on the seat. A faint, but lovely creak came from the springs. France. He felt to see if the gear lever was in neutral, stuck his right hand in under the motorcycle's belly and tickled the little teat it had there. This made a couple of drops of petrol ooze out and that made starting easier. So the dealer had said. Ash stood up, put his weight on the kick-starter: Now.

How long had he stood there stamping on the kick-starter? Five minutes? Fifteen? A century?

He didn't know. He only knew that the motorcycle wouldn't start. He tried again and again; each time there was a little rumble, then a slight report as the pedal let go, but the motor did not fire. He became redder and redder in the face. In the end he was dripping with sweat and his leg was weak from so much stamping. Now and again he glanced at the examiner. Judging by the expression on the man's face he was thinking: I thought so. If only the man would say something, Ash thought.

As he stood stamping away there, his frenzy left him for a moment and gave place to a terrifying vision. That motionless, unfeeling man on the pavement, the man with the expressionless eyes, had become symbolic of all the things that bar one's way. Ash had been riding a motorcycle for a whole week now. He could start it and he could ride it, it was all as easy as falling off a log; something must have got stuck somewhere in the mechanism and he only had to wheel the machine to a garage and get someone to have a look at it. But the man on the pavement stood there barring the way. It was the man on the pavement who had all the power. It was he who had the power to issue driving licences. A thoroughly ordinary, anonymous, unfeeling man, a nameless creature who by his lack of helpfulness, his mere attitude, could prevent Ash from getting a driving licence; could stop him going abroad, prevent him from ever getting to France, prevent him from seeing Paris, seeing the Louvre and Rodin's museum and the Champs Elysées and the Théâtre Français and Versailles and Montmartre and Sacré-Coeur and *la rue du Chat qui Pêche*, from strolling in the streets where Voltaire, Diderot, Balzac, Zola, Hugo walked— this little creature stood there barring Ash's way to the world's highest civilization! (Couldn't Ash have got to France any other way than by motorcycle? He had tried a couple of the shipping lines in the town, inquired about free passages on a cargo boat if he paid for his food, but he had been rebuffed, told that they had given up taking passengers who didn't pay; and he couldn't afford to go by train; a motorcycle *was* the only possibility, the only possible way in the whole world!)

Now this little creature stood there holding Ash's fate in the hollow of his hand, this nameless person would decide whether Ash was to remain for all time a Norwegian barbarian or be able to have a glimpse of the grace and light of culture. This stranger on the pavement was invested with a power that extended round the whole world, this man in the raincoat had greater power than God. Ash shuddered, as he realized the endless, all-embracing power of the anonymous civil servant; he was never to forget that moment; nor was he ever to forget that he, as a socialist, advocated a system which aimed at increasing the numbers of the burocrats! (Later in his life he came across a little book written by Karl Marx's son-in-law, called *Socialism versus the State*. That gave him something to think about.) But at that moment he was not thinking politically, he was thinking cosmically; he saw the stranger on the pavement from the angle of outer space.

At length movement came into the examiner's face. He came up to Ash.

'Won't start, eh?'

'No,' Ash groaned.

'Anything wrong with the ignition?'

'No idea,' Ash cried, 'I've been riding it for a week and this is the first time it's been stubborn like this.'

'Well, that's queer,' said the man.

'W-w-would you perhaps try?' Ash said. He had seen a chance and the possibility made his head swim.

'Get off then,' said the man, 'and let me have a look.'

There was nothing Ash would have liked better. He was so relieved that he could have thrown the motorcycle into the man's arms.

The man pulled the skirts of his raincoat to the side and seated himself. He inspected the machine, evidently not having seen one of that make before. Zündapp. German. Hm.

The man stood up in the saddle, thrust his foot down.

How long had the man stood there stamping? Ash didn't know. Five minutes. Fifteen minutes. Perhaps a century.

Ash only knew that nothing so blissful had ever happened to him. The man had been so calm, so knowledgeable and superior to begin with, then an element of sport had entered into it; then it had become grim deadly earnest. The man's face that at first had the yellowy grey hue of the office worker, turned slowly pink, then deep red, then purple, then peony red; when the man finally gave up, his face was the colour you can sometimes see in blue grapes.

'It *is* remarkable, isn't it?' Ash ventured to say.

The man got off the motorcycle, dropped his hat, picked it up furiously off the pavement, mopped his forehead with his handkerchief, and muttered:

'It's the queerest thing that's ever happened to me.'

Ash said nothing. After a while he ventured to suggest:

'Perhaps I might try again?'

'By all means.'

Rested, Ash settled himself astride the seat, tickled the motor under its belly, stood up, stamped.

The miracle happened.

The engine started.

Ash did not dare look at the man. If I smile now, he thought, he'll plough me. At the moment the score is one-one. If I can just remain serious and behave with absolute correctness he's bound to pass me. He saw me make a fool of myself, but I also saw him do the same.

'Ah-ha,' said the man, 'off you go then.'

Close turn to the right, wide turn to the left, arm well out. And *don't* go fast!

Five minutes later Ash had passed. The examiner hadn't asked him a single question about the inner mysteries of the engine. Couldn't bring himself to do so.

Then minutes later Ash almost bumped into a tram; he just managed to get his foot on the foot brake and stopped with a squeal.

And he had been feeling so superior and free; after all, he had it in black and white that he could ride a motor-cycle!

In the Telephone Call-box

(Information? Will you Please give me the Number of Heaven!)

For a number of days he had been wondering if it could be done, and how it could be done. It would be best if he wrote a few lines. It would be much easier in a letter. But wouldn't that look funny? A letter to someone in the same town. Stupid idea.

He dialled her number. And as he stood in the telephone box waiting for the ringing tone, his whole body suddenly became spectrally numb.

There is no silence more oppressive than the silence inside a telephone call box when you have just dialled the number of the woman of your longings, whose feelings for you you cannot guess, and are standing waiting for the ringing tone. The air in the little booth is dry and stuffy, it has a sort of greasy human warmth about it from all the previous occupants; the queer gutta-percha-like smell of the receiver tickles your nose; your inside feels like lead, your heart is thumping up by your ears, you feel that you have lost your voice, you are overcome with claustrophobia in that tiny cell, the sweat of heat and fear has already started to run down your forehead. You breathe as though you were dying. There is no answering click. No reply then. You are just about to replace the receiver with a feeling of deep disappointment and even profounder relief, when the click comes. The world goes black before your eyes.

'Hullo?' said a voice.

He could not reply. His hand holding the receiver was trembling, its palm damp and slippery. He almost wished he could die.

'Hullo?' the voice said again, now somewhat surprised and perhaps a little impatient. For a second Ash's heart sank, perhaps she was going to hang up before he could conjure up a sound.

'Hullo,' he said. He didn't know whether it was his inner or his audible voice that had spoken. He had to make sure that it was the latter. 'Hullo,' he shouted and ran his tongue over his cinder-dry lips. 'Is that Embla?' He shivered as he heard himself pronounce her name.

'Yes?' she said, and added : 'Just a moment.'

He heard that she had turned her head away from the mouthpiece at the other end of the wire, she was talking to someone else in the same room. It sounded as though she was giving instructions for something to be packed carefully, her voice sounded so right and firm, the capable voice of a person who knows what she is doing; then the voice came back to the mouthpiece and was strong and distinct.

'Yes? Excuse me, I just had to tell the girl something. Who is it?' A slight pause. 'Hullo?'

'Hullo? This is—this is Ash.'

There was a pause. To him it seemed an eternity, and he cursed himself and his ridiculous decision to ring her up. How could she remember off-hand who he was, why was he standing there taking up her valuable time . . . ? Ring off, ring off, let it be, perhaps she hadn't caught his name anyhow.

'No, is it *you*?'

His heart gave a violent leap and then died. For there was such unmistakable frankness and pleasure in her voice. But perhaps she was always like that on the telephone, to everybody. He cocked his head to one side in order to hear the resonance in her voice better; now little thrills were coursing through him.

'How nice to hear your voice. Where *have* you been all this time?'

What warmth and kindness in her voice. If it were not that life had taught one a thing or two, he might have thought from her gay, delighted voice that she had done nothing all this time but lie sleepless at night biting her fingers till they bled, that she had been moving heaven and earth and the police and consulates of the entire western hemisphere in an attempt to trace him. That was what this angel of goodness with those Mediterranean eyes and dimples made it sound like, and he had to fight hard to keep the lump in his throat from swelling and bursting.

'Imagine you being *alive!*'

He could only groan a little woolly laugh into the mouthpiece. Then he was appalled as all at once a note of panic came into her voice:

'Oh God, you're not ringing up to get me to come out on a motor-bike, are you? I daren't. I simply *daren't.*'

In some mysterious way he managed to pacify her; besides, he had had such a lot to do. There were the exams at the end of May and what with one thing and another.... He managed to fish his handkerchief out with his left hand and wipe his face.

'You're going to do well, aren't you?' she cried ecstatically.

'That remains to be seen,' he said morosely. He had a mental vision of the fat volumes in his bookcase and on his desk, the calculations, the notebooks, ruler, logarithm tables, slide-rule....

'You must, you know,' said the gay voice, now with a hint of seriousness.

'What must I?'

'Do well. We expect it of you.'

Involuntarily he shrunk back, away from the telephone. So *we* expect. *We.* There could be no doubt who 'we' were. We, the Socialist Students' Group, wasn't it? And so we expect that the young man would bring honour to the Group, to socialism, to the ideals. *We* would not like—would we?—the young man to get a bad mark and compromise socialism? 'Give us the best pass, young man, the best, and we shall give you the best.' Did none of them have any mercy? Not even Embla? Why must a person be judged by his examination marks? Of course he was going to do well at the exam, but no better than was absolutely necessary; he had *no* ambition to achieve a special recommen-

dation. All schooling throughout the world is based on con-
vention; schooling has no value, schools are instruments of torture, nothing more or less, schools exist only because the older
generation in the community is afraid of the revolution that
would come about if they let young people free. Schools are
only for backward children; that goes for all schools, primary,
secondary, grammar, and colleges and universities; the only
thing a person needs to learn is the alphabet, the rest he can
manage by himself; after all there are libraries. Nobody has ever
had anything at all out of a school but a dulled brain; all great
men have been without schooling, self-taught outsiders, great
because they had kept their brains fresh. . . . Good God, for a
moment Embla had reminded him of his mother: 'Ash, now
you must do well; do it for *my* sake.' For a fleeting instant he
had even been angry with Embla, with Embla!

(And why? Because his inmost longing was to be recognized,
liked, loved for what he was, for what he carried unspoken
inside him, not for that for which he had certificates, not for
what he might be going to do in the future! In twenty years,
he thought, I may have composed a symphony; then perhaps
people will admire me, then perhaps they will flock round me;
but it is not then that I shall want tenderness and understanding,
not when everybody can see what I am worth; it is now, now,
now while I have it all unuttered inside me! Now, when I am
twenty-three and unknown and just myself! The music that
may acquire form in twenty years is in me now; why shall the
man who can show practical results have greater recognition
than the young fellow who just goes about dreaming? Life is
bitter when one is young. For a moment you filled me with
sorrow, Embla, unutterable sorrow. You of the Group sit there
ready to catch me when I fall like a ripe orange, but you only
want me as the *best* orange, an orange that has been publicly
stamped to guarantee its quality. You make me bitter, Embla.
But all the same, I beg you to forgive me—I cannot reproach
Embla for not being God; only God, I suppose, can see into a
person's heart and know what it is worth without examination
certificates; forgive me, Embla. Bitterness is no emotion to live
on; and of all people you least of all should suffer under my
grief; forgive me.)

And the miraculous happened: the next instant his bitterness turned into warm pleasure and swelling triumph. So there was someone sitting waiting for him. A little group of people among whom he belonged, who counted him one of them, where the wanderer could settle and where the tired heart could find rest. All at once he was so moved that he had to clutch at the instrument on the wall and all but tore it loose.

'Yes,' he muttered in a husky voice, 'I'll try.'

'Fine,' she exclaimed. 'We *know* you'll do it.'

And now he swelled with enthusiasm; yes, indeed, he would get a good mark! Perhaps the *best*! No, there was another at the College, a strange fellow with a cold, dark devilish brain who never got stuck and who always solved the problems set them not only without mistake, but in such a way that the professors discovered new aspects and had to discuss the fellow's answers among themselves, this hyper-intelligent student had a stony, white face, brown eyes and was a Nazi. Ash always gave him a wide berth. At times it *had* annoyed Ash beyond measure that a damned Nazi should be so much more gifted as an economist than a socialist. But Ash had had his little triumphs; at their political discussions he had had the fellow on toast for all his intelligence and Nazism.

Suddenly a sickening feeling came over him as he realized that he had not rung her up just to listen to her rich voice and hear the resonance of her kindness. It was not her friendship he was aiming at; the superficial friendship, the comradeship, he had that already. It was something else, something quite different. He did not want it, didn't understand it; actually he couldn't think of her as a woman, the two or three times he had fleetingly thought of her body had reduced him to the wildest despair. He had been caught in the light of her big, pure, merry eyes; he went cold at the thought of ever laying a hand on her knee; to think of her as a sexual being was inconceivable, impossible; he experienced horror, almost revulsion, when he thought of her that way. Despite the fact that she was the loveliest woman he had seen. Despite the fact?

But there was in him a longing darker than night, deeper than hell and more blind than the stars, a longing that was cruel and agonizing and nameless; all men who have lived know this craving in their hearts and loins, and they shudder when they set it in motion, because where desire has trod, grass will not grow again; and his teeth were chattering when the ghastly pause was at an end, when he again heard her voice; and was there not a ring of impatience in it?

'Listen,' she said, 'did you call about anything special?'

Had she turned her head away again? Was he taking up her time? He was seized with panic as he realized that now he must say it. Now.

'Yes,' he said huskily. His voice faltered.

'What?'

He swallowed desperately; in a voice that he had to make completely unemotional to prevent it from breaking, he said:

'Yes. I—I just wanted to ask if you were doing anything next Saturday.'

Now it was said. He closed his eyes and leant his head against the wall, expecting to be overcome by faintness. But then it struck him that this was just when he must not give her the least chance to make excuses or be evasive; reeling, he pulled himself together and went on, speaking at a furious pace:

'Not this coming Saturday, but next, that is. We'll have finished the annual exams then and there's to be a big end-of-year ball at the College, and—er—I am to propose the health of the ladies, there's to be supper and various things. And dancing. And I wanted to ask if you would be my partner.'

The expression 'my partner' was too much for him. He gasped. He knew that it was a correct expression, but in his state of senseless agitation it had acquired a quite different significance. Suddenly there was a whole world, the whole world in those two words, 'my partner'. He felt as if inadvertently he had spoken his heart's inmost, unutterable secret. To check his feeling of terror he had to say something; he turned the mouthpiece towards his mouth again and shouted:

'*Evening dress!*'

'What did you say?'

'Evening dress.'

'Oh, I see.'

'Er . . .'

A note in her voice made him feel that perhaps he had been ill-advised to mention evening dress. To shout it.

'Er . . . do you think you could come?'

There was a little pause during which he felt as though he was being subjected to a pressure of thousands of atmospheres, his lungs were squeezed flat, he could not breathe. God, he prayed, dear God. . . .

'I don't think . . .' she said hesitantly.

'What?' Despair, paralysing disappointment had made him shout.

'I don't think I am doing anything particular that evening. Next Saturday, wasn't it?'

Dear, dear God, thank you, thank you. . . . He noticed a tapping sound in the call box, discovered that it was the receiver knocking against the wall, the receiver was in his hand, his hand was shaking. He grasped the receiver in both hands to keep it still. In a dull, almost inaudible voice he said:

'Fine. I'll remind you in plenty of time, you know, just to be sure that you aren't too busy. . . .'

Then his voice failed him altogether. He could not even whisper. His knees gave under him as though they were made of dough and he had to lean against the wall. He had realized that Embla had said yes.

Embla was to be his partner.

He had to use both hands to get the receiver back on the hook.

As he came tumbling out of the phone box he almost walked into one of the lecturers. The man couldn't take his eyes off the tall student's white face and burning eyes.

The lecturer thought to himself: That's one of those reading for the exam. Perhaps the curriculum *is* on the hard side. I'll have a talk with the dean.

Young Man in a Dinner Jacket

When the day arrived, he began getting ready at midday.

He had read his speech proposing the toast of the ladies for the fortieth time and he couldn't sit still. He stood up, took off his jacket and put on the dinner jacket that lay on the bed. For a moment he could not help smiling as he thought of a story about Trotsky that Doff had told him. After the Reds had carried through their revolution in Russia in 1917, Lenin wanted at any price to make peace with the rest of the world, especially with Poland. He sent Trotsky to the peace negotiations at Brest-Litovsk. But could Trotsky, as representative of the world's proletariat, wear a dinner jacket? In his dilemma Trotsky telegraphed to Moscow. The answer he received was: 'As long as Comrade Trotsky gets peace he can wear what he damned well likes. Comradely greetings. Lenin.'

Ash would glady have put on motley, draped himself in crepe or gone naked with an ostrich feather in his tail, if that could have helped him at that evening's peace negotiations.

But his heart sank deep when he saw himself in the mirror. At the shop where he had hired the clothes he had had a choice of two dinner jackets, one that fitted him round the waist, but was four inches too short in the sleeves and another that had long enough sleeves but otherwise appeared to have been made for an elephant. In desperation, he had shut his eyes and told them to give him the latter. Now, as he stood in front of the mirror surveying himself, he shuddered; the jacket reminded him of a loose mainsail in a dead calm; he could pull the thing out eighteen inches in all directions; in front, to the side or behind; he felt like a circus tent. And the trousers! They ended a good way up his leg; never had a man so resembled a mixture of fool and confirmand. A fit of hysterical laughter came over him, he tried to pull the trousers down. That was all right, except that it made him so baggy-bottomed that he appeared deformed. Also there was a gap on his belly between his waist-coat and the top of his trousers.

For a moment he fumed in immeasurable hatred of the tyranny of uniform. Who had instituted this requirement that men should and must wear dinner jackets? Whereabouts in the world did this group of spiders hang out, these grey eminences who decided in secret how men should dress? One day he was going to smoke them out, one day he would drag them out into the light, he would shoot them down with a .22, like rats. True enough, he used to want a dinner jacket; a dinner jacket was part of the rich life and world of which he used to dream; in his youth a dinner jacket would have given him more faith in himself; with his own dinner jacket he would not have felt so poor and forlorn, not such an outsider and so helpless; but his wishful dinner jacket was to have been one that he put on when *he* thought fit, not a costume that others *compelled* him to wear! He was gasping with anger. This, he told himself, is the first and last time in my life that I shall put on a dinner jacket. That will be a better revenge on the grey unknown rats which direct world fashions from their secret nest. I will never wear a dinner jacket! When they hear that, I shall not need to shoot them; they will burst with rage.

He removed the horrible black garments and laid them on the bed again. Then he began to clean his black shoes. He supposed he would have to make them shine like a mirror, like ebony. Then it occurred to him that he had not tried on the shirt. He suddenly remembered his father and how he had an old dinner jacket that he put on every Christmas. He had seen his father standing with his back to his mother abusing her because she had pulled the tie too tight. Jokes from the humorous press came back to him, drawings of fat business-men on their knees looking under the bed for their studs. In the end, with trembling hands, he tried the tie on top of the collar; the collar was so high and stiff and tight that he felt like a cow in a collar; strangely enough he managed to tie the black silk bow perfectly. He flicked the stiff shirt-front with his finger nail and it sounded like an empty barrel. Why, he thought, have the grey rats not designed a metal shirt-front? Of corrugated iron? They ought to have thought of that.

As he took off his uniform again he saw that there was a black mark on the back of the white stiff collar. He paled; his fingers must have been dirty—it must be shoe polish! With infinite caution he washed the place with soap and water, but to his boundless horror it only became bigger! He could not afford to go out and buy a new collar. He washed, rubbed, and prayed; in the end there was only a faint dark smudge at the back, but the collar was no longer stiff; there it was as soft as a wet *rag*. Good heavens, he thought, and put the collar on the window-sill in a strip of sunlight, where he went and inspected it every minute.

Then he shaved. Having no blades left, he had to use his cut-throat. He stropped it, it slipped. For an instant it felt as though he were going to cut off his whole hand, he began to tremble with delayed fright. He soaped his face, began to shave his neck and chin, came to his upper lip and then he cut himself. He made a stroke against the beard up towards his nose. For an instant there was the paralysing sensation of a razor cutting into flesh: he had cut so deep that he had to draw the edge out of his nostril, from close by the tip of his nose; he stood and saw the red drops come trickling: they ran down his lip and over his chin, he had to bend over the wash-basin, felt his head swim.

For half an hour he walked round with his nose enveloped in newspaper. Newspaper was the best, it absorbed the blood. Eventually he ventured to remove the paper. Yes, it had stopped bleeding. He looked at himself in the mirror. It had been touch and go. He had heard a story of a man who had cut off the whole tip of his nose; the man had flung himself at it, tried to catch it in mid-air, missed, whipped it up off the floor, washed it in the basin and hurriedly slapped it back into place again; then he had run to a doctor and had it sewn on. That could be done, but it had to be slapped on at once and held firm while you ran.

Two o'clock came.

The thought of food nauseated him.

He sat down and read his speech through for the forty-first time. He felt terror like a pang in his groin, not of the students and their girls, nor of the professors; but because Embla would be sitting beside him listening. He thought suddenly—and it was such a strange thought: I wonder if she will be able to read, no—hear, between the lines? I shall be standing up in front of a hundred and fifty people in evening dress about whom I care nothing, making them laugh; and the only thing I want is to talk to one person, seriously. I can speak to a hundred and fifty, but with this one person I am bereft of words.

Tell her I love her?

Despairingly he laid his head on the table cheek down. Never. Judas does not make a declaration of love to the Virgin Mary.

The only thing he could do was to follow what she said, listen to her voice, observe her manner, watch the play of expression in her dear face and read the nuance of her smile: perhaps he might be able to find a hint of response, of understanding, the fleeting shadow of a tiny hope; just enough to show that it was not utterly hopeless, the thing that he did not dare admit properly even to himself; read there a tiny, tiny little possibility that perhaps he might come back in five years' time and present himself to her, when somehow or other he had managed to wash himself clean; just a hint that it was not utterly, absolutely, impossibly out-of-the-question; perhaps in ten years?—just the vaguest idea that she was not repelled and nauseated by the idea that he was somewhere in the world, alone, and loved her; he would not visit her, not see her, not write to her; only that some time in the future, in fifteen years, *perhaps* he might be allowed to come and see her; he would not ask her, and she would not have to answer; he would not say the least thing that might put her in a difficult, embarrassing situation; he must never say anything to her that would bring sorrow into her big, good, merry eyes, for God's sake, no; he would just try to read her smile, listen to her being. . . .

He was sitting at the table in his room. All at once, he saw her wonderful face in front of him, her pale face and violet eyes came to life and he could see them. Slowly he shaped his hands into a worshipping bowl and in them took her head; tenderly, devoutly, with trembling heart he drew his hands towards his face; something snapped inside him as he felt his kiss on the palm of his own hand.

The dream was shattered; he lay across the table gasping with horror, fear and torment. At the self-same moment as he had kissed Embla's dream face, he had remembered Gunnhild's letter. Her last letter that he had received two days before. It had been posted locally. Gunnhild was here, in town.

The letter had been written in pencil. (Is there anything in the whole world so infamous as a letter written in pencil? Naturally, someone on a deathbed will seize the nearest thing to scrawl down a last message, or a prisoner in a concentration camp must consider himself fortunate if he manages to get hold of a pencil; but a grown-up at liberty in a peaceful society?— and she would certainly also have licked the point.) She had become a stewardess, right enough; this was her first trip; now she was in town; the boat was leaving again on Monday morning; she insisted on seeing him; and if he did not want her to come to him, then he must come to her; she gave a telephone number, where she was staying with an old acquaintance; Sunday would suit her best, but not until after twelve o'clock. He had better telephone.

Gunnhild is a human being too, he thought. She had a lot of good in her. She was not mean with her body. And she had a wonderful body. Her coal-black hair and strong, golden-brown body. She was a regimental whore; at the age of nineteen she had been drawn through the town, dead drunk and half naked, on a gun-carriage pulled by six soldiers. But I was young and lonely then, and she was with me in my loneliness. I had nothing to pay her with, but she was with me, gave me a hundred nights, free, because she was fond of me and she would have given me another hundred, but then there was to be a baby and I ran away. Left her in the lurch. Gunnhild is human.

He raised his head from the table and looked round desperately. His gaze fell on the cut-throat razor on the washstand.

But I mustn't see her, he thought. She mustn't come here. Never. I must write to her. I must be harder in my letters. That's the only thing she understands. I'm too polite. She doesn't understand politeness. She takes it as weakness and cowardice (which, of course, good heavens, it is!). She was twenty-six and I twenty, at that time. No excuse for me that I was six years younger than her? No, perhaps not. But there is no need for a grown woman

of twenty-six to tell a young man every time that he needn't
bother, that he can *safely* not put one on. Oh, let there be an
end to these reproaches, we cannot go on eternally weighing
guilt against guilt. My guilt weighs three hundred and seven
tons, how much does yours weigh, two hundred and eighty-
four tons? Good God, let's stop it. But what makes her persecute
me everlastingly? Her inferiority complex? Is she basically a
little, unhappy girl who has never been accepted or recognized,
who is now chock full of hate, a semi-alcoholic, who intends to
get her own back for her ignominy? How far has a man to fly to
save his soul and his independence? To the Foreign Legion?
*Why can't the State take over the cost of children's upbringing,
so that men and women can he at peace with each other?*
When in heaven's name!—*when* are we going to get a socialist
society? In a hundred years? I want it *now*! So that I can have
peace from Gunnhild! Now! These weaklings in the Group that
I've been with this year, good God, the way they sit there with
their theoretical *study* groups on the socialist society! As if
the question of bringing up small children was an *academic*
one! Why in God's name don't they get down to revolution?
Now! It only needs a little organizing talent, a group of twenty
young people could storm the assize court in every town in
Norway, thirty would take the Storting and five would do to
occupy Broadcasting House. Then it is only a question of *de-
creeing* the revolution, that henceforth every woman, married
or unmarried, shall have a grant from the State of three thousand crowns a year for every child! That at long last would
bring peace and reconcile the men and women of the country.
The workers' movement wants to see that everyone has bread,
but how is anyone to get that bread down if their throats are
all knotted with guilt? Heavens above, five hundred armed
socialists (they don't even need to be armed, toy revolvers would
be quite enough) could conquer all Norway, depose King
Haakon and his house and bring in the socialist republic. Why
don't they do it?

Again he looked across at the razor. I shall write to her, he
thought. I must tell her the position I am in. That I shall not be
responsible for what I do if driven into a corner. I have never
laid hands on anyone; but if anyone tries to shut me up in a

cell, I know that I shall kill. I must tell her that if she comes to
see me, there's a razor lying on my washstand. That I intend to
use it; she must know that it is there. Today I almost took the
tip off my own nose; I noticed how horribly sharp a razor is; a
quick cut across the throat, not mine, and that's that.

He sat there, white in the face. He thought: if I write such a
letter, I know what the result will be. She will show it to the
police and I shall get fifteen years for threatening murder. And
as for talking face to face with her, I'm done. I should just stand
feeling tortured and crazy with compassion, and would end by
stroking her black hair; I'm like that; and if she then showed me
a picture of little Astrid and asked me nicely if I could not marry
her, I'd say yes. And then I should be sunk. There is no solution.
None.

Only the socialist one.

How long are we to wait for the socialist society?

He knew that he was not going to go and see Gunnhild on
Sunday.

He would do everything, make use of every trick, honourable
and dishonourable to avoid finding himself face to face with
her. Besides on Monday he was going to France. First to Kris-
tiansand, then by ferry to Denmark and there he would be on
the European continent.

As long as he could get the motorcycle to start.

What was there in Gunnhild's letters that always made such
a tremendous impression on him? That in each she harped on
about his unending schooling, asking whether he wouldn't have
had enough soon? Pointing out that this fine college of his was
so expensive that he had had to borrow from the bank, not for
her and the child, but for himself? Yes, it was cruel to be told
that, especially since it was true; but there was something else
in her letters that was worse. What was it?

All at once he remembered:

'You talk as if you have ideals, but of course you are just as
unreliable as all the others.'

There she had touched on his tenderest spot. That was
where each time she thrust her dagger in and twisted it round.

For if there was anything in the world he did not wish to be, it was to be like all the others.

Slowly he got into his dinner jacket. Fifteen crowns for the hire. He looked at himself in the mirror with a final shudder, made sure three times over that he had the text of his speech in his pocket, put on his overcoat and hat and walked out into the hall. He went in again; he had thought of something. Supposing he and Embla, afterwards ... ? He gulped, it was the craziest idea in the whole world; beside he did not *want* to take her up to his room, even if it were she who thought of anything so incredible. He did not think of her like that. And beside his room was tainted: dirt, sin, shame, poverty, guilt. He stood for a while. There was only one thing there in which there was purity. He took off his hat and scarf; took his violin down from the wall, strummed on the strings, tuned it, put on the mute. He thought for a moment: then he bowed a few strokes, it was from Haydn, the Serenade from the F major string quartet. And as he played, he became calm. He felt the notes vibrate through his body and his mind, they coursed through his bone cavities and his thoughts. When he hung the violin back in its place he felt purified. Good old Haydn. How could a composer be so pure in his music—make music so gay, so clear, so balanced, so harmonious?

Haydn, a wheelwright's son, grew up in poverty, in his youth earned a living singing and playing in the streets. Then he went and fell in love with a pretty young girl, Therese Keller; but Therese entered a convent. Some years after that he became conductor of an orchestra and married Therese's older sister, Maria Anna. An unhappy marriage, they lived like cat and dog; Haydn wrote of his wife that it was all the same to her whether her husband was a cobbler or an artist. And to crown it all, Therese left the convent some time later and returned to the world. His young love, Therese!

Why was Haydn's music not bursting with grief, bitterness and violent emotion? It was a mystery to young Ash. But he was tremulously grateful for its purity.

Again he put on his hat and overcoat, walked out into the hall. Thought of something else, went back, got out a half bottle of brandy, poured it into a pocket flask which he stuck into his overcoat pocket.

Walking through the hall, he saw Mrs. Abrahamsen standing at her stove, smelt steak and onions.

'Ah,' Mrs. Abrahamsen said, 'the young society lion.'

He forced out a smile.

'Mrs. Abrahamsen,' he said, 'I wanted to ask you to do me a little favour. If anyone—er—if anyone should come this evening and ask for me, say that I am out.'

'Yes, of course you're out,' little Mrs. Abrahamsen said, her brown face expanding in a smile, 'the ball will go on late, I expect.'

'Yes. That's just it. If anyone comes and asks for me, I would like you *not* to say that I am at a ball; just say that I am out.' He made a helpless gesture with his hand. 'Out.' He gulped. 'It's—er—it's personal.'

'Aha,' Mrs. Abrahamsen said, throwing a searching, but understanding glance at him. 'I see. Just: out.'

'Thank you,' he said.

'And on Monday you are going to France,' she said, and it sounded as though she sighed.

'Yes,' he said. But then he brightened, because he was able to say something nice. 'But I'm coming back before Monday.'

As he walked down the stairs he thought of someone else: Constance. She had rung him at the College a day or two before; of course everyone knew that there was to be a ball at the College. He had said that he was not feeling well, had a cold, was over-worked, did not know if he would be going. Very much doubted it.

And the town was not so large a place that Constance would not know by Monday that he had gone to the ball with Embla Tombson.

Constance.

He did not know where to go. It was four o'clock and he was not to call for Embla at the Stable till half past seven.

For a moment he thought of going to the boarding house where he lunched, and playing billiards. But there they would laugh at him. Dressed already? Had he never had a dinner jacket on before? Was he running it in?

Then it struck him: I shall go out and see Doff. He won't mind if I go in and play the gramophone.

They were all at their meal when he arrived. Wouldn't he join them? No thanks, he had eaten already. He just wondered if he might go in and play a few records.

After their meal Doff came and joined him. He looked at Ash's dinner jacket and cleared his throat. Ash did not want to ask what he meant by that. Instead he had to explain that he was going to the ball with Embla.

'I thought . . .' he added hurriedly, '. . . thought I could do some small thing in return for all the pleasant times at the Stable.'

'Nice of you, my boy,' said Doff laying a big soft hand on his knee, 'really nice of you. Embla who, I'm sure, *never* goes out anywhere.'

His cheeks went red with laughter; Ash also went red, but for a quite different reason. He saw from Doff's face that he was working up to something more, he must at all costs prevent it, he cried out that he had some cognac in his coat pocket.

'*Quod felix, faustumque sit!*' gasped Doff, speaking Latin out of sheer veneration. 'At last I see a practical result of my efforts to teach you a little socialism. This is a great day. Maia! Ash has brought cognac. Cognac! Proper cognac! Bring glasses, gipsy girls and tambourines!'

Doff and Maia drank two brandies and soda each with real devoutness. Ash only drank one. He was preoccupied, kept glancing at his wrist-watch.

The time came for the children's radio programme. The two children had to listen. The boy was nine, the girl only three. The boy sat in front of the set the entire time, wide-eyed; the little girl did not understand much of what was said, but she was greatly excited and ran about all the time; the programme was evidently an event. The thing itself is nothing, the thought of it everything, Ash thought, as he looked at the little girl who was almost in a sort of religious ecstasy. The thing is nothing, the thought of it everything. All at once he thought of Embla. Then he shuddered at the philosophic thought he had just formulated. Was Embla to exist only as a notion? Was she to be nothing *per se*?

At seven o'clock Ash had to leave and the children go to bed. Ash was in the hall when the little girl came rushing out from the bedroom. She was naked but for her socks, half-off, that flapped round her toes. She grasped Ash by the trouser-leg, looked up at him, jumped up and pulled at his trouser, saying: 'Uppy man!' Ash did not understand, he asked the child what it had said and she repeated it, impatient and eager: 'Uppy man!' Ash felt quite lost, he looked despairingly at Doff: 'What is she saying?'

Big fat Doff was himself slightly embarrassed, he said: 'That means that she wants you to pick her up.' Ash gulped as he bent down; he had never held a child before, not a naked child, a little girl of three. He took her under her soft little arms and lifted her up; she was chubby and firm; he saw dimples in her flesh, there was a fragrance to her, a warm, sourish smell of child's body; she put her finger on his nose and said 'sore?' and again he looked beseechingly at Doff, but then he understood and nodded: 'Yes, sore.' And the girl pursed her mouth and said sympathetically: 'Poor man,' and the poor man did not know what to say: Doff reached out to take his daughter, because the man had to go, but the girl had to kiss the man first; she put her mouth to his cheek and gave him a wet, warm smack; for an instant he felt her little lips, then he thought: Somewhere in the world I have two little daughters, my daughters also have little mouths like this one; he almost dropped the girl. 'You have made a conquest there,' smiled Doff. There was a good-natured and proud expression on his face, Ash had never seen it so fine-looking; he wanted to say something to them all, to Doff, to Maia, to the little girl, she had such lovely round cheeks—no blemishes there—he so badly wanted to say something, for this was his last visit before the summer holidays, but he couldn't utter a sound; helplessly he held the child out to her father, groped blindly for the door-knob behind him, went out. He couldn't even say goodbye.

The Blue Chair

He rang the bell. It was a while before the door opened. He clasped his hands. Then Embla stuck her head out and beckoned him in. Her head was wrapped in a turban of red towelling and she was in dressing gown and slippers. She drew him quickly and eagerly inside. He must excuse her, but she had got so behind, it had taken her till half an hour before to get a consignment of goods away by rail; he must sit down and make himself comfortable for a while, she must just have a shower and titivate a bit ... fingers flickering in the air as though she were playing arpeggios up the keys of the rainbow, a movement out into enchanting boundlessness. . . .

Quickly she climbed the spiral stair and he caught a glimpse of her bare legs. He sat down on one of the squeaky sofas. He had not uttered a word.

He sat there with his hands in his lap, feeling that his whole universe was adrift. What had he embarked on? If he said that he had suddenly got a temperature, that it was up to a hundred and two, would she agree to call the whole thing off? Could he go home?

He heard little sounds from the floor above. Once a door opened and she called: 'You're not bored, are you? There are some magazines on the table!' He made an effort to unparalyse his throat and called out: 'No!'

He picked up a copy of *Vogue* and looked at the girl on the cover.

Then his eye fell on the big blue armchair. He listened. Carefully he got to his feet. For a moment he stood and let his hand slide over the upholstery, then he sat down in it. It was the most wonderful chair he had ever sat in. Room for a grown man. Then he stood up and went back to the sofa. He had sat in the blue chair.

Then all at once he could hear that she was having a shower. Now it was too hot, now it was too cold, now it was right, the hiss was steady; he sat listening to the hiss, his jaw dropped in awe. According to the old myth, Zeus turned himself into golden drops that fell on Diana; God, he said, let me be the drops of water that fall on Embla's shoulders! Now the hiss had stopped, she had turned the shower off. Again he could sense everything that was happening, viewing it as from above, as though he were on great stilts, high above the earth. He saw himself in his dinner jacket sitting on the sofa on the ground floor; he saw the young woman standing naked in the bathroom on the first floor drying herself: first she dried her face, then the back of her neck under her towelling turban; then she dried her shoulders, then loosely down her arms; then the towel was flung across one shoulder and drawn slantingly to and fro across her back, then over the other shoulder; then she raised her left arm and dried in one strike from wrist right into the armpit, now over her left breast that moved supply (were there drops of water on Embla's breast?) no, he was not sure of how she dried her breasts, perhaps she raised them slightly; queer to have something soft and bulging on your chest that you have to be rather careful with and which perhaps has to be lifted up a bit when you dry yourself; it must be a bit complicated being a woman. A strange tenderness towards her came over him as he sat there. Now it was her stomach and thighs, and her crutch; that perhaps was easier to dry for a woman than for a man. All at once the certainty came to him that the girl there was not embarrassed by her own body, that she did not squeeze her legs together, as he had seen other girls do when they dried, but straddled freely and gave herself the whole breadth of the towel; he could not tell why, but he suddenly felt so happy and proud, mostly on her behalf of course; then it was her knees, no, she had forgotten the small of her back and her bottom, but now it was her knees, now her legs, now she was bending forward with one foot on a stool, now she was drying between her toes, between her toes, what a joyful thought, Embla standing naked drying her toes; this imagined process of drying was one of the most beautiful performances he had ever witnessed.

And he had not lusted for her. Not for a second. He could have stood beside her in the bathroom and handed her the towel, he would not have desired her, he would have said: 'Your neck's wet,' he would have looked at her as one looks at a beautiful sculpture.

(For a moment he was frightened. Frightened at not having desired her. There's something wrong with me, he thought; that delightful performance was wonderful, like a very beautiful concert, but a man cannot look at a lovely woman and not desire her without there being something wrong with him. In fifteen years, when perhaps there will be a possibility, how am I going to bring myself to touch her? To me it seems a complete impossibility. I shall never be able to lay my hand on her bare skin in order to desire her. My attitude to her is that of a man to his daughter. Absolute purity. And there is something fundamentally wrong with absolute purity. Absolute purity is death. Am I in my relation to Embla, the girl I love, dead?)

At ten past eight she came down the stairs. He scrambled to his feet. He did not rightly know what he had been expecting: a princess in glittering golden sequins? He had to look to the side and down, down at the cement floor. She was wearing a pullover of white fluffy wool that left her arms and shoulders and a V at her neck bare, there was a brown tone to her skin; below this she wore a wide skirt with large amusing figures, mostly of animals, painted on its dark ground; he imagined that there was something Egyptian about it.

'Don't I look nice?' she said delightedly.

'Hah,' he said and almost burst into tears. For a moment he was so impressed at her being able to take such happy pleasure in herself; he thought: fancy a person having the inner assurance to be able to say of herself that she is charming! A sad thought flitted through his mind that really all people are charming. I should be charming too, he thought, if only I dared say so. But because I am uncertain, because I am tormented and sick-at-heart in my hired dinner jacket, because I am all the time thinking of the cut on my nose, because I am always painfully aware of my gluttonous person and my impossible pride—because of that I feel far from charming. Why don't I open my coat, show her my comical circus tent of a dinner jacket, dance about and say ecstatically: 'Don't I look nice?' *If I did, all my cares would be over, I should be free, we should fall into each other's arms!*

'So you'll take me along with you like this?' she said and blinked her big violet eyes comically.

'Hah,' said he.

'I made this skirt myself,' she said and swung round.

To him it was a masterpiece; he could see ibises and pyramids and hieroglyphs and elephants and black cats on it. For a moment he looked down at his own hands, they suddenly seemed so useless and clumsy, hands without purpose, hands without beauty. Why am I not wearing an embroidered shirt of many colours, he thought, a shirt that a woman has embroidered for me, or one that I have embroidered myself? Instead I go about in an anonymous ready-made affair, made by unknown people on strange machines: I have a white sheet-metal screen on my chest. . . .

All at once she was sitting beside him on the sofa. He could smell the clean smell of bath and skin and, surely there was a trace of eau-de-Cologne as well; he did not dare look at her. She sat fingering something on the table; all at once an acrid smell struck his nose, it reminded him of film cement; as a boy he had had a film projector and often used to stick bits of film together; he looked up and saw that she had a bottle of nail varnish. He sat watching the performance which was not a quick one, tense with admiration; then, all at once, she was letting all ten fingers dangle in the air; they were like little sausages and it was the funniest thing he had seen, he had to laugh; was that how it was done! She said:

'You must give me a cigarette. I daren't move till the varnish dries.'

He fumbled in his pocket, such a queer new pocket, not his pocket, pulled a cigarette out, tapped it against the table-top and got it into her mouth at the second attempt; (he missed the first time because he did not dare look, but he had to look the second time); his hand was trembling like a dowser's wand over a stream; it was so queer being near her mouth, so different; all at once he thought: It's an ordinary mouth, and felt a little gust of incomprehensible disappointment and irritation; but the irritation was an advantage, his hand was not trembling so violently as he held the lighted match for her.

Then her nails were dry; she took the cigarette from her

mouth and smiled at him. Something made him think of the remains of brandy in his flask and he told her about Doff, asked if she would like a drink, now, before they went.

'If you think we need one,' she said.

Had there been a note of surprise, a reproach in her voice? He felt suddenly uncomfortable, like a schoolboy, no, more like a representative of what is worst of all, of Night Norway, Male Norway, the Norway that cannot go to the Saturday evening dance until it has been round the corner and imbibed false strength and false laughter in the dark, the poor hearts that know no other way out than to let themselves be pickled in alcohol, the Norway that yearns (no country in the world knows what yearning is, like Norway) but is without hope; the feeling was so strong that he shivered, but he shook it off; it was as though he had been reprimanded, but perhaps she had not meant it like that; he muttered something to the effect that it was not necessary, but it might perhaps be pleasant; she went to get glasses from behind the kitchen curtain, stuck out her head with unhappy, frantically blinking eyes and said that wasn't it awful but she had no soda; he said: 'then we'll have water, water is excellent, water is the best thing there is!' When they were sitting and had said 'skaal' to each other, she said:

'I've an awfully weak head. The least thing makes me drunk and I talk nothing but nonsense. I hate doing that. And then I fall asleep. I've only been drunk twice in my life.'

With half-shut eyes she imitated a drunken person. It was so funny and such a good imitation that Ash roared with laughter. What a lot there was to her. She could change roles with the utmost ease, play a thousand parts; a continual stream of new life was always pulsating beneath her skin, always there was something warm and mysterious and variable about her that he could not grasp, and yet she was always herself, Embla.

When they went, she left her drink almost untouched. All at once Ash recalled a favourite saying of his grandfather, fat skipper Flose, which he always used when the whole family was seated round the table and one of the children did not want to finish what it had on its plate; old Flose would eat up what the child had left and say: 'Sooner shall my belly burst than good food be wasted.'

Ash shuddered. How could one ever bridge the gap between Flose and Embla?

They took a streetcar. Ash had to admit with a smile that he could not afford a taxi. They stood on the front platform. She had a head-shawl of silk and it kept slipping down on to her shoulders, then, with a comical sigh, she took it off altogether and stuffed it into her coat pocket. He stood tense with delight beside her. Then a great fear came over him. She was not a girl now, she was a woman. There was something adult and calm and wise about her, she was a woman and he felt like a little boy. This was an ordinary occurrence to her, an ordinary ball; she must have been to a thousand balls before, and much more splendid ones, she had been in Oslo and a whole year in Paris, and had she not been a short time in London too?

He was numbed; she seemed to have such beauty and elegance. He felt that he must say something, something that fitted the situation, something gallant, urbane, but all that burst from him was: 'You have lipstick on one of your teeth!'

'Where?' she said horrified, and ran her tongue over her front teeth. 'Has it gone now?'

'There's a bit left,' he said in a husky voice.

She opened her little handbag and took out a handkerchief. 'Wipe it off, Ash.'

He stood there paralysed, holding the fragrant little thing; good heavens, what a tiny thing, what does one use such a tiny thing for? Has a woman ever been seen to use such a silk postage stamp to blow her nose on? She closed her eyes and bared her teeth for him. With a silk-wrapped index finger he tried to wipe the red smear from her tooth, the streetcar lurched and swayed on a corner, but he did not dare put his left arm round her to hold her still, he had to make two attempts, surprised he thought: there is *something* about her that is cold and hard!

In that brief glimpse he had seen that two of her front teeth had porcelain fillings. Thanks, dear God, he whispered, for her not being completely perfect. There is nothing on earth more terrifying than the massively healthy, the eaters of raw foods, the open-air fiends, those who seem to have sixty-two pearly white teeth and not a hole in any of them, and who laugh with wide-open mouths; the entirely healthy are utterly stupid.

And there was a noisy, seething sea of people in evening dress, unrecognizable young men in dinner jackets and strange young girls in silk evening dresses. They were in the midst of a sea of chattering people. There was a table with cocktails in the lobby, but Embla smilingly shook her head. 'Not even a cherry?' he asked. Smilingly she took it in her teeth from the little stick he held out, and shuddered. They were late and Ash had no sooner drunk his cocktail than the sea of people was shepherded out through the lobby and down the smooth marble stairs to the club rooms in the basement, where the dinner was to be held. Momentarily they got separated and, like a drowning man, he stretched out his hand for her, got her hand in his; he had been terrified of losing her, yet he dropped her hand as if it had burned him. Embla's hand!

He had seen some people he knew. He had seen Erik Floden in a very elegant dinner jacket; he was with his enormous fiancée, Thea, and mountainous Thea was in salmon-pink tulle. He had seen Daniel and Gerda; heavens, now Constance would know about it in the morning. Well, the sooner the better. He had also caught a glimpse of Synnoeve. Thank goodness for that, he thought, so she has got to her ball. He had looked at her partner with some curiosity; Synnoeve had looked crossly at Ash and demonstratively held the young man's hand, and the young man had looked rather annoyed. Ah yes, Ash thought: life is not so easy. But then he remembered Synnoeve's chubby marzipan body and thought in an access of desire and despair: Lord, how easy and straightforward everything was with Synnoeve! No damned ideals, all beautiful open deceit. As he thought that, he hated the woman walking at his side. For one second he had hated Embla.

The horseshoe of long tables buzzed with the conversation of a hundred and fifty people. The room was filled with smoke and warmth and laughter. Were not one or two of the young men a bit merry? Their voices sounded so unaccustomedly loud and strong—normally they were well-behaved and soft-voiced.

The menu was beer and an aquavit, sausages and potato salad. Didn't Embla want her aquavit? No, why should she? Actually it was a revolting drink, so he had hers as well. (Why does it never occur to anyone on these committees that some women perhaps do not like aquavit—that it would be a good idea to serve red wine for the ladies. Have they never heard of wine?)

Ash had not approved of a suggestion that his little chamber orchestra should play at the ball; there was a time and a place for everything; they had rehearsed a small repertoire, some short pieces and the last movement of *Eine Kleine Nachtmusik*, the allegro. (Something had happened at their last rehearsal; while they were playing Ash had collapsed and had to sit down on a chair; the others stopped playing and gathered round him as he sat gasping on the chair. 'Are you ill?' He shook his head and said: 'Oh God, it was so lovely!' and they, wondering, 'What was so lovely?' and he: 'That passage where the second violins come in and frolic . . . You *got* it!' he gasped. They had stared at him and he had not been able to explain—that brief second of stupefying happiness when eight musicians get it absolutely *right*, that giddy heavenly moment, the one moment that perhaps will never come again, when they had played Mozart, had had the genius of Mozart! Trembling, he had got to his feet and embraced the student who played the flute, kissing him on the cheek; trembling, he said: 'God in heaven, it was so l-l-lovely!' then, a moment or two afterwards he thought, horrified: But I can never be the conductor of a big orchestra with an ocean of emotion in me like this; if I was conducting the Philharmonic and we came to something that moved me as greatly, I would drop my baton and break down; the audience would get their first view of a conductor standing helplessly on the rostrum, weeping!—oh, heavens, I'm useless, incapable, my whole life will be a fiasco if I can't manage to control my emotions; I must discipline myself!—after that he had been gruff and stern, 'Once more from the sixth beat,' he had ordered, but the heavenly moment had not returned; they had played it like pigs.)

No, chamber music and a students' ball did not go together, Mozart did not go with beer and aquavit. So, instead, they had a gramophone and records. Several of the undergraduates played jazz quite well and Ash would gladly play a bit himself, he said, and if they absolutely must have his choir to sing 'Little Brown Jug' (he happened to have done a new harmonization for it that he was rather proud of, written a new contrapuntal melody for the basses, in fact his 'Little Brown Jug' was quite a choral work), he hadn't any real objections to them doing that, it was only that when they began and the others joined in, no one would hear the choir, it would be swamped; and his suggestion was that they be content with community singing. And that's what was decided.

They had sung one or two of the songs and Embla sat looking through the stencilled sheets. She pointed to one she had just read.

'This is amusing,' she said.

Ash looked at the paper she held. It was a travesty on an old ballad.

'Oh, that,' he said. 'That was inspired by the lectures in political economy.' He twisted in his seat and added. 'I wrote it.'

She glanced at him. She bent towards him and said softly: 'But it's sheer blasphemy.'

'Yes,' he whispered, 'but the others don't know that.'

Their eyes met. Their secret merriment grew and grew. In the end their faces burst with great conspiratorial laughter; it was *too* funny.

'Poof!' she gasped, bit her napkin and held it clenched between her teeth. 'I think I'm going to die!' Her enormous blue eyes overflowed with tears.

'Oof, oof,' he almost bowed his head into his plate. But then he had to hush her; the dean was on his feet.

The dean was a tall thin man with a pale face, bristly hair, bushy eyebrows and a big, square, Norwegian snub nose. He was mathematical matter-of-factness personified; normally he terrified his students out of their wits, so that they did not understand a word of what he said. His was a respected name in academic circles, but now, as he stood there making his speech, a sense of violent disgust came over Ash, sorrow, horror, hatred; after a whole year of cramming and joyless lectures he now sat listening to the man speaking unctuously of the gay life of the student, his freedom and spirit, the importance of the university man as a champion of truth and justice. Ash was filled with a sickening feeling of shame at this immense discrepancy between life and theory, between the long academic year in which the man had spoken of nothing but what they must read and learn and this festive occasion when everything he said was eyewash; it seemed to him that he had heard deans say it all before, that deans must be a race apart, that one had to be born with a special chameleon-soul to *become* a dean.

Embla was touching him.

'You mustn't work your jaw muscles so,' she whispered with a little smile, 'even if you are angry.'

Aghast, he put his hand up to his face.

When the dean had sat down, she said:

'You never told me how the exam went.'

'Oh,' he said, 'it was only a first year exam. Nothing decisive. It went all right.'

'All right' was the word. All right. Done all right. And then that intolerable feeling of inner emptiness and disappointment after an examination; you have almost killed yourself reading, can scarcely drag yourself to the examination room; then you sit there for five hours writing for dear life; after that you come out and discover that you have made a few mistakes, but by and large you have done *all right*; the feeling of how nauseatingly and sickeningly *simple* it had been after all. Why all that unbearable nameless torment and examination fever?—what had that whole year meant?—all the torture of those months and weeks and days had resulted in a little mark on a piece of paper; a small hieroglyph written in ink, no larger than a speck. What about the mountain that gave birth to a mouse, he thought, and the next instant: If only I had produced a *mouse*!—for a mouse is alive, a creature that grows, but that little speck on a piece of paper, *I have produced a speck*—that's the result of one whole year!—I had life right under my nose, among friends in the Socialist Group, for four months I have known Embla and borne her face in my heart, I could have spoken to Embla, told her I loved her, taken her by storm, won her, I could have had some of that wonderful warm rich life that I have dreamed of, held her head in my hands and plumbed her wonderful eyes, that would have been living, and *only* that!—instead I have destroyed a whole year of my youth, a year that will never return, why?—to produce a speck!

He could not speak for bitterness and grief.

After a little while she asked:

'What actually are you thinking of becoming?'

And at that another stab of alarm went through him: his feeling of nothingness became twice as great; he just did not have an idea what he was going to be! And it struck him with terror that the forty-nine others had certainly used the year to make their plans, to do their lobbying, make sure of permanent, well-paid jobs for the end of the following year—while *he* . . . ? He turned a suffering face to her, smiled and said, with a shrug of his shoulders:

'Planter in Sumatra, perhaps.'

He was so depressed that he did not realize what he was saying as he added:

'Like to come with me?'

She smiled and pursed her lips:

'Might be fun.'

Afterwards he felt as though he were sinking; his question had been an unconscious attempt to discover her feelings for himself, and he had not meant that, had not dared do that. Now he sat there with her words ringing in his ear, listening to the echo of them. Her voice had been friendly, all right. But nothing more. The voice of a friend. Friend to friend. But only friend. The most terrible thing of all. Friend. The poorest thing of all. Friend. How does a man have to be made if he is to feel happy at being the *friend* of the best and most charming girl in the world? Just friend?

The time for his own speech was approaching. Most people had finished their sausages and potato salad. But not he. He was far too nervous. Now and then he glanced at the toast-master; when the toast-master got to his feet and tapped his glass, it would be to call upon him to propose the ladies. Then Ash must rise and stand there in front of them all. Numb with fear he patted his jacket, the paper was there in his inside pocket. He felt suddenly nauseated by the sight of his plate with its half-eaten piece of sausage and laid a sheet of stencilled paper over it.

There had been moments when he thought that he had written a good speech. He had worked on it, off and on, for a fortnight. He had accepted the job when he knew that he was going to take Embla. What he had thought, of course, was: I cannot do anything in the world, but I can make a speech. He had been reminded of the story of the acrobat, a good Catholic, who was so poor that he could not afford to buy a candle and burn it before the picture of the Virgin Mary, and so, in order to give her something, the only thing he could, stood on his head before her for ten minutes.

Ash had even gone to see Fiffolo, that expert master of ceremonies and writer of speeches for students' occasions. It was Fiffolo who had given him the tip that, when proposing The Ladies, you should use expressions from the professional terminology of your audience. 'For example,' Fiffolo had said, 'if I was proposing the ladies in the Norwegian Automobile Club, I would talk about warming up, clutch, ignition and a soft ride. . .' 'Hm' Ash had said and thanked him for his advice. He didn't like Fiffolo, nor his tone, but man hasn't thought it beneath him to learn industry from the ant and the art of building from the swallow, so why despise a tip or two about making speeches just because they come from a hairy billy goat?

The toast-master thrust his chair back, tapped his glass.

Ash gasped, his whole body began to quake, he closed his eyes in utter terror.

The Lad who wanted to Talk to a Woman and Managed to speak to the Ladies

There had been moments when he had thought that he had written a good speech; but as he rose heavily to his feet, he knew that what he had written was the most awful nonsense ever penned. He was so certain of this that for several seconds he stood looking out over the sea of faces, unable to grasp why he was on his feet. It was all a dreadful misunderstanding, a ghastly misunderstanding: he pushed his chair against the table, seized hold of the chair-back, swallowed, opened his mouth to say 'I'm awfully sorry ...' and to his boundless surprise heard himself say: 'Dean, Ladies and Gentlemen.'

It wasn't the students and their girls, the few members of the staff he was frightened of. He was frightened of Embla. He had written the speech for her. It was a message, a jesting, upside down message that said the opposite of what he meant; a message that never went below the surface, that did not reveal a fraction more of his true face than anyone could see, an impersonal, abstract message, but just because of that it had to be formally good; as he didn't dare show her his heart, he had to play out his talent. But the speech was all nonsense. There was nothing intellectual or witty about it, it was just an exhibition of clowning; it was a long speech without a word about the worth and dignity of man, not a word against capitalism and Nazism, it didn't have as much as a socialist comma; there he stood in a crowded forum, with all the time that he wanted, the faces of his audience turned expectantly towards him, like white flower chalices in the night—stood there on that May evening of grace 1939, a year that everyone felt was going to be a fateful one in the history of the world, and what sort of speech was he going to give them?—he was to propose the health of the ladies!

And Embla, whom he had several times caught glancing round to see what sort of strange creatures they had at the College—wouldn't she hide her face in her hands in shame, when her partner, a socialist from the Socialist Students' Group, stood up and blew a toy trumpet instead of the big war trumpet which he actually possessed?

Hadn't he, just a short while before, thought of Fiffolo with pity and contempt because he was just an empty speechifier? And hadn't he, even more recently, sat there white in the face because of the dean's *oratory*? Mustn't all the reproaches he had cast at the others now rebound on himself with ten thousand times the force?

And in his heart he knew that this was not the occasion for socialist propaganda; everyone has a right to play and to fool; without that we are lost; yet he had that inexplicable bad con science and feeling of guilt that almost all Norwegians have when they find themselves on their hindlegs in public and their faces are not grave nor their utterances profound. He heaved a deep sigh, and in a quavering voice, said:

'Dean, ladies and gentlemen.'

The repetition amused them; they clapped and he was aware of their warmth, felt a wonderful, overwhelming gratitude as he suddenly realized that they liked him. He was not an outcast. They liked him. He saw some of the students nudge their partners and rub their hands, as though to say: this is going to be fearfully funny. This Burlefoot is capable of anything, he can come out with the most outrageous things.

And all at once Ash knew that he was going to give them a speech.

'I would like to begin with a quotation from de Quincy. In his book, *Confessions of an English Opium-Eater,* he says: "In this state of imbecility I had, for amusement, turned my attention to—political economy." '

(Seventy-five dinner-jacketed students cautiously turned to look at the two professors of political economy. There were cautious chuckles.)

'Tonight, I wish to refute that insinuation. I want to go even further and show that we need this excellent subject in order to appreciate the most precious of all our treasures. *Homo poeticus* can sing woman, but only *homo oeconomicus* can really appreciate her.' (Hear, hear!)

'Therefore, this evening I intend to make a purely endogenous-economic analysis of woman.'

(Relieved laughter from the students. It was balm to recognize the curriculum in this new, unheard-of guise.)

'My first concern will be to show how the price of this particular commodity is determined by means of four simultaneous equations, where the quantity as well as the shape and base of the demand curve are assumed to be given.'

(Now they were with him; they could guess what he was driving at and groaned with delight; seventy-five students said 'sshh' to partners wanting to know what simultaneous equations were.)

'In an appendix that I have prepared, you will find details of the method of calculation used in determining the numerical magnitude of the supply. My calculations show that today there exist 53.16 million women of supplyable age. Gentlemen, 53.16 million women!'

(Now they're laughing, Embla. Do you know why I took that astronomical figure? Do you know that when I said 53.16 million, I was thinking of one?)

'Viewed superficially, one might be tempted to believe that this overwhelming supply would force the price of the commodity right down. Such is not the case. At this point it is of the utmost importance that we are clear in our own minds as to the difference between the price of non-repetitive use and that of—a fixed subscription.'

(Oh, how they liked that!)

'We must now ask: from the economic point of view, what kind of commodity is woman? What does her demand curve look like? How elastic is the demand? Is woman an essential commodity or a luxury? Is demand represented by a rectangular parabola, where xy equals a constant, or is it respectively greater or smaller than one?'

(Now they were entirely with him. A lump came into his throat as he realized that none of them suspected how serious this was for him. Some of the more gallant shout: 'Greater!')

'If we study the matter thoroughly, however, we shall see that our commodity has an inherent tendency to upset all accepted theories, since it is both a necessity and a luxury. We can consume so and so much, or be content with so and so little; thus demand would seem to oscillate between very wide limits. We know, however, that at other times demand has a tendency to be embarrassingly inelastic, and this inelasticity can be expressed thus—though I perhaps risk offending half my audience —this is a commodity with a marginal utility equal to nil.'

(Now they are bouncing on their seats with delight: this is sheer impertinence but at the same time unassailable; it's like a lecture. . . .)

'I am sure, however, that it will restore concord between me and my audience, when I add that this is tantamount to saying that the total utility of the good approaches "plus infinity"; that is to say: is infinitely great.'

(Clapping and drumming feet; now the girls are clapping too! Do you think I'm a fool, Embla?)

'I shall not in this connection touch on Senior's concept of abstinence. It goes without saying that exaggerated abstemiousness would have a disastrous effect on their normal process of price-formation—but perhaps I may add in parenthesis that you don't need to be an economist to understand that. End parenthesis.'

(Listen to them, Embla! Have you ever heard howls like it? You see, the dean's always saying 'end parenthesis' in his lectures. And look at him! He's sitting there actually laughing! So he can laugh at himself! Perhaps deans are also human after all. . . .)

'Now a glance at the structure of capital formation. Woman represents both a production- and a consumption-commodity and investment is normally made in the course of a relatively short period of years, the so-called years of youth—hm, we are considering here the different stages of supply—and the maximum woman-investment is normally found at the solemnization of marriage; compare Jevons's triangle.' (I can take a breather here. Nice to be able to pause for a bit, while they're busy laughing.) 'This plant, however, has a long life; and however much, in individual cases, one might wish to see it written off quickly, it is not advisable to exceed the rate fixed by the Revenue authorities, which is normally two per cent per annum, which, with organic depreciation of its utility value, corresponds to a disinvestment period of fifty years.'

(Oh, how they were loving it! What a pleasure it is to be able to give pleasure to others. Every one of the students was rocking with delight, and their girls were rocking with them!)

'You must forgive me, but I must also mention the commodity's possible residual value after it has been written off. Where so-called scrap-value and its influence on calculation are concerned, I need only refer those interested to page one hundred and seventy-eight of the *Student's Textbook of Cost Accounting*.'

(Have I been disrespectful, Embla? Disrespectful to the

human being in woman? It wasn't meant like that. You didn't take it amiss, did you? No? Nor have the others. Listen to them!)

'A not unknown professor in economics—whose name I shall not mention, since he is here tonight . . .'

(That's made them sit up. Especially the professor. Just look at him.)

'. . . has developed the following argument in his textbook: "In a way, one can with a certain justification say, or at any rate not deny . . ." '

(Come on! If they don't stop laughing like that, I'll never finish; but I've scored a bull's-eye there. I've hit off the professor's academic style to a T.)

' ". . . that within a certain framework, or at any rate not outside it, it is, so to speak, the aim of cultural activity to thrust the original purely organic demand more into the background, or at any rate less into the foreground, and to make room for cultural needs".'

(They'll kill themselves. If only you knew, Embla, how we've sat wondering ourselves blue in the face trying to figure out what the man meant. Now the old boy's sitting there shaking with laughter himself. Perhaps I've been mistaken about professors too?)

'However, the woman who can satisfy both the organic and the cultural needs of the consumer will perhaps be in a position to obtain the theoretical perfect monopoly price. This price can be determined purely geometrically, simply by raising a perpendicular at the point of bisection of the base of her value-triangle.'

(One student leaped up from his chair like a shot rabbit and lay writhing on the floor. Was what I said as funny as all that? It's only what we're taught in a new version.)

'In the economic game, woman will often find it rewarding to keep an eye on her own volume-index. Here, too, the consumer also employs mathematical statistics, using quadrantal deviation to chart the spread of charms round the point of bisections.'

(Oho, oho, oho! God help me, I believe they'll have the tables over. I'll have to stop or they'll be smashing the glasses . . .)

'In conclusion, let me just say that woman's influence on the balance of payments will normally be negative; but, on the other hand, she will most often have a very positive effect on the population's nett reproduction quotient!'

(Well, Embla, that's that; all that remains to be said is the obvious remark that, difficult as it may be to put a price on woman, it is much easier and more pleasant to appreciate her, as we all do, and so ...)

'Gentlemen, I give you: The Ladies!'

There's always a drop or two of flat beer at the bottom of your glass. Why? Always, when you have talked your throat dry, when you've exerted yourself to the utmost, given all that you have, when you're collapsing over the tape as though at the end of a fifty kilometre ski race ...

The applause was violent. It must have been quite a speech; they were all on their feet, clapping and calling out, some were even shouting 'Bravo!'—in a Scandinavian country!—he had stepped down off his chair, he was trembling and had to sit down; for a while he sat, confusedly staring down into his empty beer glass, then he gulped, glanced at Embla; wasn't she a bit queer about the face?—he had to ask her:

'Did you understand any of that?'

'About half, but you were awfully good.'

Swiftly and lightly she laid her hand on his arm, reminding him of a mother patting her son's arm and saying: 'Clever boy, you were fearfully good.' He did not know how he should take it. To be on the safe side, he smiled.

Ten seconds later he thrust his hand into his inner pocket. There was the manuscript of his speech. He gasped and went pale. He had spoken without his text!

A Moment of Innocence

After the tables had been cleared there was dancing.

He was dancing with Embla.

He said to himself, half dead with ecstasy: Good heavens—I am dancing with Embla.

After a while she looked up at him smiling and said:

'Do you always hold your partner so loosely round the waist?'

He mumbled something unintelligible in reply, blushed and hoped most fervently that she had not noticed. The feel of the supple play of the muscles in her back had been so intimidating. Her back was so young and she so incredibly slim round the waist. His teeth chattered quietly as he drew her closer. At that moment, when he was dancing with her, body to body, when he felt her up against him, felt her stomach and thighs, his whole being listened, he listened with all his senses. And he was aware that she was only dancing; she danced well, excellently, lightly. She liked dancing, but she was only dancing. For an instant his head swam with relief and enthusiasm: she is not a flirt, she does not telephone with her body.

Then he felt tremendously sad. If she had wanted to convey to him the least little message about her feelings, that they might possibly be a little more than platonically friendly, she could have done so now. His body was a network of listening nerves, he could have registered the most infinitesimal sign of affection from her. But there was nothing about her to say anything but that she was dancing.

To himself he decided that it was a good thing it was so.

After a while a hot swing record was put on; they stood for a few seconds listening to the music, he asked: 'Do you like swing?' and she turned to him and he could see the answer in her face and her half-closed eyes; it was as if she were in a state of semi-sleep, the rhythm was already in her body, and he became so afraid and warm and happy; this profound, feminine transport in her body even before he had put his arm round her. Of all dance-music he liked swing best, and now she stood there quivering imperceptibly and lithely to the rhythm. She came slowly towards him as he stretched out his hand, she came towards him, he took her outstretched hands and held her thus. At first there was a yard between them, they gazed smiling into each other's eyes, laughing; they danced thus, laughing, round and round, bumping into other couples, but not noticing it, laughing happily to each other, happy that their bodies had merged with the other element of rhythm; they no longer had bodies; at that moment they were disembodied and free; he was happy beyond belief, he had forgotten everything else, he was in the land of laughter and rhythm, he let go of her with one hand, drew her in towards him, thrust her out, pulled her back, their bodies danced disembodiedly, he had shut his eyes and just had the picture of her wonderful face in him, he was dancing with his eyes closed, drew her to him, held her by the elbows, danced; now she was Jewess, Assyrian, African, he was without body or consciousness, he danced wildly, panting in pure happiness; for a brief second he was aware that people were standing looking at them, that they seemed to be dancing in a circle of spectators, but then forgot it; her face was so wild and good, and the skin on her great eyelids was slightly brown, faintly brown, but now this brown was no longer deadly, dangerous colour, it was only right, right like their dance, right like their bodies, he held her by the elbows and danced, liberated, he was a spirit and this the moment of innocence. The record came to an end and he was still in the ecstasy of the rhythm, in a state of pure joy, he stopped, but the rhythm persisted, in the transition to calm he bent his head down to hers and brushed her forehead with his cheek; it was the moment of innocence, at that moment he could have put his lips to her eye as an innocent echo of the rhythm, in that moment of innocence he could have kissed her.

Then he was awake again, feeling guilty. He stared at her forlornly: what had he, for a moment, been on the point of doing? And at the same time he felt so heart-rendingly sad, felt as though his life was a failure; he could have done it, but hadn't. Something inside him reached out in a frenzy of grief for that lost second; could it ever come back? For how should he, awake and full of guilt, ever be able to touch her? God, you who are almighty, can you give a man a second back? Just one, tiny little second out of all eternity? One second? God, am I asking for too much? One single little second?

He was shaking all over; in a cracked voice he said to her: 'Come, let's s-sit down for a bit.'

And together they went and sat at a table. It was the same table at which Erik Floden and his huge fiancée in salmon-pink tulle were sitting.

A strange thought seized him as he sat listening to Embla talking with the other two. He thought: Embla and I danced swing together. We dance very well together. Swing. I shall never forget what I have just experienced with her. She dances superbly to swing. She is made to swing it and for five months we two have sat at the long table in the Stable, our brows furrowed with effort, discussing Marx and Engels!

One can without exaggeration say, he thought, that the world is utterly crazy.

He had to excuse himself for a moment.

'Shan't be long,' he said.

She smiled to him and nodded.

The 'gentlemen' was full of young men in dinner jackets. They slapped him on the shoulder.

'Magnificent speech. The funniest thing I've ever heard. Did you see the dean?'

He dodged and smiled. That was all over now. Done with.

One of them said:

'Some doll you have with you this evening. Where did you get hold of her, you old dog? What's her name?'

Another said:

'Embla Tombson? Oh, yes, she's not a bad little piece.'

Ash turned from the porcelain wall. He looked searchingly at the latter speaker. It had obviously been said as a compliment. But ... should he go after the fellow and demand an explanation?

Several others came in. Fresh praise for his speech. Fresh

questions about his partner's identity. Again he heard someone name her:

'Embla Tombson? One of the smartest things on two legs in the whole town.'

He softened with pride, the pride of the young man hearing others confirm that his chosen one is exceptional. He couldn't bear it, besides the others were standing looking him delightedly in the face; he was choking with pride, must say something, 'Oh yes,' he said, looked quickly round to see that the first speaker really had gone, 'she's not a bad little piece.' Thereupon the dinner-jacketed elk gave a coarse, hysterical laugh, rushed for the door and escaped into the corridor.

Escaped?

What came next he was to regard later as one of the most astounding things that had ever happened to him. There were even times when he could not believe that it had happened, but felt that he must have dreamed it.

In the corridor he walked into a group of girls and young men. They seized upon him and all at once he was in their midst. They too commented on his speech. He smiled wanly. Then one of the girls said something into his ear. It was a second before he grasped what she meant. The word was an allusion to something he said in his speech. And by the way the girl said it he realized that some people might have taken it as something very risqué, even coarse. Had he been coarse? Being with Embla, he would have wanted at all cost *not* to be coarse! So, he flushed, felt suddenly guilty and reluctant to meet the girl's eye. She had said only one word, but she had said it close to his ear, said it teasingly, reproachfully, provocatively. What she said was:

'The perpendicular.'

Then Ash had recovered sufficiently to be able to turn his head and look at the girl.

She was both pretty and not pretty, both pleasing and un-attractive. She had grey-green eyes and thick reddish hair, now drawn back and held in place by a narrow ribbon of brown velvet round her forehead. She reminded him of an Inca girl; he could see her ears and the whiter skin by the ears, skin that previously her hair had veiled from the sun. She was a big-boned girl with thick lips and large cheekbones; her lips were heavily made-up, her eyebrows blacked. There was a tiny scar on her top lip, too small to have been a hare lip: had she fallen once or cut herself? He could see faintly, but distinctly some reddish, almost fair hairs at the corners of her mouth; if she had had black hair, she would have had a faint moustache. He recognized her the moment he looked at her. He had noticed her at several dances in the club and on each occasion with a feeling of strong dislike. There was something challenging about her manner, she usually danced in a loud, boisterous way, had a loud laugh, seemed always to wish to attract attention, would plump down on men's knees (once she had plumped herself down on Ash's and he had stood up and put her down), on a couple of occasions she had danced the can-can on a table. To be sure there had been sexual tension between her and Ash, Ash had been distinctly aware of her; but this tension had made him feel antipathy. There was something cold and hard about her provocative attitude; Ash had never wanted to dance with her; he knew that her unspoken question would be: 'Dare you?' And Ash had not dared. Had not wanted.

He stood for a moment looking at the girl with slightly raised eyebrows.

'Come,' he said and took her by the hand.

'What?' she said.

'I want to tell you something.'

He drew her away from the others. He had no idea who her partner was. He led her towards the stairs, then up the stairs.

'What is it?'

'A secret.'

They passed some others standing by the door breathing in fresh air. He drew her out into the grounds, it was dark.

'Can't you say it here?'

'It's very private.'

They were now somewhere down in the garden. He could feel that there was no one near, no one to see them, felt their isolation in his back. He stopped, turned her towards him. Night, early summer night. He let go of her. Briefly he surveyed her and she looked back at him, chewing her gum. Then he put his left arm round her shoulder, she made a little movement, he had caught hold of her hair and was holding her as one holds a horse by its mane. He backed her against a tree; his grip on her hair was so strong that he forced her head up and back; then he laid his right hand on her breast, she squirmed, he let his hand slide down. He could feel the contour of her beneath the thin silk of her dress. She tried to kick his shins, but he held her as she was. She couldn't remove his hand. The whole time he had her by the hair. Now he bent his head towards her, looked into her face, approached his mouth to hers, got a glimpse of the scar in her upper lip. Then there was only a hair's breadth between their mouths and he could feel her hot breath laden with beer and chewing gum; he stood and looked into her eyes and all at once he saw in her face that now he could take her if he wanted to. He gave her a last clasp—and let go of her. It was like letting go of a bent willow branch.

He raised his eyebrows as he looked at the gasping girl. Then he dusted his hands.

'Lovely night, isn't it?'

He waited a few seconds, then he took her hand, led her back to the building. They did not exchange a word. As they came into the light on the open space in front of the building and were near the entrance, he took his comb from an inner pocket, and said:

'Perhaps you ought to tidy your hair.'

She took the comb, her greeny-grey eyes full of hate, and sparks flew as she combed her red hair.

They went in. The moment they were inside, she stopped, let him go first. He gave her a slight courteous bow, walked on alone. For a moment he felt a slight shiver between his shoulder-blades, he thought: she'll throw a knife, from behind.

The next second he had forgotten her.

Whenever, later in life, he thought of this strange episode about which there was always a dreamlike haze, he could never understand his own behaviour. The thought of touching a girl, no matter which girl, always made him madly embarrassed, yet here he had behaved like an out and out conquistador, had bowled the girl over in a matter of thirty seconds, he had been without pity. Was it an upsurge of hatred of the girl that had

made him so enterprising? Is hatred, then, a stronger force than
love? Was he drunk? Intoxicated by success and the goodwill
of the students?

Or?

Or had the decisive factor been pressure from the person who
sat at a table in the dance hall waiting for him, pressure from
her he loved, bitterly, desperately, impotently, pressure from
the young girl to whom he could never behave as the oppressor
and subduer?

As he opened the door into the dance hall, to Embla, he felt
sickeningly afraid: What if she was no longer there? If she was
not sitting where he had left her? If she were dancing with
someone else? If she had left him? That had happened to him,
at a dance. He had gone there with a girl, but some time during
the evening she suddenly ceased to exist where he was concerned, was dancing with someone else, had quite simply left
him and gone to another. Why? How could things like that
happen? It is a great and a cruel fear that comes over all young
men at certain moments, the fear of losing the chosen one in
inexplicable circumstances, by witchcraft, the intervention of
the powers of darkness; all at once she is there no more, the
loss is inexplicable, in his frenzied pain the young man gropes
at the empty air.

But Embla was sitting at the table.

He hurried towards the table, halted and looked at the little
group of people, saw her beloved, wonderful face and gave a
little groan of relief.

There were several more people at the table now. She was
sitting surrounded by three or four couples. He noticed how
absorbed the others were by her, how they bent forward to hear
her and see her, he saw their smiles and the happy enchanted
attention on their faces, and a lump came into his throat. When
she noticed him, she stretched out a hand towards him and
wiggled her fingers, she wanted him to take her hand.

'There you are!' she said warmly, sweetly.

Later, they danced a few more times together, but the moment
of innocence never returned.

The ball ended at one o'clock.

They were standing getting their coats and hats. He helped her on with her coat. God, dear God in heaven, he prayed helplessly, let there be one thing about Embla that isn't as it should be. One tiny little thing that I don't like, one little thing that isn't wonderful, good, true and warm. God was busy and hadn't really time: Have a good look at her hair, he muttered. Ash looked at her hair, her wonderful nut-brown hair, looked hard, stared till his eyes were popping, and deep down in her hair he saw a little piece of dandruff, one solitary piece in that wealth of nut-brown. Ash smiled, a slight wry smile, a lump came into his throat and he couldn't get himself to thank God. Nor could he bring himself to touch her hair and brush the speck of dandruff out. Besides, it was so microscopic that only God and a desperate young man could have discovered it.

Outside, in the street, they landed in the middle of a group of students, who were standing singing. When they saw Ash, they insisted that as a finale he should conduct them in 'Sing the Student's Happy Day'. Ash swallowed. He gave them a note, there were several of his little choir there in the group, yet it was a thin sound they produced. There was only one tenor, but four basses. 'No cares yet . . .' sang the basses. That made him feel wicked and evil, for he was so young that he still loved the truth.

Then the group had gone and they were alone in the street. It was one of the last nights in May, a little cold, but even so there was a hint of the mildness of approaching summer in the air.

There were some faint little stars in the sky.

He stood awkwardly beside her. Then he shut his eyes and said: 'Would you mind if we went for a bit of a walk?'

She sighed slightly, as if she were tired, and a nameless fear shot through him, perhaps it was going to end here!—but then she smiled, blinked her big eyes and said:

'It would be lovely. A little fresh air after all that heat.'

'You know,' he said, they were over on the other side of the street now and by themselves; he could hear the sound of their steps in the night-quiet street. 'You know I've scarcely had time to talk with you all evening.'

She did not reply to that. She just turned her head towards him and smiled. They walked on slowly.

A little while later he said, with difficulty:

'Do you think we could walk in the park?'

She said:

'If the gates are open, yes. But at this hour of the night?'

She looked at him with big, blue, clear, pure eyes.

He turned off with her, up the side street.

He saw the big wrought-iron gates of the park.

All at once he began to tremble.

The Night of Nights

They had been strolling in the night-quiet park; now and again they had sat on a bench; all the time they had talked together in quiet voices; they were frank and friendly with each other; they were the same age, twenty-three; they both had smiling faces; she got smile wrinkles on one side of her nose when she smiled; he got them round his eyes, he had done so ever since he was a boy. She had a quiet, sweet way of speaking, now and again she used her hands and fingers to express a thought, for long stretches at a time she was silent and just listening; his way of talking was more restless, almost staccato; he spoke quietly because of the night and the park, but he talked incessantly; it was as if he did not dare let there be a pause.

For a moment—while they were sitting on a bench—he looked at her little brown hand lying only a hair's breadth from his own. If only I dared move my hand on to hers, he thought; my God, if I dared stop this flow of fatuous words that is slipping so smoothly from my mouth; if only I dared stop—he was so incredibly near to her—then I could look at her face, he thought, and just be natural; take her warm hand in mine and say: 'Embla, I am so fond of you.'

Was it nameless fear of a possible refusal that held him back? The knowledge that if she had to say no, then the rest of his life would be without hope, life without meaning or content for all eternity? Better to live in uncertainty, than to go about for the rest of his life like his own corpse.

Perhaps too there was a feeling of shame. For he was very proud; inconceivably full of self-esteem. He knew, was aware with every bit of him, that if he bared his heart to her and said: 'Embla, I am so fearfully fond of you,' his voice would betray him; he would stand before her as a beggar. Let the words once slip out and his poverty and loneliness would be obvious; he had no one in the whole world, no father or mother whom he counted as his, no sister, no friend, no God; even the clothes he was wearing were not his; he was the most naked being on earth, his only possession was his wild, hopeless longing; this Ash-Lad would prefer to hide when he opened his bundle, because it contained only ignominy; if he said to her: 'Embla, I am so fearfully, fearfully fond of you,' he knew that he would break down and kneel before her, not with the right given by admiration and love, but in the mendicant shame of his poverty. To pronounce the words of such a declaration would be to smash the armour that was now holding him up; then he would let all his feelings pour out; even before he heard her answer, he would have to hide his face in his hands and be powerless, helpless, like a child that had got lost. And he had too much self-esteem to allow himself to sob in her lap. That was the only thing he could not do; he could not dissolve into floods of tears and beg Embla for her love. Dimly he sensed that a woman was not won in that way; she could feel compassion for a cripple and drop a coin in his outstretched hand, but compassion is not love! He wouldn't present himself before her as he was then, he could not; if they were ever to meet, it must be on a footing of equality; only a prince can ask for the hand of a princess; if it was to happen, he must come to her riding, with sunlight on his hair and strength in his heart, he would rein his charger in and flourish his plumed hat, he would lay his hand on the princess's saddle and salute her. He would greet her, in his eyes love would be sparkling, he would be trembling, but not with apprehension; he would look at her with the right of love, and victory would be in his heart, and *she* would lower her gaze before *his*.

Then . . .

For a moment he had a vision, a vision so surprising and horrible that his heart stopped beating.

(The whole time he was chatting with her in a quiet voice about irrelevant things; he kept up the flow of words as if a pause had to be avoided at all costs; if he had stopped speaking, would she have been able to hear the pounding of his desperate heart?—or was he talking in the subconscious desperate hope that he would so exhaust her that she would momentarily put her head against his shoulder?—was it a repetition of the moment of innocence he was hoping for?—earlier that evening he had been immeasurably proud of her not having shown the least sign of flirtatiousness; now he was wishing from the depths of his heart that she might show one, a tiny little one; that she would say: 'Ash, I'm a bit cold; can I have some of your warmth?' and then the miracle would happen: he would draw her to him and put his arms round her, and because it was cold and she was feeling cold, he could lay his cheek against hers, and as it was cold and she was feeling cold he could set his mouth against her cheek, the rhythm of his warming blood would bring about that same miracle of innocence as the music had, with closed eyes he would seek her mouth and her mouth would accept his. But she was not feeling cold. He talked the whole time, talked profoundly about a book by a Frenchman he had just read; he was two people, one made conversation, the other was mortally concerned with love for the young woman; while the former chatted, the latter had a strange, horrible vision.)

He had thought: never her compassion; if it is to be, I must possess her utterly.

And it was this idea of utterness that made his head suddenly swim. Suddenly, fortuitously, he had looked into man's profoundest terror.

At the bottom of things is death.

In that swift second he had recognized that love and death are life's two great demons. He used to think, for his knowledge of life came largely from novels, that love was light and easy, a dance on a flower-strewn bank. Now, he sat there knowing that at the bottom of love is death.

For a fraction of a second he had glimpsed what it would be like to possess her. If he won her, he must know her through and through, must explore every corner of her soul, just because his love was so great; he must possess every thought in her mind, because his love was so frantic. He must possess her utterly in all spheres; there would not be room for other people, not even for things; he would regard all who visited her and took up her thoughts as mortal enemies; all friendliness and understanding would be wiped from his mind; if he had Embla, it would mean that the socialists would have to have their meetings elsewhere; since she was the centre, the point that warmed the group and held it together, that could mean that the most valuable group of people in the country would be split up; if he had Embla he would make himself guilty of killing the highest ideal he knew—socialism; at that second he knew that socialism was a chimera and that any edifice of thought must fall before life's inmost demon: love.

He thought, greatly wondering, why had Karl Marx's *Das Kapital* become world famous—after all a whole world has let itself be taken in—the book of books should be called *Of Love* —why has no one written *Of Love?* He knew that he would be mortally jealous of the things she took in her hand, of her lumps of clay, her pottery, her pen, there was murder in his heart at the thought of her telephone, he would have it taken out, tear it from the wall, she must be isolated. And he must possess all her thoughts, all her memories, her early youth, her childhood. What secrets did she have? What lay hidden in the depths of her enormous deep blue eyes, beneath the dangerous brownish skin on her lids and round her eyes? Would he like *everything* about her, when he had searched the secret places of her soul and explored her past? (And he must like everything. She was the only one. And love is without pity.) What had her previous experiences been? Was it thinkable that this wonderful, charming, travelled, witty and graceful woman was a virgin at the age of twenty-three? He had not wished her to be that, for he considered virginity a disease, a disease of the bourgeoisie; but if she was not, that was synonymous with her, with her having . . .

'You had a queer look in your eyes then,' she said and smiled.

He did not know what he replied. He had turned his head aside, for he knew that at that moment his face was as full of demoniac hatred as his heart.

He knew that if he ever won her, if he reached so deep into her that she opened fully for him, he would sear his soul and die; at that same moment she must die too. Love and death, those two cannot be parted.

In his youthful moments of romantic melancholy, of romantic frivolity, he used to repeat to himself a sentence from the Bible. It had been a poetic play; the words of The Song of Songs had become fixed in his mind because of the beauty of their language. But it was only the first half of the verse he had crooned, the rest he had not understood. Now he did.

> Set me as a seal upon thine heart, as a seal upon thine arm; for love is strong as death, jealousy is cruel as the grave; the coals thereof are coals of fire, which hath a most vehement flame.

Get to the bottom? Of oneself? Of Embla?

(And now they were talking about Paris, she gave him the addresses of some people she knew there, whom he might find pleasant and profitable to go and see, sweet, nice people. He sat listening to her quiet, warm, rich voice; he had fished out his fountain-pen and a piece of paper, an envelope, to write on; luckily the writer had not written name and address on the back, but it was so queer to sit and write what Embla dictated on an envelope from Gunnhild; he wrote the names and addresses, a supplier of clips for ear-rings, perhaps he would like to call on the proprietors of the *pension* where she herself had stayed? If he had time he must ring up the owner of the pottery workshop where she was a pupil for eight months, just give him greetings *de la part de Mademoiselle Tombson*, one side of her nose crinkled with smile-wrinkles as she spoke French and referred to herself as 'Mademoiselle'; he listened to her while his other being pondered what lay at the bottom of all things.)

One should not go to the bottom of things. One should leave that to the professionals.

Only the professionals, he thought have the cynicism, the iron strength, and are sufficiently blunted to be able to go to the bottom of things and endure the sight of what they see there. Leave it to the professionals. To the prison warders, the police, leave it to those who can look into the face of a little girl of six, who has been raped and calmly ask her what the man looked like; leave it to the depth psychologists and the attendants in asylums, those who can listen calmly to the bestial shrieks from the padded cells; leave it to the surgeons, to the doctors who can calmly perform a *post mortem* on a body that has lain three months in a lake. Leave death to the generals. Leave it to the politicians. (For a moment he saw the German, Wolfgang's face in front of him. He stood five years of terror and bloodshed and concentration camps, he thought; Wolfgang is a professional.)

And the young man Ash? At that moment he understood what he really was.

He was an amateur.

He loved life when it was good, he shrank back in terror when it was bad. A lover and an amateur; a young man, so timid and sensitive that he would rather kill himself than a kitten. In that heady, sickening second he knew that he was doomed to be an eternal fugitive, the eternal broken reed when in the face of death. In spite of his height and bodily strength, in spite of his fearlessness and daring, despite the whole struggle he wanted to wage against compulsion and repression (where there is no freedom that is my country), despite all the colours on his palette and all the arrows in his quiver, despite the satyr and the Titan in him—he had the heart of a young girl.

He looked at his hands lying in his lap. Perhaps a singer's hands, he thought, perhaps a poet's hands. What importance has a song or a poem, if I drop to my knees at the first sign of death's cruelty? All at once he imagined that for some inconceivable reason his country had made him a general. Well, he thought, I could be a general and lead my troops to defend my country. But only as long as I did not see blood. The sight of the first mutilated body would make me crazed with fear and hatred of death; I would tear off my general's badges, give orders for a cease fire, demand an immediate peace conference, and do everything to avoid the sight of pointless death. To my people I would be a deserter, I would be court martialled and shot.

Slowly he turned his head towards the young woman who sat beside him on the seat in the spring night. He looked into her big, pure, wonderful blue eyes, eyes in a skin-brown frame, the ripe death-frame of womanhood, he dropped his gaze.

He was an amateur.

A little later he thought: Suppose I used guile? In love and war all things are supposed to be fair? If on some excuse or other I could draw her so close to me that I could seduce her, overpower her, take her? If only a man has the cunning, such things are possible, if you can believe what you read?

He gulped and gave himself a wan smile. Cunning?—he thought, I cannot use cunning. Well, yes, where indifferent things are concerned, things that I do not love. I managed to get fifty crowns off the price of a motor-cycle; that was a step forward. But not when I love.

And besides, if I won her by a stratagem, I would *not* be achieving the inmost longing of my heart. Let us imagine that I managed to rape her there in the bushes (unthinkable because her purity has wiped out my sexuality, tonight I have none). Then I should have possessed her body for a wretched moment; but would I have had her love? I am not asking for physical satisfaction, I am asking for the miracle. The miracle is love. Love should be a flower opening for the sun.

If I took her by cunning, I should know for all time—every hour and every minute of my life—that I had got her in an infamous way. I should never be sure, then, that I really possessed her. The victory one achieves by cunning is the most certain of all defeats.

A little while later still a word sprang to his lips and he said: 'Tananarivo.'

He said it with smiling melancholy.

'Um?' she said, 'what does that mean?'

'A word,' he said, 'a word that suddenly occurred to me. A word game. I could say "Tananarivo" and you could say, for example, "Atacama".'

'Tananarivo?' he said softly.

'Atacama,' she replied, her lips pursed with repressed laughter.

He looked at her smiling face and knew that he would always remember that moment, a moment for ever taken out of eternity and held tight. He had asked and she had answered, but of course she had not known what question she was answering.

'That reminds me,' she said, great eyes blinking merrily, 'of the story of the man who invented a word. I think it was Doff told it me. He has a fund of queer stories. Well, this man invented the word *ropopopate* and went out to see how people would react to it. First, he went into a café and said to the waitress: "Will you ropopopate today, Miss?"—"Don't you dare try!" was the answer.' (Her violet-blue eyes were sparkling with merriment.) 'The man then went into a bank and asked if the rate wasn't favourable for ropopopating: "Try 'Securities'," said the teller.' (There were smile wrinkles on one side of her nose.) 'Then the man went into a draper's shop and said hurriedly: "Would you be so kind as to tell me where I can ropopopate?" The girl behind the counter put down what she was doing and, lowering her voice, said: "I'm afraid you'll have to go round to the back. You'll see GENTS on the door." ' (Her eyes filled with tears of laughter, tears that he was to remember always, tears torn from eternity and held fast for ever.)

And so the night proceeded towards its death, something began to fade in their hearts, tired of talking, tired of walking, tired of sitting, tired of smoking, the night was in the process of dying. All the time in the park he had been listening, listening with every fibre of his being, listening for the least sign in her of sentiment stronger than comradeship.

A feeling of grim panic laid hold of him. Now, he thought. Now. The ground was slipping from under his feet. He felt the giddy fear of death creeping over him, he had to clench his teeth to keep them from chattering.

He did not dare.

But he could make an indirect attempt. With his eyes fixed in front of him (because she must not see his eyes) he asked, and he addressed his question to the one power in the world that can work miracles:

'Er—it would be fun, if we could—I mean, if you too could take a trip to Paris this summer. . . .'

The words remained hanging in the air, he did not know if he had said too much or too little, did not know if she had understood. His heart began to pound, he was terror-stricken, his lips became taut and white, his throat constricted, he stammered: '. . . If we could meet, I mean, and—er—go out together, some time. . . .'

He had meant to row back, in under the shore where the water was smooth and calm; instead, he felt that he had been quite crazy and headed right out to sea, out into the merciless deep where man is lost, where he is alone under God's eye, where man has to meet his fate by himself. The answer she gave him would be the decisive one, valid for all time, one from which there was no appeal.

Time became empty.

It was as if the universe had become a glass bell round him, an immense bell of the thinnest crystal. There was a rushing in his ears, a whispering inside the great bell. The first word would shiver the glass, the first word would cause his world to explode in a cloud of glass dust.

He held his breath.

Then quietly she cleared her throat. He clutched at the ribbed seat, time and the night had returned. Then he heard her voice:

'It's just,' she said (and then he knew), 'that I have such an awful lot to do at the studio.'

'Yes,' he said.

'I must give a little time to my parents, too,' she said, 'they have seen so little of me this last year.'

'Yes,' he said.

'Nor can I exactly afford a trip to Paris,' she said; she turned towards him, the little smile-crinkles appeared at the root of her nose.

'No,' he said, 'no, of course not.'

His hands were trembling, his face was white unto death. He had hoped, he had prayed, he had gone such a long way; and now there was only emptiness in him. A cruel, oppressive emptiness. He tried to swallow, but could not. He tried to get up off the seat, but his muscles were numbed, hard as iron, like those of a swimmer who has seen the rock that would save him far ahead in the darkness and who is lying powerless with the taste of blood in his mouth letting the waves sweep him along, a swimmer who believed for an instant that there was hope, but who now knows that his hand will never reach safety.

Then, this being the only thing a person in the twentieth century can turn to when all else has failed him, he said:

'Will you have a cigarette?'

That was the only thing in the world he had to give her now. And therefore he was to remember her answer with burning distinctness. She meant no more than what she said. But she said it as her answer to the only thing in the world he had to offer her:

'Thanks, but I've smoked far too much already.'

She said it in a sweet, feminine, kindly way.

He saw the fatigue in her face, he had worn her out with his stupid, senseless conversation, in a quick glance he had seen that her face was streaked because of him; he felt a great rush of repentance, she had certainly been working all day and must be dead tired, she had been sweet and listened to him all night because she was such a fine person, noble and courteous. Oh, forgive me, he prayed, forgive me. I did not mean to hurt you, forgive me; I have got you to lavish a whole night's healthy sleep on a fool and a good-for-nothing, Embla, forgive me....

He raised his head and drew a deep breath. He looked at her and said in a clear voice, because now the execution had been performed:

'You must be tired, Embla.'

'Well,' she said, 'a bit, you know.' She rubbed her eyes and he felt boundless concern for her, a tremendous compassion. She blinked her tired eyes, smiled heavily, and said: 'I almost think we ought to pack up and totter off to bed. If you don't mind?'

'No,' he said, 'of course not.'

They stood up.

He all but fell. The fairytale was over. The picture-book clapped shut.

The End.

He opened the big iron gate for her and let her go through. He saw her head from behind, saw her nut-brown hair and he thought such a strange thought. Never have you been loved as tonight, Embla, he thought; never will any man give you as rich a love as that in which I have enveloped you.

Embla, this was the night of nights.

And you did not know it.

Love walked at your side.

And you did not know it.

He felt a queer little warped pleasure as they came out of the park. He looked with calm indifference at the houses, the rows of windows with drawn blinds. No guilty feeling, he thought; I am coming out of a park with a young girl in the early morning and we have not done anything. If a policeman came along now, I should meet his look with equanimity. Let that be my comfort: that I do not have a bad conscience.

But at the same time he knew: If the miraculous had happened there in the park, I would now have been invincible. No policeman would have dared to stop us and have a look at us. He might have opened his mouth for a routine question, but then he would have seen my face, would have shut his mouth in awe, put his hand to his cap in a salute, and heartily wished he were elsewhere.

It had become quite light now. There was a morning freshness in the air.

It felt so strange walking through the empty streets. He was cold. The sound of their footsteps on the pavement, two people's footsteps in the night—loudest was the ring of his feet, hers not so loud, she had soft, low-heeled shoes, the uppers a mere wicker-work of narrow strips of golden leather. He had a momentary feeling that they were not two living beings walking through the streets.

For a moment he felt as if his mouth had become fixed in an

oval smile, as if it had become like one of the sound-holes in a violin.

When they had to cross a street, he took her by the arm, it would have been discourteous to do otherwise; but he felt that he must let go as soon as they reached the other pavement.

The fire had burned down. He had a taste of cold ashes in his mouth.

The Stable.

It's queer to see how much a woman has to dig through in her bag to find her key. The little Yale key.

'Now you'll be able to get to sleep, Embla,' he said.

He looked at her face, it was white and drawn; all the same she blinked gaily at him.

'Yes,' she said, 'but it's been great fun. I'm awfully glad to have been able to see what it's like up at the College.'

What should he say? That he hoped he hadn't killed her with all his talking?

She had unlocked the door now; it stood ajar.

'Well, goodnight, Ash.' Her voice changed momentarily, became gay. 'Good *morning*, I mean.'

He smiled back at her, warmly:

'Good morning, Embla. And thanks.'

She gave his hand a squeeze. Embla's hand.

'Thanks.'

They stood thus for a second that to him was a dead eternity.

'It's on Monday you go to France? Shall I see you again before you go?'

'I doubt it. I have a lot to see to. Packing.'

'Yes, of course. So we meet again in the autumn?'

'Yes. In the autumn.'

'Goodbye, then. Have a good trip.'

'Thanks. And you a good summer.'

'Thanks.'

So it was over. He must have turned his head aside as she slipped through the door, for she was no longer there. He stood and looked at the door. The door he had searched for and never found. Not until now. And now it was shut.

After a while he stepped off the slab of stone and walked off

slowly down the alley. In the middle of it, he stopped and
looked back. The Stable. The sky had become bright; he could
see a reflection of it in the big glass window in the sloping roof
of the old timber building. He stood and looked at this house; it
held all that he loved in the world; for a moment it was as though
he embraced it and covered it with flowers, with red roses, he
made it snow red roses out of the sky, a flurry of red roses, the
sea of roses mounted round the Stable like water in a lock, in
the end the house was hidden beneath fragrant red roses; he
left only the top attic window standing free, for someone might
stretch an arm out there and perhaps flutter a last farewell with
her fingers, with a hand so pretty that he would have carved it
in marble, had he been a sculptor.

But all was still.

He stood for a long time, eyes blind, head turned towards
the Stable.

Her modest, soft, gentle face. If he went to the door and rang,
she would come and stand in the half-opened door, then he
would be able to say: 'Embla, I must have you, I must'—then
she would blink her big eyes, horrified at not having thought so
far herself, with a touching gesture of horror she would put
her hand over her mouth because she had shown so little thought
and hospitality to a good companion; she would say that it was
dreadfully late and she intolerably tired, but: 'Why didn't you
say so before, Ash?' and that would be her only reproach, her
face would be soft and shy, she would take his hand in hers and
draw him inside. . . . Standing there, he knew that she would;
but he also knew that it would be as a friend she would receive
him, as a friend; he must not stay more than an hour, he must
behave as a good comrade; she liked him, a lot, he must not mess
up her life. . . .

He gulped.

He glanced round. No one must see him now. Slowly, stealthily he walked back across the open space. With thumping
heart he stood by the stone door-step. Then slowly he bent and
kneeled down. He lowered his head, he set his mouth against the
splintered woodwork; he pressed a burning and wordless kiss
on her threshold.

She was never to know that.

The Song of the Red Ruby

He did not know which way he had gone. He had not seen or recognized the streets. But he was not surprised when he opened his eyes and saw that he had come right down to the harbour and the open water. Had he made for the ships, the sea? He was at the fish market; the open space was full of fresh air and salt-laden breeze from the harbour; there was a smell of fish from the clean-swabbed tables of coarse wood and a faint smell of fuel oil from the fishing boats lying moored by the quay.

Was it that he had to see a ship?

There are moments in people's lives when they feel hopelessly lost and forlorn, when time and eternity are without meaning.

It can happen that they go to the harbour to look at a ship lying in the water. Life is a desert, the earth is a desert, but the greatest and the most meaningless desert is the sea. And right here, on the water-desert, man has put his most shining and desperate mark of will and of purpose.

The ship.

It seemed as though there were someone beside him. He did not want to look. Someone was speaking to him. Was it Gunnhild? She whom he was supposed to meet some time after twelve and whom he was not going to meet? No, it was more like a man's voice Was it God?

He was tired now. So tired that it no longer hurt properly.

'There are women in France,' said the voice. 'Many millions. There are brothels too. A man can have his fill of woman.'

Ash did not reply to that.

'What's so special about Embla?'

Ash did not reply.

'But—' said the voice, 'there must be something special about her? Something that sets her apart from all other women?'

To that Ash did not reply.

'She has wit, culture. But has she ever made an original remark? Something that no one else could have said?'

Ash drew his hand across his forehead, he was so bitterly tired, he could not collect his thoughts. He looked down at the paving stones and said heavily:

'Everything she says is new, unsaid. She is so special that all other women in the world will be laid under the curse of comparison.'

'Tell me one thing she has said?'

'A person cannot become famous for a single remark.'

'General Cambronne, in command of one of the last regiments of Napoleon's guards at the battle of Waterloo, fought like a lion. He was invited to give up the struggle. He replied with one word. That one word has made him famous.'

'But Embla never said anything coarse.'

'Tell me one thing that she said that no one else could have said.'

There was silence in the square. The only sound was the crying of gulls in the distance down the fjord.

'I remember, when we had got up off the seat and were walking back towards the park gates. We passed lots of trees. One of them was a wild-cherry. The blossom was not yet out. I said that if it had been out, I would have plucked a branch for her to have in the Stable. She turned two big, jolly, horrified eyes on me and said: "With me, inside in the living-room?" "Yes?" I said. She smiled and said: "Accordions and wild-cherry are best enjoyed outdoors."'

The square became quiet.

It was quiet for a good while.

'Are you crying now?'

'If I am,' said the young man, speaking with great difficulty, 'if I am then I am p-p-proud of my tears. This has been the greatest night in my life. I give thanks for being allowed to weep because of a woman.'

He swallowed hard and said, speaking with great difficulty: 'I used to think that the goal was the physical union of bodies. Now I know that that is the means. I used to think that the sensual pleasure was everything. Now I know that it is only a door.

Tonight I have trod holy ground.'

'Are you happy now?'

'Yes, I am happy. Everyone is happy who has been permitted to see the glow of the inner light.'

He looked up. He was alone.

He was standing by himself in the fish market, in a dinner jacket, in the grey hours of a summer morning. The sun was already striking the tops of the mountains behind the town; the sunlight sank down over the town, it was like the pink talon of some great bird slowly coming down from the roof-tops, from a high window came a flash of sunlight that stabbed at his eyes.

Then the young man shuddered, for it had been like the gleam from a red ruby.

This was where his first year, the decisive year of his youth, ended. His life's second heat was over.

For a moment he thought of those he had been with at the Stable. He thought: There I was with comrades and *among* comrades; but was I myself a comrade?'

A man came walking down the street. The town had woken to a new day. The man was a shift-worker; he wore a cloth cap and no overcoat; under his arm he carried the Scandinavian industrial worker's sceptre: the old document-case, folded in two, in which he has his packet of sandwiches and his thermos.

At that moment the first streetcar came along. It came driving down the hill. The workman crossed the street in front of it and gave the driver a salute. It was obvious that they knew each other. The man raised his hand in a comradely salute, the driver did the same.

A lump came into the lonely young man's throat; he had seen the men's faces. Their faces and their salute had carried a message of rich, tranquil, wonderful togetherness.

Coda (Dionysos is Silent)

Later he kept silent where the woman he worshipped was concerned.

He was silent in the autumn after he had come back from his
trip abroad. Silent at Christmas time 1939 when he had to go
back to his native town to get a job, his money having come to
an end, forcing him to interrupt his studies for the time being.
He was particularly silent then, perhaps, because just before
he left he heard that the woman he loved had started an affair
with another man. This affair had brought consternation to
the Stable and split the Group. He himself admired the man,
though he did not really know him; he had not exchanged many
words with him, only once had he smilingly explained to him
the meaning of the title of the German song 'A Hug is a Cosy
Thing'.

At times he also thought of the blue armchair; then he became
very silent indeed.

Then came the spring of 1940 and for a time the Norwegians
had other things to think about: German troops occupied their
country. (He had also thought for a fleeting second: political refugees whom the Nazis are hunting will have to fly from
Norway now. But he kept silent.) There was fighting on
Norwegian soil. He did not return to the College till the New
Year of 1941.

He met the young woman again early in the spring of 1941.
He knew that the Stable had ceased to exist, the Germans had
requisitioned the old building. They met each other at the meeting of an underground group, he had known that she was going
to be there. She stood up as he came in; she was wearing spectacles and did not see well at a distance, she stretched a
groping hand out towards him. They went towards each other
through the empty rows at the back of the hall, and he felt as

if he was walking across a long sea shore. They trembled slightly
as they took each other's hand: it was as if they had been waiting a long time. He could see in her face that she was a little
older, he saw a hint of grief in her eyes. They held each other
by the hand, it was as though the force of a mutual gravity made
them lean towards each other; their faces were like flowers opening to the sun; they married in 1942.

What happened to them during the rest of the war cannot be
told here. But one evening late in May 1945, when the country
was free once more, he was standing at the window of a little
attic flat where they were living, looking out over the city. The
electric lights had returned after five years of black-out; it was
a lovely evening; the smells of the spring night poured in
through the open window, was there not a smell of wild-cherry
too? He stretched up on tiptoe in order to see across the roofs;
he had happened to remember a park and it would have been
wonderful if he could see it from where he stood. The smells of
the spring night had put him in such a strange mood.

He turned as she came into the room; she had been to look
at their child; it was sleeping soundly. His eyes followed her
as she walked across the floor and went and sat down at her
work-table. She pushed up the sleeves of her blouse, so that her
forearms were free. He could never stop looking at her arms
and her hands. She smiled at him, then she put on her glasses.
She turned to the work-table, picked up a pencil, nibbled the
tip of her left thumb, whistled, began to draw on her block.
She was very pretty as she sat working.

He cleared his throat. He half turned away when he spoke,
wanting to be apart with his heart. In a low voice he said:
'The park. I can see it from here.'
She said:
'Which park?'
'The park with the swans.'
'Where we went and walked that spring? In 1941?'
'Yes,' he said. 'We went there in 1941. In the mornings. But
we went there once before the war as well. One night. A May
night in 1939. After an end-of-term ball at the College. We
walked all night talking. Do you remember?'

She took off her glasses and rubbed her eyes. She looked at him, blinked her big eyes comically.

'Did I go for an evening walk with you in 1939?'

'M'm,' he said.

'No,' she said, 'I can't remember that.'

There was such a strange stillness then; in this stillness he heard her turn on her chair and go back to her drawing. He did not dare look at her.

'No,' he said quietly. 'We didn't talk about anything very important.'

Slowly and hesitantly he turned back to the window and looked out. There were stars in the evening sky. After a while he shut the window; it seemed to have turned chilly.

Had he known it before?

He knew it now.

Love is something others do not know of. Love is loneliness.